Books by Alina

The Frost Brothers
  Eating Her Christmas Cookies
  Tasting Her Christmas Cookies
  Frosting Her Christmas Cookies
  Licking Her Christmas Cookies
  Resting Grinch Face

The Wynter Brothers
  Good Elf Gone Wrong

The Richmond Brothers
  The Art of Awkward Affection
  The Art of Marrying Your Enemy

Check my website for the latest news:
http://alinajacobs.com/books.html

ELF AGAINST THE WALL

A HOLIDAY ROMANTIC COMEDY

ELF
AGAINST
THE
WALL

ALINA JACOBS

Summary: When my cousin accuses me of stealing her fiancé—granted I did kiss him under the mistletoe, but it was a mistake I swear!—my Christmas goes from festive to disastrous. Now branded the family outcast, I have one desperate plan to fix it all: blackmail Anderson Wynter, my family's sworn enemy. Six-foot-five, ethically challenged, with washboard abs and a death wish, Anderson is the perfect weapon to expose my ex and help me get back in my family's good graces....until he shows up at my family's Christmas party in nothing but tattoos and a motorcycle helmet and tells everyone we're dating. Chaos ensues, and now I'm stuck with a motorcycle-riding bad boy who might just ruin more than Christmas...he'll ruin the rest of my life.

For anyone who's ever had to take drastic measures to survive the holiday season—this one's for you

But little do they know
They 'bout to see a show
Cause when they come up out
the house I'm gonna blast 'em
with some snow
                    —Ludacris

EVIE

"So, where's this *boyfriend*?" My judgmental cousin made air quotes.

"I bet he doesn't exist. She just made him up for attention." Her younger sister smirked.

"Or he's just some guy she's been hooking up with, and she scared him off but thinks they're in love."

"We *are* in love. He's perfect!" I protested.

But my cousins were already giggling into their cocktail glasses.

I knew what they were thinking. Evie Murphy: delusional, impulsive, disaster prone.

Chewing on my lip, I dumped pomegranate juice and champagne into the ceramic pitcher I'd made in high school art class and gifted to my mother several Christmases ago. It had been banished to the back of the cabinet, but wasn't Christmas Eve the perfect time to put it out on display?

I checked my phone. Nothing.

Braeden hadn't sent so much as an emoji in the last thirty-five hours, not since he told me he loved me as we lay on the big bed with the gray sheets in his luxury apartment that, unlike mine, had actual hot water.

Right before he'd kissed me goodbye yesterday morning, he'd said to text him the details of my mom's holiday party.

Where was he?

"Evie, why are you always on your phone? This is a family holiday party. Try to be social." My mother breezed past me, the perfect hostess, with her gorgeous red hair piled high on her head and wearing a form-fitting cream-colored cocktail dress and heels. "And use the crystal pitcher. I can't have *that thing* out on my table."

"No word?" Sawyer asked tentatively, sliding a tray of mini reindeer pizzas onto the overloaded buffet.

"He's busy, okay? He works a lot."

Defensive? *Moi?*

"Y'all work on the admin side of a company that sells luxury pool umbrellas." Sawyer crossed her arms. "It's December. I highly doubt Braeden is too busy to return your texts."

"He's not going to ghost me. Maybe he's picking out a wedding ring. He could be coming to propose." If I said it out loud, that meant my Christmas dreams would come true.

"Could he?"

"Next year, we're going to host Christmas Eve in our new home." I cut my cousin off before she could crash my sleigh of dreams. I swooned, envisioning my perfect future with my perfect man.

"You've only been with him for six weeks. Oftentimes, the men you choose don't really work out."

"Underselling it." My brother Ian pushed his way through the too-warm crush of Murphy-family holiday revelers. "Evie has the worst taste in men."

"Braeden's not like that. I don't even need Christmas presents if I have him."

"With the state of your credit card debt, you should be asking Santa for cold hard cash this holiday season." Sawyer held out her empty glass to me.

The rest of the Murphys, all successful or, in the case of my younger cousins, all with bright, shiny futures ahead of them, milled around the room, wearing their holiday best. Thinking of Braeden, I tried to keep the usual imposter syndrome and negative thoughts at bay.

I had to believe in the magic of love and Christmas.

The bells on the front-door wreath tinkled, announcing more arrivals.

Felicity—mean-girl-cousin extraordinaire—breezed in with my identical-triplet sisters. They were all immediately enveloped by their fan club, aka my family.

"Gosh, the snow is getting heavy," my cousin was exclaiming loudly while my aunts and grandmother cooed over the triplets—my mother's pride and joy.

Normally, I'd be upset, consumed by that empty feeling that I wasn't and never would be as special as my ever-so-slightly younger and definitely much thinner, smarter, and prettier sisters.

But on this Christmas Eve, it didn't matter, because there in the doorway was the most wonderful, most perfect Christmas present.

He walked in, framed by the softly falling snow outside, and took off his overcoat like a superhero's cape. His suit was a little loose in the shoulders, his tie a little crooked. And yeah, maybe it was the booze and the rose-colored glasses, but my boyfriend was the most perfect man in the world.

"Braeden," I breathed. "You came!"

"That's who you've been mooning over?" Ian muttered.

"He looks worse than his photo." Sawyer made a face.

I ignored them. They couldn't dampen my holiday cheer, because the man I loved had come home to surprise me for Christmas.

He stood under the mistletoe for a moment, the most swoon-worthy Hallmark-romance ending.

Tonight is the start of my happily ever after.

Braeden unwrapped his scarf and smiled lovingly.

I rushed to him, threw my arms around his neck, and kissed him passionately, deliriously, happily.

"Merry Christmas, baby," I murmured, closing my eyes and sinking into the familiar sensation of his body.

"Why are you kissing my fiancé!"

My neck cracked as I was yanked back by my hair.

"Ow! Help!" I clawed at the hand on my ponytail.

"You man-stealing bitch!" Felicity screamed in my face, her mascara crinkling in the corners of her eyes as she hauled me away from Braeden.

Sawyer rushed in. "What the hell? Have you lost your fucking mind?"

My heart pounded. I wanted to run to the safety of Braeden's arms.

"I should shave your fucking head!" Felicity raged. "You literally kissed my man right in front of me."

"And on Christmas, no less!" one of my elderly relatives exclaimed, fanning herself.

My cousin shoved me.

I tripped and fell in a heap of tangled hair and clothes on the floor. Palms stinging, knees shaking, I tried to stand up.

"Your fiancé?" I stammered. "But—no—he—I—we're in love. Baby, tell them. Braeden?"

My perfect boyfriend wiped his mouth with the back of his sleeve.

"You see? I wasn't cheating on you, Felicity. There's something wrong with your cousin. She's delusional. She's obsessed with me."

"You're sick, Evie," Felicity spat.

The family backed away from me, leaving me alone in the middle of the foyer to face their judgment.

"I didn't try to steal him. Honest, Felicity," I warbled.

"I warned you, Melissa, when you adopted *that girl,* that you can't undo the crimes of nature!" Grandma Shirley thundered, pointing a bony finger at me.

What the fuck? Sawyer mouthed.

"She's exactly like her birth mother—a loose woman." Grandma Shirley stared down her nose.

Ian snickered under his breath.

Mom glared at him. But she didn't counter Grandma Shirley's claims.

"Braeden, what's going on?" I pleaded to my boyfriend. "You said you loved me that night in bed…"

Felicity's face was candy-cane red.

"In bed? Why would I sleep with my employee?" Braeden scoffed. "I have a good job. I'm not ruining my life for sex. Especially not with her." The corner of his mouth lifted derisively.

Felicity's eyes flicked between him and me, like she wasn't quite sure she believed him.

Braeden laid it on thick. "Like I said, *Evelyn*," Braeden lectured in that condescending tone, "Out of respect for my friendship with your brother Henry, I wasn't going to report you to HR if you just curbed your immature impulses, but this truly is too far."

"Too far?" I was about to puke up all the holiday cocktails I'd consumed earlier. "You were going to propose to me. I have a Pinterest board with rings."

I was aware of how unhinged I sounded, but the man I loved was acting like he didn't even know me!

"Stop lying to me!" I sobbed, the tears making the festive decorations blur into a bizarre mad house. "We are in a relationship. I was in your apartment yesterday. I cleaned your bathroom."

"Don't gaslight people, Evelyn," Braeden chastised me.

"Don't use weaponized therapy-speak, Braeden," Sawyer snapped at him.

"You should have saved one of the used condoms," Granny Doyle piped up.

Several relatives crossed themselves. One woman fainted, though it might have been from all the spiked Christmas punch.

My arguing wasn't helping my case, obviously.

"Slut!" Felicity yelled at me.

Braeden took her hand gently.

"It's all lies. Your cousin has mental health issues. You know that. You were telling me all about how she's a stain on your family's good name." Braeden kissed her hand. "I would never cheat on my fiancée, Felicity. You know that. I love you and want to marry you. I'm a traditional man who wants a traditional marriage."

My father's face was a mask of disgust. "Of all the shit you've pulled over the years, Evie, stalking and trying to steal a soon-to-be-married man—your cousin's fiancé, no less—is beyond the pale."

"We're in love." The words came out heavy and desperate, but clearly, we weren't, or at least, he never was.

"Do you have any proof?" my oldest brother, Henry, asked.

"Fucker," Ian scoffed under his breath. "Of course you have proof. Right, Evie?"

"I—well, we communicated over Snapwave, and it deletes the messages after twenty-four hours, but I do have some messages still." Hands shaking, I rummaged in my skirt pockets for my phone.

"So do I," Braeden blustered, pulling out his phone. "See?" He showed everyone the last messages I sent him.

Evie: *Hello???*
Evie: *Are you ever going to respond to me?*
Evie: *I want the family to meet youuuu!*
Evie: *They don't know about us but I want to do a big reveal!*

Out of context they did look a little, well, stalkery.
I winced.

Aunt Lisa berated my mom. "Everyone told you not to bring that"— she pointed at me— "*charity case* into your home, into this family, and you refused to see reason. Now she's attacking my daughter and trying to ruin her future. Evelyn is tearing this family apart."

"Evie, apologize." My mother's green eyes flashed.

"But I didn't!" I cried, but it was clear no one in my family believed me.

"Evie." My mother shook her head. "Your father is right. Of all the terrible decisions you've made, this really does take the cake. Apologize. At once."

"I—I'm sorry, Felicity, honest. But Braeden and I are—"

Felicity's sisters had to hold her back. "Boyfriend-stealing ho. You've been harassing my fiancé. You think he wants to be with you?"

"*Liar!*"

"*Cheater!*"

"*Homewrecker!*"

The judgments flew around the room, branding me.

But I didn't know. Why didn't anyone believe me? It was like being trapped in a snow globe, screaming for help and no one to save me. I was suffocating.

"She's telling the truth," Sawyer and Ian, my ride or dies, said at the same time, stepping up for me.

I gave them a teary but grateful smile.

"Yeah, she's been talking about dating her boss for the last six weeks," Ian insisted.

"Did you see a photo of them together?" Henry asked Sawyer and Ian.

That earned him a scowl from Ian. "Whose side are you on?"

"The truth," Henry said magnanimously.

"She showed us Braeden's photo on their company's website," Sawyer insisted, "and I definitely saw messages from Braeden."

"You didn't save them, Evie?" Henry prodded.

"I didn't know he was with Felicity. I didn't know I needed to save receipts." I was hyperventilating.

"If Evie says it's true, I believe her." Granny Doyle pushed through the crowd. "After I caught my husband palling around with a forty-year-old he met on Craigslist, I know you can't trust a man, especially not one named Braeden."

My dad pinched the bridge of his nose.

"This is a very close-knit family." Grandma Shirley announced with finality. "Of course you knew, Evelyn. And how glad I am that I didn't let my son name you after my beloved grandmother like he wanted to. You are a testament to the poor household your mother runs."

"Thank you, Shirley. I will parent my daughter."

"That will be a first."

My mom's cheeks were hollowed from anger.

"I am so disappointed in you, Evie," my mom said quietly but firmly. "You need to start making better life choices. I'm sick of this behavior—not applying yourself in high school, dropping out of college, throwing yourself at the worst of men, the dead-end jobs, and now this? Maliciously trying to ruin my niece's relationship? After all your father and I have done for you, after all this family has done for you, this is how you repay us?"

"I'm sorry." My arms were clutched around me. I didn't know why I was apologizing when I didn't do anything wrong. I was full on sobbing now.

"Just..." My father made a disgusted noise and shook his head. "Just go to your room. I don't want to see you for the rest of Christmas."

"I didn't mean for any of this to happen," I said sadly as I headed to the staircase.

"Isn't that how it always is with you?" My father's words were final, dismissive.

And that's the story of how I ruined not just Christmas but also my life.

Chapter 1

EVIE

My palms left damp spots on the festive red-and-gold planner clutched tightly in my hands.

Too bad the woman sitting across the desk from me was not about to make my Christmas wishes come true. She looked down her nose at the folder of work examples I'd brought with me to the meeting.

When I'd received the calendar invite half an hour ago, I knew something was up.

"As you can see," I told the HR director in a last-ditch effort to save my job, "I am organized, creative, and have been an integral member of the admin team, helping to plan corporate events, manage conference schedules, and performing other skills required of a successful administrative assistant at Quantum Cyber."

"Except for not engaging in inappropriate relationships with your coworkers." The HR director wore a coldly polite expression.

Inwardly, I cringed. Outwardly, I tried to keep my facial expression pleasantly neutral. I was wearing fun holiday bracelets. Who didn't want to work with a girl with festive holiday bangles?

"I didn't do that with anyone here," I stressed. "You can ask all my coworkers. I only had one drink at most at happy hours and then went straight home."

The HR director frowned. "We have reports that you were stalking a fellow coworker at your previous job."

"It was three jobs ago, and it wasn't really stalking, though I can see how the circumstantial evidence might make it seem that—"

"We at Quantum Cyber take sexual harassment claims very seriously."

"If you really want to get technical, he was the person doing the harassing, since he was my superior and—"

"Please remember, Miss Murphy," the HR Director interrupted, "that you signed a morality clause upon being hired. We cannot have any member of this firm besmirching its good name."

"To be fair, this company develops high-tech drone surveillance software for Homeland Security, so…"

"You're terminated effective immediately." The HR Grinch handed me a folder. "This is your paperwork. Security is waiting to escort you out."

"But… but—it's Christmas!"

"Yes, have a lovely holiday. Additionally, please note that you are not eligible to collect unemployment. We've already notified the New York Department of Labor."

"That's it," I told Sawyer as I walked dejectedly along the sidewalk. "I'm officially blacklisted in Manhattan."

"You were too good for them." Over the phone, nail polish bottles clinked.

"I can't believe they fired me the Friday I was signed up to bring donuts. Like, why not fire me yesterday? I thought you weren't supposed to fire people right before the weekend anyway. Also, do you have any idea how expensive three dozen holiday-themed donuts are?"

"Let's concentrate on the fact that even a year later, Braeden is still trying to screw you over."

I dodged a Santa carrying a large sign telling me to buy a mattress this Christmas for my nonexistent husband.

"Felicity is behind this. I know it," I told Sawyer darkly.

I began the long, thigh-cramping climb up to my sixth-floor walkup. No, it was not my own slice of New York heaven. Instead, I was subleasing the couch.

I had been counting on my next paycheck to pay overdue bills, including the measly rent.

"Don't worry," I assured my best-friend-slash-cousin as I unlocked the door to frenzied barking from Snowball. "I'm definitely planning to pay you back."

"Don't worry about it." Her tone softened. "It's an early Christmas present."

Tears prickled in my eyes as it hit me.

I was at rock bottom, a horrible end to a horrible year during which my family ostracized me at the various family events, no matter how many themed desserts I baked or how many gatherings I planned.

Now here it was, Christmas, my favorite time of the year, and I was broke, miserable, and unemployed.

"I am totally going to pay you back," I said stubbornly, blinking back the tears. "They didn't even pay out my PTO." I sniffled as I thumbed through the packet the Quantum Cyber HR Grinch had given me. "Legally, they have to, right? I earned that PTO."

Sawyer sighed.

"Let me ask my roommates if you and Snowball could crash here for a little bit. Annalise has a couple big weddings happening in the spring, and she's always shorthanded. There's always a bridesmaid who thinks she can do her own makeup, and she absolutely cannot. If I promise Annalise I'll be on standby, she might let you come back. Maybe you can show her how much more home training Snowball has…"

"No." I grabbed my patched duffel bag and tossed in the handmade Christmas decorations that festooned my couch. "I don't want to make things difficult for you." I stared up at the cracked plaster ceiling. "Maybe I can just stay at my parents' for the next few weeks."

"Are they seriously going to let you?"

"I'll pretend like I'm just there to help out and working from home, and then after Christmas, maybe I can waitress while I get my bartending license."

"I don't know…"

"It will work out, right? Maybe I'll get a Christmas miracle."

"Screw Christmas miracles. You need to fight back. Braeden is ruining your life. You can't survive in this town with waitressing work alone."

I grabbed the glass pan of Christmas caramel cinnamon rolls that were proofing for a treat tonight. After scrounging for paper, I wrote a note to my soon-to-be-former room-mates, apologizing profusely for bailing on rent, promising I'd pay them back, and *Oh, here are the world's best cinnamon rolls. Icing is in the fridge.*

After giving the cinnamon rolls one more longing look, I finished packing up my stuff, not that there was much. I had already sold anything that had even the remotest amount of value the last time Braeden got me fired from an admin job. Also, you were a more attractive couch guest when you traveled light.

Then I braced myself and sent my mom a text message.

> **Evie:** *Hey! Since I know you and the fam have all these holiday events coming up, I was thinking I could come home early to help out. My job says I can work remote.*
>
> **Mom:** *Your cousin Irene already informed the family that you were fired from yet another job.*
>
> **Mom:** *I don't appreciate being lied to.*

I slumped down on the couch, phone landing next to me on the saggy cushion.

On the bright side, this was confirmation that there definitely was a family group text that I was not included in. Love being talked about behind my back.

> **Evie:** *I was planning on telling you in person.*
>
> **Mom:** *Your father is going to drive you home once he's done with the press conference after the big surgery. Be at the university hospital early so that you do not keep him*

*waiting. He's in the middle of conducting a
very long, very strenuous medical procedure.
Do not add to his stress.*

Feeling like garbage, I finished packing up my things, and I zipped up my coat.

I wanted to take the subway or, better yet, an Uber, but Snowball needed a very long walk, and I need to save every penny I could.

The tiny white Pomeranian practically vibrated with energy. Her white hair stuck straight out from her in a poof, only her black eyes and nose visible. The shiny rows of needle-sharp teeth let everyone know she was not a cuddly stuffed animal.

The old man who lived below me thumped on his ceiling with a broom handle while Snowball barked her head off.

"Don't worry. We're about to be out of your life for good," I yelled at the floor as I tried to wrestle the tiny dog into her harness.

"Never should have spent all this money on a custom Frosty the Snowman leash," I grumbled as I stuffed Snowball's legs through the harness and fastened it.

After hoisting my duffel bag, I let Snowball pull me out the door and down the narrow flight of stairs.

Outside in the cold, it smelled like snow.

Maybe we'd have a white Christmas, though I wasn't sure that even snow would keep this from being one of the worst Christmases in memory.

Snowball strained at the leash as we began the long walk toward downtown. My feet were numb as the Empire State building loomed closer and closer.

Snowball never let up the pace. She either pulled furiously at the leash, tried to dart into the street to attack a yellow cab, or charged headlong at a pedestrian who dared to get in her personal bubble.

The dog could have walked the hundred blocks back uptown when I finally arrived sweaty and red-faced outside the university hospital.

I hovered outside the large lecture hall, which had a sign on the door for the press conference about the recently completed surgery for the teenage son of a famous hockey star.

The doors opened, and the journalists streamed out. Ducking behind a large plant, I hid there, waiting until my father, white coat over his crisp suit, strode out with his fellow surgeons.

They shook hands and congratulated each other. Then he held up his wrist, looking at his watch in annoyance.

"I'm here!" I darted out from behind the plant.

Snowball flung herself at him, practically hovering in midair as the leash kept her in check.

"Someone who doesn't have stable employment should not have a dog, Evie," my father said by way of greeting. "Why don't you drop her at a rescue society?"

"I know, I know, but I thought I had stable employment," I explained as I hurried after him. "Besides, I don't want to get on the naughty list for abandoning a puppy."

He frowned in confusion.

Sweat pooled under my bra. "You know, it's a joke because it's Christmas…"

My father buttoned his suit jacket and grabbed his overcoat from a coat rack in a side alcove.

"Are those all of your things?" he asked, looking pointedly at my overstuffed duffel bag and backpack with

Snowball's toys. "I'm not bringing you back to New York City if you forgot anything."

"All ready for a festive holiday season!" I chirped.

My dad grunted. His phone rang, and he answered it, talking rapidly in medical jargon as I trotted after him back out into the cold.

He handed the valet his ticket.

Christmas carols filtered softly from hidden speakers outside the medical college.

My stomach growled. I wondered if it would be too much to suggest grabbing a bite to eat before heading to Maplewood Falls.

The cold calm was broken by hip-hop music, the loud bass rattling my teeth as my dad's Mercedes screeched up in front of the entrance, almost knocking over the valet stand.

The valet sprinted up behind the car.

"Granny Doyle!"

Gran hopped out of the car with more energy in her eighties than I had at twenty-one. She wrapped me in a big hug.

"Merry Christmas, babe! I stopped at that Italian place, Camelli's. Food's in the back. Don't give me that health-food nonsense, Brian," she warned my dad. "You'll pry my pasta out of my cold, dead hands. Let's bounce, kiddo. Traffic is a bitch, and people in this city can't drive."

I sank into the deep leather seat behind Gran. Snowball climbed in my lap so she could see who to bark at through the window. The car smelled like cheese, garlic, and fresh bread.

I reached into the bag on the floor and pulled out a piping-hot container.

"Have a cocktail back there for you too, Evie. Heard you got the boot. Figured you'd need it. Let me know if you want me to TP anyone's house."

"Give me the keys," my dad ordered his mother-in-law through the car window.

"Hell no." Gran put the car in reverse, almost running over the valet.

My father cursed and raced after the car, wrenched open the passenger-side door, and climbed in.

"It's dangerous for you to drive when you're tired!" Granny Doyle shouted over the hip-hop music blaring from the speakers as she merged into traffic. "Eat some gnocchi, bro. You're too high-strung."

My dad ignored her and turned around in his seat to give me a stern look. "Evie, you need to start taking responsibility for your life. You're not going to drop out of college, make terrible career choices, then expect you can move back home with your mom and me and take advantage of our hard work."

The pasta was a rock in my stomach.

Gran flipped off a driver in a Porsche then took a hard left turn. "Don't worry, Evie. Screw your dad. You can live with me."

"No, she can't, because you live with us." My father was exasperated.

"I'd rather have gone to prison!" Gran shouted, laying on the horn.

"Your grandmother has your and Ian's old room. You're in the attic."

"Just like Kevin McAllister," I joked.

"Evie, you need to take this seriously. Your mother and I have cut you too much slack over the years."

Had they?

"After discussing it, your mother and I agreed that you can stay with us only if you find a job by Christmas. If you do, then you have an additional two weeks. Otherwise, you need to move out."

"You're going to throw me out on Christmas? I don't even have till the end of the year?" I asked in a small voice.

"No one is hiring after Christmas. If you cannot find a job by the twenty-fifth, then you're certainly not going to do it by New Year's Eve. This is tough love, Evie." My father turned back around in his seat. "Our support of you stops in sixteen days. Plan accordingly."

Plan how? I didn't have an icicle's chance in hell of getting a good-paying job in New York City, not after Braeden and Felicity had spent the last year painting me as some gross sex pest.

I'd been hoping I could at least bum at my parents' for a few months, doing odd jobs in Maplewood Falls, and save up enough money to pay back people who'd helped keep me limping along last year. Then when the spring hit and tourists started coming, I could find a job at a cute bed-and-breakfast a la Lorelei Gilmore.

Instead, there was a ticking clock hanging over my head, ominously counting down the days until December twenty-fifth.

Forget having a perfect Christmas—I wasn't going to have any kind of life without a holiday miracle.

Chapter 2

EVIE

"Yes, he's legally your cousin, but you're not actually related, so I don't see why you can't just go on a date with Wendie."

"Mom," my cousin whined, wiping his nose with his sweater sleeve, which was cute when he was eight but not so much now that he was a college sophomore. "I told you I don't want to date someone like her."

"You mean someone with the nicest tits on the east coast?" Granny Doyle crowed, topping off my wineglass.

"Gran, I appreciate the confidence, but I'm not dating my cousin."

"Especially not one on Shirley's side." Gran glared across the room at my father's prim and proper elderly mother.

I clutched my drink as one of my uncles jostled me accidentally.

Aunt Jennifer's house was packed with our family.

"You'd be lucky you have Wendie." Aunt Abby was offended. "My baby is going to be a software engineer." She pinched his pimply cheek. "Evie, you need someone to take care of you. I heard you got fired from another job today. And you're homeless. You can't be choosy."

"If you're going to go all *Sweet Home Alabama* and date your cousin, don't waste it on Whiney Wendell," my cousin Nat slurred, her spiced Christmas wine sloshing out of her glass. She draped a toned arm around my curvier shoulders. "Go for Sean."

"You're seriously pimping out your own brother?" Sawyer yelled over the techno-remixed Christmas carols.

"Is Evie on the prowl? Better hide your husbands. Justin!" Meghan, one of my married-in cousins, raised her voice and yelled to my second cousin, "Stay away from Evie. I don't want her breaking up my marriage. I spent a lot of money on our wedding."

"Justin is our actual cousin, so I think you're safe," Sawyer clapped back.

"Mom." Felicity turned to Aunt Lisa. "I thought I told you I didn't want her here."

"Christmas is about helping the less fortunate," Aunt Lisa said soothingly to Felicity.

"She's not less fortunate. She's a home-wrecker."

Yeah... I was never ever living that down. Felicity was going to make sure that last Christmas's kissing incident stayed burned in the collective Murphy-family memory.

"She isn't less fortunate. She made bad choices." My mom came up behind her sister-in-law and tilted her head prettily.

The frumpier Aunt Lisa scowled. If Aunt Lisa weren't so mean, I'd feel sorry for her. I knew what it was like to have a family member who set a standard I could never meet.

My mom looked at me and sighed, pulling at the sleeve of my too-tight sweater. She didn't have to say anything, but the sigh said it all: Why can't you be more like the rest of the family? Why do you have to be a college dropout with a dead-end job and a Chinese-food-delivery addiction?

"You should go to the adoption agency and get your money back!" Uncle Kevin chortled.

His wife elbowed him sharply, and he looked ashamed.

"Just joking. Sorry, Evie. We love having you in this family. No one makes stuffed mushrooms like you." He popped one into his mouth.

I wanted to shrink into myself. "Thanks. I fry them in duck fat and make my own breadcrumbs."

"Why don't you go to culinary school, dear? You could get a job for a wealthy single billionaire and fall in love." Aunt Amy gave me a pained smile.

"More like sleep with him and get pregnant." Felicity turned up her nose.

"She didn't get pregnant at fifteen, so she managed to make one good decision," Uncle Kevin quipped.

"You'll get there, Evie. Some people are late bloomers," Aunt Amy said soothingly.

"And some people are home-wrecking stalkers."

I mumbled my excuses, pretending like I needed to deal with Snowball, who was racing around with her dog cousins, mainly the beautiful Irish setters Grandma Shirley bred and that several family members had been gifted.

Then I fled to the kitchen to put more of the appetizers in the oven to crisp up.

Christmas used to be my favorite holiday, but I didn't think I was going to survive this December with everyone in my family hating my guts.

Maybe when my dad kicked me out on Christmas day, I'd just move. I could go to California or buy one of those old Victorian houses in a dying rustbelt town.

Who was I kidding? Like I had enough money for a bus ticket, let alone a whole house.

The pastry was turning golden brown, and I pulled the tray out of the oven.

"Brava, Evie! You bring those cranberry-brie bites over here," Aunt Trish called when she saw me come out of the kitchen with the platter. "In case you missed it, I brought a cheese platter that I made myself on my farm retreat. Evie? Evie, where did you put the cheese tray?"

Aunt Jennifer had made me throw out the goat cheese.

"Trish doesn't know how to cook," Aunt J had said, "And she sure as fuck doesn't know how to make cheese."

Aunt Trish cupped my face. "I'm doing tarot readings. I have sage and my cards in my purse. You, my dear, are in need of guidance."

"She needs to go back to school," my father muttered under his breath. Then a smile lit up his face.

Speaking of family successes...

He spread his arms, delight on his face as three identical redheaded young women entered the living room.

I quickly made myself an extra-strong eggnog while my parents fussed over the triplets.

"Look at how much you've grown!" my mom's second cousin gushed over my ever-so-slightly younger sisters.

Great-Aunt Gladys and Great-Aunt Eleanor also shuffled over.

Yep, family members who had missed the drama last Christmas were coming out of the woodwork. Guess everyone wanted to be there in person to see how much I'd fuck up this year instead of being forced to watch the aftermath on Facebook like a commoner.

We're not going to screw up, I reminded myself as I downed my eggnog and made another. *We're going to be a helpful niece-slash-cousin-slash-daughter, and hopefully after another ten years of that, we'll be back in the family's good graces.*

"What a blessing to have such wonderful daughters." Eleanor's hearing aid gave a loud beep.

"I love my girls." My dad tucked the triplets under his arms.

My parents had had three boys then had trouble conceiving and really wanted a girl.

Enter yours truly, stage right.

It wasn't six months later that my mom gave birth to surprise triplets. And not just any triplets—they were her doppelgangers, little mini-mes with model-good looks, sparkling personalities, and the ability to breeze through even the most advanced chemistry coursework.

The perfect daughter my mom always dreamed of, and she got three of them.

Too bad she and my dad were stuck with me. I looked nothing like my lithe Scottish-Nordic parents who could be elf extras in *Lord of the Rings.* I was a sun-swarthy fifty-year-old Italian peasant woman who subsisted on carbs, garlic, and cheese and could grow a mustache better than my fair-skinned, redheaded brothers when I was thirteen.

"They graduated early from Brown University," my mother gushed to Great-Aunt Gladys, "just like me and

Brian. And Henry and Declan, of course." She blew a kiss to my eldest two brothers. "You remember Henry. He almost died in the war. It was heartbreaking."

My mom's sisters rolled their eyes. "Like you'd ever let anyone forget."

"A war hero and three beautiful daughters!" The great-aunts congratulated my mom.

"They're not just beautiful. The girls already have job offers," Dad gushed.

"We're all working at Svensson PharmaTech!" Alissa gave an effortlessly beautiful smile—with dimples.

"Just got our offer letters." Alana held up an envelope.

"We already told them we accept!" Alexis was giddy.

My three sisters shrieked and hugged each other.

My dad whistled appreciatively as he inspected their letters.

"Look at that salary. Guess you're going to be buying us nice Christmas presents this year."

"Oh, stop it, Brian!" My mom swatted him playfully then kissed him. "You girls don't have to get us anything. We're just so happy to have you home for Christmas. Your rooms are all ready."

Yeah, they were, because I'd spent all afternoon cleaning and putting on fresh sheets.

"Seven children." Great-Aunt Eleanor turned to her sister. "Seven children, and she looks like that." They marveled at my mother's willowy body as she pretended not to bask in the compliments. My mom lived for these moments.

"She didn't birth all of them," Aunt Lisa butted in. "Don't give her that much credit. She adopted that one."

All the attention was now on me.

Slowly back away. Hide under the table.

I pretended to be heavily invested in my plate of appetizers.

"There she is." Aunt Gladys tapped her sister excitedly. "I missed the big finale last Christmas. I can't believe she slept with her aunt's husband."

"No, it was her sister's husband."

"It was my fiancé," Felicity interjected.

"It sounds more exciting than the Christmas of fifty-four." The hearing aid gave another loud beep. "Remember when Mildred showed up pregnant, not married, no boyfriend, and told everyone it was Aunt Dee's husband's baby?"

"Lord, and then Great-Granny Mae keeled over, dead as a doornail. Now, that was family drama." Great-Aunt Eleanor thumped her walker on the carpet.

"Are you pregnant?" Great-Aunt Gladys demanded, pointing her cane at me.

"Uh, no?" I rasped.

"Who's going to get her pregnant?" Felicity demanded. "I mean, look at her."

Aunt Trish, reeking of spiced rum, hugged me to her chest.

"Let their negative energy flow over you. It is perfectly natural for a woman to have facial hair."

"Sawyer didn't do a waxing for you? Honestly, honey." Sawyer's mom peered down at my face. "If you're going to shame the family and become a back-alley beautician, you could at least keep your clients on a regular waxing schedule."

"I waxed her two days ago," Sawyer stated.

Aunt Virginia shook her head. "They have these little face razors you can get from Korea. Why don't you order her some, Sawyer?"

"You need to find a man that loves you just the way you are." Aunt Trish tossed her tie-dye scarf over her shoulder.

"Yeah, a furry." My brother Declan snickered.

Sawyer kicked him, and he grabbed his shin, wincing.

"You're a father now and, for some godforsaken reason, a doctor. Can you act like an adult?"

"My bad, Evie. Guess I can't make a request for the next holiday dinner?" my brother begged.

"Let him starve." His wife glared at him.

"Just text me what you want," I said weakly.

Great-Aunt Gladys patted my hand. "I'm looking forward to what you have planned. I'm not missing a holiday party this December just in case. I have a feeling this year's going to be a doozy!"

My family was biting back laughter, giving each other snide looks and whispering my name.

There it was... the shame, moldy and rotten in my gut.

I was the gross marzipan-filled chocolate truffle in the box next to all the more desirable ones—never living up to the promise, not worth the hype, not worth the money.

I was never going to belong in the Murphy family, was never going to be forgiven.

My life was as good as over.

Witness the last dying gasps of Evie Murphy's hopes and dreams—forced to perform holiday party after holiday party, listening to my parents' relatives make passive-aggressive remarks until the final door opened on the advent calendar and I was kicked out onto the street.

I was trapped. The room was closing in. It was too warm.

I shoved my plate of snacks and my drink at Sawyer. "I'll be right back."

Chapter 3

EVIE

Chapter 3

Evie

Snowball started growling as soon as we approached my parents' house.

The Christmas lights hadn't been put up yet, and the house was dark.

Snowball's white fur was puffed out even more than usual.

"Can you please just be calm for once?" I begged the dog.

I'd snuck out after the family went back to fawning over the triplets.

It made my heart ache to watch them get what I wanted—the unconditional love and admiration of our parents.

Is it really unconditional if they're legitimately prettier, smarter, more successful, and more charming than me?

I wondered as I stuck my key in the lock on the oversize door of the restored Victorian house.

That seems like it's conditional and they met the requirements. Performed as advertised.

I frowned as the key jumped in my hand. The front door was already unlocked. I must have forgotten when we left earlier for the party.

Dummy.

Good thing I came home early after all. Otherwise, my dad would be pissed if he found out.

Setting Snowball down, I stepped into the dark foyer.

She was acting weird, little body low to the ground, teeth bared as she crept through the faint yellow glow of the porch light that shone in through the windows.

"Come, Snowball," I hissed, trying to get her to follow me into the kitchen, where I was going to make some tea then disappear with the snacks I'd stolen from Aunt Jennifer's holiday party and hide up in my drafty attic bedroom and lose myself in a book.

"Seriously, can you not act like an elf cracked out on hot chocolate and candy for one freaking night?"

Instead of turning into the emotional support lapdog I'd always hoped she'd become, Snowball revved her engines then rocketed into my father's dark study off the generous foyer.

"Snowball!" I yelled. "I swear to god!"

I raced after her, then I screamed as a menacing shadow loomed in front of the French doors that led to the wraparound porch. A headlight from a passing car illuminated it briefly.

There was a man—a huge man!—in my father's study, all in heavy black motorcycle gear, a helmet hiding his face.

Snowball had her needle-sharp teeth latched onto the robber's pant leg, and he was batting at her roughly, trying to knock her off.

"Don't you hurt my dog!" I screamed, picking up a priceless wood statue my parents had brought back from their anniversary trip to Japan and racing after the attacker.

He grunted in surprise but raised his arm too late to block the statue from crashing into his motorcycle helmet, shattering the tinted visor.

Eyes like a raging winter storm glared back at me through the broken glass.

I hefted the statue again, and it connected with one of his massive arms.

The hit didn't even knock him off-balance.

"Oh shit," I whimpered as he took a step toward me.

The huge arm came up, knocking the statue out of my hands to split on the floor.

I spun to escape but tripped on the corner of the rug and crashed to the floor, yelling unintelligibly as he pounced on me, pinning me on my back. His huge gloved hand covered my mouth and nose so I couldn't scream. I could barely breathe.

"Shut up," the deep voice ordered, slightly muffled by the broken motorcycle helmet.

I struggled under the massive male body that had me

trapped on the floor, clawing ineffectively at him.

"What the hell?" he growled. "Fuck, I need to do something with you."

Was he going to hurt me? Or take me with him to be— *Gulp*—disposed of somewhere else?

Don't let yourself be taken to a second location!

But I couldn't budge all the muscle and sinew holding me down.

"Motherfuck—" he roared, snatching his gloved hand back from my mouth as Snowball bit him, her sharp teeth sinking through the gloves into his thumb.

Sucking in shuddering breaths, I pummeled the man's helmet as he shook his hand, Snowball not letting go as he flapped her around.

Scraping my nails on his neck, I managed to drag his helmet off his head and hoisted it, banging it on his face and shoulders as he cursed, finally shaking the dog and the glove free.

His tattooed hand made a fist and punched the helmet out of my grasp. His knee pinned my hip to the floor. As he raised himself slightly, his face was lit up by passing headlights.

"Oh my god," I whimpered, eyes bugging out of my head as I took in his chiseled face, strong jaw, black hair, wintery gray eyes, and scars on his cheek and across one eye.

"You're the... the... the..."

"The... the... the..." he mocked as he catalogued my dawning recognition.

The Grinch!

"You're *him*."

"Your family's sworn enemy." The baritone had a mocking lilt.

Anderson Wynter.

I hadn't seen him since the military trial my whole family had attended almost eight years ago, where my sisters all sobbed on the stand and my mom had clung to my tense father. Those pale-gray, almost-silvery eyes—*Snow-demon eyes*—had bored into me as they led him away to prison.

Those eyes used to give me nightmares after seeing them for weeks in the courtroom.

"You tried to murder Henry," I choked out. "You almost got my brother killed in battle. Oh my god, you're here to kill us all, aren't you?"

I tried to push him off me, to escape. But that massive body didn't budge "Are you going to hurt me? Are you here for revenge because Henry put you in jail?"

He could kill me. Easily. I mean, look at the size of those hands. Though he'd seemed big at the trial, now he was absolutely monstrous.

No one knew I was here. I'd snuck out of the party. It would be hours before anyone realized I was missing, and then it would be too late.

"You aren't going to get away with this," I warbled as he looked down at me coldly. "I'm going to call the police." I tried to dig in my jacket pocket for my phone.

"You threatening me, Gingersnap?" He grabbed my wrist with that tattooed hand, fingers squeezing hard.

I blinked furiously. I refused to let Anderson see me cry.

"No," I whimpered.

His fingers slacked.

"Honest, just please let me go. I promised Aunt Amy that I'd help prep breakfast casseroles." Yet another of my ham-fisted attempts to worm my way back into my family's good graces.

"I don't like being threatened," he continued.

"I'm not. Please don't hurt me. I won't tell anyone," I babbled.

Don't tell anyone...

Suddenly, I didn't feel afraid anymore.

Instead? I felt inspired, like a star lit up on the top of a Christmas tree.

He peered down at me as a smile twitched on my mouth.

"What? What are you doing?" I heard a twinge of apprehension in the deep voice.

"I take it back." My smile widened.

"No."

"I a—"

"*No.*"

"*I am threatening you!*" I raised my voice. "Help me or else!"

"No. No you're not." He shook his head, his dark hair falling into his eyes.

"Look, I'm being gaslit by my ex. He lied to my whole

family, saying we weren't in a relationship, and he's ruining everything, my entire life. I'm about to be disowned! You're a criminal. You must have... I don't know..." I made little Tinker Bell hand motions. "Skills? Know the right people? You can help me clear my name. You can save Christmas! All for the low, low price of my silence."

A scowl set in on his face.

"We can help each other out."

"I don't need anything from you, Gingersnap."

"It's Christmas. The season of giving," I wheedled, totally convinced that blackmailing my family's sworn enemy was the ticket to a merry Christmas. "We can pretend the breaking-and-entering episode never happened. I'll even dust off your footprints in the snow when you leave."

He shifted his weight. His hand fumbled at my hip.

I strangled a gasp as he reached into my pocket, pulled out my phone, and dropped it on my chest.

"Hard. Fucking. Pass. Go ahead and call the police. I'd rather be in jail than help you get your ex back."

"Then," I said, spreading my arms, "you will have to kill me. Right here on my dad's floor."

He swore loudly and stood up, taking his helmet.

"You don't understand." I clambered upright.

Ignoring me, he bent down to grab the glove Snowball had removed and worked it onto his tattooed hand.

"Snowball, attack!"

My dog latched herself onto his boot, snarling.

It didn't even halt the heavy footfalls.

I raced after him into the foyer.

"You have to accept my blackmail offer. Please, it's my only chance! Besides, I will ruin you."

He gave me a dismissive look. "Doubtful."

I puffed myself up to my full height, which admittedly wasn't much. "I have half a semester's worth of a marketing degree. I will make sure you're the most hated man in America." I jabbed a finger into his rock-hard chest. "You have a criminal record. You'll go back to jail. You almost killed an American hero."

"Is that what they're calling him now?" He slipped the helmet onto his head.

I grabbed his wrist as he reached for the door.

"I swear," I hissed at him. "You don't know what it's like to have your back against the wall, to have everyone hate you, to believe you're a liar. I'm desperate and crazy."

The helmet turned toward me.

"I'm on a sinking ship, buddy, and I will take you down with me. If you aren't going to help me clear my name, then I'll be forced to deploy Plan Blitzen. I'll be the hero that caught the villain and saved Christmas."

Anderson zipped up his jacket and made a disgusted noise.

"I'll tell everyone how you cast me to the ground, and…" I floundered, thinking about my grandmother's old bodice-ripper romance novels. "And threw yourself onto me in a violent passion."

In half a second, he had me pinned against the wall, gloved hand at my throat.

"Word of warning, Gingersnap. You don't blackmail someone like me," he hissed into my ear. "I will fuck you up."

"Desperate and crazy." I pointed at myself. "Right here. You'll be in jail for the rest of your life," I rasped. "Or you could just help me. You know, mutually assured destruction."

He drew back.

Those ghostly silvery-gray eyes bored into mine.

I shivered, unable to break my gaze away as we stared at each other.

The grandfather clock chimed.

Wordlessly, he lifted his right hand and extended it to me.

I slipped my smaller one into the rough glove, and he gave me a crushing handshake.

Then he was gone, disappearing out into the wintery night, leaving me feeling like I'd slipped a leash on the devil and I was about to regret it.

Chapter 4

ANDERSON

"You fucking idiot." My oldest brother, Hudson, didn't even look up from his computer when I walked into the abandoned auto service garage I'd turned into a makeshift field office.

"How the hell did you get caught?" Jake, the second youngest, demanded, approaching me, coffee mug in his hand.

"Why the fuck do you care? I didn't ask you all to be here." I slammed my helmet onto one of the tool-laden tables, sending one of the wrenches spinning.

The scent of machine oil hung in the air. Usually, the smell calmed me, but not today. I worked the heavy gloves off my fingers, wincing at the bite on my hand.

Fucking dog. Fucking girl. Fucking job.

Talbot, the fourth youngest, was hovering in front of an oversize TV screen, watching footage from the drones Lawrence, the third youngest, was operating—Lawrence aka the *only* Wynter brother that I'd asked to come help me tonight.

"I thought you were watching my six," I snarled at him, resisting the urge to bodycheck him so he didn't lose control of the drone and send it crashing into the Murphys' roof.

My brother grimaced.

"I was, but then..." He gestured to my other three brothers, his eyes never leaving the screen.

The drone feed was a little hazy from the snow, but with the infrared, we could make out Henry Murphy's little sister sweeping away my boot prints, just like she'd agreed to, the little demon dog hopping around like a possessed windup toy at her feet.

"Aw, look at the little doggie! Did you see the little dog, Anderson? Anderson?" Jake nudged me. "Did you see the dog?"

"Yeah, it bit me."

"Aw, let me see that." Hudson took my hand, inspected the puncture marks, then flicked the bite wound hard with two fingers.

"Ow!" I shoved him.

"You deserve it for being caught."

"I was careful," I snarled at him.

"The fuck you were." My older brother was up in my face now.

"This isn't your fucking job." I didn't back down. "Why the fuck are you all here?"

"It's my goddamn company, and your fuckup is about to cost us a huge client. So yeah, I say this shit show is absolutely my business," Hudson snapped.

I ran an angry hand through my hair. "She wasn't supposed to be there, and Lawrence was supposed to be running comms."

"Mea culpa! Jake brought sandwiches. I thought you would be good for three minutes."

"You should have had two people, one watching the party, one watching the house," Hudson said flatly.

"I know how to run surveillance," I forced through clenched teeth.

"Then act like it."

Ignoring him, I plugged in the hard drive that I'd used to copy all of the data from tonight's three targets, including Dr. Murphy.

"The point of this exercise is to make money, not waste it." Lawrence jumped to my defense. "You don't get red-carpet service to cover up a mistake."

"Now it's worse." Hudson berated us as I started copying over all the files for analysis. "That girl's going to call the police. Word will get out that we were involved with a break-in at a beloved sports surgeon's family home. He's done operations on half the NHL. He's a fucking New England hero."

"Even if she does, there's no evidence," Lawrence countered. "We cut into the Ring camera feeds, and Anderson didn't leave a trace. See? No footprints."

"Why... is she cleaning up after you?" Hudson inclined his head to the screen, where Evelyn Murphy, or Evie, as she was listed in her father's phone contacts, was tramping back from a detached garage, a little bottle of quick-acting glue in her hands.

I looked up then quickly back at my screen.

"She and I have an understanding."

"Did you threaten her?" Jake scoffed. "Because I'm sure that's going to hold."

"No, I—" Frustrated, I tapped my fingers on the mouse. "We made a deal."

"A deal? What deal?" Hudson was back in my face now.

"I have it under control."

My brother grabbed the collar of my motorcycle jacket roughly. "I am sick of you fucking up."

I stared mulishly into eyes, which were identical to my own.

"And I'm sick of you lying about it to cover up your mistakes." Hudson shook me.

"Fine. She tried to blackmail me. I'm going to make her regret it."

"You fucking better." He threw me back down into my seat.

Evie was back out on the back porch, shaking out the rug I'd had her pinned down on.

Her dog didn't seem to like that very much and jumped up to clamp its sharp teeth onto the corner of the carpet while Evie yelled at the animal, trying to shake it loose.

I winced, remembering the dog's teeth in my fingers.

"What's its name?" Jake wore a shit-eating grin.

"Snowball," I muttered.

"Snowball!" Jake collapsed with laughter. "Snowball the Pomeranian took down one of the most feared men in America."

Talbot grinned and sat down next to me with a first aid kit.

"Hope you're up-to-date on your tetanus shots." Jake tousled my hair.

"Fuck all of you. If you're not helping, you can leave."

Hudson grabbed his laptop and sat next to me, glowering, but he did log into the server where I was copying the files and began wordlessly analyzing them.

"What are we looking for?"

I ignored him.

"The usual," Lawrence said when he realized I wasn't answering. "You know what Aaron Richmond wants."

Jake and Talbot also grabbed files to work through while Lawrence recalled the drone and swapped the feed to one with fresh batteries.

Hudson took a breath, held it, then said, "I know you have a hard deadline for December twenty-fourth. I can ask Grayson if he could convince Aaron to give you a stay of execution."

"That's just going to piss him off. You know how Aaron feels about his older brother. Anyway, I have it under control," I promised. "The Nick Steppes files definitely have what we need. The Bergeson Real Estate files should yield something, and if we're lucky, the Murphy files will be a gold mine. Then problem solved."

And I could ghost Evie and her deranged little dog.

"St. Nick hath blessed us!"

It wasn't even forty-five minutes into reviewing the files that Jake got a hit on one of the Steppes files.

"It's a smoking gun for insurance fraud."

Talbot went to stand behind him.

"Can you—"

"Backtrack it to give the Van de Berg fraud investigators a legitimate opening for relitigating the claim? Already on it. And he acts like this is my first day on the job."

"It's been amateur hour tonight. You can't blame him," Hudson said snidely.

"Family incoming," Lawrence announced.

There on the screen was Henry with the rest of the Murphys, all coming back from their holiday party. The world's most perfect family.

"Now he can actually announce incoming civilians," I remarked dryly.

I absently wondered if Evie managed to fix the statue. From reviewing all of her father's files, he was a meticulous man with a laser-focused attention to detail.

The lights flicked on in the house. Shadows moved in front of the windows.

The light in the round attic window stayed on as the rest slowly winked out.

A few hours later, Talbot got a partial hit on the Bergeson Real Estate files.

"I think there might be something here, based on the text-message log. These people were better about covering their tracks, though."

"Which means that they definitely were trying to commit fraud. We just need the proof."

"Might want to see if you can't send Skylar to fish it out of this Braeden Wallace," Talbot suggested. "It looks like he was in contact with the Bergeson Real Estate head honchos. Based on this tragic company headshot, he's a shallow douche."

"This is not an official paying job," Hudson interjected. "Skylar is expensive, and she's busy doing actual work. You need to investigate it yourself, Anderson."

I sat and stewed as the night progressed into morning. It was becoming more and more obvious that Dr. Murphy at least had conducted business aboveboard, and there was zero chance of insurance fraud.

"Fuck." I leaned back in my chair.

"You can cut the drone feed. That house is clean," Hudson told Lawrence.

"Wait. Just—"

Lawrence looked at me expectantly.

I stared at the screen as Evie, dog spinning crazily at her feet, carefully maneuvered an empty rolling grocery basket down the wide porch steps like it was a normal Saturday, like she and her family weren't out to ruin my life.

I swore under my breath. The irritation, the lack of sleep, the stress of the impending deadline—fury at her boiled in my normally ice-cold veins.

"Blackmailed by a girl, bitten by a dog, and you didn't even get the files we needed." Hudson tossed his pen onto the table. "This is not a great start to the holiday season."

"I have this under control. She's going to learn what it means to try to fuck me over. Just..." I added. "Don't tell Aaron Richmond."

A cold smile spread across Hudson's face. "I don't have to tell Aaron anything." He leaned in to whisper, "Because he already knows."

I swore again.

Dr. Murphy's social calendar was up on the screen.

"I know how to bring that girl to heel."

Chapter 5

EVIE

"And this year's Murphy Misfit award goes to... drumroll please..."

Sawyer rapped the serving tongs on the marble counter of my mom's kitchen.

"Evie Murphy!" Ian announced.

"Whooo!" Sawyer tossed red, white, and green M&Ms at me. They were the official candy of the Murphy Misfits, a club consisting of me, Ian, and Sawyer—the black sheep.

"Don't eat those," I chided Snowball. "I'm unemployed and don't have money for a vet bill."

Sawyer scooped up the chocolate.

"It's not the end of the year, guys," I reminded them as I carefully plated the holiday-sweater-shaped sugar cookies I'd spent all afternoon baking for my mom's party on the antique tiered-glass tray.

Did the Murphys not just have a holiday party?

Why, yes. Yes, we did.

However, when you're part of a big family, what's more fun than passive-aggressively one-upping your siblings and/or cousins at being the perfect hostess?

"It's close enough that I'm calling it, folks." Ian used a dead-on sports announcer voice, holding a candy cane up to his mouth as a microphone. "Not only did Evie come off strong from last year, what with kissing Felicity's fiancé, but she's shown another strong finish this year with her third firing of the season *and* an official notice of disownment from the Murphy parental team leaders. Ian, with his low-paid understudy role, just doesn't have the runway to make up the ground."

"Because Ian is at least getting paid."

"Allegedly." Ian switched back to his real voice and stole a piece of cheese off the charcuterie board.

"Wasn't the director absolutely for sure letting you dance the Nutcracker Prince?" Sawyer rearranged the cheese on the board.

"He was." Ian's face went dark. "He's a cheap wad. You should have seen who he hired to repair the expanding Christmas tree. I think Snowball could have done a better job."

The Pomeranian yipped.

The doorbell rang with the first of my mother's ugly-holiday-sweater-party guests.

"Showtime!"

"I hope everyone likes the snacks," I fretted.

"Just give it up." Ian pulled on the sweater I'd crocheted for him, with its array of holiday appliques of Rudolph and his friends. "You keep bending over backward for these people, but they're never going to see you as anything other than the interloper who tried to ruin Felicity's relationship. Even when you moved in with Declan and his wife and provided night nursing and general housekeeping for free, he didn't say one nice word about you to the family."

"They're busy with their new baby."

"This family doesn't deserve you." Ian patted his hair in place.

"Come December twenty-fifth, it's over one way or the other," Sawyer reminded me as she smoothed down her bright-blue sweater with a snow scene on it. It wasn't my best work, but Sawyer insisted she loved it.

"Don't remind me." I felt sick. I shouldn't have eaten all those cookies. Mouth dry, I pulled on my own red-and-white holiday sweater.

"Might want to go change." Sawyer pointed. "People already think you're a ho ho ho. Don't want to advertise it."

I raced the three flights of stairs up to the attic and rummaged in a cast-off trunk for a different holiday sweater. Yeah, these were all holiday sweaters I'd crafted for my parents and non–Murphy Misfit family, and they all had ended up here.

It's the thought that counts on Christmas, right?

The makeshift attic bedroom was drafty. The round window that looked out over the front yard was single paned and needed to be reglazed. The cracks were big enough that I could hear Snowball's furious barks.

Dammit.

My dad hated it when Snowball barked and would always remind me that the Irish setters didn't howl like they were deranged.

Pulling the cold iron handle of the window, I finally tugged it open, sending paint flecks drifting into the winter wind.

Leaning out the window, I sucked in a breath of cold winter air to yell at Snowball then almost fell out the window when I saw what she was barking at.

Or rather, who.

"Nope. Not today, Satan." I grabbed the first sweater in the pile and clattered down the stairs, pulling it over my head as I raced down to intercept him.

I'd half believed I'd dreamed last night. My dad hadn't noticed the repairs to the statue, and I'd erased all evidence that Anderson had even been in the house.

Now he was here? Why?

What if he really had been out for revenge? Maybe I'd interrupted his big Murphy annihilation plan and he was here to finish what he started.

I needed to stop him.

But I was too late, I realized as, wheezing, I rushed into the living room, where my family was crowding around the new arrival.

Anderson cut a chilling figure against the cheery Christmas décor.

Thick black leather motorcycle pants rode low on his hips. Tattoos snaked up the V of muscle that led to parts of him that I was totally not interested in exploring. More black ink trailed up the washboard abs, up the swell of pecs, to the broad shoulders and crawled along the tendons of his neck to disappear under the dark black motorcycle helmet that swiveled around slowly to survey my family.

You can fix this, I told myself, taking an unsteady step toward him. *They haven't seen his face. He could be anyone. You just have to get rid of him. Now.*

"You can come down my chimney anytime, Santa!" Nat whooped, causing the rest of my female cousins to hold on to each other, jumping up and down and screaming. Phones out, they recorded the impending carnage.

"Now, this is a holiday shindig!" Granny Doyle whooped appreciatively. "Glad to see you removed that stick up your butt, Melissa, and actually tried to throw a fun holiday party for once. Life is for living!"

Granny Doyle poured out shots, splashing vodka on the table. The smell of fake eggnog coupled with the monster in the middle of the living room was making it hard to keep from tossing my Christmas cookies.

"You brought a stripper to your holiday party?" Grandma Shirley was appalled. "Why am I not surprised?"

"He's not for you." Granny Doyle handed my cousin Lauren a shot glass wrapped in dollar bills. "We all know you wouldn't know what to do with a man like that if he popped up naked out of your toilet." Gran and Lauren knocked their shots back.

The helmet swiveled to her.

"Mom, *please.* Of course I didn't hire a stripper, Shirley. Brian, do something," Melissa hissed.

My dad rolled up his sleeves. "Excuse me, who hired you?"

The helmet inclined slightly.

"Dad, don't." Henry's voice was sharp as the shirtless man took a step toward me, wood floors creaking under the heavy boot falls.

"This is all just a horrible misunderstanding." I tried to shoo him to the door. "A prank gone wrong."

"You brought this…" My mother gestured helplessly. "Here?"

"Gingersnap," the deep voice rumbled from under the helmet. "I thought you'd be happy to see me. I came all this way for you."

"I'll just give you your payment outside."

"You did hire him, Evie Murphy." My mom's voice was shrill. Better her anger than her heartbreak.

Desperate, I shoved my shoulder against the massive chest but couldn't budge him.

A tattooed arm reached up, twisting the black helmet slightly then removing it… and unleashing complete bedlam at the holiday party.

"St. Nick, stick me on a spit and roast me like a marshmallow!" My female cousins and most of my aunts yodeled like horny cats.

Henry immediately let out a line of expletives and shouted, "I knew it was you!"

My mother grabbed my father, wailing like the Grinch had just crash-landed in Whoville.

"Cute party," Anderson announced over the fray, fixing those ghostly eyes on me.

"How could you?" my mom screamed, tears streaming down her face.

"Disowned!" my father thundered. "You're disowned, Evie."

"Miss me, Gingersnap?" A smile sliced Anderson's face. He reached out to grab my waist possessively, the rough palm of his hand sliding briefly under the frumpy, misshapen sweater.

Bending down, he growled against my ear, low so only I could hear,

"I told you—fuck with me, and there's hell to pay."

"Motherfucker." Henry shoved the tattooed man off me. "You don't have any right to be here, Anderson."

"I was invited," my Christmas nightmare drawled.

My father's eyes were round with shock. The triplets cowered next to Declan.

"Man." Granny Doyle whistled. "I know Anderson tried to kill Henry and all, but damn if an attempted murderer never looked so good."

My mother made an indignant noise.

There was a scowl stamped on Anderson's mouth.

"But he's stacked the game in his favor," Nat purred.

"I'm sure Evie didn't tell you, but this is an ugly-holi-day-sweater party," Lauren added, literally licking her lips.

"Naughty boy," Nat hummed. "Someone isn't wearing a sweater."

Slow smile spreading on his face, he reached up one tattooed hand to his neck and ran his fingers lazily along a jagged tattoo.

"You can't make an exception?" the deep voice rumbled.

"Oh, we can!" My cousins panted.

Braeden, who, unlike Henry and Anderson, was not an ex-Marine, stepped up next to my eldest brother.

"Braeden, what in God's name are you doing? Sit down. You're not going to fight Anderson Wynter," Sawyer said derisively. "Go away."

"Boo! You're blocking my shot!" Lauren yelled, phone out.

"Felicity, tell your lame-o fiancé to move it!" Nat hollered.

Anderson took a menacing step toward Braeden, who held his position for a split second then thought better of it and scuttled out of the way. The large man banged his shoulder into Henry's as he passed him to get to me.

My family seemed to take a collective breath, waiting in anticipation for what was going to happen next.

"You," my mother said, voice trembling as she pushed off my father, "are not welcome in this house, and you are certainly not dating my daughter."

"I don't date girls. I fuck them." Anderson slowly rolled his shoulders. "And in my defense, I didn't know she was your daughter the first time she begged me to fill her up."

There were shocked gasps from the family.

"She doesn't look anything like you," he added, flat gray gaze flicking dismissively over my mother. "Thank fuck, because I like a woman with big tits I can come all over and an ass that I can hold on to when I'm raw-dogging her pussy."

The flat of his large hand connected with my backside, making me squeak.

The color drained from my father's face.

Anderson smiled maliciously, a bad elf standing in the middle of the North Pole with a smirk on his face, holding a gas can and a cigarette lighter. He was here to blow up my life.

As I looked around at my horrified family, it was then that I realized I had, in fact, fucked up.

In a lifetime of bad decisions, blackmailing Anderson Wynter was hands down the worst.

"Trust me," Anderson continued, deep voice rumbling around the room, "holiday parties aren't what I typically fuck with, but Evie really wanted me to come, and I really wanted her to choke on my dick tonight, so here I am."

This isn't happening. I'm going to pass out.

"Stay the hell away from her."

Declan and several of my male cousins had to hold back Henry as he tried to take a swing at Anderson.

"She doesn't have anything to do with what's between us. If you have a problem, you come to me, not my sister."

Anderson was unbothered. "So much for the holiday spirit." He turned to me, horrible delight in his eyes. "Next time you want to fuck, Gingersnap, just stick your ass out of the kitchen window, and I'll take care of it. I don't want to get tied up in your family issues, and your mom doesn't want me in her living room."

"I want you in her living room!" Aunt J whooped.

"I demand you leave at once," my father said firmly.

"Whatever. Gingersnap." Anderson snapped his fingers at me. "Let's go."

I shook my head. I couldn't speak.

He looked me up and down. Cold. Unfeeling.

"Want to disobey me? Fine. I'll take it out of your ass tonight." He turned, helmet swinging from one hand.

"Someone call the cops!" Braeden yelped as Anderson slipped the helmet back on and disappeared out into the winter night.

"Someone call animal control." Aunt J fanned herself.

"Fuck that!" Granny Doyle hooted. "Call the fire department. That was hot, hot, hot!"

Finally able to shake off the paralysis, I raced after him, my flats slipping and sliding on the icy walkway.

Anderson was twisting on his jacket as he made his way toward the black motorcycle.

"Bastard!" I yelled at him, the tears freezing on my face. "You ruined my life! You ruined it more than it was already ruined. No deal. Fuck you."

The faceless helmet peered over his shoulder at me.

I hurled myself at him, fists flying. "Did you see my mother's face? They hate me now."

"Calm down, Gingersnap." Large hands trapped me, one on my waist and one on my arm. There was the brief sensation of warm leather under my palms as I twisted against him.

"Get off of me." I struggled, my feet sliding while his boots stay firmly planted.

"Stop fighting me. I don't want them to think we're breaking up." The deep voice mocked me behind the motorcycle helmet. "Mutually assured destruction, remember?"

"The deal is off." I sniffled. "I'm calling the police."

Hollow laughter came from behind the helmet.

"I saw your family in there, Gingersnap." He released me with a shake. "If you go back in there and tell them that you tried to blackmail the Murphys' sworn enemy so that you could make your cousin's boyfriend admit he loves you, then you're just digging that hole deeper for yourself."

Damn him, he was right.

"You wanted to play with the wolves. You can't be upset when you get bitten." He spread his arms. "Looks like you did a fantastic job of alienating your entire family back there. Guess you're stuck with me, Gingersnap. Now give me a kiss." He leaned toward me.

I slapped the helmet. "You're as horrible as Henry always said you were."

"And don't you forget it." His huge gloved hand grabbed my face, shaking it softly like you'd do a dog. He released me before I could hit him again then straddled his motorcycle, making a big show of adjusting his Christmas package as he settled on the dark-leather seat.

"I don't ever want to see you again!" I shouted at him.

He revved the engine then popped the visor briefly to pin me with those snow-demon eyes.

"Something tells me you're going to come crawling back to me. You made a deal with the devil and all."

The visor slammed shut.

I breathed hard, my breath clouding around me as I slowly made my way back to the house.

I shouldn't have done it. I should never have done it. I should have known that you can't leash a man like Anderson Wynter. I needed to get rid of him, needed to break his hold on me, neutralize his angry fixation.

I slipped back in through the front door.

My mother was waiting.

"*You.*" Melissa grabbed my arm, her nails digging into my flesh as she dragged me to my dad's study.

"Young lady." She addressed me like I was a middle schooler again and had gotten yet another D on a math test. "I am so disappointed in you."

Tears filled my mother's eyes. "How could you be involved with that... that criminal? He almost got your brother killed. *My baby.*"

My mother broke down in my father's arms.

I felt like a worm, like a little slug. There was no argument about it. Anderson was pure evil.

And he was trying to break my family apart.

No. Correction, he was trying to break me apart from my family.

"You don't understand what it's like to birth a perfect child then have someone try to kill him."

"Mom," Henry began. "Don't you think this is a little excessive?"

My mother barreled on. "And then to have the girl that you invited into your home, loved like your own child, throw that love back in your face and start dating—"

"Sleeping with," one of the triplets, Alana, corrected before she could stop herself. "Anderson said they weren't actually dating, just hooking up."

"Fucking, really..." her identical triplet added then trailed off. "He said the F-word..."

My mother took a shaky breath and looked up at the ceiling. "I've never been more ashamed to call you my daughter, Evie."

A crowd of family members on the porch peered through the open French doors into the study, addicted to the dramatic *telenovela* that was my life.

"So glad I didn't skip this party," one of my dad's cousins whispered to her sister-in-law.

"I know, right?" The other woman sipped her wine. "It's always so boring, but this? Totally worth the Uber fare."

My father tapped in to the Evie emotional beat down. "You need to break it off right now with Anderson Wynter," my father ordered. "I just—" He turned around then back to me, frustrated. "I don't understand, Evie. What were you thinking?"

"I'll tell you!" Granny Doyle hollered through the doorway off the foyer. "It looks to me like she's thinking with her vajazzlebiscuit. Can't say I blame her. I thought menopause had dried me up, and now here I am, about to have to change my underwear."

"Mom, not helpful, and it's not even seven o'clock. Why are you already drunk?" my mom fussed at Gran.

"Because like all of us, she thought this party was going to be torturously boring—oh!" my dad's sister chirped. "Did I say that in my outside voice? I love the charcuterie board, Melissa. Sooo cute!"

"I actually made that." I slowly raised my hand then put it back down at my mother's withering glare.

My aunt toasted me with her hand-painted cocktail glass.

"Hopefully, this means the mandatory party games are canceled," one of Dad's brothers joked to Uncle Hugh.

"That dick must be fire, though." Lauren and Nat fanned each other.

Cousin Irene, face flushed, said breathlessly, "I can't imagine what it must be like to be in bed with Anderson. He's an animal, crazy and dangerous. He has no soul."

"Massive dick, no soul." Aunt Jennifer made a weighing motion with her hands. "I don't need a man to respect me to fuck me."

"Then why did you bitch me out," her boyfriend du jour complained, "when I came home with the wrong brand of yogurt?"

"He tried to kill my son!" my mother cried to noises of disgust from her sisters.

"You're going to milk that until the day you die."

"Drama queen." Aunt J coughed into her glass.

My dad's jaw was tight. "Evie, do you have anything to say for yourself?"

Sweat dripped from my armpits under the sweater. I tried my hardest not to look at the hastily repaired wood sculpture on the side table.

Just come clean.

Honesty is the best policy.

Get it out of the way, then I could go back to being strongly disliked as opposed to actively hated.

"Well, I, uh... you see..." I tapped my two index fingers together.

"Think of Henry!" my mother cried, interrupting me. "Did you even think about how he would feel? This is traumatizing for him."

"Mom." Henry rested a hand on her arm, centering himself. "Please. I think everyone is overreacting. Clearly," he said, cutting off my mother's arguments, "Evie is just doing this for attention. It's a phase, and we need to just ignore it."

Ian scoffed under his breath, "What a twerp."

Henry's mouth turned down at the corners.

"My wonderful son is right." My mother rallied and clapped her hands. "Everyone, ignore Evie's desperate cry for attention. We'll indulge her little fantasy, and she'll see that she can't co-opt the Christmas holiday season with her juvenile nonsense."

"Nothing juvenile about that man." Aunt J and Aunt Virginia toasted each other.

Nothing human about that man. He was pure evil. Chaotic evil, really.

I couldn't believe my family—or at least some of my family—was fawning all over him and acting like I was actually with him. Like I would even willingly be with someone like Anderson Wynter.

Under the angry gaze of my father, I escaped through the crush of drama-hungry family members back to the kitchen, where I slumped down next to the oven... where my clam chowder bites were burning.

"Shoot!" I scrambled back up and yanked them out of the oven, fanning them.

Then I bent over, feeling lightheaded.

I was completely, totally, effed.

Chapter 6

ANDERSON

The big, burly muscle flicked the sterling silver lighter, holding it up to the cigar in the mouth of the Mafia boss. The grizzled older man puffed the cigar, catching the flame, then leaned back in the chair, smoke swirling around his face. Bulgarian? Croatian? Ex-Yugo Mafia?

It did not matter.

He was not who I came to see. He was smoking that cigar like a toddler sucked a pacifier to keep from crying for his mommy as he faced the expressionless man in front of him.

Aaron Richmond.

The Mafia boss's men were draped menacingly around the windowless New York City bar. It was exactly the sort of place you'd think a midnight Mafia meetup would occur.

Except Aaron had no bodyguards.

The Mafia boss puffed his cigar.

Aaron waited.

I kept my mouth shut and my helmet on. It was not my business.

Beside Aaron sat his assistant, Betty, who was about a thousand years old, four feet tall, and eighty pounds soaking wet. She'd swapped her usual hot-pink sun visor for a green-and-red holiday edition. The polyester tracksuit, straight out of one of those eighties JC Penney catalogues my little sister, Elsa, used to cut up for her paper dolls, rustled as she loaded paper into the portable typewriter in front of her.

Coke-bottle-thick glasses were perched on her nose. She raised her hands over the typewriter keys. The toes of her feet in their orthopedic shoes barely brush the floor.

"Your bodyguard's late," one of the Mafia boss's men chortled, breaking the tense silence and slamming his shoulder into me.

The Mafia boss inclined his head. One of the handlers backhanded the muscle across the face.

"He means no disrespect, Mr. Richmond," the boss assured Aaron.

"That's actually my twelve thirty." Aaron glanced up at me then looked back at the Mafia boss.

"Wait in the corner, love," Betty called.

One of the mob boss's men handed Aaron a folder.

Aaron opened it and pulled out the paperwork inside.

The Mafia boss began, "I want to make sure that you know exactly what you're insuring, no funny business from our side."

Aaron thumbed through the papers.

Betty typed rapidly on the typewriter, bony fingers flying over the keys.

"We'll launder money from illegal imports through our in-house construction company, paying laborers in cash. Additional cash will be funneled through the bar, club, restaurant, and on-site parking lot, contributing to an initial operation fund and a twenty-percent rolling maintenance fund. It doesn't need to be said that we can't just open our books to any insurance company."

The mob boss laughed.

Aaron didn't.

I watched my sometimes-employer review the documentation.

People thought that the Mafia ran New York City.

Maybe fifty years ago, sure, but today?

Try getting anything done without insurance. Want to launder money through a pizza joint? Insurance. Running a shady shipping operation? Insurance. Even casinos depended on insurance. Overworked government officials often relied on insurance companies to vet businesses, assuming that if an insurer issued a policy, the business must be legit.

Once an insurance company like Van de Berg had their hooks in an enterprise, you better not piss them off. They could expose your dirty operation to the FBI while claiming ignorance. The government wouldn't challenge them because if a giant like Van de Berg collapsed, it took the whole economy down with it.

The mob boss shifted in his seat, his cigar almost burnt down to his lips.

"Make it twenty-seven percent." Aaron crossed out a number with a red pen. "And we'll work out an insurance policy." He closed the folder.

The boss visibly relaxed and stubbed out the cigar.

"Pleasure doing business with you, sir." The boss stood up and gave Aaron a little bow.

The typewriter clanged.

Betty loaded in a new sheet of paper and handed Aaron a large black book as the Mafia boss and his men cleared the windowless bar.

Aaron opened it flat on the table

It was a ledger. Old school. No digital records for Aaron, not on business like this.

He looked up at me. "Next."

I approached the oversize table and removed my helmet. "Evening, Betty."

"What's shakin', sugar?"

Aaron ran his capped fountain pen down the hand-written ledger.

"Anderson Wynter," he began. "On June 24 of this year, you fucked up." His glittering green eyes regarded me.

I stared at the spot above his head.

"I hired you," he continued, "to investigate a nonprofit for fraud. Instead of delivering the evidence that I *know* you found, you destroyed it, lied to my face about it, and cost me 5,342,010 dollars and five cents."

I ground my teeth together.

"Because I hate to burn a good investigative firm, and your brother's come through for me when other firms have failed, I gave you a second chance. I granted you mercy. Pay back the debt in six months, and all would be forgiven. Now here we are. December 10, and you still owe me"—he tapped the ledger—"exactly 745,632 dollars and sixty-four cents. Where—" He steepled his hands. "Is my money, Anderson?"

"I'm working on it."

"Not good enough."

"I've cleared through dozens of potential fraud cases," I reminded him, "dug up evidence your people overlooked, and," I added, slipping the printouts from my jacket, "I just cleared a little over two hundred fifty thousand. The Steppes account."

Aaron flipped slowly through the evidence.

"You're still short."

"In progress."

"Is it?" Aaron asked mildly. "Because I heard that you were caught. America's pride and joy, apprehended by a college dropout with a toy rescue dog."

"It had very sharp teeth."

Aaron raised an eyebrow.

"You're lucky it didn't latch on to your willy." Betty peered up at me through the thick glasses.

"It's actually going to work in my favor."

"Enlighten me."

I pulled out the list of names, many of them crossed out, the majority of them with a dollar figure noted neatly to the right.

"These last ones here on the list? The girl, Evie, is related to them, and I have her under my boot. She'll get me access to these last few names. I'll dig up the evidence of insurance fraud and done. It's the last half a million. I have two weeks. It's nothing. I'll clear the list with time to spare."

"By dating some girl who's blackmailing you? Color me not confident."

I clenched my fists. Forced myself to relax.

"I would never actually date her. I can't stand her. Or her family."

Aaron gave me an assessing glance. "My mistake."

"She's a tool to be used. Believe that."

"Can't say that I do."

"I will pay you back by Christmas," I promised Aaron. "I give you my word."

The typewriter dinged.

"You better."

As the winter landscape passed me by in a blur, I wondered, as usual, what the hell was wrong with me.

How had I fucked up my life so bad?

I wished I could just ride and ride, as fast as the motorcycle could take me. Away from it all—out west.

Just escape.

Instead, I rode to Maplewood Falls, to the good part of town.

"Bro, you're late." My younger brother Talbot slapped me on the back when I walked into the big commercial kitchen, where I tossed my jacket and helmet into a locker.

I grabbed an apron from the hook on the wall, tied it around my waist, and pulled the silk tie out of my pocket.

Talbot took it from me and popped the collar of my starched white dress shirt.

"If you see anyone from the Kingsley-Alden job, give me a heads-up, okay?" He deftly tied a Windsor knot. "Look at you in your little monkey suit."

"Did yous get more tattoos?" the manager demanded when he saw me.

"Stop riding him, Mac. He's been up all night."

The manager cracked his neck. "I always tell you kids to get more sleep. Yous gonna to wake up like me with aches and pains one day."

"Gets colder every year, don't it, Mac?" one of the cooks called.

"I have some extra firewood. I'll bring it by your place later," I promised Mac. "Have to borrow my brother's truck when he's not in town."

"I'm good. You kids don't worry about me."

I shrugged nonchalantly. "It's just from another job," I lied. "Rich woman decided it was too rustic. Felt like someone should use it so it doesn't go to the landfill." Mac wouldn't accept it if he'd known I'd chopped it just for him.

"All right, all right, but it still doesn't change the fact that you have five minutes to eat, Anderson," he barked at me.

"Like I want to eat your shitty food," I said with a smile.

"Your brother's an asshole." Mac slapped a towel into Talbot's hands.

"Always!" Talbot quipped as I grabbed a bowl of the eggs, potatoes, and bacon Mac had left for me, then I wolfed it down.

A hundred fifty years ago, the Wynter family had been this club's most prominent members. Now I cleaned the tables they used to dine at.

"The bridge club is coming in at eleven," Mac told me. "I'm putting them in your section. Zeke says he's going to quit if he has them again. Put those tattoos to work. They're a big draw with some of the neglected housewives."

"I don't know why you're complaining. You did some of them," I reminded him.

"Just the shitty ones. Hey," he added, serious, "you haven't been picking up that many shifts. I can schedule you in for more if you need."

"Doing some work to pay back some money I lost." The lie slipped out easily.

Talbot, walking by, made a slot machine noise.

Mac slapped me on the back of the head. "Make better choices."

I stacked waters on my tray and headed out into the ornate Gilded Age–era dining room, my face professionally neutral, and took orders for the first of the brunch rush—mostly cash-flush retirees out with whiny grandkids.

Even though it no longer was the gathering place for one sixth of the world's wealth, it still was the country club of choice for a number of high-status individuals. Regular access to them was worth the hassle.

Usually.

I peered out over the privileged elite as they complained loudly about the state of their grilled fish and *beurre blanc* sauce, demanded to speak to the manager, or let their little dogs and ill-mannered children run around the dining room.

"Fuckers," I mumbled.

"Hey!" Mac grabbed my jaw. "Leave it. This is a job. They're a paycheck."

But that girl in a red-and-green pinafore sitting in front of the sparking crystal glasses and fine china, fidgeting with the ends of her hand-knitted scarf?

She wasn't just a paycheck.

Chapter 7

EVIE

As my parents sat in front of me, my father cleaning his silverware with his napkin, I was met with the sudden realization that I was woefully unprepared for this meeting.

Why, oh why, were we even here?

As the parents of seven kids, my folks didn't want to be like those other big families—you know, the trashy ones like the Svenssons where the parents just let the kids run around feral and didn't even know their names, let alone anything about them.

My parents prided themselves in always making time for their children as individuals.

Hence the mandatory quality time.

Great in theory, especially for golden children like Henry, Declan, or the triplets.

For yours truly?

You ever had one of those interviews where you know from the moment you step into the room that you are *so* not getting the job offer? But it's too late to turn around and walk out?

Yeah. That's this.

Maybe we would all just psychically agree to sit here in uncomfortable silence—a continuation of the world's most uncomfortable car ride ever.

Perched on the edge of my seat in the stuffy country club dining room, I reached for my cardstock-printed menu, sending a fork crashing to the floor.

My father took a breath.

"I see that you have been baking a number of holiday confections in the last week that are different from your usual fare. What inspires you to create new recipes?"

And so it begins.

"That's really a great question," I said, stalling.

Normally, before my mandatory quality-time days, I prepped funny anecdotes, practiced my "I'm interested and happy to be here" face, and tried to anticipate the congressional-inquiry- level questions my dad might ask.

Between holiday delusions of grandeur, blackmailing an extremely dangerous man, and pretending like I wasn't getting thrown onto the streets Christmas morning, I'd been a little preoccupied.

"I've just been drinking leftover wine and trawling through TikTok at night." This was not the right answer but the only one that my brain seemed able to supply.

"Studies show that excessive social media use, especially short-form content, has a negative impact on your attention span." My father frowned.

"If you used the energy you spend on social media looking for a job, you'd have one right now," my mother added, unfolding her napkin and placing it neatly in her lap. "Don't think your father and I won't hold this boundary. You have to find a job by Christmas, or you're moving out."

"Hence the social media," I joked, my mouth running away from me before I could think. "I just need to attract a man who has a good job and wants a stay-at-home girlfriend."

My dad's frown deepened. "Evie, that is not a plan. It's not realistic. You're not a classic beauty. I work with single men who have well-paying jobs. They desire a wife who's highly educated, who prioritizes health and fitness. They don't want a college dropout raising their children. Now, you need to get serious and find a job. You like baking. Why don't you go work at a bakery?"

"Gran says I have amazing tits and could make a killing on OnlyFans."

"You do that, and we will send you back to the orphanage."

"Ha ha!" I laughed awkwardly then screamed bloody murder as a tattooed hand grabbed me under the chin and a rough jaw nuzzled my neck.

Everyone in the posh dining room turned to look at me.

Anderson gave me a self-satisfied smirk then set glasses of water down in front of me and my parents.

"Is this why you suggested the country club?" my mom demanded.

Friends, it was not. Had I known that Anderson worked here, I would have suggested a long, cold, miserable hike in the sleet.

"I just wanted eggs benedict and those crispy potato stacks." My voice was faint.

The tattooed hand slipped into his apron pocket and pulled out a leather-bound notepad. He briefly tapped me on the head with it then scrawled out my order.

"Do you want anything to drink with that besides water, Gingersnap?"

Out of instinct, I turned my head to speak to him then snapped it back, eyes forward when I came face to well, *bulge* of his crotch.

"Mix all of the alcohol you have back there with orange juice, please."

"And for you, Dr. and Mrs. Murphy?"

"I want to be placed in a different section." My mother had had too much Botox to frown, but she was scowling in spirit.

"All the sections have been reserved. You're free to go elsewhere," Anderson's deep voice rumbled.

I sat ramrod straight, trying to ignore the heat, testosterone, and aggressive male energy radiating behind me.

"I do want to kindly remind you that there is a monthly minimum spend on food and drink at the country club, and you placed a reservation, and that has a cancelation fee. I'm happy to process all of that for you right here. Shall I put it on your tab?"

"Hurry up and order!" an elderly woman hooted from two tables over.

"Mel, why is your mother here?" my dad grumbled.

"Hey, Hot Stuff!" Granny Doyle hustled over to our table.

"While my daughter tries to fight her inner Karen and get you fired, I need you to bring a couple pitchers of mimosas for the table." She lowered her voice. "If I have to listen to Shelia tell the story about how her so-called hot doctor stuffed her prolapsed uterus into her abdomen one more time, I'm going to lose it. I've met her doctor. You wouldn't catch his hand up the snatch of my cold, dead corpse."

She grabbed Anderson's arm, pulling him down, and looked around furtively.

"Now, listen. You gotta tell the kitchen staff not to lump me in with these losers. Nothing but stuck-up old people. I hate bridge. I hang with the cool gals. We just drink and talk shit about the other members and trade porn links." Granny Doyle slapped Anderson on the very firm behind.

"You should think about doing porn. You'd make a killing. More than working at this joint, I bet."

"Gran…"

"I need to find the manager and get your boyfriend's schedule, Evie. I'm only coming here when he's working from now on."

"Gran, you can't sexually harass the wait staff." I regretted the words as soon as I said them, looking up guiltily at Anderson.

But there was only malicious delight in his eyes.

"You sexually harassed me."

My dad wanted to die.

"Evie, you're going to get us all banned from the club," my mom complained.

"I didn't—"

Anderson's hand was possessive on the back of my neck. He leaned slightly forward over the table.

"That's how I met your daughter last summer. She jumped me while I was cleaning the sauna. Didn't even ask my name, just knelt down to suck my cock then got on her hands and knees and told me to fuck her up the—"

I lunged for his arm to stop the next word and only succeeded in banging my knee on the underside of the table, spilling my ice water in my lap.

His large hand tipped my chin up. His thumb ran over my lower lip.

"I saw she was back in town. Got in contact." The tattooed hand slipped down my shirt for a brief moment and squeezed me through the bra. "She was just as good a fuck as I remembered."

He released me then clicked the pen.

"We have a grilled monkfish with *beurre blanc* sauce and roasted turnips. Today's special."

"That's fine for them," Granny Doyle interjected while my parents tried to recover from their shock. "Bring a stack of those peppermint chip pancakes for the table too. You need to eat something, Melissa," Gran said to her daughter. "A man wants a woman with some meat on her bones. Dammit, Peggy." She stood up to hustle over to her table. "People come late, then they want to take other people's seats."

I busied myself mopping up the water that was soaking into my dress so that I didn't have to look at my parents, steaming in fury at Anderson as he left to put in the order.

"I hope," my mother began, "that you are using protection. You don't want to end up like your birth mother—pregnant with a degenerate's baby, chained to man who has no job, no prospects, and who's going to abandon her. Because I will tell you right now I am not taking care of that ingrate's child."

"You don't get pregnant doing anal, so no worries there," I snapped before I could stop myself.

"I think now we know why her behavior has taken a nosedive," my father said, carefully nudging his silverware so that it was evenly spaced next to his plate. "Anderson is a terrible influence on you, Evie. You are the lowest common denominator of the company you keep."

"Don't waste your breath," my mother declared. "Look at her. She's completely obsessed with him. She can't keep her eyes off him."

It was hard not to look at Anderson.

The biceps in his crisp white shirt bulged as he carried two heavy trays on his massive shoulders.

Unlike the last time I'd seen him, his hair had a severe side part and was slicked into place, the savage beast tamed, at least for a little bit.

With the black slacks, the shiny dress shoes, and the tie, he was looking a little too close to my type for comfort.

No. Not my type.

Anderson was going to help me clear my name, so help me St. Nick, then I was kicking him to the curb.

Also, he was not going to keep treating me like a little sex toy.

"I need to get some paper towels from the restroom. I'll be right back." I excused myself, pretended like I was going to the restroom corridor, then hung a right to the kitchen.

"Back for seconds?" Anderson thrust the empty tray he was carrying at another waiter with similar coloring to him.

Then the huge man grabbed the front of my sweater, hauling me toward him.

"Get off."

Anderson's large hand covered my mouth, and he dragged me to a little alcove, cornering me against the wall.

"You here to give me the riot act, order me to clean up my act, stop the sex talk in front of your parents, Gingersnap?"

"You're rude and horrible and—"

"And I'm making you fucking wet, and you can't handle it? Is that it?"

"You're not—"

"Please." Those ghostly eyes narrowed. "Like you don't lay in your bed at night, your fingers under your panties, and fantasize about me destroying your pussy."

"You're the one who's fantasizing about me." I fought back. "You're the one who can't stop touching me, who can't stop telling me about all the humiliating things you want to do to me. You're the one who's obsessed with me and my family."

His head tipped back, and he let out a hollow laugh.

"Don't flatter yourself, Gingersnap."

"I bet you jack off in the shower like a teenage boy."

He grabbed my hand, fingers large on my wrist, and pressed my palm to his mouth.

"You think you make me hard? You think I'm obsessed with you?" The words were hot against my fingers.

Still gripping my wrist, he slipped my hand down his chin, down his chest, down the silk tie slippery under my fingers. My breath caught in my chest.

"You think you make me hard for you?" he crooned as he forced my hand lower... lower.

I swallowed noisily as my hand scraped over his belt buckle to rest on the heavy canvas of the black apron.

"You feel that?" he whispered in my ear. "*Do you feel it?*"

"Um…"

His hips rocked into my hand, and all I could think about, because I was a horrible person, was those hips doing that into me.

"I said do you feel that?" He pushed me back against the wall roughly.

"Um, no?"

"No. That's right. You do nothing for me. I don't desire you. But you?" His head raised so he could stare into my eyes. "I'd bet my whole paycheck that you're soaking wet right now."

"I am not," I croaked.

"I bet if I put my hand in your panties, your cunt would be so fucking juicy for me."

"Not true."

"You want me to find out?"

Yeah. Yeah, I did.

"Anderson!" barked a man with a military-short haircut and crow's-feet around his eyes.

I scrambled away from him.

When I looked over my shoulder, the older man was chewing out an unrepentant Anderson.

Those gray eyes pierced mine, and he drew his hand across his throat like a knife.

Chapter 8

EVIE

"**Y**ou are a queen, sis!" Ian tossed a handful of poinsettia petals at me. "Take a bow."

"You didn't tell us you were dating *Anderson Wynter*." Sawyer pulled up a stool.

"Fucking," Ian said, enunciating both syllables. "They are *eff-uck-ing*, and I am here for all of it. Did you see St. Henry's face?" He cackled.

"It was a recent development." My mouth was dry.

"'Once you have a murderer's dick, you can't go back' type of thing?" Sawyer joked.

I licked my lip, looked around furtively, then whispered, "I'm blackmailing him."

"You're blackmailing a murderer?"

I raced to shut the kitchen door. "Attempted murderer, and he's had a recent career change. He's a waiter at the club."

"At the country club." Ian slowly snapped his fingers.

"Our origin story is that we had a stranger-danger hookup in the sauna."

"I need to tell my parents we're going to the country club for my birthday if they have guys like that on staff." Sawyer fanned herself. "Gawd, did you see his eyes when he talked about coming on your tits?"

"He was just doing it to humiliate me. He wouldn't actually."

"That man would totally come on your tits if you let him." Sawyer pressed a cold can of Coke to her neck.

"You totally have to sleep with him." Ian grabbed me.

"He's not my type."

"He's every woman's type."

"And gay boys'." Ian pulled at his sweater collar. "There are probably some straight guys who would cross the aisle for him too."

"Not me." I dumped the washed cranberries out onto a towel. I'd adapted my stuffed pork loin recipe for the holiday season.

"My dream guy is a billionaire who wears fancy suits and likes to throw money at problems to make them go away. Not a bad boy with a loud motorcycle and a nasty temper." I cut thick slices of the French bread for croutons.

"It's hard to find a billionaire IRL. You get tased if you get too close to one." Sawyer began whipping the softened cream cheese and herbs in a bowl. "A bad boy? You can stumble on one breaking into your parents' house."

"Take advantage of the walking dildo that just appeared in your life," Ian said sagely, dipping a piece of French bread into the herb-and-cheese mixture.

"When you do decide to take advantage, let me know first so I can wax your nipples." Sawyer slapped Ian as he tried to steal more cheese.

"I'm not taking advantage of anything. Anderson ruins Murphys. He put Henry in the hospital, and he's trying to get me kicked out of the family for good. It's a complete disaster," I groaned as I set garlic butter on the stove to melt.

"No, this is genius," Sawyer corrected. "No one is going to be talking about you trying to steal Boring Braeden after you paraded none other than Anderson Wynter around your mom's living room."

"Instead, they're talking about how I'm a traitor and need to be drawn and quartered." Using a mallet, I banged the pink meat.

Wrong visual. Absolutely terrible visual.

"You can't give up now," Ian urged me. "Go big, like full-on animatronic-nativity-scene-on-your-roof big. Get pregnant with his baby and announce it at Felicity's wedding. Have sex with him under the Christmas tree as everyone's coming down for presents."

"My life is already a shit show!" I shrieked then lowered my voice. "I cannot afford to keep dealing with Anderson. I need him out of my life, not to be chained to him with a baby."

Miserable, I salted the pork loin.

"You saw how everyone was last night, how our parents were. They hate me. I'm never going to be welcome at Christmas again. I need to ghost him. Forget I ever saw him."

"That leaves you worse off than before," Ian argued. "At the very least, stage a big breakup at the next family holiday party with an impassioned pro-Murphy speech."

Laughter sounded from the hallway that led into the sunlit kitchen as Henry, the triplets hanging from him, giggling, waded into the kitchen, the heavy wood door thumping against the nearby shelf.

"Happy twelfth day of advent." I tried to keep my tone chipper and not like someone who had just spent all morning envisioning disaster scenarios.

"Ooh, are you making Cesar salad?" Alana breathed in appreciatively at the umami smell of the garlic butter.

"I know it's your favorite."

Alexis grabbed the pot of eggnog-spice coffee I'd made earlier and poured out three cups.

"Just black coffee for me." Henry waved them away when she offered him one.

"I have to make some more black coffee," I said. "Sawyer took the last of it."

"I can do it," Henry offered. His demeanor was stiff, as you would expect if you thought your sister was dating the man who'd tried to kill you.

Gosh, I was a horrible sister.

Anderson and I were done.

Totally done.

I was cutting my losses.

I brushed butter onto the croutons while a cast-iron skillet heated up on the stove.

"You don't need to help, sweetie." My mother breezed into the kitchen, making a face at the amount of oil I had in the cast-iron skillet. "Henry, you work too hard at that big military drone company. Let us spoil you."

"Maybe you could get Evie a job there," Alissa suggested to Henry as she and the other triplets tag teamed to steal more croutons. "They're letting you work remote, which is awesome. Then Evie could do holiday cooking and still get a paycheck."

Alissa stole a swipe of the herb-and-cream-cheese filling. "*So good.*"

"I think Evie needs to lower her expectations," my father interjected from the doorway. "After you finish prepping dinner, you should go out and see if anyone is hiring at one of the local restaurants, Evie. You might want to go too, Ian. Dance isn't a real career."

My middle brother narrowed his eyes. "Technically, neither is working at a restaurant."

I ducked my head, busying myself with making more coffee.

"Forget what your father says." Granny Doyle hustled into the kitchen. "You and Ian are good-looking kids. You need to find a rich husband."

"And then kill him?" Grandma Shirley interjected sharply as Braeden helped her to the kitchen, Felicity hovering possessively next to him.

"You said it, not me. But if you do," Granny Doyle told us conspiratorially, "Don't wait too long. You don't want to give him a chance to burn his retirement savings on women and poker."

"If that's your goal, I don't think Anderson fits the bill, does he?" my mother remarked as she removed the plastic wrap off the veggie tray and dip I'd assembled early that morning. "Someone with a criminal record isn't employable."

"Uncle Brian did say she should lower her standards. Sounds like Evie should go for it, then." Felicity slid a coffee cake onto the kitchen island.

Mom glared at Dad, who made an apologetic face.

"Are you making sausage stuffing, Evie?" Felicity's sister Ashley asked.

"She doesn't need to make it if she's getting it delivered!" My younger sister cackled as the rest of my family, attracted by the twin allures of food and family drama, piled into the kitchen.

I poured glasses of holiday sangria, tried to keep Granny Doyle from spiking it with brandy, and rolled the stuffed pork loin, trying to blend into the background while my family traded good-natured ribbing.

I was browning the pork when phones started beeping and buzzing with an incoming message. Then the screams started from my female relatives.

My father's normally pale face had angry splotches of red on it as he looked at his phone.

"Oh my god, your boyfriend is so fucking hot!" Nat and Lauren drooled at Nat's phone.

"What?" I peered over her shoulder at her phone screen... and saw the picture... and the message.

Unknown number: *Bad girl.*
Unknown number: *You didn't let me come down your throat last night.*
Unknown number: *Guess you need to be punished.*

On the screen was a photo of a man—tattooed chest, huge arm with a prominent vein, hand in unbuttoned motorcycle pants pushed down his thighs, the photo strategically cropped so you could only make out the base of the thick shaft.

"If I had him, he would not be coming down my throat. Let's just make that clear." Aunt J screenshotted her phone. "It would be a white Christmas all up in my—"

"Seriously?" My mom turned on her sister.

"Melissa." Granny Doyle poured a splash of rum into her mug of coffee. "Your vaginismus has clearly spread to the rest of your body."

"Lighten up, Mel." Mom's sister smirked at her.

"Don't feel like less of a man if you catch my daughter having some quality time alone with her phone tonight, Brian." Granny Doyle hiccupped, almost falling off her stool as my cousins howled with laughter.

"Did Andy go to art school?" Aunt Trish asked me while several of my other female family members crowded around, wanting to know if I had the rest of the photo.

"This is such a creative piece." Trish was in high-school-art-teacher mode. "Look at the lighting."

"Damn right." Granny Doyle raised her glass. "A work of fucking art, this is."

"Evie, you need to break up with him now. This is obscene!" my father thundered. "There are children in this group chat!"

"I don't know anything about a group chat. I'm not in the group chat!" I yelled at my father.

"You're not?" He seemed a little confused.

My thirteen-year-old girl cousins did not seem at all concerned about having a very risqué photo of Anderson on their phones and were giggling and texting it to their friends.

"Yeah, that's going to be all over their high school Facebook page in like three seconds." Nat and Lauren collapsed in drunken giggles.

"Kids don't use Facebook these days." Sawyer passed her glass to Gran for some rum.

"I'll put it on Facebook," Granny Doyle promised. "This picture has to be shared with the people." She slammed the bottle on the counter, sloshing amber liquid everywhere.

"I can't. I just can't!" My mother threw up her hands.

"Don't work yourself up." Braeden tried to comfort my mom. "We know that Evie is prone to spiraling into delusional behavior. Like Henry said, we're just going to ignore her. She will eventually see the errors of her ways and realize she made a horrible miscalculation in allowing herself to fall in with bad company. Just like her being fired from her jobs for immoral behavior." He gave me a patronizing smile, but his eyes were reptilian. "Karma always comes around."

"Until then, keep the photos coming!" Aunt Virginia toasted Granny Doyle.

"Melissa, you need to get your daughter under control. I do not want photos of that man on my phone unsolicited." Grandma Shirley thumped her coffee cup on the counter.

"I heard Evie was soliciting him at the country club."

All my aunts and cousins erupted in squeals of laughter.

"This is why you can't ever keep a job, isn't it?" my mom demanded. "You're—" She groped for the words. "Soliciting your bosses."

"That's just what I heard Janice from HR say to Amber," Irene clarified, spooning caramel sauce onto the coffee cake. She sniffed it. "Oh, gross. What is this? Why does this cake taste so weird, Evie?"

"She didn't make that cat food. Felicity brought it and jarred caramel sauce," Sawyer said, grabbing the plate and heading to the trash.

"I have a job. I cannot spend all day baking." Felicity grabbed the plate from her.

My nails dug into the palms of my hands.

"But you have enough time to spread rumors and lies about me all over Manhattan!" I shrieked at her.

Braeden placed a protective arm around Felicity. "It's sad that you're still tied to your girlish imaginary fantasy. You and I will never be together." My former boss regarded me like he was a patient older professor and I was some unhinged teenage girl. "We were all there last Christmas Eve. You can't deny that you were trying to break up my relationship because of your insecurities. Understand, Felicity and I are setting a boundary here. You can't control us. We will speak our truth."

"Braeden, just drop it," Henry snapped.

"A stain on this family!" Grandma Shirley was shouting as more messages came pouring in.

"Oh my god, that bike," my aunt gasped, staring, face flushed, at her phone.

"Does he always go commando, Evie?" Lauren demanded. "Or is this just for the photos?"

One of the triplets held out her phone to me. "Aww, Anderson said oops, that he meant to send it only to you. He's sorry for the confusion, and he didn't mean to be a bother."

"He can get me all confused and bothered." Aunt Jennifer fanned herself.

"I don't know why you wanted to steal Braeden from Felicity when you're capable of scoring this." Cousin Nat kissed the screen.

Score? Hardly.

I ducked around my aunts to grab a bottle of schnapps in the pantry.

My phone vibrated in my pocket.

Unknown Number: *Ready to get on your hands and knees and come crawling back to me now?*
Evie: *Go to hell.*

Hands shaking, I twisted the cap off the bottle and took a noisy swig.

Anderson was the biggest mistake in a lifetime of mistakes.

He was fucking with me was what he was doing. He was targeting me.

Well, guess what. I was not going to roll over.

I stared at his text message, blinking back the angry tears threatening to form in my eyes.

I meant what I'd said: if I was going down, Anderson Wynter was coming with me.

Chapter 9

ANDERSON

"Thanks for staying through the dinner rush."

"Tell Cade he owes me," I called, turning to walk backward so I could yell at my coworkers. "I hate the late shift."

"Hey, it's a good shift when you didn't kill anyone!" Dav, one of the cooks, said cheerfully, slapping me on the shoulder.

As much as I despised the country club and everything it represented, there was something easy, something normal about the camaraderie of getting off a long shift. Just you and your coworkers after the place had closed down in the early hours of the morning, the night crew coming in to clean and get the place ready for the early-bird club members at seven a.m.

Much better than breaking into people's houses, stealing their data, and hanging a knife over their heads, just waiting for the insurance company to cut the string.

"You working tomorrow?" Dav asked.

"Day after."

"Ah, I see. You have to make it up to your girl for staying late. Don't worry!" The cook raised his voice. "Anderson's just been balls deep in mop water tonight!"

"What?"

"She's cute." Dav punched my arm. "Crazy. Unhinged. Probably going to end up with you walking naked along a highway. But cute."

"Goddammit."

Evie, wearing the most ridiculous over-the-top ginger-bread-girl costume, stood in the middle of empty foyer of the country club. She jumped up and down when she noticed me looking. In the low-cut bodice, the effect was, well... I did not like the appreciative looks from the rest of the guys.

Evie didn't seem to mind. She held up a basket. "I thought you boys might be hungry."

My coworkers immediately flocked to the basket, which had what smelled like grilled cheese sandwiches, homemade chips, and cookies.

"Merry Christmas!" She handed the basket to Dav. "Pumpkin Muffin!" she squealed, clapping her hands together then practically jumping into my arms. "Surprise! Are you surprised to see me?"

"What the hell are you doing?" I grabbed her by the apron strings of her costume.

"Mutually assured destruction, asshole," she whispered into my ear. Her soft, round tits pressed up against my white dress shirt.

I tried to untangle her from my arms, but she was back on me.

I finally slapped her hand away when it reached for my belt buckle.

"My little Pumpkin Muffin is shy," she said to Dav, who was standing next to Talbot, who was munching his grilled cheese around a shit-eating grin.

"I never knew that about you, Anderson." My brother's grin widened.

"Don't you mean little Pumpkin Muffin?" He and Dav collapsed with laughter.

"He pretends to be a big bad military man, but he asked me to give him a cute pet name." Evie made an exaggerated kissy face then slapped me right on the crotch.

I strangled a curse.

Talbot was dying laughing. I knew as soon as this shit show was over, he was going straight to the rest of my siblings to give them the full humiliating play-by-play.

"Can I have the last one?" a line cook asked, looking into the basket.

"Oh yes! I have a different kind of dinner planned for Anderson. It's pussy," Evie stage whispered.

"What the fuck?" I grabbed her and dragged her out to the parking lot to the roars of laughter from my brother and coworkers. "We had a deal. We shook on it. This? This wasn't part of the deal." I climbed onto my bike.

"Neither was the fake anal sex or the strip tease at my mom's holiday party." She clawed at my jacket as I revved the engine

"Don't ever show up here again." I shoved her off, and she landed in a snowdrift, sputtering and cursing behind me as the bike roared off.

"Motherfucker!" Jake yelped as I sent the puck flying toward his face.

"He's still mad about earlier."

"I thought you weren't actually sleeping with her." Hudson sent the puck flying back to me.

"I am not."

Is it crazy to play hockey in the early, dark morning?

Who do you think you're talking to?

Besides, in hockey-obsessed Maplewood Falls, this was the only time the outdoor rink was free.

We weren't the only ones out either. A bunch of loud college guys played on the half rink next to ours, a happy-looking German shepherd enjoying the cold next to their bags.

The beer and the ice and the workout had done nothing to dent the aggravation and frustration around Evie.

"Who the fuck does she think she is, showing up in that outfit at my job?"

"I'm not complaining." Talbot laughed as I dodged around Lawrence with the puck. "I should have taken a picture."

I banked hard, crashing into him. We both went down heavily on the ice.

"Oof! Hudson," Talbot wheezed, "help. He's trying to kill me."

I kicked my brother in the shin guards as I stood up.

"He's just afraid you're after his girlfriend." A smirk twitched on my older brother's mouth.

"I am not." I skated around in an agitated circle. "And she's not my girlfriend."

"Then why is she here to be your puck bunny?" My youngest two brothers howled with laughter.

I made a disgusted noise as I looked over.

There in the bright floodlights Evie was, slip-sliding in her boots across the ice toward me, Snowball's tiny legs working overtime to keep pace.

"What the fuck are you doing here?" I roared.

"I thought that's what we were doing. You know, showing up at other people's family time uninvited, just taking off our shirts!" she shrieked.

"Take it off!" Talbot whooped then cursed as I swept my hockey stick out, swiping him off his feet to land face-first on the ice.

"You say one more fucking thing to her," I snarled softly at my brother, "and I'm knocking your front teeth out."

"Not his teefs!" Lawrence clapped a hand over his mouth.

Jaw clenched, molars about to crack, I skated over to Evie.

"So you're just driving around, trying to find me?"

"For your information, I do not drive. I lost my license—ran one too many stop signs—and didn't have the money to get it back." She turned up her nose. "The bus doesn't run that often at this time."

"Yes, but why are you here?" I enunciated the words.

"Christmas miracle?"

"Duuude." Lawrence drawled, "I bet there's a tracker on your bike."

"What? No. I don't get trackers on my stuff."

My brothers took off on their skates, me racing after them, Evie sliding after me.

They reached my bike before me, and the four of them checked it over, each trying to be the first.

"Found it!" Jake held up the Air Tag triumphantly. "It was glued under your wheel well." He tossed the little metal tracker to me.

"You keep fucking up, Anderson," Hudson warned me.

"Don't give me that shit."

"This little girl put a tracker on you." Hudson pointed with his hockey stick as Evie puffed up, red-faced, legs a little wobbly.

"Damn right, and I'll shove one up your dick!" Evie yelled, dancing around me. "You want to fight dirty and turn my whole family against me? I'm going to make your life as miserable as you made mine. I will haunt you for all your days, like Jacob Marley's ghost."

"Go ahead and trauma dump on me. Tell me about how your mom wronged you when you were a tween!" I shouted.

"My mom is not the problem. You're the one who ruined my life."

"I didn't fuck up your life, Gingersnap. You're homeless, you have a possessed little gremlin for a dog, no fucking money, and your whole family hated you long before I showed up."

"She's the cutest little gremlin ever," Jake cooed, reaching for the dog.

"Be careful. She—"

"Fuck!" Jake yelled as Snowball took a chunk out of his protective gear.

The dog growled up at him from the snow while Evie and I screamed at each other in the middle of the cold dark.

"You see? You are the author of your own fucked-up life, and you're here to ruin mine. Your dog tried to kill my brother."

"Really? Did she *really*?" Evie hollered back. "Maybe she bit him because he looks like you."

"I'm better looking and younger." Jake rubbed his hand.

"Why are you acting like a *lunatic*?" I roared. "I said I was going to help you."

"Too bad. You fuck with me, and I'm hitting the big red button. Mrs. Claus is coming to town, and she's going to fuck your shit up!"

"We had a deal."

"No deal!"

"*No deal?*" Hudson growled.

What was unsaid?

Wasn't this part of your big plan?

And *Does Aaron know about this?*

"Look," I said, mind spinning as I tried to salvage this because fuck it, I needed access to her family, needed the fast track, because otherwise, I was well and truly fucked.

"Why don't we—"

"Snowball, no!" Evie screamed as the dog took off, racing toward the German shepherd.

"What the hell?" one of the other hockey players yelled drunkenly.

"Dammit, Snowball." Evie ran after the dog. "Come back!"

"You gonna go get that?" Hudson looked at me pointedly.

I rubbed my jaw. "Just give it a moment."

The German shepherd had taken off at a sprint around the periphery of the ice rinks. Snowball rounded the tight curve, making up the distance.

"Fantastic technique," Jake remarked.

Evie was falling behind as she raced around the lake after Snowball. "Come back heeere!" Her voice was distant in the cold. "Snowbaaallll!"

The German shepherd had longer legs, but Snowball was fueled by pure, distilled hatred.

The little dog was a blur of white.

My brothers watched, awestruck, as the tiny Pomeranian closed the distance on the larger dog as they made the last round of the turn.

Evie had only made it halfway around the rinks.

I twirled the hockey stick as the dogs barreled toward us.

The German shepherd passed under Hudson's legs right as Snowball was about to chomp her pointy little teeth in the poor dog's tail. I scooped her up with the stick like a flyaway puck, tossing her high into the air. The dog did an aerial flip, then I caught her as she barked her head off at the retreating German shepherd.

I waited patiently for Evie to huff up.

Snowball vibrated in my arms, keeping a long, steady growl going while her head twitched between the panting German shepherd and a red-faced Evie.

Wheezing, hand clutched to her chest, Evie stumbled up to me and my brothers.

"Frickin' hell, Snowball," she gasped then coughed. Her fingers grabbed at the thin ribbon laced on her bodice, all that was keeping her tits from falling out. "Can't breathe."

Bet her nipples are hard as fuck in this weather.

"St. Nick's balls, it's hot out here." Evie fanned herself, then hands on her hips, she leaned over to suck in deep breaths. In the loosened bodice, her tits almost fell out.

"Whoops!" She giggled then coughed, clutching at her chest.

"I'm not looking!" Talbot hollered, hands over his face. "Lawrence is, though. You should have heard him."

"I did not! Ow!" Lawrence yelped as I brought the hockey stick down on his back. "Fuck." He crashed to the snowy ground, the protective padding catching the brunt of the fall. "Why are you acting like that? I thought you'd never sleep with a Murphy. Hey!" He dodged my skate boot.

"Are you trying to be intimidating, Anderson?" Evie demanded as I tried not to notice the undone state of her clothes, the little straps holding up what was left of the bodice.

It was too much—I hadn't had enough sleep, I owed Aaron too much money, and now Evie was doing a strip tease in the middle of what was supposed to be my mental health hockey time.

In the nearby parking lot, tires screeched. A car headed straight for us.

And I was going to die here.

"Fuck!" I threw myself in front of Evie as the car made a hard right turn, honking its horn.

"I can't stop the car!" Granny Doyle yelled out the open window. "It's cold, and the thingamajigger is stuck, and my knee can't handle the gear shift. They don't make knee replacements like they used to. You have to run for it, Evie!"

The car made another erratic circle in the parking lot as my brothers and I watched, stunned.

"Snowball, let's go!" Evie yelled, taking off at a run toward the car.

"You have to time it!" Granny Doyle hollered. "Run, Evie! Your dad doesn't know I stole the car. We're on the clock."

The Mercedes screeched on the asphalt as it made another turn to head back toward us.

"I can't get the door open. You have to come through the window," Granny Doyle called.

Snowball had no problem making the leap into the car. Evie sprinted then jumped, clinging clumsily to the open window as she scrabbled.

I winced, praying I didn't watch her get sucked under the wheels.

"This is insanity."

There was a flash of bright-red panties, and she was safe in the car.

Evie's grandmother blared the horn and yelled a parting greeting.

"Take off your shiiirts! Woo!"

The Mercedes almost crashed into a newspaper delivery truck as it squealed out of the parking lot.

Hudson worked his jaw.

"So." Lawrence rocked on his skates. "That's your super-secret plan to keep Aaron Richmond from torching our livelihood and our skins?"

Hudson made a disgusted noise.

"Welp," Jake said, "I'm going to go find a new job."

Chapter 10

was on coffee-fueled hour seven of blowing up Anderson's phone with memes, gifs, and pictures of puppies wearing holiday sweaters. All to the number one of his coworkers had given me, which was different from the one that he'd used to send the risqué photo.

I dumped espresso into my coffee as I hit Send on the next batch of text messages I had lined up to fuck with Anderson.

I was on a mission.

I might have rolled over for Braeden, but I was done.

Anderson wasn't going to boss me around.

At the very least, I was going to force him to get a new number. Then he'd have to update his bank accounts. *Muhahahah!*

Anderson: *You are so fucking juvenile.*
Evie: **Buddy the elf meme**

Anderson: *For someone who claims she hates me, sending a thousand text messages makes me think you actually care.*

Evie: **Gif of a cat knocking over a Christmas tree**

Anderson: *At least respond in English like a normal person.*

Evie: **Nonsensical paragraph of Christmas emojis**

The phone rang.

"Hi, Pumpkin Muffin!" I greeted Anderson with an exaggerated squeal.

I could practically hear him wince over the phone.

"Since you ruined my fucking life, just go ahead and impregnate me so I have a cute baby to exploit on social media and I can afford somewhere to live after I get evicted."

"I am not and will not ever get you pregnant. You make me want to cut my dick off."

"No, I don't. I make you want to come all over my tits."

Anderson made a noise of deep irritation. "Meet me for coffee. Let's put this desperate cry for attention from you aside and tackle this problem like adults."

"Oh yeah, I'll meet you," I snarled into the phone, the lack of sleep, the coffee, and the sugar making me feel dangerous and on edge. "I'll meet you in a dark alley. You need to bring five thousand—no! Manhattan rent is expensive. Ten thousand! Wait... I owe Sawyer money. *Fifteen thousand dollars* in twenties. Otherwise, this is just a taste of how much hell I can rain down from Santa's sleigh." I knocked back the rest of my coffee. "Mutually assured destruction, asshole."

I needed to be careful. The house creaked as people started to wake up.

Anderson blew out a breath. "I'm not giving you fifteen grand, Gingersnap."

"Why? Cause you don't have it? Better get a job. There's a strip club off the highway exit. Gran goes there."

"Shirley?"

"What? No. Of course not. Granny Doyle—she constantly spends money there."

Another snort.

"You could," Anderson drawled, "let me help you. Wouldn't you rather see Braeden tossed out into the street, your family on their knees, begging for your forgiveness?"

Stay strong.

I knocked back another espresso. "No dice."

"If you don't, I'll tell your fun grandma that you're being mean and trying to extort me for cash," he taunted.

"She'll choose me over you. She loves me." I was stubborn.

"I'll promise her dick pics for life."

"Oooh, you..." I fumed, the caffeine making me literally vibrate.

"Mutually assured destruction, Gingersnap. I'm texting you the address."

"No!" I shrieked. "I'm texting you the address. And guess what? I know you're going to loathe it."

Chapter 11

ANDERSON

hate Christmas. I hate the songs, I hate the decorations, and I especially hate the Christmas cafés with their holiday-themed sugar-laden drinks that seemed to be all you could buy in Maplewood Falls between Thanksgiving and New Year's.

When Evie finally scuttled into the café, an irritating ten minutes late, she was dressed to fit in with the Christmas vomitorium surrounding us.

She slid into the seat across from me in the booth, ducking her head, her lopsided knit hat low over her forehead, scarf up around her neck.

From the mound of her sweater, something growled.

"They don't allow dogs in here, Gingersnap."

"Shh!" She looked around furtively, hand covering the front of her jacket. "Snowball is my emotional support pet."

Snowball struggled out of the sweater, freeing enough of her muzzle to snarl at me.

Evie wrinkled her nose. "Guess this is not the beginning of our star-crossed romance, considering my dog hates you."

"I'd bet money she shares the same feelings as her owner."

"Damn right."

"And yet." I leaned back in the booth. "She comes crawling back to me."

"This is not crawling. Don't flatter yourself, Anderson. This is blackmail."

"You need me more than I need you." I pulled out the burner phone that I'd used to send the photo. "Your family adores me, loves me like they never loved you."

"Give me that." Evie snatched the phone out of my hand. "Oh my gosh. These are so thirsty and inappropriate." She slammed the phone onto the table. "Don't answer any of these messages. Especially not from Aunt J. Her current boyfriend is about at his expiration date."

"Someone's territorial. Jealous, Gingersnap?"

"As if. I wouldn't be caught dead with you."

"That's not what your family thinks." I crossed my arms. "And not what I think, especially after that little display on the ice. Your tits half out, you did everything except beg me to come on them."

With the way her lip curled, she was about to lay into me. "That was for your much hotter brothers, not you."

"Pretty sure I could convince you otherwise." I let a sly grin form.

Her mouth pinched into an angry pucker. "You're filthy."

"Say that again. I liked it."

She let out a huff.

"I bet you lay awake all night, thinking about how 'filthy' I am, Gingersnap." I used air quotes.

"Stop calling me that!" she practically shrieked. "Ginger is for redheads."

"Gingersnaps aren't red." I reached over and yanked one of the curls of hair that had escaped her hat. "They're brown. Chestnut, really."

"I—" Her hand came up to her head.

"Welcome to the Cozy Cocoa Cottage!" a waitress dressed in a Mrs. Santa costume chirped. "Can I get you all started with one of today's specials, a Frosty's Frothy Eggnog or an Elfspresso Explosion?"

"Both of those sound revolting. Do you sell alcohol here?" I asked her.

"Don't mind him." Evie kicked me under the table. "He was raised in a barn."

"I'd literally take anything. I'm not choosy." I let a slow, smoldering smile creep onto my mouth.

"How about a Reindeer Rum Raisin Brownie?" the waitress offered, fanning herself.

"We'll take that and both specials." Evie handed back her menu.

"Unless you have something else in the back you're willing to share?" I let my voice deepen to a purr.

The waitress melted.

"I might be willing and able."

"Stop being such a Scrooge McDuck," Evie shot at me after the waitress left.

"You need to stop being childish. You can't pick Santa's Holiday Hellscape for a meeting of sinners." I brushed away the red and green sequins on the table.

"This isn't some criminal meeting."

"Blackmail, sexual extortion…"

"No one's having sex. And what's wrong with this place?"

"Aside from the nauseating amount of holiday cheer? It doesn't have good sight lines."

"This isn't some opportunity for you to LARP around and pretend to be some sort of romance hero Navy SEAL." Evie leaned toward me. "This is my life. My life that you are ruining."

"Don't forget, Gingersnap, you're the one who tried to blackmail me first. Choices have consequences." I poked her nose, making her recoil.

"You don't call the shots. You owe me—fifteen thousand dollars or Braeden's head, but you owe me."

"I owe you?" I snarled, slamming my fist on the table. Despite what I'd told Aaron, December twenty-fourth was screaming down the highway at a hundred miles an hour. I could not miss that deadline, which meant I needed Evie under my boot.

There was a flash of apprehension in her brown eyes.

"You seem to be under the mistaken impression that you hold the cards, Gingersnap. You think that photo sent your family in a tizzy? Wait until they wake up on Christmas morning and realize that thumping noise coming from the attic isn't Santa but instead you getting fucked within an inch of your life."

She swallowed hard, her eyes big and wide in her head.

"If you sneak into my bed, I'm going to scream."

I smiled toothily. "That's what I'm hoping."

"Stay away from me." Her voice had a slight tremble.

She was off balance. Good.

"Look, Gingersnap." I picked up the spoon resting on the napkin by my forearm. "We've already established that you are in way over your head here. Now, I'm going to help you. We shook on it," I reminded her, "and I am a man of my word. But you"— I pointed the spoon— "are not calling the shots."

A stubborn set of the chin. If she wasn't Henry's little sister and wasn't trying to blackmail me, I might, after I'd had a lot to drink and no sex for a year, *might* say she was cute.

I held out my hand.

Cautiously, she rested hers in it.

"Trust me?"

"Never." She snatched her hand back.

"Two specials and a brownie!" the waitress sang, arriving with a tray laden with the disgusting-smelling drinks.

An oversize coffee mug festooned with what looked like gummy Santas sloshed froth onto the table.

"I saw your cute little dog," the waitress whispered and slid a cup of whipped cream onto the table. "On the house."

"Yum!" Evie beamed. "Say thank you, Snowball."

The dog licked its small black nose.

"Er…" Evie added before the waitress had a chance to leave. "I don't suppose you're hiring?"

The waitress looked me up and down. "We are for a stock boy. Night shift."

"I thought you might need a waitress."

"Maybe this summer for tourist season. Come by in a few months."

Evie snuck the cup of whipped cream down onto the booth seat. Slurping noises were heard.

She seemed suddenly sad.

You don't care. You don't care how sad she is. We are done falling for bleeding-heart charity cases.

"This is why I need your help," she said dully. "I'm getting kicked out on the twenty-fifth unless I have a job. But if I can prove that I'm not a complete fuckup, that I didn't lie about Braeden, then maybe my parents will let me stay a few extra months."

I scowled down at the sickly-looking cup of eggnog.

"Do you want the elfspresso instead?" she offered.

"Espresso is supposed to be served in a small cup, no sugar and definitely no gummy bears. That noise is the collective scream of baristas in Rome as they all spontaneously combust."

"I like it," she said defiantly, picking up the gigantic mug and using her thumb to keep the candy cane bobbing among the mountain of whipped cream from hitting her in the nose.

She licked the froth off her lips, her pink tongue darting out. "What's the plan?"

"The plan for what?" I asked.

"Nabbing Braeden."

"Just give me whatever evidence you have, and I'll work on it."

"I want to help take him down."

"You couldn't even handle being in the same room as me for five minutes." I crossed my arms. "How are you going to survive with me alone, for hours, on a stakeout?"

"I can handle it. You don't scare me." Her mouth set stubbornly.

I huffed out a laugh. "Yes, I do."

Ignoring me, she pulled out her phone.

"Here's my evidence. It's not much," she explained hurriedly as I scanned the screenshot. "But it's a start, right? See? I used Snapwave. He was my boss, so I wanted to be careful about not sending him emails or using the company chat app so he didn't get fired." She laughed sadly. "Guess I shouldn't have been so nice."

I swiped to a photo of her and her dog.

"Where's the rest of it?"

"That's… it."

I sighed heavily and handed the phone back. "I'm not a miracle worker, Gingersnap."

"You're my last hope."

Was she about to cry? I couldn't take it if she started to cry.

Stay focused on the job.

I didn't need to help Evie. This was all for show until I got the evidence I needed for the real job. Then I'd dump her like an unwanted Christmas puppy.

"Braeden Wallace." I rubbed my jaw.

Evie nodded.

Before I could stop it, my mind immediately started churning, running scenarios, as if I was actually going to help Evie Murphy, of all people.

"There is evidence out there." I spun the silver spoon around on the reclaimed-wood tabletop. "Braeden's cautious but full of himself. He made a mistake somewhere."

The Christmas lights glinted off the spoon as it rotated.

"How was the sex with him?"

"What kind of question is that?" Evie sputtered.

I looked at her coldly. "Don't worry. I don't need to hear your lackluster bedroom activities to get off." I tilted my head to the waitress, who was making bedroom eyes at me from across the room. "I could get laid in the storage room right now."

Evie's cheeks flushed.

"I guess it was okay," she mumbled.

"So worse than being fondled by some teenage boy under the bleachers in high school. Got it. If Braeden sucks that bad at knowing what women want, then he likely believes he's God's gift in bed and thinks sleeping with you was fantastic. He'll want a souvenir. Something to remember the conquest. Did you send him topless photos, used underwear, anything like that?"

"I—" She bit her lip.

I pushed the eggnog latte over to her to coax her to talk and to get the smelly concoction out from under my nose. "I can't help you if you don't give me all the information. Any small detail could be what nails this guy."

She held up her napkin to block her face from the crowded café.

"I sent one…" She held up a finger. "One topless photo, but my face isn't in it. It's an artsy photo. Just…" She motioned around her ample chest area.

I could almost imagine what it would have looked like, those huge tits, dark-pink nipples. Was she touching herself in the photo?

She gulped down the latte.

"Do you have any tattoos, scars, birthmarks, or piercings that could identify you?"

"I photoshopped out the mole," she admitted.

"Great." I rolled my eyes up to the ceiling. There was a collection of demented-looking inflatable reindeer up there. "Did you do anything else to make this difficult job more impossible?"

"I had to! There was a hair growing out of it. Er—" Her face burned red.

I snorted. "No judgment here. I've slept with plenty of witches."

Evie balled up her napkin and threw it at me.

I batted it down.

"Shit, the dog. *Your dog*, Evie."

The dog lapped up the last of the elfspresso.

"That was mine, Snowball." Evie tried to pry the slobbery candy cane out of the Pomeranian's mouth while I gagged.

Finally giving up, Evie made a disgusted noise.

Wordlessly, I handed her a napkin to wipe her sticky hands.

"You're going to be sorry later," she told the dog as its sharp little teeth crunched the candy. "All that candy isn't good for doggies."

I wasn't going to make it till Christmas.

Snowball practically vibrated in Evie's lap. From the sugar, the caffeine, or because she was about to launch across the table and attack me—who knew?

"You got red all over your white fur. Yes, you did." Evie dabbed the napkin on the dog's muzzle.

"Can you please focus, woman? Both of you have had too much caffeine."

"Sorry." She saluted me.

"You need to write down all of your conversations with Braeden," I ordered. "And give me a list of his friends, family, acquaintances, and favorite places to go. It's been a year, so the trail's going to be pretty cold."

"Oh my gosh, it's like a spy movie." She impulsively grabbed my hand. "You're going to save me. I'm so glad we worked this out," she gushed. "Obviously, you're not going to be showing up at my parents' house unannounced, so we should set up some meeting times. Do you have a secret lair?" She shrank at the expression on my face.

"Gingersnap, I plan on showing up to all your family holiday parties. Just because I'm helping you doesn't mean you get to fuck with me and get away with it."

Chapter 12

You would think I would learn my lesson, that my instincts were never correct, that my impulses led only to disaster.

What I should have done was sit in that café and told Anderson we were over, blackmail was off the table, pay me my fifteen grand, have a merry Christmas and a nice life, and stay out of mine.

Then I would have spent my free time hunting for a job so I wouldn't get evicted on the night before Christmas.

Instead, in between prepping the snacks for the Christmas tree cutting, I racked my brain for any scrap of information I could give Anderson to help clear my name.

Though I'd made a fabulous lunch and Pinterest-worthy snack bags, maybe I should have spent more time on the job hunt, because it was clear from my measly half page of notes that I was kidding myself if I thought Anderson was going to make any headway on clearing my name.

He was right.

The trail was cold.

I'd spent months after last Christmas poring over everything, trying to find any shred of evidence to clear my name.

Short of tying him up and torturing a confession out of Braeden, I didn't see how Anderson was going to find proof that my ex was lying.

I slammed the cabinet door closed.

My mother appeared in the kitchen doorway.

"Evie, the triplets have a big day tomorrow, and I really need you to check the attitude."

"I'm not," I protested, feeling like a little kid again. "I'm just trying to find—"

"I don't care, Evie. Brooke Taylor was my roommate at Brown University. I want this house and my children to look perfect for when she comes to film her update on the girls."

I bit back my argument. "Sure thing, Mom."

The picnic basket I needed wasn't even in the kitchen.

I tried not to hold the triplets' position in the family as the favored daughters against them. I really did.

Ian would never be able to make peace with Henry's position as the favorite son, but I was really striving to stay in my lane. However, I would have given anything to be in their place just so that Brooke Taylor would be coming to film a big holiday special about me.

I fantasized about it as I climbed up the three flights of stairs to the attic.

Brooke was the ultimate cool girl—awesome talk show host who had dabbled in acting and had her own makeup line. When I was a kid, Brooke Taylor was who I had secretly wished was my birth mom.

But I would never be as exciting as identical redheaded triplets.

When they were born, Brooke had used a segment about my younger sisters and Mom to launch her talk show into the stratosphere. The segment had been an early viral video pre-YouTube. Brooke liked to do updates on them periodically.

Now that the three famous Murphy triplets had graduated early and were on their way to a fabulous new life? Who didn't want that wholesome holiday content?

The woven wicker snowman-shaped picnic basket was wedged in the back of the attic, wrapped in a blanket. I blew the dust off, snapped a photo, and sent it to the Murphy Misfits group text.

> **Evie:** *Can't believe you all are missing the annual Christmas tree cutting.*
>
> **Ian:** *You mean the death march in the snow while Mom gets her Oedipal fix on St. Henry cutting down the tree? No, thanks.*
>
> **Sawyer:** *Someone's feeling spicy.*
>
> **Sawyer:** *Save me one of those custard-filled snowmen éclairs. Two bikini waxes stiffed me on tips today already.*
>
> **Ian:** *Maybe Evie can send Anderson after them and get them to pay up.*
>
> **Evie:** *Don't even joke like that. I can't make him do anything. It's like I'm running around with a glitter bomb that's about to go off at any moment.*

I hauled the oversize snowman picnic basket downstairs. It had been a gift from my father to my mom when I was little and included a set of custom plates and utensils that were snowman themed.

For all of Anderson's faults, I wished he was there at that moment just to carry the heavy, bulky basket downstairs. He at least had longer arms than me.

Not that I would ever actually consider dating him, murderer or not.

I started stacking the carefully wrapped Christmas sandwiches made with leftover smoked turkey from the holiday party, spicy stuffing, cranberry sauce, and gravy.

A doughy hand reached around me to grab one of the sandwiches.

"Don't touch that."

Braeden ignored me and unwrapped the Christmas-wreath-decorated butcher paper encasing the sandwich.

"Those are for the picnic." I ground my teeth.

He took a noisy bite. "You got any of those éclairs, you know, the ones I like?" My ex smirked at me.

I hadn't been alone with him, not all year, not since two days before that fateful Christmas Eve where he'd blown up my life. I hadn't wanted to face him or the probability that my family would see me alone with him as a scarlet admission of guilt.

Now here he was.

I didn't feel any of those warm, fuzzy feelings from back when we would lie in bed, daydreaming about our future.

All I felt was the cold-snow-down-your-neck realization that Anderson was absolutely right. He was an evil bastard and on Santa's naughty list, but he was right.

Braeden was enjoying this, enjoying breaking me down, tormenting me. He liked winning. He liked knowing that he had complete control of my life.

Maybe if I could get a confession out of him on video, then all this—Anderson, my parents' disappointment, my family's anger—could all just go away.

Trying to be subtle, I felt around in my pocket for my phone.

"You mean the ones I made you to celebrate your big bonus?" I croaked. "The Holiday Eggnog Éclairs?"

Braeden laughed. "You wore that little elf outfit. You were so horny for me. I should have known you'd spread yourself for someone like Anderson. I bet all he had to do was lie to you and call you pretty, and you put out for him, didn't you?"

There was something unsettling about his gaze. Jealousy? Envy?

"I'm surprised you remember, considering you seem to have forgotten everything else about us."

"I knew you still missed me." Grabbing an éclair, he winked at me. It was not anywhere near as sexy as Anderson's. "Don't worry. Keep trying, and maybe I'll take you back or at least give you a pity fuck. Depends on how much you beg."

Hands shaking, I finished packing the basket after he left. I hadn't been able to get my phone to record in time. I should see if Anderson had a mini tape recorder.

"You should have brought your big, hunky boyfriend to come carry that for you," Alana joked as I lugged the basket out to the car.

"We will not make light of Evie's bad behavior."

The triplets shrank under my mom's gaze.

"Evie is a bad influence on you three."

When you came from a big family, you didn't all fit in one car. Sure, you could buy a minibus, but my dad wasn't going to be caught dead in a sprinter van, and so the family split into multiple SUVs.

I had been left after the rest of the cars took off, lugging the large container of spiced hot chocolate. I used a little bit of chili pepper to give it some kick.

Now I was wedged in the very back of Henry's car with the snowman picnic basket, an irate Snowball, several Irish setters, and the various tools needed to cut down the trees to decorate the house in time, not for Santa but for Brooke Taylor.

I stared ice daggers worthy of Elsa from *Frozen* at the back of Braeden's head.

Why now? Why was he showing his hand now?

Because he saw that he had finally succeeded in turning my family against me. Now all that was left for him was to roll around in the spoils of my ruined life.

Dramatic? Sure, but then, I'd just been gaslit for the last year. I was owed it.

The jeep jumped over a rut in the road.

Off in the trees, I thought I saw a dark shadow move.

I'm losing it. I'm going crazy.

I desperately wanted to talk to someone. Scratch that. I wanted to talk to Anderson. Sure, it was cathartic to complain to Ian and Sawyer, but Anderson had a plan. Anderson was going to help.

You're going down, Braeden.

Henry pulled up to the circle of cars in the clearing. All we needed were the giant bows to make this Christmas-tree-cutting outing look like a holiday car commercial.

I stumbled out of the car after Snowball, who saw something in the trees and immediately raced off into the woods.

The magnificent Irish setters loped gracefully through the snow over to my father while I dragged the picnic paraphernalia to a nearby table that overlooked the rushing water that gave Maplewood Falls its name.

All under the angry gaze of Felicity.

"Of course you snuck your way into the car with my fiancé." She hovered behind me as I cleared snow off one of the picnic tables.

"He wormed his way in there with me," I argued then clamped my mouth shut.

I finally had a potential way to get Braeden to admit he had been gaslighting me. I didn't want to tip him off.

"I mean, it was just an honest mistake, Felicity."

"It better not happen again," she warned me, nose in the air.

I passed out steaming cups of hot chocolate as my family milled around, snapping photos of the wintery landscape backdropped by the snowy falls.

Several of my cousins bounded over to the picnic basket and loaded up on snacks while my mom handed out assignments for the Christmas tree event.

"Everyone, pick out a tree. We need a large one in the living room, then I want one in the foyer, one in the dining room, and one in the sitting area upstairs." My mother straightened, and you could see where Ian inherited his dancer's posture. "Evie's finding greenery. We need garland for the banisters, the mantel, wreaths." My mother ticked off the list.

I didn't mind that I wasn't selecting a tree. I was just happy to be out soaking in the festive atmosphere. It was just what I needed to recover from Anderson… and all that caffeine and sugar I'd consumed.

As If I'd summoned the demon himself, a black shadow materialized in the shadow of the trees behind my mother.

Black skullcap over his dark hair, rifle slung over one shoulder along with a large backpack, scarf partially obscuring his mouth—Anderson stepped out of the forest.

"He's here to murder us all." Grandma Shirley pressed a trembling hand to her chest.

"He can murder me any day!" Nat giggled.

"If he brought booze, he can stay. My nipples are freezing off," Granny Doyle complained.

"This is a private event," my mother declared.

Anderson's silvery-gray eyes slid over her to me.

"Did you get a permit?"

My mom's lips thinned.

He adjusted the rifle and stalked through the snowy clearing over to me.

"This" —he held out a glove, from which a tiny, growling white dog hung—"belongs to you, I think."

"She ran off," I explained weakly, trying to detach Snowball from Anderson.

"Are you stalking Evie?" Alana asked.

Henry glared at her.

Anderson gave my younger sister a bemused look. "Of course not." He turned back to me. "You left the fridge open, by the way."

I desperately wanted to tell him what Braeden had said.

I hesitated, then I threw my arms around his neck. He grunted in surprise, then his hands slid down my red coat to rest on my hips.

"I think I have a breakthrough. We need to meet in private," I whispered in his ear. I thought I felt him shiver, but it was probably my imagination.

"I'll tell you when." The stubble on his jaw was rough against my cheek as he pulled away.

For that brief second, it was like we were the only two people in the world.

I shook off the feeling. Anderson was my mortal enemy. We were working together because the enemy of my enemy, yada yada, but I needed to stay focused. I had run out of fuckups.

My mother cleared her throat pointedly.

"Do you want some hot chocolate or a sandwich before you go?" I offered.

"I'm sure he doesn't," my mom said firmly.

"I'm good," Anderson said.

"I made extra. You can't tramp around the woods on an empty stomach."

Stop it, Evie.

I could feel the anger rising within my parents, but it was bumping up against my pathological need to feed people.

I stuffed a wrapped sandwich half into Anderson's pocket. He gave me an odd look then hoisted the rifle over his shoulder.

"Sorry." The apology was whispered as soon as Anderson melted back into the trees.

My mother didn't acknowledge the words.

"Henry, don't forget I want to get your photo for the Christmas card."

I headed in the opposite direction from my family. The freshly fallen snow crunched under my feet. The scent of maple trees and smoky fires from distant cabins transported me to a peaceful, perfect Christmas wonderland.

I loved coming up here and wished I could have a big house on the lake like my uncle.

Snowball practically disappeared against all the white as she bounced through the powdery snow.

I dragged a sleigh behind me, heading deep into the woods, and trimmed off the best-looking boughs for garland, including juniper and other evergreens. The sharp scent of pine really made it feel like Christmas.

The trees were all loaded on the cars by the time I dragged the overflowing sleigh back to Henry's Jeep.

"Did you get any boxwood?" my mother asked, surveying the boughs as the triplets helped me load them into the back of Henry's car.

"I saw some a little way back. I'll grab some," I promised, making sure my shears were in my pocket.

I hurried off to the boxwood I'd seen. They were just going to be accent pieces, so I was able to clip enough. Hoisting the bundle onto my shoulders, I tramped back through the snow to the clearing.

The empty clearing.

"Hello?" I stood in the silence, snow falling around me. "Anyone there? Hello?"

Did they really leave me?

Chapter 13

ANDERSON

"I really," I said into the satellite phone, "need you to keep better track of your shit."

"Not every drone is a winner," Lawrence replied lightly. "The GPS says it should be like fiftyish feet in front of you."

I cursed as I tramped through the ankle-high snow.

Overnight, the clouds had dumped a fair amount in the mountains around Maplewood Falls.

The mountains surrounding the north side of town were favorite spots for camping, hiking, and of course secret meeting places for affair partners.

Why not take your mistress into the romantic secluded woods around the falls? Who's going to find out?

Me, that was who.

I'd taken a break from clearing off my ledger to do some actual work.

Hudson had dumped several cheating-scandal jobs on me. Rich, spoiled Manhattan investment bankers thought that Maplewood Falls in Rhode Island was far enough away from New York City that they could safely stash and visit their mistresses without their wives and children finding out.

They could not.

We had hours of very clear footage of a man living out his midlife crisis with his brother-in-law's nanny. We'd gotten the evidence we needed, then an eagle had seen the drone in its territory and attacked. It had come down in a tree, and I had to use to fancy rope work to retrieve it.

"We're fair and square now," my brother said cheerfully on the call. "When's the next big break-and-enter?"

I swore as I slid down the embankment, the drone secure in my backpack.

"I have Evie primed. Need to do a little on-site recon, then I'll let you know the go date."

"Are you going to make it?" Apprehension filled his voice. We all knew who Aaron really was—and who his father was.

My eyes narrowed as I peered through the snow flurries. "Yeah, I'll make it."

On the ridge above me, I saw a lone figure in a red coat, hand extended above her, jumping up and down.

"I'll see you back at the field office."

Evie was shivering slightly and jabbing her mittened fingers at the touch screen of her phone when I finally made it to the clearing where she and her family had had their dumb little picnic.

Glad my brothers and I didn't do festive shit like that— though Hudson's girlfriend was threatening to make us decorate the Christmas tree at their house.

"Little girls in red coats shouldn't be out in the woods all alone," I said by way of announcing my arrival. "There are dangerous men out here."

Evie yelped in surprise, which set off Snowball, who charged at me.

I was ready for the little dog and scooped her up to my chest, where she thrashed.

Evie swung her feet over the bench to stand up.

"You are stalking me, aren't you?" she demanded.

I handed her the Pomeranian. "Like I don't have anything better to do with my time than follow you around while you get all bent out of shape trying to have the perfect Christmas."

"You're just jealous."

"Of what?"

"I have years of happy Christmas memories, and you have none. I have a big family, and we do fun events together. We're close-knit," she rattled off like she was parroting the party line. "Everyone wants to be part of the Murphy family. In high school, our house was the one everyone wanted to hang out at. My family is the greatest. We have big reunions and holiday get-togethers, and it's a warm, loving family."

"It sounds like a fucking cult. You all have children trapped in the basement?"

"You're the one with a criminal record." Her words were a whip crack in the cold. "You're the one who has a history of violence. You're the one who's trying to ruin my family."

My lip curled up in a sneer. "News flash, Gingersnap, I don't have to ruin anything. They suck. Your whole family is fucking toxic, and so are you for making excuses for them."

"You take that back!"

"Sure, I'll take it back just as soon as they remember that they forgot you out here and come pick you up. I'm sure it will be any minute now." I tapped my military orienteering watch.

The wind whistled forlornly through the trees. In a few hours, it would be dark.

Her face fell.

"They're coming back." Her words were emphatic, but her eyes looked worried.

Don't get involved. Remember what happened the last time you got involved.

"Good luck with that." I hoisted the rifle over my shoulder and turned to leave.

Snow crunched behind me. "Wait. Uh…"

I looked over my shoulder expectantly.

"I just was wondering"—she shivered as the wind picked up—"were you out here hunting?"

"This?" I tapped the rifle. "This is just in case I see a mountain lion."

"We don't have those in Rhode Island."

"Not officially, no, but I've seen them. Mostly rogue male cats looking for territory they can claim."

She trembled.

"Poor choice of words." I gave her a toothy smile.

Evie looked up through the trees at the sun low in the sky.

Leave.

I took a step toward the tree line.

"Did you…" Her voice sounded small in the vast snowy landscape. "Did you like the sandwich?"

You mean one of the best fucking things I've ever eaten? And it was somehow miraculously still a little warm?

"When you're done ruining people's marriages, Gingersnap, maybe you can open up a café."

She stuck her tongue out at me.

"I bet it was Felicity's fault I got left out here." Evie headed back to the picnic tables and slumped onto a bench. "I guess you want to go home."

Home? I didn't really have any place to call home. Hadn't in a long time.

Snowball jumped onto her lap, tucking her small paws under her belly so that she looked like her namesake.

It was freezing. Evie'd been out here about as long as I had, which was hours at this point. Just sitting there at the picnic table, not moving? She could easily get too cold, then it was all over.

"If you don't mind walking, I can drive you home. To your parents' house." I forced out the offer.

"Thank you, but they're coming back for me. They have to realize eventually."

"Did they call?" I asked, but I knew the answer. Phone signal up here wasn't great, and with the snow? I'd bet she hadn't managed to send even a text message out.

After marching over to her, I grabbed her upper arm, hoisting her out of her seat. She already felt a little stiff.

"You don't have to tell me," I said as she protested. "I already know the answer."

Evie's shorter legs were having trouble keeping up with me through the deep snow. Not to mention that she insisted on carting a big bushel of branches with her.

"Just dump the greens, and let's go," I called back. "I'd have already been at the truck by now if I didn't have this dead weight."

"You're a horrible knight in shining armor," Evie retorted, adjusting the branches on her back. "Just go on ahead if you're that annoyed."

I made a disgusted noise.

"Yeah, that's really going to look good when yet another Murphy child turns up half-dead in my company."

I walked back and took the branches from her. After taking out a bungee cord from my backpack, I secured them to the bag and adjusted it on my shoulder.

"Thanks," Evie said. "You didn't have to."

"I did if I don't want to be out here all night."

I looked down at the tiny dog, steam clouding around its nose like the world's smallest, cutest demon.

"You sure you don't want to carry her?"

"She will outwalk us all then eat our frozen bodies," Evie declared.

My mouth twitched into a smile before I could stop it.

Evie was trailing farther and farther behind me.

"We aren't actually walking that far," I told Evie impatiently as Snowball raced back to her then spun and raced a few feet ahead of me.

"This is far. We've been walking for ages."

"It's only been two miles, and I'm carrying all your sticks and leaves."

Evie rallied to catch up with me then kept pace for a few minutes until she started to lag.

"Do you really think you can help me?" she asked, breaking the muffled sounds of our footsteps. "My family is already freezing me out." She sniffled. "Next year, I'll be completely alone."

"Save the crying for someone who cares."

"You're an asshole, you know." She rushed again to catch up with me.

"Damn right."

"I hope you never have a girlfriend or children. You'd make Christmas miserable for the whole family."

The words stung more than I wanted them to, dredging up memories of my father being a dick while we were just trying to scrounge something together for the younger kids to have a Christmas.

"Like Christmas would be any better with you." I went on the attack. "You'd force your poor kids to be subjected to your mother while she spoiled her real grandchildren and left your kids to fight for crumbs."

"That was mean," she said after a moment.

"Don't forget who you're talking to."

Crash!

Evie stumbled behind me, falling face-first in the snow.

"I can't fucking take this anymore."

"Sorry." She wiped at her face with snowy mittens. "I have phone signal now, but none of my family even noticed I'm missing. No calls or messages or anything."

"I'm not your therapist, Gingersnap. I don't care. You want to cry over those people, that's between you and your personality disorder, but I'm not going to freeze to death out here with you while you self-actualize."

"Don't touch me!" she yelped as I grabbed her around the knees then tossed her over my shoulder in a fireman's hold. "Put me down." Her legs kicked ineffectively.

Between my annoyance and the desire to finally get the hell out of these woods, I traversed the next mile easily.

"You can put me down now. I see the car." She tapped me on the head with her mitten.

I ignored her.

"Why'd you even park all the way down here, anyway?"

Because I didn't want to tip off the cheating banker.

"Because I didn't think I was going to be leaving with extra cargo." I set her down next to the passenger door of my brother's truck, which I'd borrowed.

Opening up the cover on the bed, I stuck in her branches, my backpack, and the rifle, then I got into the cab of the truck.

As soon as the truck rumbled to life, Evie turned the heat and the radio on full blast.

Snowball howled along with the chipmunks singing their hearts out for a Christmas present.

I turned it off.

Evie turned it back on.

I snarled at her.

She sighed loudly and hit the power button.

"You are the least fun person I have ever met." Evie crossed her arms and stared out the window at the snowy woods.

"People don't hire me for fun, Gingersnap. Speaking of—"

Her phone rang.

"Finally! Oh my gosh, I—" Her voice fell as someone spoke angrily on the other end of the line. "No, I didn't—" She sighed. "I'm on my way."

"You can just drop me off here," she said as the truck approached her mom's house.

"I can drop you at the front door. It's not like you're really saving me time if I drop you off a few houses down."

"I insist." Her voice was shrill.

I ignored her and pulled up in front of her parents' house.

As I was unloading while she was antsy next to me, the front door opened, and an angry redhead stormed out.

"So even though you knew that the triplets have a very important day tomorrow and that Brooke Taylor is coming. Instead of helping, you ran off with your boyfriend," Evie's mom scolded her.

"He is not my—" Evie puffed up.

"I told you, we're just sleeping together," I interjected before she could blow my cover, especially since Braeden was approaching with Henry, because of course those two would be friends.

"Mel." Dr. Murphy put a hand on his irate wife. "Evie, we don't care if you want to ruin your life with *him*." He looked at me like I was a slug that had crawled onto his perfect lawn. "But you are not putting him before your family commitments."

I barked out a laugh. "Seriously?"

"Yes, seriously, *Anderson*." Her father said my name like a curse. "Unlike you, we Murphys instilled honor, decency, and loyalty into our children. Or we tried to, anyway."

Evie was shrinking into herself.

This is not your battle.

But when could I ever resist a lost cause?

"Honor? Loyalty? Fuck you. You all left her in the middle of the woods to freeze." I moved in front of Evie.

Her father took a hesitant step back.

"Anderson, just drop it."

I ignored Evie's hands on my back. "You're lucky she's here at all."

"Is that some sort of a threat?" Henry snarled at me, coming to stand next to his father.

It took everything in me not to punch him in the face.

Unlike his father, he didn't step back when I got in his face.

I lowered my voice. "'Forget' her in the woods again, and we'll find out."

"Evie!" Three identical redheaded young women raced out of the house to gather around the shorter woman.

"Oh my gosh, stop fluffing your boyfriend and come help us decorate!" one of them, wearing a green shirt, teased.

"Yeah, we can't make the garland like you do."

"Mom was trying to show us—"

"But it looked so bad when Alissa tried."

"There's, like, twine sticking out."

"Also, we want to do the lights like the Jefferson mansion."

"Yeah, Brooke Taylor always does, like, an intro shot, and we want it to look cute!"

"I'm coming," Evie said, giving me a look I couldn't read.

I dragged the bundle of sticks and branches out of the back of the truck and brushed past Henry to follow Evie into the house.

In the kitchen, there was garland strewn all over the place. Christmas carols blared, and cookies were burning in the oven.

"Shoot!" Evie ran to grab them.

The smoke alarm shrieked as soon as she opened the oven.

"They were trying to bake," one of Evie's cousins said from where she was painting her nails at the kitchen island.

"The oven's too hot. Did you even read the recipe?"

"Couldn't find it, and you wouldn't answer your phone."

"Guess we know why." At least one of her sisters had the wherewithal to look guilty.

"Yeah, sorry, Evie."

"We honestly thought you were in another car and maybe had gone over with the rest of them to Uncle Ross's house to watch the hockey match."

I opened the door to the back porch and reached up to fan a towel at the smoke detector until it stopped beeping.

Evie was giving me that weird look again.

"What?"

Her sisters giggled.

"You're very tall," one of them said.

Evie rocked on her feet.

"No."

"Just a few lights?" She gave me a pained smile. "I'll feed you."

"She's a great cook." Her sisters yapped over one another.

"Please?" one of them begged. "We're already behind. Brooke's coming early tomorrow."

"Your lack of planning is not my emergency."

One of her cousins giggled. "I mean, it is a little bit. You were responsible for at least some of the delay." She waggled her eyebrows at Evie, who pursed her lips. "Besides, you have a whole tool shed on your truck."

Hudson was in the process of renovating his house. As such, he did—it was true—have a tool shed in the truck.

"Just two strands, then you can leave?" Evie clasped her hands together.

"Depends on what's for dinner."

"Roast beef with a really rich, creamy gravy, pan-roasted carrots, garlic-and-cheddar mashed potatoes, green beans, caramelized onion rolls, and cinnamon twists for dessert."

Unbidden, my stomach growled.

Did I really want to eat another soggy sandwich and stale chips for dinner?

"Fine. Two strands."

I followed Evie back through the house, where her family was haphazardly hanging decorations.

"This is what we're going for." Evie showed me a photo on her phone when we stood in the yard in front of the house.

"That is more than stringing a few lights, Gingersnap."

"But it's Brooke Taylor!"

"Not sure why you even need me. Looks like you have it under control." I nodded up to the dramatic roofline.

On the roof, Braeden was working hard to make a puncture wound that would eventually leak water into the Murphys' precious historic Victorian house.

He raised the hammer for the killing shot...

Not your problem.

...then missed, the motion sending him sliding down the slate tiles.

Evie winced as her ex landed in a heap on a snowy bush next to the house.

I went over to the groaning man and dragged him up by the collar of his shirt.

"You dropped this." I handed him his iPhone back after taking a long look.

He took it, scowling at the snickering onlookers who had arrived.

"I bet the dash cam caught the whole thing," a young man who looked like a leaner version of Henry said.

Braedon stomped off.

"Not staying for the tree trimming?" the woman who'd arrived with the redhead asked.

Braeden ignored her. The baby in her arms babbled.

"Ooh, the real celebrity showed up." Evie cooed a hello at the baby with its shock of red hair.

"I promised Declan I'd come for the tree trimming," the young mother said to Evie.

"I'm just going to get the lights strung up, then I'll join you, Raegan. It will only take a minute."

"Like hell you're climbing up on the roof," I growled to her. "You could barely manage to walk in the snow."

In the photo, the lights were looped like icing on a gingerbread house.

"I'll do it," I said, twisting off my jacket and heading to the truck for the tools.

"You're going to be sorry," I warned one of Evie's sisters, who was trying to hang a heavy bough of greenery over a doorway. I headed back through the house from grabbing more clips from Granny Doyle, whom Evie had sent to the store. "You need to use a tap screw, or you'll bust the plaster."

"Just do the bows." Melissa chided the girl.

As much as I disliked Evie's mom, at least she was effective at decorating. Her areas of operation were neat, clean, and organized, and she hung garland with military precision, though she kept getting sidetracked with questions and micromanaging.

The rest of her family? They sucked.

They spent more time drinking and eating the snacks Evie had prepared than actually decorating.

"Here's the next run of garland." Evie hurried into the foyer as I was halfway up the stairs, three dozen feet of garland draped around her like a shawl.

Her sisters untangled it from her, then Evie raced up the stairs after me.

I paused on the stairs, box of lights in my arms, waiting for her.

She grinned at me. "Open your mouth."

"No."

"Just open it."

She jammed in two fingers, then there was an explosion of flavor on my tongue.

"Thought you needed a snack."

"What is that?" The words were muffled around whatever food witchcraft she'd given me.

"*Knodel!* A German dumpling. I stuff mine with a little gravy, some red cabbage, and pork belly. Good, aren't they? You were looking a little hangry."

"I'm not hangry. The Christmas music is giving me a migraine."

"That's what I was saying!" Granny Doyle yelled.

"It's not the music," Evie's angry grandmother shouted back. "It's the amount of peppermint schnapps you're drinking."

"Evie, something's wrong with the lights on the tree!" Melissa was shrill.

"Did you check the bulb?" her daughter called from below me, where she was feeding me strands of the oversize light bulbs in between twisting garland.

This wasn't my first rodeo of festooning a house in Christmas lights. Any blue-collar male in Maplewood Falls between the ages of thirteen and thirty-five counted on the extra money he made installing Christmas lights on the houses in the rich part of town to pad out the year-end finances. I could and had done it in my sleep.

"I'll come down and take a look in a minute," Evie promised as I reached into my leather tool belt for another black plastic clip to attach the lights to the roof ridge.

"Braeden thinks it's something Anderson is doing out here."

"I didn't touch the breaker, if that's what you're asking," I called down, still not fucking believing I was putting up lights all over Evie Murphy's parents' house. But what could I do? Let her on the roof and have her break her neck, costing me my one shot to clear my ledger?

Swinging down from the roof of the dormer, I tucked then jumped into the bedroom through the window.

"And no jacket." Her mom tutted.

"Do you want me to look at your lights or not, lady?"

The living room was in a state of disarray, half-empty boxes of Christmas ornaments and tissue paper strewn everywhere.

Evie disappeared to check on dinner, which was filling the house with mouthwatering smells.

Melissa flicked a switch. The tree stayed dark.

"I think he tripped a breaker," Braeden said from where he was looking up incorrect information on his phone.

"We checked all the lights, of course," Melissa said as I used a voltage detector to test the strand.

"Just buy a new set of lights," I told her.

"But all the ornaments are on the tree," one of Evie's siblings protested.

"This site says it's the plug," Braeden insisted. "You just need to splice it."

"And then burn down the tree and your house?" I opened up the toolbox. Hudson was like me. He had never escaped the habit developed from decorating hundreds of houses and kept all sorts of little bits in the toolbox for fixing light strands.

"Look." Braeden held up another strand of lights and a wire cutter. "We're just going to splice this new plug onto the old one—"

"Drop it!" I bellowed.

Granny Doyle slapped Braeden.

"Bit—" Braeden caught himself at my furious glance. "Ow!" He rubbed his head.

I grabbed the wire cutters from him along with the strand of lights. "This was plugged in."

"You should have just let him cut it." Granny Doyle cackled. "Then we'd really get a light show."

"Gran," Evie said from the living room doorway.

Braeden glanced up at her arrival. I wanted to punch the possessive expression off his face.

After checking to make sure that none of the lights on the tree were plugged into anything hot, I used a tiny screwdriver to pop off the plastic housing on the plug.

"I told you it was the plug," Evie's ex brayed as I worked out the tiny fuse. "I could have done that."

In two seconds, I had a new fuse in and the cover back on.

"Let there be light," Declan said dramatically as I plugged it in.

The tree lit up.

"Wow!" Evie's eyes sparkled in the colorful light from the tree. "You fixed it!"

"Sure is nice having a man who's *actually* useful around here," Granny Doyle declared.

Dr. Murphy took an annoyed sip of his drink.

"You should put the star on the tree." Declan's wife held out the tree topper to me. "Since you saved Christmas."

Melissa snatched it back. "He will do no such thing. Besides, we're not done decorating. The tree topper is the last thing to be done."

Raegan and Declan exchanged tense looks.

"Mom, can you just let Anderson do it?" Declan asked in a resigned tone. "He did save us a lot of time. It would have been a nightmare to try to take off all those ornaments."

I wasn't going to be dragged into the middle of their family shit.

"Hard pass. I don't actually do Christmas, and I certainly don't hang tree toppers."

"You must really be putting out, then," Granny Doyle said to Evie, "to get a man to do this much free labor."

I did not finish before the dark set in.

"You know, I don't blame you, Brian," Granny Doyle said to her son-in-law. "Your father never got off his lazy ass to do any of the fem work, as the kids say. So of course you don't know how to lay down Christmas lights."

Declan whistled. "Look at how straight they are. It's like a machine did it."

"It's only half-done, and Brooke is coming in the morning," Melissa complained.

"I think it's good enough, Mom." Declan sighed.

"Some of us don't leave jobs half-done."

"You're not exactly paying the man."

"Evie is." Granny Doyle waggled her eyebrows at her granddaughter.

"Is it dinnertime yet?" Evie's cousins complained.

"I need to make the gravy and warm up the rolls. The meat should be done soon, but it has to rest. Oh!" Evie exclaimed as I headed to my truck. "You're not staying for dinner? I guess you probably had plans. At least let me make you a plate."

I cranked the truck and turned on the high beams.

Evie's family groaned as the lights blinded them and lit up the whole front of the house.

I slipped on a pair of sunglasses and scrambled back up the ladder to finish the lower parts of the roof.

Like I said, not my first Christmas rodeo.

"Let's do this." I couldn't help the twitch of my mouth as Evie's family, sans her parents, all cheered.

"Lights." I clapped my hands at Evie.

She handed up the next roll of lights. "How did you—"

"Some of us plan ahead, Gingersnap."

It took another two hours to finish the house.

Evie came out as I was stashing the ladder in the bed of the pickup.

"I can't wait to see!" She jumped up and down in excitement, riling up Snowball, who barked, her four feet lifting off the snow with each yip.

I tried hard not to let her joy infect me as I flipped the switch and lit up the house.

Evie's eyes were shining as I went to stand next to her, but she wasn't looking at the house. She was looking at me.

No, she's not. She's looking at the house, dipshit.

"This is the best it's ever looked," she breathed as we stood there staring up at the house decorated like a postcard.

"If I was twenty years younger, I'd have been up there with you." One of her uncles chortled. "Fantastic job."

"You shouldn't get so bent up about a bunch of lights." I crossed my arms.

Evie thumped her fist on my ribcage. "Don't be so modest. You did amazing." I could hear the smile in her words.

"He's never going to do another thing for you again unless you feed him!" Granny Doyle called.

"Steak and a blow job at a minimum," one of her uncles joked as he handed me a beer.

His wife glared at him until he shrank.

Evie was crestfallen when we walked back in through the living room.

"You put the star on the tree without me?"

"It was a contentious political issue." Declan's wife rolled her eyes.

"Don't smile at the bad man." Grandma Shirley was cooing to Evie's niece, who babbled, reaching toward me.

"Grab a plate," Evie said as her brothers herded their family in varying states of inebriation into the massive dining room, where garland was draped from the chandelier along the ceiling.

The scene was beautiful—Evie there, holiday apron on as she handed out china decorated with vintage Christmas patterns.

"I thought you said I could take mine to go," I reminded her over the din of her hungry family.

"Oh!" She was taken aback. "You don't want to stay and eat while it's hot?"

"I just spent the last five hours dealing with you and those lights. No, I don't want to eat dinner with your fucking family."

Chapter 14

EVIE

"**M**erry slutmas!" Brooke Taylor blew into the Murphy house in a cloud of perfume, wearing a big fur-lined designer coat and sky-high heels. She hugged my mother.

"Mel! God, I'm always so jealous of your figure. Look at you! Your tits are still so perky. You have to give me the name of your plastic surgeon." Brooke pulled off her matching fur hat, letting down a cascade of glossy curls.

As someone who had soldiered on through middle school sporting ill-shaped, cheap haircuts, I was in awe of how Brooke had tamed her curls.

I resolved then and there to give the curly-girl method another go.

Brooke shrugged off her coat like Cruella de Vil and breezed through the house, calling, "Where are they? Where are the little darlings?"

I picked the coat off the floor, shaking it out.

A harried-looking producer threw himself in front of me before I could follow Brooke and my mother.

"Ms. Taylor requires chilled Perrier on hand at all times with a selection of lime slices. Slices. Not wedges. Not chunks. Slices."

"Already prepared! I know all her tastes," I chirped. "I follow Brooke on Instagram. I have pomegranate seeds and mint as well. I also have snacks."

The producer turned up his nose. "Ms. Taylor doesn't do anything as pedestrian as snack while she's working."

In the living room, Brooke was admiring the decorations, complimenting my mother. "And look at all these cookies! So festive! So fun!"

"It was nothing," my mom said modestly. "Honestly, I wasn't going to go all out this year, but I wanted to make sure we didn't tank your show."

"You're such a perfect hostess. Mel does all this, raised seven kids, and has a very successful career." Brooke gave her famous laugh. "Can you believe"—she turned to an imaginary audience—"that this woman is a grandmother? Spin around, Mel. I mean, look at her."

"It has been very exciting."

"And all your little mini-mes," Brooke cooed at the triplets. "So, so fun! Let's get started. I'm thinking this shot, Zane. Maybe move this table out of the way."

I opened my mouth to offer Brooke something to drink.

"Don't talk to her directly," the producer hissed, grabbing my arm.

The camera guys rolled their eyes as they set up for the shoot.

I mimed zipping my lips to the producer then tiptoed back to the dining room to set up. After this initial interview, Brooke wanted to get festive holiday B-roll of the family. I had been up since three, cooking dishes that would look amazing on camera.

"Where is Brooke's water?" the producer demanded, rushing into the dining room.

I set down the tongs I was using to rearrange a tray of Frostberry Delight pastries and wiped my hands. The producer trailed after me as I grabbed the glass bottles of sparkling water from the fridge and placed them on the tray with the garnishes.

"Your water, Ms. Taylor." I set the tray on the coffee table and smoothed my apron. "I'm also almost done setting up in the dining room," I added to my mom. "I'll let you know when it's ready for inspection."

Mom waved a hand to dismiss me.

"Thank you, dear. Oh, look at this tiny little spoon for the pomegranate seeds!" Brooke cooed. "Such attention to detail. It's the little touches that set the professionals apart. I should hire you away!" She gave me a friendly smile. "I'm sure you're tired of working for Melissa. She was my roommate at Brown. Did you know that? You should have told me you hired a housekeeper, Mel. That's your little secret."

My stomach sank.

"It's a good job, and the family is nice," I stammered out, not wanting to be awkward and correct Brooke Taylor. "I like working here."

My mom looked like she was about to have an aneurysm at the lie.

The front door slammed, and a man's footsteps thudded in the hallway.

"Evie!" Anderson bellowed. "Your fucking dog."

"'Scuse me," I mumbled, but it was too late.

Anderson had appeared in the doorway to the formal living room, Snowball held out in one large hand. "You need to take better care of your shit."

"Can we just go—"

"Seriously. This is insane." Anderson raised a knife-hand in front of me. "I did two tours in Fallujah with some of the craziest motherfuckers you have ever met, and no one there was as batshit as this dog. I had to pull her off a FedEx truck *five goddamn miles* from your parents' house." His arm extended sharply to the window.

"She doesn't like the FedEx guy." I gingerly took Snowball from Anderson and tucked her under my arm like a football.

"No shit."

"Your... parents' house?" Brooke's eyes widened.

Anderson scowled.

My mother pressed her hand to her mouth.

"This is the baby I adopted, Brooke. You remember Evelyn?"

"I am so sorry!" Brooke immediately rushed over to me. "Evie! Of course, Evie! I didn't even recognize you."

"I didn't think I gained that much weight," I joked.

Brooke let out a peal of laughter. The tension was broken.

"Same girl, same, although mine's all the stress-drinking from ratings week last month. What are you up to these days? Your mom would not have had these miraculous triplets without you, and I wouldn't have my top-rated show." She tossed her glossy curls exaggeratedly. "You know what they say—adopt a baby, and the next thing you know, you're pregnant. You're in college, right, in Virginia?"

"I went to college to get my MRS degree," I joked self-deprecatingly, "and flunked out on both counts, so now I'm just trying to be the neighborhood cat lady, though at the rate I'm going, I think I'll have to settle for possums."

"You are so funny! Is it rolling? It was rolling on that?"

Zane gave her a thumbs-up.

Brooke's bright-red lip caught in her teeth briefly, then she looked Anderson up and down.

On any other man, the tennis shoes, jogging shorts, and gray zip-up hoodie would make him look like a schlub.

Not Anderson.

The muscles in his arms bulged against the gray fabric as he crossed them. Not that I found it in any way appealing—just, you know, stating an observation.

"Seems you didn't need to go to college at all to find a husband." Brooke looked him up and down then back up.

"Evie is going through that phase," my mother interjected, "where she is attracted to the wrong sort of men."

Brooke twirled a perfect curl on a French-manicured finger. "That phase is a necessary learning opportunity. You might not be such a stick-in-the-mud if you'd lowered your standards and your panties back in college." She winked at my mom.

My sisters giggled.

"Once you're done with him, can I have him, Evie?" Brooke joked.

"Have me how?" A slow smile spread across Anderson's mouth.

I elbowed him sharply.

Seriously, why were women falling all over themselves for him? The man consisted of nothing but muscles, ego, and disregard for women, for god's sake! Susan B. Anthony was rolling over in her grave.

"Back up, sister! I'm first in line if he wants a May-December romance," Granny Doyle hollered, barreling into the room, my father rushing behind her.

"We are not done filming. You were supposed to be babysitting her, Brian."

My father gave my mom an apologetic look.

"Brian!" Brooke air-kissed him on each cheek.

"I know you and Mel are concerned about Evie and her—" There was that frankly lecherous look at Anderson. "Terrible taste in men. You remember it took me a second to find myself. I should have dropped out of school instead of wasting money on a journalism degree. If you think about it, Evie's doing better than me at her age. I had no man, no dog, and tons of student loan debt." She fluffed out her hair. "Now I buy myself diamonds and hookers for Valentine's Day."

"You're overpaying, then," Anderson purred to her.

"If you're buying jewelry, you should get him some for his cock," Gran added loudly. "I bet you got ornaments all up your dick like a Christmas tree, Anderson."

The huge man grabbed the back of my neck before I could scream, *Your dick is pierced?* because if I was his not-girlfriend-slash-hookup, I really should know that.

Anderson palmed his crotch. "Why would I poke a hole through that?"

Gag.

"Speaking of holiday romance." Brooke turned to the triplets. "Are you three looking for identical hunky boyfriends? That's next on your checklist of having it all."

"If any other hot men try to kill Henry, we're so down," Alexis joked.

Brooke held up a hand. "Excuse me? Ex-*Cuse* me?"

"Yeah," Alissa added, "Anderson is the guy who went to jail for almost murdering Henry in battle."

"Girls." My mother's voice had a hysterical edge.

I longed for the safety of the kitchen.

"Oh my god." Brooke was immediately drawn to the drama. She shooed one of the triplets out of the chair. "Sit, Evie. Tell me more about dating your family's enemy." She tried to drag me into the seat.

I balked. "I don't think there's much to tell," I squeaked. Just because I'd fantasized about being the star of a Brooke Taylor segment didn't mean I actually wanted to be. I was still in yesterday's makeup. I was pretty sure I could feel a hair growing on my chin at that moment.

"Dating is a strong word. We're not putting labels on it. He's just…" I gestured helplessly to Anderson.

"Of course! How could a girl resist?"

Barf.

"So sorry, Brooke. Maybe another time." My mother inserted herself between me and her old roommate. "Anderson was just leaving. As you can see, we have a lot going on. Not to mention we're trying to find Evie a job, and having all this on camera won't help that at all. So let's just delete all that footage, mm-kay?"

"Spoilsport. I always had to drag your mom to have fun, even in college," Brooke said with a theatrical sigh.

"Evie, finish the dining room." Melissa snapped her fingers at me.

I shoved Anderson toward the kitchen and slammed the door.

The rest of my family had started arriving. The hum of conversation was muffled a bit by the closed kitchen door. Braeden's nasally voice could be heard talking loudly in the dining room with other relatives.

I leaned against the kitchen island and faced Anderson. Cold gray eyes narrowed.

"Brooke Taylor. Your family is fancy."

"Why are you here?"

"And here I thought you'd be happy to see your hot boyfriend—'scuse me, the guy who bends you over the table and fucks you on the regular."

For once in my life, I was thankful for my olive complextion, because it hid the rush of blood to my cheeks.

His hands came up to circle my waist.

Too close!

"No one is here," I croaked. "You don't have to pretend."

"Honestly, Gingersnap?" he whispered in my ear, pinning me against the counter. "Most of the fun for me is watching you fight yourself, fight how much you secretly want me."

"I hate you," I whispered.

"I know, but you still want me. Even if you're a bad daughter and a bad sister, you want me bad."

Chapter 15

ANDERSON

The metal hanging lamp creaked as I pulled the chain, flooding the room with bright-white light.

I set the phones down in a neat row. Two of the latest iPhones, one red, one silver, last year's Samsung, and a white iPhone from two years ago.

I quickly tapped in the PIN numbers I'd memorized then disabled location sharing.

While her family members were drunk and distracted by the filming, I'd swapped my targets' phones with identical phones that were bricked. At first, they would think the battery had run out and they'd try to charge it, but they would never really work right. At the next holiday party, I'd swap the phones back out.

After I got all the data I needed.

Braeden wasn't the only person on my list. Two cousins, an aunt, and her father's second cousin had all potentially had a hand in securing fraudulent insurance payouts from Van de Berg Insurance.

Normally, I'd space this out—swap out one phone, wait a bit, then swap the next. But time was of the essence.

Santa Claus wasn't coming to town, but Aaron Richmond was, and I'd be lucky if all he did was leave a lump of coal in my stocking.

Was it easier to perform a sleight-of-hand trick when I was standing face-to-face with these people, pretending like I was just squeezing past them to the wet bar, instead of sneaking into their houses at night?

Sure.

But at the very least, the slow method would mean I didn't have to deal with Evie. Or her family.

I was starting to think that it was a mistake to punish her for blackmailing me. I should have just taken the hit and strung her along on finding proof from Braeden.

Because it was pure torture being in that house with those people.

I couldn't scrub off the looks of hatred, the disgust, the anger.

Sure, a few of her female relatives wanted to throw their panties out the window for me, but the rest?

I was the Grinch's shitty older brother.

I wanted to shed my own skin after leaving the house.

The worst, though, was Evie.

Maybe it was so hard to keep her at a distance because she didn't look like the rest of her hateful redheaded family, with her big brown eyes and the tangled hair that kept escaping from the haphazard bun. The way she looked at me was like needles under my fingernails—the mix of fascination, loathing, and desire. It was a toxic brew, and I kept wanting to dip my head to lap it up.

Somehow, I had fucked myself again, just like with trying to get one over on Aaron.

I turned back to the task at hand.

My brothers were busy with paying jobs. As much as they annoyed me, the field office was cold and lonely without them.

People thought hacking was exciting. They were wrong. It was more like archeology. Armed with a tiny paintbrush, you had to carefully uncover fragments to piece together into a dinosaur.

I stood up, flexing my arms, and picked up a Sharpie, marking a red *X* on another day on the calendar hanging on the wall.

I was no stranger to blowing through sleepless nights. But between all of my normal contracts for Hudson and this, it was starting to add up.

I just had to make it until Christmas, then I was going to sleep until New Year's.

And block Evie's number.

She was blowing up my phone: complaining that I had shown up at her parents' house, fretting that Braeden was going to think something was up, demanding to know if I'd liked the puff pastry galette she'd baked, and asking if precious Snowball had *actually* caused any damage to the FedEx guy or the FedEx guy's truck because she didn't want Snowball to spend Christmas in doggie lockup.

Now she was assuring me that she totally wouldn't be mad if I did sleep with Brooke Taylor but if I did to please send her photos from inside her house.

Anderson: *If you don't leave me the fuck alone,
I'm going to show up at your parents' house
and jack off all over that demented-looking
Rudolph statue your mom has on the front
porch.*

Evie: *Go pierce your dick.*

Annoyed and irritable, I shoved the phone into my
pocket then grabbed my keys and motorcycle helmet.

Time to stop fucking around.

Chapter 16

EVIE

I yelped when my phone rang, the sudden noise causing me to drop a stitch on the table runner I was crocheting.

Anderson's name flashed on the screen.

"Merry Christmas!"

"Downstairs now."

Sighing, I looked around the room. I'd tried to make the drafty attic space as cozy as possible. Candles were lit, music played, and I was finally warm in my bed.

"Can't we do this tomorrow?"

"Now, Gingersnap."

I peeked out the window. Across the street and one house down was a dark figure on a motorcycle.

Hopping around in the cold, I pulled on black yoga pants, my boots, and a black sweatshirt. Well, mostly black. I had been trying out my ill-advised purchase of an embroidery machine, and it was festooned with Scottish Terriers in their Christmas best.

I stuffed Snowball into a small backpack then tiptoed down the stairs, praying no one in my family woke up and caught me sneaking out to meet a boy.

Anderson made a big show of uncrossing his arms to look at his watch when I huffed up in the cold to his motorcycle.

"You need to give people more of a heads-up."

"We're at war, Gingersnap." The deep voice was muffled by the black motorcycle helmet. "Readiness is your most powerful weapon."

He handed me a black helmet slightly smaller than his own. I looked at it… and looked at it.

"Does this strap thingy go on first?"

"You're killing me. Come here," he ordered, taking the helmet. "Haven't you ridden a bike before?"

"A bike? Yeah, but I've never in my life ridden on a motorcycle."

He set the helmet on my head, then his fingers deftly tightened the strap under my chin.

"Get on. Let's go." He held out his hand for a fist bump.

I tapped his fist. "On, Dasher! On, Dancer! Go, team!"

Anderson blew out an annoyed breath. "No, Gingersnap, I'm trying to help you get on the bike."

"Oh. Ha ha! I thought you wanted a fist bump for, you know, solidarity."

The helmet regarded me silently.

"Right." Gingerly, I used his extended arm for leverage as I straddled the bike.

"Closer."

"Uh, sorry." I shimmied forward.

"I said closer."

He reached behind him to grab my waist, pulling me forward so my chest was pressed against his back and his hips were snug between my splayed legs.

Even though it was freezing out, the heat from him radiated through the heavy leather protective jacket.

I rested my hands on his shoulders then his ribcage then his hips, unsure what I should do with them.

He grunted as my hands brushed over a bulge.

"Not there." He grabbed my hands, moving them up to clasp snugly around his waist. "At least, not while I'm driving." There was a smile in the deep voice.

My heart thudded against Anderson's back as he revved the engine.

The wind whistled past us as the bike picked up speed.

I clung to Anderson, adrenaline making my heart pound, eyes tightly shut, and tried to keep from screaming as the bike roared through town.

Every so often, his hand came up to stroke my thigh.

"I knew you couldn't stop thinking about me!" I shouted at him at a red light. "Sorry to disappoint you, but I'm not sleeping with you tonight."

The helmet looked at me then returned forward. "Don't flatter yourself, Gingersnap. I'm giving you a heads-up so you don't fall off when I make a turn and scrape pavement."

"Oh. That makes sense."

Snowball barked. His hand was back on my thigh. The light changed, and the bike jumped, sending us flying down the empty street.

By the time Anderson pulled up in front of the narrow two-story brick building where he lived, I was getting the hang of riding a motorcycle. I had even opened my eyes to watch the industrial buildings whizz by as we rode through the Gulch, aka the bad part of town.

Gravel crunched, then Anderson turned off the bike.

"That was intense," I said, feeling a little lightheaded as I tried to lift my leg over the bike as elegantly as I'd seen him do it. I couldn't quite make it, though.

I grabbed my boot, trying to hoist my foot over the bike, then tried to grab on to something for purchase as I felt myself keel over and thud on the ground.

Snowball yelped her irritation and struggled out of the backpack.

"Seriously?" Anderson looked down at me from the bike. He gracefully lifted his leg over the saddle—was that what it was?—and stood in front of me, arms crossed. "If you're going to work with me, you can't make me look bad." Reaching down, he grabbed my arm, swinging me to my feet.

"You can take the helmet off," he said when we were inside a high-ceilinged space that had lifts, chains, and other car-related machinery hanging from the ceiling.

"I can't." I motioned helplessly.

"Why do I even bother?" he muttered.

I tilted up my chin so he could unfasten the helmet.

Fluffing my hair out, I took in the space. "He actually brought me to the bat cave. I feel so special." I walked around the converted garage and stopped in front of a bulletin board with Braeden's headshot in the center. "You're going down!"

Snowball barked.

"Focus, Evie."

Anderson arranged himself on a plain metal stool, one boot on the floor, the other heel caught on a rung of the stool, leaning forward slightly. He held a little notebook in his hand. "You said you had a breakthrough?"

"You were right." I bounced over to him.

"Imagine that." He cocked one eyebrow slightly.

I ignored it. "Braeden is doing this because he's getting off on it." I rehashed the conversation from the kitchen while Anderson listened with an intense expression on his face.

"You need to keep him off-balance. Make him slip up."

"What I need is a recording device. Like a spy."

Anderson stood up and headed over to a desk with a lot of little drawers. Metal clinked, then he shut the drawer he was looking in and padded over to me, hand outstretched.

"Is that a vibrator?"

"I don't bring a woman to my place and offer her a vibrator, Gingersnap." A smile played around his mouth.

I snatched the little gold tube from him.

"You're terrible in a crisis. This is easy to use," he said.

"Can't you give me something that's on all the time?"

"You mean a wire?" he shot back. "Do you have wire money? Because those require a whole team monitoring twenty-four seven."

"I could bake cookies."

He took the vibrator-slash-microphone from me.

"Just press it to start recording. You don't need to look at it at all. And if someone's searching through your things, they will think you're just sex starved." He tapped the USB-C port on the side. "Make sure you keep it charged."

"Don't you have anything that looks like a Tamagotchi?" I was panicked at the thought of walking around my nosy family with a vibrator-shaped object.

"Do you want to be kicked out on the night before Christmas? Because I'm telling you right now, you're not going to try to worm your way in here on Christmas morning."

"As if! You don't even have a tree."

He glared.

I put my hands on my hips. "Reporting for duty. Ready to follow instructions, sir. Do you want me to shave my legs and wear a cute miniskirt around Braeden?"

"Absolutely not."

"Ooh, someone's jelly!"

His hand slammed down on the table. "You will not," he said, deep voice tense, "go in there and act like a sex kitten. Braeden will immediately know something's up, and then you've lost."

"So I just go about my business normally?"

"No." He straightened. "You need to act like prey."

"What?"

He worked his jaw. "Enticing."

I was confused.

In a split second, Anderson was in my personal space, backing me slowly against the table.

"You're so trusting and dumb, letting him use you like that. Though I'm not surprised, considering how I could practically smell it on you—the desire. If I pushed you over this table, you'd spread your legs, begging me to fuck you."

"*Stop it.*"

"You'd take my cock, and you'd like it because you're a terrible person."

The tears were immediate, threatening to spill out of my eyes.

"You like this." He whispered the horrible words. "You're soaking wet at the thought of being held down and fucked by the man who almost murdered your brother.

You're a selfish little cunt. You'd sell your whole family down the river for my cock."

My heart was pounding in my chest, and he was right—I could feel the warmth bloom between my legs. What was wrong with me?

"That feeling?" Anderson whispered. "Where you feel like you're small and insignificant, and you just want to curl up and wait for this all to be over? That's being prey. For a certain type of man"— Anderson's voice had a rough edge—"that shit's addicting."

His hand came up, hovering like he was going to rest it on me, then he turned away. "No, you want him to feel like he's broken you down. Like you're almost afraid of his touch but still crave it."

I wiped my eyes.

"You're like three cluster B personality disorders in a trench coat."

"Bottle that up." His tone was immediately cold, professional. "Use it. Be prey when Braeden's around. He won't be able to help himself. He'll slip up, say the wrong thing—"

"And then we've got him!"

"Wrong. We have a piece of evidence."

"Seriously?" I complained. "I'd have a voice recording of him admitting to lying."

"A singular piece of evidence can be hand-waved away. People will make all sorts of excuses in order to hold on to their preconceived notions," he argued. "We need a stack of evidence that's irrefutable, that paints the picture of Braeden as a manipulative liar."

"And all before Christmas." I sagged. This was impossible.

Anderson gestured to the bulletin board. In addition to Braeden, there were a number of other photos of people I recognized.

"While you were wasting time baking cookies, I was analyzing your family members' phones for connections to Braeden."

"We're going to hack them?"

"No, we're going to social engineer them. You have family holiday parties coming up, yeah? Sit next to them. Get them talking."

"I usually stay in the kitchen. But," I added hastily at his annoyed expression, "there's no time like the present to stretch those social muscles."

"Don't forget to set the bait for Braeden."

I shivered as I thought about Anderson that close to me, calling me a slut as he practically had his leg in my crotch.

"Yep!" I squeaked, "I'm going to be the best prey there ever was. Just me and my fake vibrator."

Chapter 17

EVIE

I shouldn't bait Evie.

There was no reason for it.

Shouldn't even bother helping her clear her name.

I just needed to string her along and make her think I was going to help her prove to her family that her ex was a lying scumbag.

I needed to keep my emotions out of it. That was how I'd screwed myself over the last time.

Baseball cap low on my head, I hustled into the Christmas market, losing myself in the crowd then ducking behind a stall to change jacket and hat.

Adjusting my gait, I walked back out to meld into the crowd again.

Overkill? Maybe, but I'd just been in Evie's cousin's house to hunt down a final piece of evidence, a whole backed-up treasure trove of chat app messages sent to her by her boss, that spelled out that the company lost money not from a hacking attempt but instead because the boss let her twelve-year-old into the office because she didn't have a babysitter. The kid had plugged her sketchy label printer into one of the company computers, compromising the entire system.

It wasn't as much damage as I needed to clear off the ledger, but it was a good chunk. Every bit counted.

I just had to kill time until tonight, when I would make contact with Aaron and hand over the files.

I walked through the crowded Christmas market, feeling like I was Scrooge from that Charles Dickens story, observing the townspeople going about the holiday but not really experiencing it. They all looked so happy, so joyous as they examined the wares of the stalls, greeted friends and neighbors, and drank their holiday drinks.

Maybe I'd just head down to New York City early, crash at Hudson's place there. Get away from this oppressive holiday.

There was one person, though, in the Christmas market who, ironically, didn't exhibit a deranged level of holiday cheer.

Evie was slumped on a bench next to a man in an inflatable Rudolph costume trying to foist free samples of something called Reindeer Ribbon on people.

"You look like you eat protein, bro," the reindeer said, shaking what looked like individually wrapped jerky at me.

"Don't eat it," Evie told me dejectedly. "His sister bakes the jerky in their kitchen. None of it's licensed."

"Why don't you take his job?" I suggested.

"They aren't hiring. I already asked. Anyway." She stood up, brushing off her skirt. "I need to finish handing out résumés. I'll leave you to your Christmas shopping."

"I'm not Christmas shopping."

"Just soaking up the holiday atmosphere, then?"

I kept pace with Evie as we headed through the Christmas market, dodging people carrying firewood, wrapped packages, and wreaths.

"Going old school, huh?" I nodded to the paper bundle in her arms.

"My parents don't believe me when I tell them I've been applying for jobs online. They're technically not that old, but they act like they were born in the 1930s. They're all like, 'You need to go meet the manager and hand them a résumé.'"

I plucked one of the résumés printed on cream-colored paper out of her hand.

"Evelyn Murphy. Let's see, high school diploma, okay. Gaps in work history, a smidge of waitressing experience. Three-month stints as an office assistant." I handed it back to her. "Gingersnap, no one is going to hire you with this. Why don't you join the military?"

"You really want me running around with a gun?"

"On second thought..."

"Besides, I am not in shape enough for all that."

"You'd look cute in the uniform and the hat."

"Maybe I'll have to steal your hat and try it on the next time I'm at your place," she joked, her bag banging into my leg.

"Good luck. As soon as I got out, I collected my dishonorable discharge, doused my dress blues in gasoline, and lit it up."

"Oh, right. Yeah, I guess you would."

"Why don't you apply there?" I said, jerking my head toward a yarn store.

"There be dangerous waters. You really do like to live on the edge."

I grabbed the door handle before she could, ushering her into the brightly lit store.

Evie's eyes lit up like a kid's on Christmas morning.

"I need all of it! Come home with me, my pretties!" Evie trailed her fingers along the soft yarn.

Snowball was eyeing a box of white yarn the color of her fur.

I scooped up the dog, tucking her under my arm and keeping my fingers away from her sharp teeth.

Evie didn't have any money, and I didn't need the scrutiny, which meant that I would be paying for any yarn Snowball ruined.

Evie thrust her bag and her résumés at me then picked up a shopping basket.

"You're supposed to be applying for a job," I reminded her.

"They are having a sale, Anderson."

Into the basket went several bunches of Christmas tie-dye yarn.

"I saw these yarn Christmas trees on Pinterest, and I've been making them as gifts to give to people."

"I think you're past the age when you can give your friends and family handmade gifts."

She stuck her tongue out at me. "You're never too old to hand make a gift. Last year, I knitted Christmas tree ornaments. They were a big hit."

"I didn't see any of them on your mom's tree."

"Okay, so they were mostly a big hit," she said defensively.

She rifled through the next bargain bin of yarn. I, of course, had to hold the basket through all of this.

"Here's the good stuff." She held up a pack of pale-gray yarn and tossed it into the basket.

"We have to go to this cute toy shop next," she told me, excited, as we headed up to the cash register.

I set the basket down.

"Merry Christmas!" Evie chirped to the clerk.

"You got some good finds." The clerk, wearing what looked like a hand-knitted Christmas vest, rang up the purchases.

I cleared my throat pointedly.

"Right, um, are you all hiring at all?"

"Check back in January," the clerk said brightly. "And we'll definitely be hiring for the summer rush."

"Will do!" Evie said with forced cheerfulness.

"That was something, at least," I told Evie as we stepped out into the cold.

"I need a job in hand by Christmas," she explained dejectedly.

I set Snowball down and took Evie's shopping bag from her.

"I thought you said you were unemployed and broke," I reminded her as we walked down the bustling sidewalk.

"I might be able to sell my holiday sweaters on Etsy."

"I'm sure that was what your dad meant when he said he wanted you to make something of yourself."

She fished in her bag of yarn for her purchases and held up the pale-gray yarn to my face.

"It matches your eyes. It's a sign. I had to buy it."

"You should just shave that dog and use her fur to make sweaters."

Evie wrinkled her nose. "I had to do that when I first adopted her. I was living with a trust-fund girl who was slumming it for a year and wanted the full impover-ished-artist experience. Rent was free, but the water pressure wasn't high enough to get all the gunk out of her fur, so off it went. Snowball's never forgiven me."

"You didn't want to take her back to the orphanage?" I asked, repeating her mom's comment from the country club.

Evie looked down at the little dog.

"I'm Snowball's last chance. I found her in one of those boxes of free stuff people put out on their brownstone steps. Her owner told me I could have her when I knocked on the door."

I ducked under a low-hanging sign welcoming people to the historic Main Street for the holidays.

"When I tried to take her to a Pomeranian rescue, they refused and told me that she'd already burnt bridges at multiple adoption homes. She's a biter," Evie explained, twisting toward me then back. "She's on her last chance."

"So you're trying to keep her off doggie death row. Guess I'll keep the chunk of flesh you took out of my thumb between us, Snowball," I said to the dog.

The Pomeranian was walking next to us, head on a swivel, alert for targets.

"If that dog was a German shepherd, she would have been unstoppable in combat," I observed.

Snowball snapped at a snowflake in front of another colorful Main Street store.

"This place is so cute! I need to buy a toy for Reagan and Declan's little baby."

The chime above the door jingled as Evie and I entered the toy shop. It was like being transported back in time, to when things were simpler and my family still celebrated Christmas.

"That is an epic train set." I couldn't keep the wonder out of my voice as a miniature train chugged past me on its way to make a delivery at a tiny post office.

"You like trains!" Evie was gleeful. "The Grinch does have a heart."

"It's perfectly normal to like trains. Any red-blooded American male likes trains," I argued. "Railroads built this country."

"You're like a little kid," she gushed.

"These miniature trains are marvels of craftsmanship. Look at this." I pointed as the train chugged into the station in front of the miniature mail depot. A hidden mechanism sprang, and a tiny bag of mail was thrown out of the train car onto the depot platform.

"Isn't that amazing?" I asked her. "See, today, we'd just use a computer chip, but back then, it was all handcrafted mechanics, like those old Victorian windup toys. Impeccable craftsmanship."

"You need to embrace your inner child and build a big model train set." Her small hands rested on my chest for a moment.

"I can't." I turned away. "I don't have time."

"There's always time for joy."

"Isn't that how you ended up broke, living at your parents' house, and blackmailing a guy your mom hates, Gingersnap?"

She didn't throw back a snide retort. "Life's too short not to do things that make you happy." She rested a hand on my arm. "You deserve to be happy."

"I don't."

She made a noncommittal noise.

"Which do you think the baby will like?" We moved to a shelf of infant-appropriate wooden toys. "These are cute!" She held up a set of natural wood toys shaped into Christmas items like a tree, an ornament, and a Santa. "My niece is going to get loaded down with presents this year."

"You look like a man that's been dragged to Christmas hell and back." The shop owner was cheerful when Evie placed her finds on the counter. "Is your girlfriend treating you right? You can't run him ragged."

"She's already maxed out her card. Not too much more damage she can do. Besides—" I smirked at her. "I can take it."

As Evie paid, I noticed a small basket with what looked like broken toys. The sign said they were to be rehomed.

"Maybe this would be more your price range," I joked to Evie, digging through the pile of broken toys.

"Ha ha."

My fingers brushed something metal.

"A doggie!"

"Ooh, she is not friendly." Evie rushed over to the little girl who was infatuated with Snowball.

I grabbed her receipt and bags.

"I tried to fix it," the shopkeeper told me, nodding to the little metal miniature locomotive in my hand. "But." He shrugged. "I have a lifetime of projects in my garage."

"Yeah." I reached to put it back.

"Take it."

I hesitated then pocketed the little metal locomotive.

"Is no one hiring?" Evie asked with a sigh when we were back on the sidewalk after she dragged Snowball away from the crying girl who just, quote, "wanted a puppy exactly like that one for Christmas."

"I know!" Evie grabbed my arm. "Can you get me a job at the country club?"

"Members' kids can't work there. It makes people uncomfortable."

"Crap."

Ahead of us was a shop with a black-and-white-striped awning and pink decorations in their window of pink poodles having a Christmas tea party in front of a Christmas tree.

Snowball's pointed ears perked up.

"You were nice to that little girl, and you didn't bite Anderson when he picked you up, so I think someone deserves a treat!" Evie gushed to the dog.

I reached for the door handle.

"She's actually banned from this store. Could you wait outside with her, please?" Evie winced.

"Banned?" I raised an eyebrow.

"She went after a Doberman. His owner wanted me to pay for his therapy. It was a whole thing."

"Damn, Snowball." I looked at the tiny Pomeranian with newfound respect.

Blocking the dog with my boot, I held the door open for Evie.

"Wait! Résumé." I handed her one.

She made a face.

I waited, watching Evie through the glass as she selected dog treats. To one side of the door was an advertisement for the town's annual holiday parade this coming weekend. Santa would be there, as would the high school marching band. Henry Murphy was going to be the prince of the holiday parade, to honor all his service for his country. The small-town hero.

Fucker.

Looking around, I ripped the poster down, crumpled it up, and tossed it the few feet to a nearby trash can.

When Evie came back out, she held a white paper sack with the store's logo on it and the résumé.

"They said Snowball was a liability and they weren't going to hire me." She tossed the little dog a snack.

"We have to get you a treat, though, Anderson," she said, walking backward in front of me. "There's a stall nearby in the Christmas market that sells the cutest cake pops."

I couldn't help the bemused smile. "Gingersnap, every single time I'm with you, you're stuffing me full of desserts. I'm not going to be able to run a mile by New Year's at this rate."

"It's not like you ever eat them." She punched me lightly on the chest. "But fine, we'll go to Fern and Froth. They have herb-and-cream-cheese-stuffed pretzels. You can also get plants there. But you can't let me buy a plant," she warned me.

"I can't?"

"I have spent way too much money on succulents, and they all die."

There were more posters up as we walked down Main Street.

"I can't wait for the parade," Evie chattered. "Snowball, I can't leave you at home because Dad doesn't want you there unsupervised, but if I bring you, you have to behave, okay? It's Henry's big day."

I tried to keep my expression neutral but couldn't stop the noise of disgust.

Evie shot me a dark look. "Hey, you made your bed. You can't get mad when people want to celebrate him."

"Is that what you tell yourself to get through those god-awful brunches with your parents? That you deserve to be treated like that?" I growled.

"I haven't made the best choices."

"You haven't made the worst either."

She shrugged helplessly, rubbing her arm.

"Why don't you just ditch your family? Screw them. Leave. Run away. Go find your birth parents. Maybe that's your holiday miracle, reuniting with your birth mother."

"Except, like Snowball, I've been striking out on rejections," she said, swinging her bag. "Found my birth mom a few years ago. She was pretty pissed I showed up to ruin her perfect life. Apparently, she found some awesome rich guy to marry, and she has a cushy life as a stay-at-home mom with nannies and maids and everything."

"Birth father?"

"He's from a good family."

"Ah."

"And you know how that goes. His parents apparently didn't know I existed, and he wanted to keep it that way so as not to jeopardize his multimillion-dollar inheritance."

"Did you blackmail them too? You should have a pretty cushy fund from the payout for your silence."

"No, uh, no. I didn't."

We walked in silence for a moment.

Evie turned to me. "You're the first person I've ever blackmailed."

"Don't I feel special."

We walked into a coffee shop overflowing with poinsettias, wreaths, succulents, ferns, and other broad-leafed plants.

It was warm and humid in the shop. The smell of dirt and coffee and cheese was almost overwhelming.

Snowball sneezed.

I unzipped my jacket.

"Merry Christmas!" Evie greeted the two older ladies behind the counter while I watched Snowball to make sure she didn't mistake the plant array for a park.

"Grab a seat anywhere," one of the old ladies said.

Evie looked up at me.

I tried to silently communicate that I was suffocating in the coffee shop rainforest.

"We'll just take them to go," she said. "Two herb-and-cheese-stuffed pretzels, please. A black coffee for him and a Winter Wonderland frosted latte for me."

The ancient toaster oven behind the counter heated up, adding yet another layer of conflicting smells to the humid shop while Evie chatted with the shop ladies about the upcoming parade and when the street closing was going to happen, and they'd better make sure the delivery truck came early because Evie thought the streets were closing at midnight, and the old ladies thought five a.m.

"Two stuffed pretzels." The shorter-haired old lady crumpled the top of the paper sack and set it on the counter while her friend set down the coffees.

The old lady kept her hand on the coffees when I tried to reach for them.

"Shame on you," the old woman scolded me. "Trying to ruin a nice family like the Murphys."

I tensed up.

Evie didn't say anything, of course, just stood there while I had to take it.

"I used to babysit Henry," the other lady added. Now the tears were starting. "You shouldn't even show your face around here."

"It's a free country." I put a snarl behind the words.

Her hands didn't budge on the cups.

I wrenched the coffees away from her. "Evie already paid for these."

"Sorry," Evie said guiltily when we were back on the sidewalk. "I didn't mean to—"

"I have to go," I said abruptly.

"They just…" Evie made a helpless gesture. "It's just everyone loves my family, loves Henry and the triplets, anyway. They're just doing what they think is right."

"You don't need to explain it to me," I said coldly, handing her the coffee. "Your family is the Maplewood Falls nobility. And you're their court jester."

"You're just jealous."

"And you're delusional." I rounded on her.

"I don't want to hear it. My choices are my own. Take your pretzel."

"I'm not hungry."

"Fine. I'll eat them both."

We stood there, fuming at each other.

"Why are you so… so…" I searched for the word.

"So what, Anderson? Spit it out. I have to go haul food for fifty to Aunt Trish's house."

"You were just being nice to me so that I'd drive you around? Is that it?" I demanded, getting in her face.

"God no. Of course not." Evie wasn't intimidated. "I was about to say that today didn't totally suck, but obviously, you were going to ruin that eventually. Just go away."

"I'll drive you." And return the phones I'd stolen.

178 • Alina Jacobs

"No."

"Yes, I will," I said hotly. "It's all part of the deluxe blackmail package."

Chapter 18

EVIE

I was tense in Anderson's truck as he drove me and Snowball back to my parents' house.

"That's an awful lot of résumés still left, Evie," my father called when he saw me, then he grumbled when Anderson came in behind me, jingling his keys. "And now we see why."

"As the aging patriarch, confused that paper résumés no longer work, confronts a digital world, he is unable to cope and resorts to lashing out at the younger females of his troop," Anderson narrated in a fake British accent.

"Anderson," I warned him before he said something that would really set off my father.

I pushed the larger man toward the back of the house. "There's a cart in the mudroom. Just pack up the trays that are in the fridge. I have a cooler too. You can put the ice in it."

Snowball followed Anderson as he stalked to the kitchen.

"The yarn store said try back in the summer and she might have something."

My father folded his newspaper.

"It's your life, Evie. But you have until December twenty-fifth, and something tells me that you're not going to be as appealing a prospect to Anderson once he actually has to support you, since you seem averse to doing it yourself."

"If you're going to glom on to me as my boyfriend," I told Anderson as we carted the food up the walkway to Aunt Trish's rambling Victorian house painted in red, green, and white, "can you at least try to act nice to people?"

"You mean like your siblings that your whole family worships? Just because you have low sense of self-worth doesn't mean I do, Gingersnap."

Using my elbow, I rang the doorbell.

An elf shot out of a holiday-themed cuckoo clock, screaming, "It's time! For! Christmas!"

Anderson cursed, crouching down like he was about to reach for his gun a blow a hole in Aunt Trish's door.

"She's an artist," I explained as, inside, Aunt Trish was yelling at her yodeling family of foster cats to get out of the way, that it wasn't safe outside for kitties.

Anderson was digging deep into his military training as the door was thrown open.

"My niece! Look at my niece and her big handsome man. Oh." Aunt Trish sniffed then wafted her hand in front of Anderson, inhaling deeply. "You're wearing cologne. Evie, he's wearing cologne."

What the fuck? Anderson mouthed.

Aunt Trish tossed her scarf over her shoulder dramatically. "I feel a migraine coming on."

"Maybe it's all the cats."

I glared at Anderson.

"You know I cannot with the strong smells." She breathed in noisily. "It's definitely a migraine."

I sniffed Anderson's neck.

He kicked me with his boot. "Don't sniff me."

He smelled a little woodsy, like smoke and snow and male.

"I don't smell any cologne, Aunt Trish."

"It's there. Maybe he wore some yesterday."

"Are you wearing cologne?" I whispered to Anderson.

He shook his head wordlessly.

"I need to lie down. I'm entertaining tonight, and I cannot with my sisters and the cologne and this migraine. Get down from there, Evermore. You're afraid of heights!" Aunt Trish yelled at a white three-legged cat that was balancing precariously on the banister.

Snowball stood guard at my feet, puffed up, as the dozen pairs of feline eyes watched us enter the house.

"We'll put these in the kitchen. Let me just clean the cat hair off the counters." I pulled cleaning supplies out of my bag.

"I'm not eating anything this woman has made," Anderson said flatly.

"That is why we brought food," I told him.

I shoved the cat toys out of the oven and turned it on to keep the savory appetizers warm. Aunt Trish's parties tended to go better if people had something more substantial than cookies and fondant to eat.

Snowball growled as several cats materialized in the doorway. One cat snuck in through the back way and was getting close to Anderson's boots to sniff the strange man.

The Pomeranian rocketed, barking at the cat, which yowled and skittered away. Then the little white dog parked herself in front of Anderson's feet, keeping guard as he helped me ferry the food into the kitchen. All while Aunt Trish rested on the bright-purple fainting couch, hand over her eyes.

"Could you help me grab the folding tables?" I called from the mudroom.

Anderson pushed his huge shoulders through the narrow doorway.

"I'll take this end and—oh!" I exclaimed as he just lifted the whole rack of folding tables, carrying them like they were nothing into the open kitchen and dining area.

"I have new decorations, Evie." Aunt Trish pointed at a bulging closet.

I hauled out the centerpieces.

One of the cats yowled as a striped box fell off one of the stuffed closet shelves.

"Looks like a Christmas present. Do you want me to put it under the tree?" I offered.

My aunt opened one eye.

"That's for you, Evie. I received several signs that you needed this in your life. You remember I took that sculpting retreat."

"This is an interesting centerpiece," I said, turning the misshapen object around. It had a ribbon around it. "Is this like an infinity symbol? It almost looks like... oh my god!" I almost dropped the ceramic dildo.

Because that was what it was, complete with a giant set of balls, the name *Evelyn* scrawled on them in red script.

"Aunt Trish, I don't need this, I have…" I gestured toward the kitchen, where there was clanking as Anderson checked the oven. "*A man.* This is…"

"Just because you have a boyfriend," Aunt Trish said, raising herself up slightly, "doesn't mean that you can't also take charge of your sexuality. It's reinforced, so it's perfectly safe for use. It's got hematite embedded for positive energy."

She sank back onto the couch and pulled her scarf over her head. "I must convalesce for tonight."

Holding the dildo out in front of me, I prayed it would just disappear. I couldn't take this. What the hell was Trish thinking? Also, why was it so girthy? That shouldn't even fit in a woman.

"Evie?" Anderson's heavy boot steps came around the wet bar, which partially divided the kitchen from the living room.

Crap! Could I hide it in the cat bed? The box of decorations? I sprinted to a window and pitched the dildo out into the yard, making a mental note to retrieve it later.

When Anderson found me, I was pretending to be busy rummaging through a box of table linens and cloth napkins.

"These need to be ironed," I blurted out, holding up a wad of linen.

"I am not ironing those," Anderson said emphatically "I don't like you that much."

I shook out the white-and-green tablecloths.

"Snowball, run a perimeter," Anderson ordered the dog as I set out the Christmas centerpieces, which could be politely described as avant-garde.

"Kids won't be at the party, will they?" Anderson bent down to whisper into my ear. "Because I think these are going to give them nightmares. Also, these cats are going to make people sick."

"I'm going to try to lure them to a bedroom."

"We need to buy her a spiked collar," Anderson said as Snowball ran in defensive circles around the table, keeping the cats away.

"Afraid of a few cats?" I teased.

"I don't know how Trish is able to sleep. I'm afraid if I lie down, they'll all eat me."

I set out all the trays of cookies. I'd spent all my free time the past couple of days baking them. There were pieces to make miniature sugar cookie gingerbread houses and other cookie art ornaments. Along with twenty different colors of frosting, I also had fondant ribbons for hangers.

"You made these?" Anderson marveled.

"It's not that hard," I said as he inspected all the little pieces. "I just had to design custom cookie cutters. One of my many jobs after I dropped out of college was running a 3D printing rig at an ill-advised startup. They didn't pay me for three months, but they let me keep the printer. I had to sell it, though. Whomp whomp. But not before I made these custom cookie cutters."

The timer rang in the kitchen, and he immediately went in to check on the food.

I wasn't sure where we stood, but then, was there even really a *we*? Maybe this was how Anderson was. Anyone who could attempt to murder their fellow Marine in battle was clearly not the most mentally stable person. After raging at me on the sidewalk, now he was as helpful as one of Santa's elves with setting up the party.

"Sorry we're late!" Ian and Sawyer announced, armed with red wine and coolers of craft beer.

"No understudying tonight?" I hugged my brother then Sawyer.

"There's something shady at that theater," Sawyer said. "Did they ever fix the bathroom?"

"How about 'Did the director ever give me a lead role?' He's such a liar. This was supposed to be my big chance." Ian set the cooler down and looked around. "Wow, did Aunt Trish actually help?"

"She has a migraine, but Anderson was here to pick up the slack."

"Anderson?" Sawyer peered over my shoulder to where he was manning the appetizers and giving orders to Snowball in a clipped tone.

"Evie." Sawyer lowered her voice. "You can't treat him like your boyfriend. He hates you and our family, and you're supposed to hate him too."

"Yes, she can," Ian whispered. "It's killing St. Henry, and I am here for all of that."

"She can treat him like her sex toy, but, Evie, I know you. We've been over this. Braeden wasn't the first not-so-great guy you were convinced you were in love with. Remember Dean in high school? You were certain you were meant to be because he had the same name as a *Gilmore Girls* character, and then he broke your heart."

"I swear." I held a hand to my heart. "I have zero, nada, no feelings for Anderson. Definitely not love."

"Then why is he setting up a Christmas cookie party for you?"

"He's a grown man. He can make his own choices. Have some meatballs." I opened up one of the Crock-Pots and shoveled mini meatballs in a rich spicy-sweet sauce onto a plate for Sawyer.

"I need to hydrate before this party." Aunt Trish swanned in, pushing her glasses down to peer at Sawyer and Ian.

"Thank the goddess. The cool people are here. You two are an inspiration—living your dreams in New York City. You cannot worry about money at your age. You have to live. Don't give in to corporate pressure. You don't want to turn out like my sisters."

I poured Aunt Trish a glass of wine.

"Yum." She took a long drink and made a gimmie motion. "Protein. I need protein and an Advil."

The rest of my family was starting to arrive. The younger kids raced to the table, excited at the mountain of cookies.

"My class!" Aunt Trish clapped her hands twice. "Just because this is a scheduled activity does not mean you need to be afraid let your creative flag fly. There are no wrong answers. I want to see risk. I want to see bold choices. Yes, we do have purple frosting, Katie!"

My parents and siblings set up at one end of the table, giggling and laughing as they decorated ornaments. With their matching red hair, they always reminded me of the families in the dollhouses I lusted over as a kid and never received for Christmas. Even Ian, who was often agnostic on our family, looked like he belonged with them.

"I'm firing two more trays of the ham-and-cheese pin-wheels," Anderson said, coming up next to me. "Do you want the bar paced, or you just going to let them drink alcohol at will?"

"I think there will be a riot if we try to limit it."

He grunted.

I turned to him.

"Thanks for your help. Once again, couldn't have done it without you."

His tattooed fingers traced the collar of my sweater then gently tugged me toward him.

"You're kicking me out? Not even going to force-feed me dessert first?"

"Have to keep your *Playgirl*-worthy figure." I grazed my hand up the tight T-shirt then thought better of it and hid it behind my back. "You can stay, though," I offered. "I know Christmas isn't your style, but decorating cookies is fun. It looks like not everyone is making Christmas-themed ornaments, anyway."

"And tell me about your piece." Aunt Trish hovered over Granny Doyle's shoulder.

"It's Santa's little orgy." Granny Doyle held up her ornament.

"Mom, you are supposed to make a nativity scene out of that." Melissa snatched the cookie from Gran. "Evie." She waved me over. "Get rid of this."

"I quit," Granny Doyle declared then ripped off her apron and threw it at Anderson as she headed to the bar. "I only have so many holiday seasons left on this earth. I am spending them drunk."

"I love that woman," Anderson whispered around a grin. He took Granny Doyle's spot, and I sat across from him, assembling the little cookie houses.

"You don't want to put a little color on those ornaments?" Granny Doyle asked Grandma Shirley, who was carefully decorating a cream-and-white bell.

"Some of us like traditional Christmases."

"*I'm dreaming of a sad, beige Christmas!*" Granny Doyle sang then burped.

"This is about family, not newfangled notions about holidays. There is a traditional way of doing things," Grandma Shirley lectured. "Not that some people respect convention—"

"Oh, shut up, you shriveled labia."

"—What with people fraternizing out of wedlock."

"Mom," Dad begged.

"Anderson's not fraternizing. He's making edible ornaments, Ma." Aunt Trish breezed by, tossing glitter over everyone.

One of the cats sneezed, sending Snowball on the offensive.

"Anderson's got the only edible ornaments I want." Granny Doyle poured scotch into a glass.

His eyes widened slightly.

Henry and Braeden were exchanging annoyed looks.

With Aunt Trish's open floor plan, I didn't have an opportunity to get Braeden alone. I was secretly glad. I didn't know if I could keep it together enough to both lure him into thinking he'd broken me and try to turn on the microphone.

I wished that this was just a normal family Christmas and Anderson was a normal boyfriend and I was a normal daughter instead of this disaster of a half-baked revenge plan.

"Wow, these are ornaments I can actually gift people." I marveled at the intricate detail on the tiny town hall cookie ornament Anderson was working on.

Anderson had a neat line of them along the table.

"Oh-Em-Gee!" Nat and Lauren exclaimed, phones out. "Can we put you on our Instagram stories?"

"Take off your shirt first," Granny Doyle ordered.

"There really should be a separate room for those of us who want to have a wholesome cookie-making experience," Grandma Shirley said pointedly.

"Guess that vagina's not as defunct as we thought, eh?" Granny Doyle asked while Shirley sucked in a sour breath. "You just want to be alone with Anderson so you two can make cookies together."

"Why, I never—"

"Don't worry, Hot Stuff." Granny Doyle pinched Anderson's cheek. "I won't let her sink her claws into you. Some of us haven't made the transition to widow as gracefully as others." She reached for a sleigh cookie.

"No, Mom. You cannot make any more cookies." Melissa slapped her mother's hand away.

"Fine. I'm going to try to make a halfway-decent cocktail, then."

"Evie, pull out the bitters that you and I made this summer. They're in the root cellar." Aunt Trish breezed past with paint that I wasn't sure was edible.

I stood up, wiping my hands.

When I came back with the admittedly somewhat cloudy bitters for the cocktails, more arrivals were streaming through the front door.

"Look who decided to grace us with his presence!" Nat, wineglass in hand, greeted her brother and his new wife as they unwound their scarves.

"Can't miss the famous cookie festivities," Madeline said. "We brought wine."

"Thanks. I can put this by the bar. Sawyer and Ian brought some too."

"Oh, did they? This is imported French wine. I'm sure everyone would probably rather have that." Madeline tossed her glossy blond hair. "It's the holidays. We splurged since it's family."

"Not all of us are family." Grandma Shirley harrumphed.

Granny Doyle hooked two fingers in her cheeks and made an ugly face at her. "It's a wonder your husband lasted as long as he did."

Madeline air-kissed me.

"Another homemade sweater. So chic."

"Thanks," I gushed, probably with way more enthusiasm than the passive-aggressive comment warranted.

"I heard about your job," Gabe said, making a sad face.

"Yeah, that's awful," his wife added. Gabe and Madeline were actually acting friendly to me for once.

"You know me. I'll land on my feet."

My cousin was sympathetic.

"I'd say you landed on something else." Madeline inclined her chin.

Anderson was working like a machine, assembling and decorating cookie ornaments. He glanced up, those gray eyes watchful.

"Since you're currently between jobs, Gabe wanted to talk to you about an opportunity," Madeline said.

"At Svensson Investment?" I perked up. "They pay well. I could move back to Manhattan."

My cousin and his wife exchanged looks.

"This is a different opportunity, but you can still come back to Manhattan."

"We're looking for a surrogate. We could go to California, but it's just so expensive, you know," Gabe explained. "We can't start a family two hundred thousand dollars in debt."

"And I just can't take off of work," Madeline added. "Nine months of pregnancy and all the fourth-trimester inconveniences?"

"You're having a baby!" Gabe's mother cried, swooping in, frosting still in hand, to hug her son and kiss him noisily on the cheek. "Did you hear that? I'm going to be a grandma after all! And I thought you weren't having children."

"Thank god, because it sure as shit wasn't going to be me." Nat toasted her brother.

"Only if Evie agrees to be the surrogate."

All eyes were on me.

My aunt hugged me. "You'll be a great surrogate. You have the family history and the hips for it."

"That's what we were thinking. And since we aren't, you know, actually related, it won't be weird. Since it will be my sperm," Gabe told me.

"Like we'd have to have sex?" I squeaked.

"God no. I don't want your genetics. Madeline would use her eggs," Gabe said quickly.

"Obviously, we wouldn't pay you. That's illegal in New York, but you'd get free rent," Madeline stated.

"You mean the converted closet that doesn't have a window?" Sawyer demanded.

"We can't put her in one of the bedrooms. One's the nursery, and the other is for guests," Gabe argued.

"Evie, you cannot seriously be considering this," Sawyer demanded.

"Rent is expensive." I wavered.

"We'd meal plan," Gabe added pointedly.

"You'll have to keep her from eating so many chips. We'd better start feeding her prenatals," Aunt Kerry added. "She has the worst diet."

"I'd need to think about it," I hedged.

"Seriously, Evie? No way!"

"Your womb is fertile. Embrace your feminine spirit." Aunt Trish bent down and pressed her cheek to my belly.

"I guess just send me a—"

"No." Anderson's deep voice cut through my family's excited chatter. "Evie is not your surrogate. The only man impregnating her is me."

"Whew! Now I'm dreaming of a white Christmas!" Granny Doyle fanned herself.

Anderson turned to my dad. "Real father-of-the-year shit right there, Dr. Murphy, pimping out your own fucking daughter for a breed mule."

"Fuck off. He didn't have anything to do with it." The table rattled as Henry jumped up.

Anderson snorted and continued to decorate the cookies.

"Evie, get over here and bring me a beer."

Ducking my head, I hurried over with a cold bottle.

Anderson hooked two fingers in the waistband of my skirt, pulling me to him. The scrape of his nails on my bare skin sent a thrill of pleasure through me.

"Thanks, Gingersnap."

"So you just come when he calls now?" Henry asked me, voice tense.

Anderson pulled me off-balance so I half landed in his lap. "She does if she knows what's good for her."

The hand at my waistband slid under my shirt... up... up...

I tensed against Anderson.

The hand slid back out from under the sweater.

Anderson grabbed the beer.

I released a breath.

Anderson reached down and knocked the bottle cap off with his boot. The cap clinked on the floor. The cats raced for the new toy.

He took a long draught of the beer.

"You can't just bully your way into this family and try to steal my sister away."

"I don't have to steal her." Anderson grabbed my chin, forcing my head to face him. "When I'm done with you and all your shit, she'll leave willingly with me."

Is he going to kiss me? I screamed internally. I wasn't sure what I would do.

My eyes darted from his gray ones to his mouth to his jaw.

I was totally going to scream if he kissed me, because I was so not attracted to a man I hated and my family despised.

Right?

My heart raced.

His breath was slightly cool on my mouth.

He ran his thumb over my chin.

"Evie'd do anything for me. She's obsessed with me."

Chapter 19

EVIE

"It's a good thing he didn't kiss you," I whispered to myself as I climbed the dark, narrow staircase to my attic purgatory. I'd left Snowball with the Irish setters. After guarding the table from the cats all evening, she was ever so slightly tired.

I was already on thin ice with my family. Making out with the most hated man in Maplewood Falls in front of my grandmother wasn't a good look.

"Good thing I'm not attracted to him," I reminded myself as I turned on the lamp in the attic.

I mean, I wasn't, right? Especially because Anderson was just acting. When he had his hand up my shirt, it wasn't because he was attracted to me. When it seemed like he was about to kiss me, he wasn't.

Because he hated me.

As he'd said repeatedly.

But I bet it would be good, right?

As I pulled my sweater over my head, I tried not to think about how it would feel to have him run those tattooed hands over me—surely, methodically.

I slid off my skirt. The bra followed.

My hands circled my breasts. I was glad to be out of the underwire that dug in my rib cage.

Instead of grabbing my nightgown, I slipped under the covers, aware I was about to cross some line.

"We're just staying warm," I lied to myself, trying not to gasp as the sheets scraped over my pebble-hard nipples, making me wonder if that was what his teeth would feel like *there*.

I stroked myself through my soaking-wet panties, not ready to slip my fingers under the lacy band to touch my clit, to fully accept that I was in fact attracted to Anderson and, even worse, that I wanted to know what it would be like to have those tattooed fingers stroke my clit while he sucked on my tits, those silver-gray eyes never leaving mine.

I let out a whimper, and my hips surged against my hand.

I imagined it was his hand there.

I summoned up the memory of him next to me in the garage, his voice rough and hot against my neck as he told me how he'd bend me over and how he'd take me.

That word—he'd *take* my pussy with his cock.

I gave in.

My fingers were hesitant as they slipped under the fabric.

Closing my eyes, I imagined Anderson watching me stroke myself. How he'd talk dirty to me, tell me to come for him, tell me how he wanted to fuck my pussy raw, spill his cum all over my tits.

My fingers had just barely brushed the hot wet slit when the floorboards creaked. Was it Anderson? Did he come for me?

"Don't be shy," Braeden said from the doorway. "You can't pretend like you were doing something wholesome."

My eyes flew open. Strangling a scream, I pulled the cover up to my chin.

Braeden closed the door behind him. "Remember how you used to do that for me? Put on a little show on FaceTime when I was traveling?"

I didn't have to pretend to be prey. I felt so vulnerable, so helpless.

"Don't you want to keep going?" my ex mocked.

I wordlessly shook my head.

The vibrator microphone was in my purse across the room, along with my phone.

I wished suddenly, desperately, that Anderson was there.

"You were thinking about him, weren't you? That fucking white-trash piece of shit. You're a stain on your family's good name. I was always going to be the best you were going to do." He took two steps to the bed.

"I miss your tits, you know. None of the women in your family have tits like yours. Probably because you're not really part of the family." He reached for the covers.

"Go away."

Swearing at me, Braeden grabbed a fistful of the covers. I held on tight as he tried to yank them down.

"You know you want to show me."

I finally managed to swallow enough to force out, "You had your chance with me. We're done."

He released the quilt but not before brushing his hand down the fabric.

I shuddered.

Braeden was revolting. How had I ever thought I was in love with him?

A slow smile spread across his face. "I knew you still wanted me."

I lay there frozen after Braeden left, worried he was going to come back. Finally, I talked myself into scurrying out of bed so I could collect my phone, nightgown, and the little microphone.

I held it clenched in my hand like a talisman, waiting for Braeden to come back.

I was so stupid. I should have kept it on me.

I wanted to call Anderson, wanted to hear his voice, wanted to tell him... well, what exactly? That I was having extremely inappropriate thoughts about him and was caught fluffing my pillow?

He would just berate me and tell me I should have had better situational awareness.

But he'd still come, right? He'd helped me with the cookie party and gone shopping. Some little part of him cared about me. There was a human under all that evil.

My finger hovered over his name in my phone, then I turned it over.

Anderson didn't care about me.

No way, no how.

I finally gave up on sleep at five, killing my alarm as I tiptoed down to prep for the parade. In the spirit of Brooke Taylor, I was embracing my curly hair. After my shower, I wrapped a T-shirt around my conditioner-soaked hair to let my curls set a la the Curly Girl method.

Today was the day of the Christmas parade, one of my favorite holiday events in Maplewood Falls. I couldn't wait to see all the floats, the marching bands, and the dancers. There would even be horse-drawn carriages.

I hummed along to the Christmas carols playing softly from the radio, mixing the orange-colored dough for the spicy cheese straws and sipping a peppermint hot chocolate latte.

If I forgot about my impending eviction and Braeden's newly kindled creepy obsession and the microphone that I wasn't sure how to work and Anderson and his tattoos, I could almost pretend that this was just another cozy holiday morning.

"You're making those sandwiches with store-bought rolls?" my mother remarked judgmentally, coming into the kitchen when the sky was just starting to lighten.

"I always use Hawaiian rolls on the Christmas cracker sandwiches," I argued. "I am using homemade pickles, though."

"This is Henry's big day."

I sighed, took out the flour, and started measuring.

"You're not using Hawaiian rolls, Evie?" Henry asked, walking into the kitchen in jogging pants and taking out his ear buds as he saw me measuring flour.

My oldest brother poured himself a cup of coffee.

"Of course she is," my mother assured him. "Evie, make sure those cheese straws aren't burning."

Mom checked the oven while I put the flour back in the pantry.

Henry grabbed a hot cheese straw and wandered into the living room, where my father was already set up with his coffee and the newspaper.

Using a long serrated knife, I sawed through the Hawaiian rolls, swiped spicy horseradish spread over the bottom half, and laid them out over the kitchen island. I was layering the Swiss cheese, thick-cut ham, and pickles on the sliders when happy voices from the foyer announced the arrival of family.

"These are for the parade," I warned my cousins as they piled into the kitchen.

Sean tried to steal a sandwich, and I hit him with a spoon.

"Ow! You should have made breakfast."

"There's breakfast casserole in the oven."

"I knew Evie wouldn't let us starve!" His brother put him in a friendly headlock and ruffled my hair.

"You'll make a good wife one day, Evie," Aunt Heather told me as I pulled the bubbling casserole out of the oven.

"That's about all she'll be good for unless she goes back to college," Uncle David said pointedly to my tween cousins. "This is why I keep telling you girls to do well in school."

"Someone has to make the sandwiches," my aunt scolded her husband. "School isn't everything." She beamed at me then followed me as I carted the casserole out to the buffet in the dining room.

"Not worth it!" Granny Doyle was raging at inexplicably inebriated family members in the dining room. "Even if your husband is nothing but a blobfish, the Christmas parade won't let you strap his cheating corpse to a pickup, Marc-Antony-returns-to-Rome style."

"Now, Evie." My aunt was still following close behind. "You remember Preston, don't you?"

I almost dropped the casserole, burning my hand as I slid it onto the hot pad. My cousins didn't even wait for me to move before they dug in.

"Oh, Preston!" my mom exclaimed. "Henry, you used to be friends with him. He was always over here when you were in high school. You remember?"

"His wife left him." My brother poured orange juice for the younger kids.

"Exactly." Aunt Heather beamed. "And I told him all about Evie and how she's well-meaning but boy crazy and just needs a good man to help steady the ship."

"Because that's a wonderful message to send to all the young girls present," I said.

"Nothing wrong with being a wife. Especially if you don't have any other skills. Now, Preston's meeting us at the parade with his four children—"

"No wonder his wife left," Granny Doyle quipped, tipping vodka into her glass of orange juice.

"Some of us appreciate the fine art of homemaking," Grandma Shirley declared, looking down distastefully at the plates. She flicked an invisible speck of dirt off one.

"Evie would be an excellent stepmother—"

"Aren't his boys, like, older?" Henry asked with a frown.

"They got married young." Aunt Heather smiled wanly. There was lipstick on her oversize veneers.

"The last time I hung out with him, his kids were a holy terror." Henry took a plate.

"Just be forewarned, he's not as good-looking as Anderson," Uncle David added.

"Really selling it there, Aunt Heather," Sawyer stated dryly.

"Again, I'd be out the door." Granny Doyle took a swig of vodka then shoved the bottle down her nightgown.

"Can you please dress for breakfast?" Grandma Shirley was incensed.

"You can't think I'm going to marry Preston," I protested.

"Don't be rude. He has a job, a house…"

"I think he's mortgaged up to his eyeballs on it," Henry interjected. "Not sure that—"

"*Henry,*" my mom snapped at him, using the tone that she usually reserved for me.

My oldest brother clamped his mouth shut and turned to his food.

"Now, Evie, I know you think that you're in love with Anderson, but rest assured, your feelings are not reciprocated. Men like Anderson do not stick around," my mother lectured me.

"I don't think she's with him for the happily ever after." Granny Doyle made a vulgar gesture, which set off Grandma Shirley.

"You should try to get to know Preston," my mom urged me over the angry shouts of my grandmothers.

Get to know Preston? I didn't need to. I already knew him far too well.

I'd lost my freakin' virginity to him.

Chapter 20

ANDERSON

" Oh, Santa, baby! I want you to come down my chimney after this."

Grunting, I carefully extricated the woman in the skimpy red outfit from my neck.

"How far down do those tattoos go?" an equally scantily clad woman asked, twirling her baton around.

"I knew you were full of shit."

"Ooh!" Another of the performers giggled. "I want both of them for Christmas."

Henry grabbed my arm and shoved me against the brick wall of the town hall.

"I knew you were just using my sister. You don't love her." He slammed me back against the wall again. "You don't even respect her."

It took everything in me not to punch him in the face. I was working security at a parade practically thrown in his honor. That would not be a good look.

"That's what she likes about me, actually."

"If you know what's good for you, you'll stay away from Evie." Henry gave me one more shove then turned away.

"Is that a threat?" I called after him, taunting. "From you? As if you ever follow through on any of your promises."

He ignored me and kept walking. Off to be the inflatable hero.

Sirens blared as the fire department cruised up in their big trucks to take their spot in the parade.

I was assigned to watch the periphery as the baton performers walked down Main Street and keep any crazies from attacking them.

Shoving the skullcap low on my head, I took my position.

The mayor made some sort of windbag speech then climbed onto the float next to Santa Claus and Henry.

I tuned out the off-key Christmas carols wailed by the high school marching band as I trailed the performers down Main Street, keeping an eye out for any potential threats. It wasn't like the parade was heading down through the Gulch. There were dog treat boutiques, for Chrissake. But it had been a thing, apparently, at city council. The more well-to-do citizens felt better with additional security.

I ignored the baton girls and focused on the crowd—lots of families with kids excited to see Santa. There was cheering up ahead as the main float with Henry passed by a particularly packed section.

The Murphys. Out to support the golden son.

I half wished Evie had grown some balls, had just stayed in bed and told her family to fuck off. But then part of me also wanted to see her. Make sure she was okay.

What did I care? She wasn't my problem. Henry was right. I was using her.

Then why did I want to blow a hole in something when I saw Evie feeding a bite of sandwich to a balding man wearing a fanny pack?

Who the fuck is that?

Evie noticed me staring and gave me a guilty look.

As she should.

No, she shouldn't.

Even if I had wanted to kiss her, it was only because I wanted to freak out her family, not because she was a girl I'd want to fuck.

The parade moved past the Murphys. I stared straight ahead then finally realized what I was doing and forced myself to continue to visually sweep my side of the street.

Good thing I did, because there was someone pushing through the crowd, causing ripples in the onlookers.

My hand twitched.

Did I go for the gun I had holstered under my jacket?

"Anderson!" Evie called, pushing through the crowd to the barrier. "Hey, Anderson!"

Of course.

I ignored her.

Main Street wasn't that long, and the parade petered out near the entry to the Christmas market. Townspeople were already streaming into the market for post-parade shopping, to buy gifts for people they merely tolerated for the holidays.

206 • Alina Jacobs

"*Anderson!*" Evie, breathless, grabbed my arm. "Happy parade day! I didn't think you would be or wanted to be at the Christmas parade."

She still looked guilty and hopped back from me.

"You could have told me you were already in a relationship," I forced out.

"Oh my god." She doubled over for a second then righted. "I was right. You're jealous of me talking to Preston."

"Preston." The scowl settled onto my face. "Of course that's his name."

"Someone's territorial." Evie walked next to me.

"If you want to shoot your shot with some guy who can't just bite the bullet and shave his head, that's a you problem. We've already established you're a terrible decision-maker."

"Contrary to what my mom believes, I tend to not make the same mistake twice."

I pounced on her words.

"What did he do to you?"

"I didn't think giving a shit about me was part of the deluxe blackmail package."

Turning, I grabbed her and shook her.

"Tell me. *Now, Gingersnap.*"

Her lips thinned. Then—

"I lost my virginity to him."

"Preston?"

"He used to have a lot more hair." She was defensive. "My mom always wanted to have the big fun house, you know, where all the teens would gather and hang out. She would always have drinks and snacks and beanbags in the rec room in the basement with a big TV. Henry was captain of the hockey team. After games, the varsity team would come over and hang out. Teenage me thought they were drool worthy."

"No offense, but teenage you had bad taste."

"To be fair, adult me also has bad taste." She made a face. "Anyway, I had been ineffectively flirting with Preston. He saw an easy opening. I wanted male attention and to be like the cool girls with boyfriends, like in one of my books. We hooked up a few times. It was awkward. And bad."

"Of course it was."

She shoved me. "Then he got a real girlfriend, a high school girl friend, and refused to acknowledge me. I was so dumb." Evie laughed sadly. "I really thought he and I were going to be a couple and live happily ever after."

"That's not dumb. He sounds like a creep and a loser."

"He wrote a book."

"Any idiot can write a book these days," I muttered as we approached her family.

Preston was trying to keep one boy with his same doughy cheeks from taking a singular bite out of every goddamn cupcake Evie had made.

"So, this is the uneducated brute you were telling me about, Braeden?" Preston had that privileged-yacht-boy man-child voice.

The fact that he had treated Evie, *my Evie*, like she was disposable, like she was nothing, made me want to kill him.

"Yeah, this is the fucking brute." I drew up in his face.

Preston backed away, stumbling over the cooler.

"Let's get one thing straight. Unless you want to see just how much of an uneducated brute I can be, that"—I pointed a knife-hand at Evie—"is my girlfriend. Mine. Do you understand?"

Preston's protruding eyes bugged out even more.

What the hell had Evie even seen in him?

"I don't want to see you near her. I don't want you talking with her. I don't want her feeding you food. Yes, I fucking saw that. I don't even want you in the same fucking room as her. So stay the fuck away from her. You and your little brats."

"Um—I—" he stammered.

"Do. You. Under. Stand?"

He nodded rapidly.

The correct thing to do in that moment was kiss Evie, stake my claim.

I pulled her to me possessively, felt the pulse in her neck jump.

Her brown eyes were wide.

Her tongue darted out, licking her lip. Intoxicating.

She wasn't even my type. Which was anyone not a Murphy.

But the way her curvy body leaned into me, I wanted to feel all of her, turn her to putty in my hands.

I had self-control. I wasn't going to ever think about this kiss again. It was just because I had a reputation to uphold. It *wasn't about* her.

My hand reached up to tangle in her hair. I wanted to kiss her like no man had ever done. Certainly not Preston or Braeden, whose time on this earth was quickly dwindling.

There was crackling and snapping under my hand.

"Evie!" her cousin screamed. "Your hair!"

Evie grabbed the frozen icicles of her hair.

"Don't look at me!" she cried, running to hide behind her cousin.

I stood there blinking in the winter sun, looking down at a frozen chunk of curly chestnut hair in my hand.

Chapter 21

EVIE

"They need to put a warning label on those Curly Girl Method books," I complained as Sawyer hovered around me in the bathroom while Ian passed her different pairs of scissors when requested.

"You can't go out in the middle of winter with wet hair."

"I had to! It had been hours since I washed it, and it still wasn't dry. What was I supposed to do?" I wailed.

"Use a blow dryer?"

I threw a wadded-up napkin at my brother.

"Anderson is never going to want anything to do with me."

"I don't know. He seemed pretty territorial at the parade." Ian dug through Sawyer's beauty bag. "With the way he was acting, I kind of thought you put out already."

"Same." Sawyer nodded.

"What? Why would you think that?" I cried.

The Murphy Misfits shrugged.

"Let's be real. You have a track record of sleeping with terrible men as soon as you meet them." Sawyer grimaced.

"Not immediately as soon as," I argued.

"You've had a lot of first dates turn into casual hookups, Evie." Ian made a face. "No judgment, but this is the longest you've been with a man and haven't slept with him."

"I'm not with Anderson," I argued.

Ian nibbled his cheese straw and made a noncommittal noise.

"Anderson's not like the others."

"Where have I heard that before?" Sawyer ran a comb through my hair.

"I don't mean he's my dream man," I protested. "Just that he hates me. He hates the Murphys. He'd never actually lower himself to—"

"Lower himself on you?" Ian completed.

"Hate fucks can be good." Sawyer ran her fingers through my hair.

"I just want a hate fuck, baby." Ian handed Sawyer the electric razor.

"Whoa, whoa, what are you doing with that?" I twisted on the stool.

Sawyer slapped my hands. "I'm going to have to even it up on both sides and go with your curl pattern. Hold still."

Ian winced as more chunks of my hair fell to the newspaper on the floor.

"Is it bad?" My eyes were squeezed shut.

"You've got some cute little side bangs now." His tone was forced cheer.

"Ian, Evie." My mother stuck her head in. "Oh god, Evie, what did you do to your hair?"

"Ian said it didn't look bad!"

"Can't you flat iron it, Sawyer?"

"Evie's going au natural, Aunt Mel."

My mother pinched the bridge of her nose. "Ian and Evie, your guests are here. Come down and say hello."

"Hashtag can't." Ian sighed.

"Try to be social." My mom slammed the bathroom door.

"What other friends are you bringing over?" Sawyer sounded a little hurt.

Ian and I burst out laughing.

"You mean the triplets' friends?" Ian scoffed.

"It's like the world's largest, most enmeshed friend group."

"They wanted a little reunion since, for most of them, it's their last year of college before they all get well-paying jobs, marry each other, and live happily ever after." Ian pretended to puke.

"I should have spent more time trying to get in that friend group and less time sleeping with Henry's friends," I admitted as I helped Sawyer clean up from the impromptu hairstyling session.

"You slept with more of them besides Preston and Braeden?" Ian demanded.

"Don't you think that was more than enough?" Sawyer asked as we headed downstairs.

The triplets' close-knit high school friends were all giggling and happy to see each other in my parents' living room, reminiscing about the good times in high school, which usually occurred in the advanced classes, in which yours truly did not find herself.

"Hi, everyone." I waved awkwardly, while Ian offered a wan smile.

"We're having a sleepover for old times' sake," Alana gushed.

"And I will have fun sleepover snacks ready for you for old times' sake."

We all stood there for a long, silent beat. Then I gave a half wave and sidled away to the kitchen. Behind me, the laughter and cheer started up again.

"You shouldn't just run away from them," my father remarked as I passed him in the hallway. "You could learn something from the triplets and their friends. They all buckled down, applied themselves, and are about to enjoy the rewards of their hard work."

"Thanks, Dad. I'll definitely drink the creamy milk from the tit of their wisdom right after I finish setting up the chip-and-dip bar."

He made an annoyed noise then went in to greet the guests.

You might think, *Oh, poor Evie, having to cook for a party she's not even welcome at.*

Hardly.

The kitchen is my safe space. Back when my mom wasn't on the Evie-is-ruining-Christmas bandwagon, we semi bonded over our love of elaborate dinner parties.

Sleepover snacks were the perfect excuse to be antisocial.

Humming Christmas carols, I set up the table in the downstairs rec room with sliced veggies, pita chips, and ceramic snowflake dishes piled with various dips like buffalo chicken, spinach artichoke, and of course, the cookies and frosting dip.

"Are those Chips Ahoy?" one of the triplets' friends asked when the group all clattered down the stairs.

"Please." Alexis snorted. "Evie wouldn't be caught dead serving people store-bought cookies."

"These are chocolate chip cookie sticks," I explained, pointing at one of my hand-lettered info cards.

"I wish I had time to bake cookies all day," another of their friends said.

"She doesn't just bake. She also cooks." Alissa grinned. "She made all these dips herself."

"It's just recipes on Pinterest."

"Is your boyfriend coming?" The girls in the group all erupted into a fit of giggles.

"I saw the pictures." More giggles.

"There aren't any guys like that at Harvard."

"There is that one professor—"

"What kind of photos is he sending you that compare to Evie's hunk of meat?" Alissa demanded.

Harvard? Professors? All it did was remind me that I'd flunked out of college. I fled upstairs as soon as I could, mumbling excuses about needing to put the food away.

As I snapped lids on the containers, the back door opened.

"Anderson?"

"You really are obsessed with him. You think he actually cares about you? You are such a child."

"I'm busy, Braeden."

"Expecting that criminal?" My ex was in front of me now. "What was it? You let him come up your ass at the country club?"

I tried to follow Anderson's instructions and be prey.

"How did you—" I fumbled in the pocket of my apron, hitting record on the microphone.

"Your mom was complaining. She's very disappointed in you, and so am I." Braeden leaned in to whisper into my ear, "You never let me come in your ass once. I should have known a girl like you would want a guy to do that."

"Felicity not putting out?" I asked before I could stop myself.

But Braeden wasn't suspicious.

Instead, there was a slimy, smug smile.

"You know," Braeden added—his breath stank of stale beer—"it would be perfect if you married Preston. Felicity is looking at a house in his neighborhood, then maybe you could make it up to me."

I stood stock-still in front of the fridge. This was it. *I did it!* I had Braeden on tape admitting not only that we had been together but also that he was actively plotting to cheat on Felicity.

"You are still obsessed with me. I bet you're parading that ogre around just to try to get back with me." He grabbed one of the leftover breadsticks and took a noisy bite, chewing with his mouth open. "I knew you'd get desperate."

After he left, I hurried into the walk-in pantry, trembling with the thought of this nightmare finally being over, my name finally being cleared, my family finally loving me again. But when I hit Play on the recorder, the only thing that played was a garbled mess.

I sank down to the floor, stuffing my fist into my mouth to keep from wailing.

"I'm never going to escape this. They're never going to believe me." I tried to muffle the sobs. "I'm going to be trapped here forever. What am I going to do? Why can't I do anything right? What's wrong with me?"

"Evie? *Evie*." Leather motorcycle gloves cupped my face. "What happened? Who did this? Who hurt you?" Anderson demanded, kneeling in front of me, resting his motorcycle helmet on the floor. "Tell me." The gloves were rough on my face, wiping away the tears. "It was Preston, wasn't it?"

I shook my head.

"It didn't work," I coughed out as Anderson stroked my hair, making soothing noises. "I tried to record him, and it didn't work."

I played the recording.

"Hmm." He cocked his head, listening, then said, "Play it again."

I wiped my eyes with the apron as the garbled audio played.

Anderson cupped my cheek briefly then took the device from me.

"Braeden was whispering, like really close to me," I explained, fishing out a napkin, "and the microphone was in my pocket."

"It should have picked up something." Anderson slipped it into his jacket pocket. "I'm going to see if I can post process it at all. We might get lucky."

I blew my nose. "Don't bother. I've already given up. I'm just going to cook holiday dinners until I get old and wrinkly. Maybe one of my siblings will have pity on me and let me live in the shed in their backyard."

"You don't get to throw in the towel, Gingersnap." He grabbed my arm, dragging me to my feet.

I must have been imagining the look of concern on his face.

Anderson did a quick check outside the pantry then waved me out.

"You done here?"

"No, I have to clean."

He made an annoyed sound and shrugged off his jacket.

I stuffed a cookie into my mouth to give myself something to do other than stare at the tight T-shirt stretched over his rippling muscles as Anderson scrubbed the heavy pan I'd used to make the sliders this morning.

"Hurry up. We have a mission tonight," he said in a low voice.

"A mission?" I squealed.

"Keep it down." He forced his hand over my mouth.

"A super-secret you-know-what."

Using my finger, I scraped out the last of the fluffy frosting in the bowl, needing a pick-me-up, and stuck my buttercream-covered fingers in my mouth. "Yum, frosting."

Anderson's eyes tracked the movement.

"Don't say anything. I need sugar and carbs. There's extra buffalo chicken dip in the fridge. I know you're a protein guy."

I grabbed the container of leftovers and slid it onto the countertop then sat across from him with my frosting bowl.

"This is so exciting." I rested my elbows on the counter as Anderson used a carrot stick to swipe up some of the cheesy buffalo chicken dip.

"We're spies like James Bond."

"Not like James Bond," he argued in a low voice. "We are not getting in fights. We're not stealing anything. We're getting in and getting out."

"I need a disguise."

"No disguises."

"I am so wearing a disguise."

"You're going to do exactly what I say. All we're doing is copying data off of computers then leaving."

"We're going to be hackers! I need a cute outfit."

"No. No hacking." He sighed. "I really shouldn't take you with me."

"I know Braeden's house plans. I can be a good spy. Fine," I said to his dirty look, "nonspy. Ooh, I need to make Snowball an outfit."

Anderson reached over to comb his fingers through my short side bangs. "You're a fucking disaster, Gingersnap. You know that? And we're not going to Braeden's house."

"Wait. Why?"

That earned me a cold smile from my sworn enemy.

"Because. We're going to Preston's."

Chapter 22

ANDERSON

No, we weren't breaking into Preston's house because he was after my fake girlfriend. That would be crazy.

His name was on Aaron's list. I'd written it off because the amount was so low. But now it felt personal.

Which was dangerous.

It killed me to think about Braeden and Preston plotting to manipulate my girlfriend.

"Fake girlfriend. She's fake. She means nothing to you."

Not even when she was sobbing on the floor?

Right. Absolutely nothing.

Preston's house was dark when I rode by, kit on my back.

He wasn't the type of man to cook for his children. They were all at his mother's house for dinner. I'd ridden by and checked.

Still, I was cautious as I paused down the street, keeping to the shadows as I pulled on a balaclava to hide my face.

The rest of the houses were dark as well, with the exception of a holiday party far down the road.

Preston's house had haphazard loops of lights strewn along the roofline. I wouldn't have put those lights up like that. And the inflatable Christmas displays in the weedy yard—a Santa Claus with his reindeer, a sleigh, a Frosty the Snowman, and several oversize ornaments? Trashy. Especially for a neighborhood like this.

No sign of Evie. She probably got cold feet.

It was for the best. I had only offered to let her come to try to cheer her up, to stop that awful crying that made me want to cut my heart out and give it to her.

It was better this way. I needed to get in and get out, especially since, even in the best-case scenario, I wasn't making much money off this job.

The fans whirred softly in the inflatable decorations as I headed up the walkway. Lawrence had already cut the feed on the Ring camera.

As I passed the snowman, I caught movement in my peripheral vision. I turned, studying the yard. The snowman watched with lifeless, painted eyes.

This job was getting to me. I needed more sleep.

Adjusting my bag, I took two more steps.

Something rustled.

I whirled around.

The snowman was still facing me, but... that couldn't be right... it seemed somehow closer...

"Did you see that, Lawrence?" I asked softly.

My brother was chewing something.

"You know I hate when you do that."

He swallowed. "I didn't see anything. Hurry up. I got shit to do, like paid shit."

I peered into the dark. "The wind moved it the few feet farther away from Rudolph."

"Moved what?"

"Nothing."

Yeah, that was what it was. Nothing.

But I didn't turn around, just kept walking backward, only putting my back to the yard when I reached the porch stairs.

Plastic rustled against snow. I whirled around to a snowman bearing down on me.

"Shit!" I strangled the curse, scrambling backward, almost losing my balance on the icy steps. In my ear, I heard Lawrence laughing his head off.

"Surprise! Don't you like my costume?" The snowman waved his stubby arms.

"Evie?"

"Isn't this a great costume?"

"I told you no disguises."

"But it was a great disguise. I blended in."

"She got you, man."

"Shut up," I hissed.

"Oh." The snowman's shoulders sagged.

"Not you," I said to her, "my brother."

"He's here?" The snowman looked around wildly.

If she wasn't about to fuck up my plans, it would almost be comical.

"He's watching."

"He knows when you are sleeping…" she sang.

I pointed up to the sky, where a drone hovered, blacked out against the night sky.

The snowman squealed, "It really is like a spy movie. Hi!" Evie waved up at the drone. "Hi, Anderson's brother. Is it the cute one?"

Lawrence guffawed in my ear.

"It absolutely is not." I grabbed one of the inflatable arms to hoist her up the steps. "Take that off while I pick the lock."

Evie was still struggling with the inflatable costume when the front door swung open. I scooped her up and deposited her inside the dark house, untangling her from the white nylon.

She stepped out of the snowman feet, balancing her arm on my shoulders for support, then looked around. "It looks like a frat house."

"Smells like one too."

We silently made our way through the messy room.

Well, I was silent. Evie kept banging into things.

"Shh!"

"I'm doing the best I can."

"It's fucking embarrassing."

She banged her knee into a table.

I glared at her in the dark then led her to the home office upstairs.

"What do you want me to do?" she whispered.

"Go to the other rooms. See if there are any electronics."

Preston had left his computer unlocked, and I plugged in the external hard drive. While the files copied, I navigated through his open tabs.

He had his text messages linked from his phone to his desktop computer. I scrolled through the messages with Braeden. A little suspect but no smoking gun. I looked through the list of who Preston had recently sent messages to: complaints to his mom, passive-aggressive messages to his ex, ham-fisted attempts at flirting with coworkers...

But there was one that showed an unknown number. I clicked it, opening the message thread. It showed a gray box with the word *DELETED*.

"Did you find a clue?" Evie was back, chin brushing my shoulder.

"Not sure." I stared at the message.

"It could be nothing. Could be a spam message," Evie suggested.

"Then why an outgoing message, not incoming?"

I copied down the number. After all my years of working insurance fraud for Aaron, I had learned to trust my instincts when something seemed off.

"The boys' room is a dumpster, but I found these tablets," Evie whispered, handing them to me. "But I don't know if you can download the information without a password."

"I'll run some decryption software."

"You're going to hack them?"

"No. No hacking. For fuck's sake."

"Sounds a little like hacking to me."

I blew out a breath and unzipped my backpack.

"You're going to steal them?"

"I'll bring them back."

She pulled out her phone and started punching a number.

Then I realized *which* number she was calling. "Dammit, Evie."

One of the tablets lit up with an incoming call. She grabbed it, swiping up.

"Preston was messaging one of those fake virtual numbers. It's linked to one of the kids' tablets."

"Fine." I tried to grab it back from her. "I will start with unencrypting that one."

"Won't that take forever?"

"We don't have a choice."

She played keep-away with the tablet while I tried to snatch it back.

"You'll lock us out, then we're fucked. Give it." I grabbed her around the waist.

Her legs kicked while she quickly typed in a number.

ERROR showed on the screen.

"Just let me try one more."

"Evie—"

She typed in 1-2-3-4.

"That's not going to—"

"In!" she said triumphantly.

"Who uses one-two-three-four as their password?"

"A ten-year-old boy. You, sir, need more young idiotic cousins." She navigated to the text message app.

I peered over her shoulder, pulling a piece of her hair out of the way so I could see the screen better.

"Whooo!" she crowed.

I clapped a hand over her mouth. She bit me gently.

"Santa brought a whole hippopotamus for Christmas! Look." She shoved the tablet in my face triumphantly.

There was a screenshot of a Snapwave message.

"That's Braeden's name right there!"

Braeden: *...this chick I'm seeing. You ever seen tits this nice?*

My blood boiled.

"He sent your photo to Preston. I'm gonna fucking kill him."

"Yes, he did," Evie stated.

I cupped her face.

"I am so sorry, Evie. I will make him pay."

"Yeah, we will!" She sounded way too calm about this whole thing. Maybe she was in shock.

"Damn, I'm so glad I sent him that topless photo. Now we have proof!"

"You aren't..." I fumbled the words. "Upset that he shared a..."

"Photo of my boobs out on full display? Call Grandma Shirley. She'll keel over dead. Uncle David is waiting on his inheritance."

"It would be a Christmas miracle."

"And he can get in the holiday spirit." Her shoulders sagged as she stared at the tablet. "A teenage boy is jacking off to a photo of me. Guess my dad was right. I am dumb. My parents told me not to sext."

I rested my hand on the back of her neck then slid it down to squeeze her shoulder. "That kid wouldn't know what to do with them."

"I'm the queen of embarrassing events." Her back straightened. "This is a price I'm willing to pay if it lands Braeden in the doghouse. Quick. Here's my parents' number. Send it to them."

"We can't send this to them." I slipped the tablet into my backpack.

"No, don't burst my happiness bubble."

"The photo doesn't even have your name."

"Or the mole. *I know.* But this is progress!" She squeezed my hand briefly. "At the very least, we can prove that Braeden was cheating on Felicity with someone."

"Or that we're very good at Photoshop. We need more evidence."

"Negative Noel. Let's get drinks," she whispered as I took the stairs two at a time.

"You need a pity cocktail?" I glanced back at her.

"A celebratory drink. I'm taking this as a win."

We got one of the last free tables at Nick's Noshery.

"Order whatever you want. My treat," Evie announced as we slid across from each other in the booth, drinks from the bar in hand.

"You don't have any money, Gingersnap."

"I have a credit card."

"I will get up on this table and sing 'Rudolph the Red-Nosed Reindeer' if your card isn't declined."

"Meanie. I'm getting the Santa's Stack-Up pancakes. You should order the Sugar Plum Platter so we can split it."

"Sounds like diabetes in a gun."

"It's not. It has sugar-roasted chestnuts and sugarplum pancakes. I've always wanted to try those."

"Merry Christmas!" A smiling waitress in a reindeer-themed vest arrived with waters.

"Can I just have the Christmas-morning platter but sub bacon for the pancakes?" I asked after Evie ordered.

"That's not festive," Evie complained.

"I'll give him Canadian bacon cut up like Christmas trees. How's that?"

"Perfect."

"I need another drink."

"Coming right up. You want the same thing, or"—she winked at me—"do you want something special?"

Evie grabbed my hand before I could answer.

"He just wants the same. A whiskey."

I raised an eyebrow at her. "I hope you're not thinking you're protecting my virtue, Gingersnap."

"I didn't like the way she was looking at you." She turned up her nose.

I snorted. "How do you know I didn't want to get laid in the storage room tonight?"

She stammered, "I-I guess I didn't think."

I savored her shock. "Relax, Gingersnap." I took another sip of my drink.

"You don't have a girlfriend, right? I'm not that bad of a person, am I?" She winced.

I reached across the table. "I don't have a girlfriend, and I never will. I'm not husband material."

"That's okay. I'm not wife material."

"Seriously? You spend all your time in the kitchen. You decorate. You knit... semicompetently."

She kicked me under the table.

Grinning, I grabbed her ankle.

"I can't find a decent man, let alone keep one," she admitted.

"You'd be a good mom at least."

"Eh." She looked over the busy restaurant. "Debatable."

"You'd be better than your mother."

"My mom has a lot on her plate. She works, she's married, and she has seven kids."

"And my mom had six kids and a pill addiction."

"Overachiever." She took a breath. "I always secretly wanted to adopt kids—not fight a bunch of other couples for an infant but adopt the older kids no one wants. The boy with an attitude problem, the girl who bounced around twenty-five foster homes. I'll have a nice big house. They can have their own rooms. I want to give them a place where they aren't judged, where they can just be."

She seemed so sad as she folded her napkin into a snow-flake shape.

"That sounds like a dream." I suddenly wanted to give that to her and make all her wishes come true just to see her smile.

"It's a dream unless I win the lottery or Santa really does come through for me."

"I wish I'd had someone in my corner like that."

"You were in foster care?" Her brown eyes melted as they looked at me.

"Explains a lot, doesn't it?" I quipped desperately.

Fortunately, the waitress came by, sliding the hot plates in front of us.

"Look at all this Christmas cheer!"

"That thing needs to be killed with a flame thrower." I scowled at the unholy sculpture of whipped cream over a stack of pancakes shaped to look like a snowman.

"I think it's cute," Evie cooed. "Look! It even has a little Twizzler scarf and chocolate chips for the coal eyes and buttons."

The eggs, bacon, and fried potatoes and onions had been arranged in the shape of Santa Claus's face.

Evie took a sip of her toxic syrupy-red cocktail then dug into the snowman. I scowled as a glob of whipped cream plopped onto the table.

Evie held out a forkful of pancakes. "He just wants to get to *snow* you!"

"We are so going to blow up Braeden's life." Evie was drunk and giddy next to me as we walked in the cold toward her parents' oversize Victorian house.

"Shh," I whispered, not exactly sober myself. "This is supposed to be a secret."

"Our secret," she agreed. "What am I going to do when I'm finally free?" She twirled in the snowy night air. "I'll get so many apologies. I bet my father even apologizes."

"Apologies are overrated. Get cash."

"It's Christmas. We can't be materialistic." She swatted me with her hat. "You can't be Ebenezer Scrooge. I should come over and decorate your house for Christmas."

"Hard no."

This was a far cry from my days in the alternative school, sneaking out of class, everyone trying to self-destruct.

Evie was so much more wholesome than any of the done-with-life shitheads I used to hang with.

"We're the dream team! Team Save Christmas!" Evie stumbled and tipped over in a snow drift, her red drink spilling onto the white snow.

"I can't walk," she gasped through the giggles. "These things are strong." She downed the remainder of the drink she'd stolen from the bar, sitting back in the snow.

"Honestly, Gingersnap, you couldn't walk straight when you were sober. I can't count how many times you've banged into stuff or fallen down."

"I am not that clumsy." She reached up for me.

I took her hands, swinging her upright.

She wavered on her feet, staring at me with this happy, dopey smile like I was everything she wanted for Christmas.

"You're not going to make it." I grabbed her and tossed her over my shoulder.

"You can't carry me."

"I've done it before. In the snow. Backward."

"Uphill both ways." She giggled as I wrapped my arm around her ankles, keeping her in place on my shoulder.

The Murphy house was dark when I stamped up the wooden steps.

"My key's in my pocket," she whisper-shouted.

There was more giggling as I fumbled around her waist, her ass curving under my hand.

"*Not there*. My pocket." She snorted, trying to contain her laughter.

My hand slid under her skirt. "There?"

She slapped my back.

My lip caught in my teeth, then I fished the house key out of her skirt pocket. It scraped in the lock.

"Ow!" she yelped as her head thumped the doorframe.

"Told you you're always banging into stuff."

"That was you," she hissed, sliding off my shoulder to stand in front of me.

"Evie." I was too drunk for this. It was too late for this. There was too much hurt for this. "*Evie.*" I cupped her face.

"Shh!" she whispered loudly as the front door slammed shut behind us. "My parents will hear."

"That's what I'm counting on. I'm your boyfriend, remember?"

"Yeah." She sounded a little breathless and not just from the cold. "You're my boyfriend." She said it like it was the most wonderful thing in the world.

The ice on my heart threatened to crack. I rested my forehead on hers, wanting to give in and drown myself in her.

"We hate each other, remember?" she whispered to me in the dark.

"Yeah, and I've never hated anyone the way I hate you."

Our noses brushed together. My hands drifted down the collar of her jacket.

The sconces flipped on. I winced at the bright light.

"I told you it wasn't a robber!" Granny Doyle hollered. "Honestly, Brian, why do you have to cockblock people?"

Evie tried to duck from under my arms.

I wasn't ready to let her go. I turned, my arms still wrapped around her, her hands grasping my forearms.

Footsteps thumped up from the basement rec room.

"Damn." One of Evie's sisters' little friends whistled. "If I'd known you could get a man like that by dropping out, I wouldn't have tried so hard in college."

"You cannot come stumbling home at all hours of the night, Evie. If you live here, there is a curfew." Melissa drew her robe tighter around her.

"She's a grown-ass woman," Granny Doyle argued.

"She's not an adult if she's living under my roof." Dr. Murphy frowned.

One of my hands slid up Evie's legs under her skirt.

"No, sir," I drawled to her father's angry face. "I can guaran-fucking-tee you that she is a grown adult woman." I slapped her ass then shoved her toward her father.

Evie tugged at her skirt.

I grabbed her jaw, turning her to face me.

"I'll see you tomorrow."

"You're awfully satisfied for someone who still owes me half a million dollars."

Aaron didn't sound angry. In fact, he sounded almost pleasant.

That wasn't good.

"I'm working on it. Have some leads."

"Leads on my job or the one you're working on for your latest charity case?"

"Preston is on the list." I hated being on the defensive. "I have proof. Last night was fruitful." Sort of.

"Preston... Preston... ah yes, the man who, let me consult my notes, was in receipt of a certain photo."

"You don't have any right to look at that," I said tersely, trying to keep the anger out of my voice.

"You are so transparent." Aaron laughed.

"You're an asshole."

Be calm.

"I don't need you to question my methods." I modulated my tone.

Aaron was silent for a minute.

Had I gone too far?

I had only seen him angry once and had vowed to never let it get to that point again.

I steeled myself.

I could practically see him leaning back in his high-end leather desk chair.

"I'm starting to wonder if you're even cut out for this line of work anymore, Anderson."

"Of course I am."

Wasn't I?

Chapter 23

EVIE

"You know," I said as Sawyer and I dragged a table closer to the wall, "I really feel like Anderson is just misunderstood. Maybe all he needs is the right woman to fix him."

Ian rapped his knuckles on an oversize vase he was filling with poinsettias for the table centerpieces.

"Hear that? That is an alarm bell."

"I don't mean me! I am not that woman. Just making an observation."

"Can we worry about our own lives?" Sawyer took a steadying breath.

"She says as we sit here decorating the Canal Club for Grandma Shirley's big holiday party." Ian waved around a roll of ribbon. "Without the help of any of the party beneficiaries."

"It's good to do things for family," I protested.

236 • Alina Jacobs

"Fight! Fight! Fight!" Granny Doyle hollered from the couch. "What the hell is the point of a hockey game if you're not going to fight?"

"See?" Sawyer pointed at Granny Doyle. "They could at least come and watch the game and pretend to work."

"Honestly, I'd rather not have them underfoot."

"Uh-huh." Ian rolled his eyes.

"What's that supposed to mean?"

"This entire year, you've been trying to make people like you again with acts of service. It hasn't worked yet," Ian said. "Cookies can't counteract the smear campaign waged by Felicity and Braeden."

"Instead of blackmailing him to help bust Braeden, you should have paid him to sleep with Felicity and ruin her relationship," Sawyer said.

"She's a victim too." I threaded hanging wire around a wreath. "Braeden was lying to her."

"In the event that the murderer you're blackmailing miraculously comes through, Felicity is still going to hate you." Sawyer unwound a new packet of Christmas lights. "The only thing that topless photo proves is that you are a homewrecker."

"But I didn't know!" I cried.

"Then you'd better hope that armed and dangerous sex toy you're parading around family functions is actually going to come through." Sawyer plugged in the lights to test them.

"I have faith in him." I turned back to adjusting the garland on the chandelier of the Canal Club.

"I love this venue. I've always dreamed of getting married here—a white Christmas wedding. Wouldn't it be magical? The view across the snowy lake, Dad proud of me as he walks me down the aisle to the man of my dreams."

"I hope you're not envisioning Anderson," Sawyer warned me.

"Of course I'm not." I squashed the vision of Anderson in a suit.

"He's hot, and you should totally tap that, but Anderson is not marriage material." Ian positioned a ladder. "He is covered in red flags."

"Maybe he's just dressed up for Christmas." I pick up the box of cloth napkins I'd starched and folded into snow-flake shapes earlier and carted them over to a long table near where Granny Doyle was still watching the hockey game and drinking spicy holiday margaritas.

"You have terrible taste in men. It's cute but toxic." Ian made a heart shape with his hands.

"This is not the first time we've had this conversation," Sawyer reminded me, hoisting up the Christmas lights. "You scrapbook whatever joker you're lusting after into your fantasy life, and then he breaks your heart."

"Anderson doesn't have my heart, so he's not going to break it." I looked around, the daydream fading away to my cold, harsh reality. "I'm falling behind. Mom was only a couple years older than me when she had Henry. She had a college degree, a handsome husband, a nice house. I have nothing. I'm officially a failure."

"You have a dog."

"You have us," Ian said, and he and Sawyer sandwiched me in a hug.

"Neither earns me cred with the parents or rent money. I should have tried harder to get a boyfriend when I lived in New York," I said, extricating myself to set the head table.

"Like an investment banker or something. Everyone would be impressed if I brought home a rich guy. Bonus points if he was hot. I shouldn't have been so picky."

"I'd say you could actually afford to raise your standards," Sawyer said pointedly.

"I told you to sign up for that escort service." Ian inspected the half-decorated ballroom.

"Don't let your mother hear you say that," Gran called, tipping more tequila into the pitcher. "Didn't I tell you she made me delete my OnlyFans account?"

"One of the dancers in my company met his boyfriend through an escort service. He quit," Ian said. "Now he's a stay-at-home dog dad."

"I wanted the romantic meet-cute, when our eyes meet across the room and we know we're meant to be together." I sighed wistfully, wishing I could be in love, wishing for the happily ever after, the perfect life.

The door on the far side of the ballroom opened, the daylight darkened by a lopsided shadow.

Then Anderson came in, blinking in the low light. His silver-gray eyes locked with mine, and he mouthed, *Seriously?*

I put my finger on my nose and pushed it up, making a weird face at him. "I'm a Who in Whoville! Merry Christmas!"

A laugh escaped his mouth before he could stop it. "Not funny, Gingersnap. You have a problem."

Last night had been easy, magical, *dangerous*. Because for a moment in time, Anderson Wynter wasn't my family's sworn enemy. He was just a hot, fun guy who seemed like he was into me.

No need to keep that up. A little cringe was just what the doctor ordered.

The tools on his belt clanked as he adjusted the ladder on his shoulder, his tight gray T-shirt riding up to expose the tattoos that scrolled around his hip. Over the other shoulder was slung an oversize tool bag.

"Damn," Sawyer said as she and Ian watched appreciatively. "Even if he is a murderer, the man is fine."

"I got a report the air wasn't working," he said as he set down the ladder.

"You work here too? How do you have time to break into people's houses?"

"I only do that part-time, Gingersnap." He tugged a piece of my hair.

I rocked on my heels. "Is the Canal Club hiring?"

Anderson looked down at me. Rubbed his jaw. Sighed.

"I own it with my brother. But that just means that I do free maintenance work," he warned me.

"You can't hire me?" I wheedled.

"You're already blackmailing me, and I have a photoshopped picture of your tits on my computer and not because we're dating. I'm as enmeshed in your life as I'd like to be." He looked around the half-decorated space. "Where are the rest of the helpful Murphy elves?"

"You mean the motherfuckers in this family who don't do shit? Currently receiving very nasty text messages from me," Sawyer said loudly.

"I'm not helping on principal," Granny Doyle said from her spot on the white couch Aunt Trish had dropped off as her contribution. "I'm drinking my way through the tequila."

"That's not Christmassy, is it?" A smile played around Anderson's mouth.

"If you put it in a red glass, it is. You want a tipple on the nipple?" Gran offered.

"Can't drink on the job."

"You're not getting paid."

"You have a point." He took the offered shot glass, drained it, then wheezed. "Jesus, that is not tequila. That tastes like kerosene."

"It's the stuff Aunt Trish made," I explained.

"You need to stop accepting food from that woman." Anderson made a face then pulled a cat hair out of his mouth while Sawyer gagged.

"If you can't get the heat to work, sonny, then we can just light this tequila on fire." Gran hoisted her glass. "Sure, it might take the garlands with it, but at least Shirley's party will actually be exciting."

My friends and I worked on the rest of the decorations while Anderson was up and down the ladder, checking the ductwork and testing the heat.

Though I definitely preferred a man with a lean, emo-boy body, soft hands, and the money to pay people to clean, I had to admit I did see the appeal in a man who could fix shit.

"Seriously? He's just showing off at this point." Ian stood next to me as we watched Anderson straddling a ladder, tipped backward, shirt riding up to display a ribbon of muscular torso.

"Are we ogling Evie's latest bad decision?" Sawyer stuck her head between us.

Anderson swung down off the ladder gracefully.

"Offer to suck his dick." Granny Doyle, in a cloud of booze, popped up next to me. "Then you can finish this shrine to Shirley's ego, and we can head to the bar before this party."

"Shirley's having a dry party?" Anderson sauntered over to us, lifting up his T-shirt to wipe his face and exposing an expanse of tattooed six-pack.

Sawyer and Ian drooled.

"As if anyone would come. It's lame enough when you're drunk. Sober, and you'd have people slitting their wrists in the holiday punch bowl."

"I'm shocked you got an invitation."

Gran sniffed. "Only because she knows I'd throw an even hotter, more kick-ass party, and no one would come to hers."

The furnace kicked on, and warm air started flowing into the chilly ballroom.

"Thanks, Anderson," I told him.

He reached out and smoothed back one of the curls that had escaped my bun. "Don't want you all to freeze out of your party."

"Can't be too warm. Aunt Lisa is having an ice sculpture of Felicity as an ice princess delivered."

"That's her Christmas contribution?" Anderson frowned.

"It cost seven grand."

"The fuck?"

"Our family is privileged and spoiled," Ian said solemnly.

"I'm chipping off her nose to put in my drink," Sawyer declared.

Anderson looked down at the eight oversize reindeer made out of wicker and festooned with poinsettias that we had to somehow suspend from the ceiling. "Do you want me to carry those somewhere before I go?" he offered.

"Are you going to do it shirtless?" Granny Doyle cackled.

Anderson smirked.

"Ignore her. She's been drinking since ten."

Anderson reached down to pick up the closest reindeer while Granny Doyle whooped, "Look at that gun show!"

"We're going to have to hang them up," I said hastily, trying to take it from him. "The theme of the party is 'home for the holidays.' It's about tradition and family."

"Ah yes, the traditional poinsettia-covered reindeer. How could I forget?" He smirked.

"I spent a lot of time placing these flowers."

"I believe it, Gingersnap."

I reached for the reindeer.

He jerked it away. "Just tell me where you want them. You're a walking disaster, and the last thing I need is for you to drop this reindeer and put a hole in my floor."

After securing the reindeer using some sort of lift machine on wheels, Anderson helped us finish stringing up the lights and garland.

Family members chattered excitedly as they entered the ballroom while Anderson was draping white ribbon across the ceiling. Grandma Shirley was explaining loudly where she wanted the ice sculpture.

"That table isn't in the right spot," she said loudly, not even greeting us as she walked into the space, mouth pinched, inspecting our handiwork.

"You there." She snapped her fingers at Anderson. "Come down and move this table at once."

The rest of my family didn't even notice it was Anderson. To them, he was just the hired help.

"Stop pretending like you're helping," Sawyer said loudly to Felicity as she made miniscule adjustments to the table settings. "We've been here freezing our tits off and setting up the venue."

"It doesn't even look that good."

"I want the buffet lined up on this side," Grandma Shirley said while I trailed her.

"But, Grandma, the sketch you sent over—"

"That was a suggestion, Evie. I asked you to see how it looked in the space. Obviously, it looks terrible. Hurry up, boy," Grandma Shirley demanded, not looking at Anderson, as she was preoccupied with the table arrangement.

"You can't come in here and boss him around!" Granny Doyle came screaming over in a drunken rage. "He doesn't work for you. Evie's the one sucking his dick. You should ask her if her boy toy can move your table."

"I beg your pardon?"

"You're sleeping with the laborer too?" Felicity sniffed. "Why am I not surprised?"

The platform lift finished lowering. Anderson stepped off.

"You brought him here to my party?" Grandma Shirley sputtered, indignant. "He must leave at once."

"He was helping us, Grandma," Ian interjected. "Since none of you bothered to show up."

"We're here now!" my cousins protested.

Nat shrieked, "I would have come to help if I'd known there was going to be eye candy!" Then she lowered her voice and asked Sawyer, "Did he take off his shirt?"

"If you'd been here, you'd know."

"Oh-em-gee, he did!" Nat clapped her hands on her head.

"Just move these tables!" Grandma Shirley thundered.

"Evie, where do you want these tables?" Anderson asked.

Grandma Shirley's wrinkled mouth puckered in annoyance. "I wanted them on the other side."

Anderson was still looking at me, waiting for my instruction only.

"Just line them up over there, please. I'll grab the centerpieces." I hurried to the nearest table.

"No college degree, not good for anything except manual labor," Grandma Shirley was saying not softly, "and he can't even follow directions."

And this was why I didn't want the family over when I was trying to decorate.

"Thanks, Anderson." I felt awkward.

The gray eyes were cold, his body language aloof.

Why did my family have to be so rude to him? I mean, sure, there was the attempted murder, but you know, aside from that?

"I'll see you at the party, Hot Stuff," Granny Doyle called after Anderson finished moving the last of the furniture.

"The party?" Grandma Shirley was horrified. "He is not invited."

"Kind of a shitty thing to do, use Anderson for free labor then kick him out," Sean said into his glass of tequila.

"Is anyone surprised? That's how her husband died," Granny Doyle declared. "She'd just lie there on the bed and make that poor old man do all the work, and it took out his heart. We should go have a party at my house." Gran poured Sean another splash.

"Evie's not going to come if her boyfriend can't come," Uncle Jacob argued with his mother. "She's supposed to make the crab-and-cheddar potato bites."

"I'll make them," Felicity offered.

Nat made a retching noise. "I've been saving up my calories, and I'm not wasting it on the dog food you call cooking."

"And the punch," Lauren added. "Who's going to make the punch?"

"There is a dress code." Grandma Shirley's voice was shrill. "Anderson has to wear a suit, which I'm sure he doesn't have."

"I'll lend him one of Ross's," Aunt Kerry offered.

"Uncle Ross is a good head shorter."

"I can let out the hem."

"A nice suit. Well fitted. Tailored." Grandma Shirley raised her voice. "I'm sure you understand, Anderson." My grandmother's mouth curled up on his name.

"Even if he showed up in a trash bag, he'd still be the hottest man here," Nat observed.

"Yeah, it's not right that Anderson can't come."

"Let him come," her adult kids and grandkids said.

"I really don't want to come." Anderson picked up his tool bag.

"You see?" Grandma Shirley nodded. "He doesn't want to come."

"Because you're bullying him!" Granny Doyle booed.

"There's a game on anyway." Anderson took a step to the door.

"There's a game on?" My uncles perked up. "We could have a party at—"

"No. This is Granny's annual holiday party," Felicity snapped.

"But there won't be any punch!" a cousin wailed.

"Fine," Grandma Shirley spat out. "If he finds a suit, he can stay. *If* he finds a suit."

Chapter 24

ANDERSON

My brother hissed like a rain-drenched cat as I took the three-piece suit out of its garment bag.

"You're going to wear that?" The disgust twisted Hudson's face.

"Some of us are grown adults and can wear a suit without complaining."

"They're itchy."

"You're a toddler. I don't know how Gracie puts up with you." I shook out the trousers.

"You're supposed to be her murderous boyfriend. You could wear jeans," Hudson argued.

"Someone's jealous I can pull off the James Bond look better than they can."

Jake came at me with a small pair of tweezers. "Just let me get a couple of those nose hairs."

"No. Get away from me. I don't have—ow!"

He'd jabbed me in the cheek with the tweezers.

"Get out of my room."

"I put condoms in your wallet," Jake called as he walked away. "I see how the Murphy women drool all over you. We don't want to be back here in nine months while you juggle your baby mamas. You need to start putting him on those jobs that require flirting, Hudson."

"The problem is that he's good-looking, but the minute he opens his mouth, you realize he's a complete imbecile." My eldest brother smirked.

"I said out!"

I combed my hair back with a severe side part then gelled it in place and inspected my reflection in the cracked mirror hanging above the dresser propped up on repurposed 1970s encyclopedias.

Maybe if my ancestors hadn't lost the family fortune, I would have been a billionaire with women falling all over me. Not a walking failure.

I pulled on the suit jacket and let it settle on my shoulders, forcing my posture military straight.

Hopefully, if all went well, this would be the last time I had to deal with the Murphys.

"You look like a terrorist," Talbot remarked cheerfully as I took the metal staircase two at a time down to the field office.

Christmas carols blared from Jake's laptop as he set up a command center with multiple computer monitors.

"Cuff links." Lawrence dropped the heavy pieces of silver in my outstretched palm.

"Those are mine," Hudson growled.

"You're never going to wear them," Lawrence shot back. "Getting you in a clean Polo requires a written edict from heaven. Gracie said he could borrow them."

"He has to look the part," Talbot quipped as he rolled the little locomotive around on the desk. I'd been working on repairing it and was waiting on a new switchboard.

"Aren't the Murphys going to think something's up if you show up like this?" Hudson was concerned.

"They're used to me now. Mostly. Once they're all drunk, I'll just have to bait them into talking. They'll only see the suit. I'll get confirmation of the fraud they committed then done, all wrapped up in a neat package. Merry Christmas."

"What about Evie?" Lawrence looked at me expectantly.

"What about her?" I fastened the cuff links.

"You still have to find proof that her ex threw her under the bus."

"That is not the priority this evening," I warned my bothers. "Clearing the ledger is."

"You're just going to bounce on her?" Talbot seemed worried.

"She is not important." I hardened my heart as I said it.

"You could have a celebratory hookup," Jake goaded. "I bet she'd be fun."

"She'd totally be down for riding you like a motorcycle."

I kicked Lawrence in the back of the knee with the sharp heel of the dress boot, making him yelp.

"Make sure you all are watching on comms." I checked my watch then stuck the comm radio in my ear.

"I am not lending you my truck," Hudson warned me when he saw me near his keys.

I picked up the motorcycle helmet.

"I don't want your dumb truck, Hudson. I'm making an entrance."

Chapter 25

EVIE

" I'm a shitty girlfriend," I told Sawyer as she applied hot wax to my upper lip. "Maybe this is why the universe hates me."

"Shitty fake girlfriend." Ian took a sip from his wine-glass. We were pregaming for Grandma Shirley's holiday party.

"I'm sure Anderson is chilling in the bat cave, drinking a beer and watching the hockey game," Sawyer said. "Don't feel bad for him."

"I don't even like hockey, and that sounds delightful." Ian took another sip of wine.

I shrieked as Sawyer ripped the wax off my upper lip.

"Buckle up," she warned me. "We haven't even got below the neck yet."

"I can't take it." I sobbed.

"You picked out that dress. Friends don't let friends wear dresses like that without mowing the lawn down to a dirt patch."

"I feel like all of us," Ian said, pouring more wine, "are way too close."

I arrived back at the Canal Club as hairless as the day I was born, stuffed into several layers of Spanx and sky-high heels. I immediately headed for the bar to grab a drink to numb the stinging pain. Not for the first time in my life, I looked at the triplets and my mom and wished that I, too, had been blessed with the hairless-body gene.

"It's so unfair." I downed the wine. "The actual hair on their head isn't even thin. Santa emptied his whole haul all over them."

My mom and her daughters were posing for photos.

My stomach churned. I poured out another glass of white wine, some sloshing over the table.

"Let's take one with your husband and children," the photographer said as my mom waved to my dad.

The party was getting crowded with the Murphys plus Grandma Shirley's friends, neighbors, and anyone else who needed her success rubbed in their faces.

I stood there awkwardly, sipping my drink. Practically all of my same-aged family were coupled up.

I desperately wished Anderson was there.

Not because I wanted a boyfriend, especially not him, but I was just so sick of being alone, being the outsider. Sure, my entire family—well, most of them, anyway—hated

Anderson. But it was kind of nice not to be the most despised person at a Murphy-family holiday gathering for once.

I shouldn't have dressed up. I should have worn a pant-suit instead of this strapless cocktail dress. The saleslady said it made me look like Jessica Rabbit with the low-cut sweetheart neckline and the little flare at the calf-length skirt. In hindsight, I probably needed a little more support in the bust area.

"The light is better outside." Aunt Trish swept by. Her dress looked like it had been patched together with cast-off rags from Santa's workshop. "Let's all head outside for family photos."

Family photos. The tenth circle of holiday hell.

Scrooge-like?

Did I make the Grinch cringe?

Worse, did I sound like Anderson Wynter?

You would, too, if you were the odd ugly duckling in your beautiful swanlike family.

I made my way as slowly as possible to the French doors at the entry of the ballroom, emptying my glass of wine as I did so.

The front of the historic beaux-arts building had been decorated like a Christmas palace, its grand sweeping stair-case leading down to the terrace overlooking the water.

"I'm sorry," the photographer said as I walked out to join the rest of my fashion-model-esque family. "We're taking family photos."

My mother sighed. "That's my daughter. Hurry up, Evie."

I slunk in next to my sisters, who were stunning with their perfectly glossy red hair that sported deliberate and subtle waves.

254 • Alina Jacobs

Meanwhile, the Curly Girl Method had completely failed me, and I had used two packs of bobby pins to secure my poofy bun as close to my head as I could.

"Stand up straight." My mother jabbed her fingernail between my shoulder blades. "Don't you have a shawl? Girls with bigger chests shouldn't wear strapless dresses."

The photographer snapped a few token photos of the entire family. Then it began.

"Let's do one of me with the grandkids." Grandma Shirley waved as her children's generation headed down the steps, out of the shot.

My stomach churned knowing what was coming next.

"Who has Grandpa's photo? Come on, girls," she motioned to the triplets. "You stand by me. Look at that beautiful red hair."

The photographer snapped a couple of pictures. "Let's do one with everyone making a funny face."

Grandma Shirley was impatient. "No need. Do one with just the real grandkids."

I dutifully held down the hem of my skirt to keep it from riding up and maneuvered down the steps to the side terrace.

"You can't just kick Evie out of the photos," Sawyer said.

"It's fine," I said softly, not wanting a repeat of the family reunion fight from the Fourth of July.

"You see? Evie doesn't mind." Grandma Shirley waved to the photographer.

"Dad!" Ian called to our father.

"We already talked about this, Ian. Grandma Shirley is from a different generation and stuck in her ways."

"Evie's not really a Murphy." Felicity joined in with Grandma Shirley. "She doesn't look like any of us."

"Thank god, because who wants to be as flat chested as Shirley?" Granny Doyle yelled from the bushes.

"I'm not going to be in a photo if Evie's not in it." Sawyer grabbed Ian, and they started heading off to the side terrace.

"Ian, just stay there," my father begged. "I will pay you twenty dollars."

"I can't be bought!" my brother declared.

"You have to pay that jaywalking ticket," I reminded him.

"Make it a hundred."

"Sellout!" Sawyer shouted at Ian.

"No one wants you in the photo anyway," Felicity yelled at her. "We can see your tattoos."

"Oh, come on. What is this? The 1950s?" Sawyer argued. "Everyone has a tattoo. It's practically standard issue to every basic bitch at this point, and Ian, if you don't walk out of this picture, I'm going to put a rat in your apartment."

"I will pay both of you five hundred dollars," my dad said.

"Wait, Uncle Brian. I want five hundred dollars to be in the photo," Lauren complained.

"You're ruining Grandma Shirley's holiday party!" Felicity shrieked.

"You see what you did, Evie?" My mother was furious.

"I didn't—"

We heard the motorcycle before we saw it.

The roar of the engine cut through the cold winter evening. Tires crunched on the gravel drive as the black bike carried a black rider. One gloved hand on the chrome handle bar, the other on his hip, he navigated the bike in front of the Canal Club staircase.

The engine cut with a purr.

"Oh my god!" My female cousins started screaming and clutching each other. "Who is that?"

The rider, face hidden behind the black motorcycle helmet, leaped gracefully off the bike. Instead of heavy gloves, he wore thin leather ones. He briefly smoothed down the front of his jet-black three-piece suit as he approached the wide stone staircase. Reaching up with one hand, he pulled the helmet off his head.

The confused murmurs morphed into gasps of surprise.

Anderson Wynter.

My family was tall, but Anderson was six-five and cut through them like a tank as he casually took the steps two at a time.

As if he couldn't help himself, the photographer started snapping photos of Anderson as he moved up the steps like a panther.

"Santa Claus is coming to town!" my cousins hollered.

Anderson ignored them, eyes only for me. He stopped in front of me when he reached the terrace.

I cowered, stunned, in the doorway.

Anderson looked—well, he looked like he had just stepped out of my deepest, darkest fantasy.

His mouth twitched as he approached me.

His gaze clocked the exaggerated red lip, the cleavage that was propped up by duct tape and a shelf bra, and moved down the fitted skirt to the sparkly shoes and back up to settle on my mouth.

"There's mistletoe," I croaked. "We should probably move."

"Move?" He took another languid step closer. "Nah." He closed the distance. "I don't think so."

His gloved hand came up to grab the back of my neck, and he tipped me backward under the mistletoe over the doorway.

I shouldn't kiss him. I had terrible taste in men, and he was the worst, but when he crushed his mouth to mine, it was like the two of us were alone, trapped in a snowstorm, and all we had was each other. I suffocated against his soft lips, let myself be carried away, swept along by a blizzard of conflicting desires.

I vaguely heard Ian shouting, "Get it, girl!" as Anderson deepened the kiss.

I clung to Anderson's rock-hard shoulders as his tongue slipped into my mouth. The kiss was as thrilling and magical as a cold swim on an icy dawn.

Right when I thought I was going to drown in him, he slowly ended the kiss, his mouth lingering on mine, like the last melting snowflake. His silver-gray eyes, luminous under dark lashes, gazed at me like I was everything he'd ever wanted wrapped up under the tree on Christmas morning.

My heart was *thump-tha-thump* in my chest.

It was the first kiss I'd always dreamed of, sleigh bells chiming, perfect under the mistletoe.

Too bad it was with a man who had walked out of my family's worst nightmare.

The world around us slowly came into focus. But I didn't want to step out of our magical little snow globe just yet.

I ran my fingernails, cranberry red with little white snowflakes, courtesy of Sawyer, over the smooth-shaven jaw, the strong brow.

"Kissing under the mistletoe? That's a little clichéd for a bad biker boy," I teased.

His lips brushed mine—on the mouth, quick, then under my jaw. "You smell good," he murmured against my neck.

He kissed me again, savoring my mouth. "And you taste even better. You done with family time?" He still had eyes only for me.

I nodded, trying not to faint.

His arm circled my waist. "Good. I need a drink."

Inside, the 1940s brass band that Grandma Shirley had insisted on and shockingly still had elderly members alive struck up a big-band rendition of "White Christmas."

Anderson set the motorcycle helmet on a nearby table then in the same motion spun me around in time to the music.

Friends, I am not a good dancer, I am an enthusiastic dancer, especially after drinking my weight in red wine.

But Anderson knew what he was doing—light on his feet even though he was a freaking giant. He did fancy footsteps, one or the other hand always on my waist, shoulder, or neck to keep us moving in unison.

"Now, that's how we danced in my day!" Great-Aunt Gladys shouted over the music. "None of this grinding hip hop nonsense."

"Don't act like you wouldn't wear those yellow panties to light up your rear end when the sailors would toss you over their head!" Her sister cackled.

The trombone kicked off the final verse of the song. Anderson picked me up in his arms, spinning me around over his head while I shrieked, then set me back down like I weighed less than an empty eggnog carton.

"May all your Christmases be black and gray!" I sang along with the end of the song, smoothing my hands down the lapels of his jacket.

"You didn't think I'd find a suit, did you?" His eyes narrowed slyly.

"I didn't think you'd actually show up."

His head was turned slightly, like he was listening to a song. Then he smiled at me. "We belong together. I can't leave you. Besides." His lower lip caught on his teeth. "I'm not going to let you ruin Christmas without me, Gingersnap." He took my hand, his fingers caressing mine.

"You look—" *Perfect, like a dream, like everything I've always wanted.* "You look good."

"Good?" A dark eyebrow rose. "I was going for panty-dropping."

"Great-Uncle Horace has incontinence, and usually, the Depends end up on the floor at some point."

Anderson blinked hard. "Gingersnap, if you care—" He kissed my mouth. "About me." Another kiss. "Even one shred in your cold little heart, please tie me up in Christmas lights and toss me off your parents' roof if I ever get that bad."

"Granny Doyle thinks Uncle Horace wouldn't have such a problem if he cut back on the alcohol. She says with the number of pills he's taking, it's a recipe for disaster."

"She killed her husband, right?" he whispered into my neck. "So I guess she'd know."

"Rumors. Baseless rumors." Granny Doyle appeared next to me. "Pull up your top," she whispered out of the corner of her mouth.

I adjusted my dress.

Gran handed Anderson a glass of scotch.

"Higher." She gestured. "Us bigger girls need to wear 'em high and proud." She grabbed my boobs, hoisting them up.

Anderson tried to hand her the glass back.

"That's yours, sonny. I was saving it for you. You can't believe the people here. Already stealing the refreshments to take home. Bettie came with five Tupperware containers in her bag."

A large glass bottle fell out from under her dress and landed on Anderson's boot.

He grunted.

"I earned that." Granny Doyle hurried to grab the bottle and pressed it against her dress. "You wouldn't believe the nonsense I have to put up with. There are people coming out of the woodwork. Folks I haven't seen in a decade. They'd do anything for a free meal and hot gossip."

Relatives I barely recognized were flocking to me. Granny Doyle tried to run point, explaining in elaborate detail with interpretive dance moves what had gone down last Christmas then how Anderson had materialized.

Appreciative noises were made when the picture of him was passed around.

A pack of little boys raced up to him, wanting to see his tattoos. My tween emo cousins stood off to the side, trying to be sneaky about taking photos of my fake boyfriend. A gaggle of elderly women from the local DAR hobbled by to feel up Anderson, giggling as he lifted his arm, one little old white-haired lady swinging like a school girl.

"Now, you hold on to that one." She wagged her finger at me. "When you're young and your tits aren't down to your knees, you think men like that grow on trees."

Anderson accepted his adoring fans with smirks, smoldering glances, and a hand firmly on the curve of my back.

That hand slid down the low-cut dress to my ass, settling in the little pocket between my legs, then coming around to rest on my hip.

"Did I ever tell you," he whispered into my ear, so low and rough that I almost thought I was hallucinating, "that dress makes me want to fuck you? And not even to make your parents mad, just because I want to feel your cunt clench around my cock as I make you come."

He straightened back up, his hands running up the curve of my shapewear-cinched waist.

I stared straight ahead at the stage for a moment then dared to look at him.

He was pleasantly waiting as my dad helped Grandma Shirley up to the stage.

Anderson winked at me.

The microphone screeched.

"My husband, may God rest his soul..." Grandma Shirley broadcasted, my father standing beside her.

"It begins," Granny Doyle muttered then took a swig from a bottle.

"Would be so thrilled to have us all together for Christmas." She clasped her hands to her chest. "He loved these holiday parties bringing together family and friends—"

"And prisoners!" Granny Doyle shouted.

"Wait. Are you out on parole, Anderson?" Several of my college-age cousins on winter break gathered around him.

"Do you have an ankle bracelet?" my little cousin Alfie demanded.

My dad glared at me from across the room.

I made a *What-can-I-do?* gesture.

"The holiday season," Grandma Shirley continued loudly, making everyone wince, "is about family, it is about faith, and above all, it is about traditional values. Christmas was never about presents. Rather, it—"

"A puppy!" a little girl in her father's arms squealed. "Daddy, it's a puppy."

"Isn't that nice. Someone surprised their kid with a—*fuuuck!*"

Snowball, melted ice dripping off of her fur, pranced into the ballroom, big red bow in her hair to try to make her look cute and not like a dog that couldn't be trusted home alone by herself.

Her fluffy white tail was held high as she trotted up to the stage and dropped her prize right at Grandma Shirley's feet.

The ceramic dildo rolled twice then came to a rest, the large balls with EVELYN emblazoned on the underside in bright-red paint turned to the audience.

My tipsy sisters and cousins all erupted in shrieks of laughter.

Should I run out the door? Die right here on the floor? Hide behind Anderson?

"Oh, good," Aunt Trish said loudly in her teacher's voice, which carried all the way through the ballroom, "you like the gift, Evie! I'm so glad! It's not an art piece. It's designed to be used."

"Ugh, gross. Is that why it's wet?" Irene blurted out.

"Remove this at once!" Grandma Shirley thundered. She turned to my father. "Your daughter has ruined this event. I need to lie down."

"It's not wet from me. The dog was slobbering all over it!" I yelled, finally picking the literal worst option as per usual and running, not very fast on account of my too-tight dress and heels, to pick up the dog-slobber-covered ceramic dildo and the dog.

Well, I tried to pick up the dog.

"Snowball, come."

She panted I made desperate *come* motions.

"Snowball." Anderson whistled sharply, and the dog leaped off the stage to run and sit at his feet. "Good girl."

My female relatives chattered.

"If he talked to me like that, I'd be his good girl."

"Can't believe she's using a dildo with a man like that."

"It's a damn shame."

"Youth and a tight vagina are wasted on young girls these days."

Beside me, Anderson's shoulders were shaking.

"I'm literally dying here. You cannot be laughing." I pinched him.

Anderson bit back a smirk. "I didn't know you wanted cock that bad, Evie."

Chapter 26

ANDERSON

"Snowball, what the hell?" Evie bent down in front of the little white dog, giving me a good view down her cleavage.

Braeden was trying to steal a peek too. Fucker.

Suddenly, I wanted to throw it all away, just to fucking own him, drag him face-first through the sharp gravel and expose what a lying creep he was to the Murphys, who were oh too willing to slaver all over him and believe every word he said.

Par for the course for that family.

Evie gave up trying to corral the wiggling Snowball, who didn't seem at all the worse for wear from her four-and-a-half-mile sprint from the Murphy house through the snow, carrying a dildo the same weight as her.

Snowball raced off, keeping Evie's smaller cousins busy so their parents could enjoy a free few hours of food, drink, and fun.

"Bet you wish you'd saved the money on the suit rental."

"Hardly." I leaned over to kiss her.

I would have dug up a corpse to steal a suit to be at the party. It was a gold mine.

And the suit was the perfect disguise. Once they were drunk, all her family members saw was the suit and the interested expression on my face.

I was wearing a wire—I'd promised Jake my first-born child—and he was cross-checking in real time the information Evie's family was drunkenly spewing.

Disasters made good cocktail conversation, and everyone liked to brag about getting one over on the insurance company.

Evie kept bringing me drinks and little bites to eat, smiling up at me with unfiltered adoration.

I kept slipping the alcohol to her elderly relatives, who were all too happy to accept drinks from me disguised as flirting. Even though I wanted to unwrap her out of that dress and fuck her in the nearest storage room, I had a job to do.

Would it be bad to sleep with her?

I was the villain of her Christmas story. Wouldn't the villain fuck her then ghost her?

"You're going through these like water," Evie joked, handing me another scotch as her uncle who worked for an alarm company, and just admitted to lying to Van de Berg Insurance about the cause of the big customer-database breach, finished his story.

"I'm actually going to hand this to you," I said to her uncle, swapping the drink with his empty glass. "Hell of a story."

"Fuck the insurance companies, man."

We did a complicated handshake.

"If you can get info off Braeden about Bergeson Real Estate," Jake said in my ear, "we'll be in the clear with extra to spare."

Braeden was sloppily drunk with the rest of the obnoxious Murphy frat-boy cousins.

My hand settled protectively on Evie's waist as we passed them. I angled us so she wouldn't have to feel the slime of his gaze on her. Then just because I could and just because I was an asshole, I bent down and kissed her hard in front of Braeden, grabbing her ass possessively when I finally released her.

"I love having a girlfriend who puts out." I tipped her head up with two fingers.

Her eyes were dilated with desire, anticipation.

"Yeah," Braeden sneered, giving Evie an ugly look. "She does do that. On the first date, too, I hear. Don't feel too special. She lets anyone fuck her."

Evie grabbed my arm before I could slug him.

"Did you get that?" I asked.

"I didn't have the microphone on." She looked up at me, unhappy and guilty.

Jake said at the same time, "Hell yeah, I did! Too bad we didn't have video, though."

I tucked Evie under my arm, grabbing her a glass of wine, then led her outside into the cold.

"He's right." Evie took a long pull of her drink.

I took the radio out of my ear and slipped it into my pocket without her noticing.

"I always put out on the first date," she admitted sadly.

I shrugged. "So do I."

Evie made an unhappy noise.

"You probably do it because you can get any girl you want, so why not have the sampler platter? I just do it because I'm afraid guys won't like me if I don't."

"Between the territorial dog, the disaster-prone life, and the general state of homelessness, what's not to like?" I trailed my fingers along her collarbone.

"Yeah," she huffed. "In high school, anytime a guy showed interest in me, it turned out he just wanted to get with my sister or..." She shuddered. "My mom. I tried, I really tried, to be a good girl like my mom and get a boyfriend, a real nice one from a good family, who knows what a mutual fund is and has life goals. They never seemed to click with me on dates. They'd just ghost me. But I found out if I slept with them, they called me back, so..." She took another sip of her wine. "Sorry. I have clearly had too much to drink if I'm not fun drunk or even sloppy drunk. I'm just sad drunk."

I reached over to pull one of the curls that had escaped from her bun. "All I heard was someone humblebragging that she's such a good fuck that guys crawl all over themselves to get another taste." I leaned back against one of the massive marble columns, pulling her toward me to rest on my chest.

"That's not going to impress Grandma Shirley."

"Who gives a fuck what she thinks? I bet Granny Doyle thinks you're the shit."

"I bet you're secretly judging me."

"Like I said, I don't like you enough to lie to you about what those men wanted or promise you that you'll find true love," I reminded her, feeling my heartbeat reverberate around her.

I tipped her face up to kiss her before I could convince her to hook up with me, wanting to feel her curvy thighs around my waist as I fucked her up against the wall, losing myself in her.

That was what the Murphy's deserved, right? To have the man they hated fuck their daughter then break her heart? Hurt them like they hurt me?

Though I didn't think that would actually hurt them. They'd just blame Evie—probably already did.

My chest clenched in pain when I thought about her family angry and abusing her for being with me, even if it wasn't real.

I didn't have to show up at her mom's party. This was my fault, right? I was making Evie's life worse.

Man up. Stick to the plan.

Snowball strutted out from under a snow-covered bush, chewing what looked like a slab of roast beef and shaking the snow out of her fur.

I whistled to the dog and took Evie's hand. "Let's get the fuck out of here." I grabbed my helmet and my gloves.

Evie balked when we stood in front of the large motorcycle.

"My dress is too tight." The pulse in her neck fluttered when my gaze swept down the tight red bodice of the dress.

"And more humblebragging about her sexy figure." Then I picked her up, straddling the bike, then set her crossways on the seat in front of me.

"We are going to crash."

"We're not going to crash if you just hold still. I've ridden with bags like this before." I stuffed Snowball down the front of my suit jacket, her little front paws sticking out. "Hold on."

The bike roared, Evie screamed, then we were racing through the snow.

Her parents lived in the good part of town, and they were fairly close to the Canal Club, just up the tree-lined river walk.

Evie was gasping and laughing as we pulled in front of her postcard Victorian house.

The headlamp from the bike illuminated the Snowball-sized hole in one of the windows when I parked the bike.

"Crap, crap, crap."

"I'm impressed, Snowball."

The little dog jumped out of my suit jacket onto Evie then into a nearby snowbank, sank, then rocketed out.

"I'll come by tomorrow and fix it," I promised, setting Evie on her feet.

"I'll do it." She sighed dejectedly.

"You?" I was incredulous. "You know how to fix a window?"

"I think I could figure it out. It can't be that hard, right?"

I couldn't stop a grin. "You are so completely delusional."

She kissed the motorcycle helmet, leaving hearts of red on the shiny black as I carried her up the short staircase to the front door.

I should just leave her there, should go back to the field office, shouldn't take off my helmet, shouldn't kiss her until she was gasping and breathless and shivering but flush in the snowy cold.

But I couldn't stop kissing her.

It was intoxicating the way she just yielded to me, like all she wanted as for me to fuck her raw, damn the consequences.

"My decision-making skills have been lax as of late." She gasped.

The helmet dropped at my feet.

I held her hands above her head with one gloved hand, the other cupping her through her bodice, which barely held her huge tits in place.

She moaned as I kissed the mound of her breast above the bodice.

"I want to come all over your tits." I tugged at the zipper on the back of the dress. "I want to fuck you right here, your tits out, your skirt above your hips, your pussy dripping all over my cock as I pound into you while you scream against the glass."

Evie didn't register the approaching headlight.

I did.

But I didn't stop.

I couldn't get enough of her tits, which were huge and heavy.

"Your nipple will be so hard when I put it in my mouth." I nipped at her lip.

"You could make me come just like this," she said in that breathy voice.

The words went straight to my dick.

Footfalls crunched on the snow, then came angry words.

Evie yelped against my mouth, trying to push me off so her dad, brother, and ex didn't see her, face flushed, with my hand down her dress.

"Your dog put a hole in my window, and now this?" Her father sounded disappointed. "Evie, you know Mrs.

Charleston is going to call your mother and complain. You need to think before you act. You're not a teenager anymore. Why haven't you grown out of this behavior?"

I turned around, carefully blocking her from view.

"Just because your wife doesn't put out doesn't mean Evie has to join a nunnery."

Dr. Murphy sputtered.

"This isn't the first time she's been caught on the porch, exposing herself in the middle of the night." Braeden held a carton of what smelled like leftovers.

"Might not be the first time she's been caught, but it is the first time she's been with a real man." I caressed her tits through the bodice one more time, my thumb lingering. I picked up the helmet. "I didn't want to leave without seeing your tits, but I don't think your dad's going to let you invite me upstairs." I let my gaze slide down her—predatory, possessive.

Yeah, I could definitely lower myself to fuck Evie Murphy.

Chapter 27

EVIE

"Psst! Got your dildo out of the trash can."

"Gran!" I slapped the hand she was using to prod me with the ceramic dildo. "I don't need that. I threw that away for a reason."

"You put on a big show so Surly Shirley would get her granny panties untwisted."

I turned back to the window. I was trying to piece Plexiglas from my dwindling craft supplies over the hole. After Anderson had left me clothes askew, panties soaked, and with a potential public indecency charge, I'd tacked up a garbage sack on the broken window.

As soon as I'd woken up hung over and horny, my father had pointedly reminded me that I needed to fix the window. Today.

"Don't get cocky." Granny Doyle waved the dildo at me. "You can't bank on Anderson being there when you need him. Besides." She poked me in the side with the tip of the dildo. "If he knows he's got some competition, he won't get complacent."

"I don't even have anywhere to live. I don't have room for a custom ceramic dildo. Get rid of that before Mom sees and freaks out." I grabbed it from her and threw it into the street, expecting it to shatter.

It didn't. Because of course it didn't.

Instead, it bounced, sailed... and crashed through the passenger-side window of a big black pickup truck.

"Dammit."

The pickup truck rolled to a stop in front of the house.

Anderson got out into the snowy street to regard the broken window, his hand clasped over his mouth. He rubbed the back of his head as he approached me. "Gingersnap..."

"I'm sorry!" I blurted out. "I don't know why I don't have better decision-making skills."

"At this point, I don't think it's bad decision-making skills. I think it's bad luck." Anderson grabbed the front of my jacket, pulling me to him for a deep kiss. When he broke it, he was smirking. "If you show me your tits, I'll fix that window for you."

"Well, that is an easy trade." I grabbed the hem of my sweater and gave Anderson a nice, long view of the girls.

His mouth dropped open, then his head tipped back, and he roared in laugher, collapsing against one of the ornate porch columns, slapping his leg.

"Look, man..."

He gasped in laughter from the porch.

"I called around for some quotes." I pulled my sweater back down. "That's like a fifteen-hundred-dollar fix. I owe a lot of people money, and I'm at the point in my life where I'm A-okay with trading mild sexual favors for cash."

"Damn right." Granny Doyle fist-bumped me. "You gotta use those things for currency while you still can. It's like having your own personal ATM."

"Damn, it's cold enough to freeze your tits off." I rubbed my arms.

"I'll warm you up." Anderson wrapped me in his strong arms, spinning us slowly and kissing me long and slowly.

I melted against his soft mouth. "Yeah, I could get used to this."

He laughed against my mouth. "You're fucking one of a kind."

"Evie!" My mom was shrill.

I jumped away from Anderson guiltily.

My mother, in chic brown calfskin boots, stepped out onto the porch.

"I just had a very long conversation on the phone with Mrs. Charleston down the street."

"That nosy old shut-in." Granny Doyle made a rude noise.

"She said that she saw you out here last night, with him." Mom pointed at an unapologetic Anderson. "Engaged in intercourse."

"I wasn't railing her, ma'am, just feeling her up."

"You're probably going to get another call from her because Evie just flashed half the neighborhood," Granny Doyle said proudly.

My mother closed her eyes and gave a shuddering sigh.

"In my defense," I said with a grimace, "Dad told me I had to get the window fixed. Anderson isn't working for free anymore."

"That is a man who knows his self-worth. We love a king who practices self-care." Granny Doyle gave a little bow.

"You need to make extra Christmas cakes to take Mrs. Charleston to apologize," my mom instructed me.

I saluted her. "Cake duty starts at eleven hundred."

"Ian, let's go," my dad called from inside the house then joined Mom on the porch.

"Evie," he said, glaring when he noticed Anderson hulking in black against the cheery Christmas decorations on the house. "Remember, you are supposed to—"

"Already have it covered, Dad!" I chirped, jerking my thumb at Anderson, who was using a knife to prod at the window frame.

"He's handsome and handy." Gran gave my dad a pointed look.

"Ian!" my dad yelled again.

The door slammed.

"Someone doesn't sound excited for mandatory quality time," Ian whispered out of the side of his mouth as he passed me and Granny Doyle. My brother had his jacket draped over his shoulders like a cape just to make our dad mad. "You're going to leave Evie here by herself with that baby-making machine?"

"If Evie wants to make life-ending choices, she's an adult, and that's on her." My dad plopped his hat onto his head.

"Between the two of us, I'm the only one who seems to have figured out how to use a condom," Anderson drawled, flipping the knife in his hand and doing some fancy maneuver to make it spin in the opposite direction, where he caught it.

"Eight days until Christmas," my dad announced loudly as he, my mom, and Ian headed to the car.

"Yeah, eight days until Christmas." I sighed.

"I found a drainpipe in the woods you can stay in," Gran said conspiratorially. "I'll help you chase out the hobo."

"Thanks, but no thanks."

"Your loss."

"So, can you fix it?" I asked Anderson.

"No problem," he assured me. "This is historic single-pane glass. I brought some glazing to cut down. Just give me a couple of hours. Do you know the paint color of the window frame?"

"We have some extra cans in the back garage. I'll grab it."

"And then I might need another top-up." He tugged the neckline of my sweater.

Gran piped up, ruining the moment. "You think I can nab that dildo out of your truck, Hot Stuff, since Evie here isn't using it?"

Anderson squinted. "My brother's going to kill me."

Anderson had set up a makeshift shop on the back of the pickup bed, and the saw whirred as I started the Christmas cakes.

I loved Christmas cookies, pastries, and all kinds of desserts. Christmas cakes, though, were my favorite. They were a Murphy family tradition. When I was a kid, I had practiced with an icing piper and shaving cream to create perfect, intricate designs for the miniature cakes.

The sheets of cake—a recipe from Grandma Shirley's grandmother—were baking in the oven. The house smelled like Christmas.

Several cousins had shown up to help with the cakes. However, they'd all promptly gone back outside to gawk at Anderson.

I flipped one of the thin sheet cakes over onto a cooling rack, put the next set of cakes in the oven, then wiped my hands.

Outside, Anderson was carefully filling in putty around the brand-spankin'-new pane of glass.

"Don't wreck this one," he was saying to Snowball while my female cousins swooned.

"That just needs to dry, then I can paint it," Anderson said, standing up when I poked my head out of the front door.

"Do you want a snack while you wait?"

"You offering?" A slow smile spread across his handsome face, earning him catcalls from my cousins.

A car pulled up, and Grandma Shirley was helped up the porch steps by Felicity and her mom.

"I'm not sure why I expected a wholesome afternoon of Christmas-cake decorating at Melissa's house," my grandmother said tartly.

"We should have had the party at my house," Aunt Lisa simpered.

"Then Felicity would try to bake the cakes, and that would have been a disaster," Lauren said while sending someone the photos she had taken of Anderson.

"I moved all the leftovers to the cooler," I told Anderson as he followed me to the kitchen. "Help yourself. I have to get the cake assembly line moving."

Anderson fished out a cold slice of roast beef and rolled it up then ate it in two large bites. "What do you have on deck?" The water ran at the sink.

"Christmas cakes, four inches," I said, slipping into the easy rhythm of cooking, where you could just turn off your brain, focus on baking two hundred miniature cakes, and not have to worry about evictions or blackmail or the mad crush you had on the guy your family absolutely hated.

"Christmas cakes? You mean fruitcakes?" He looked over his shoulder.

"Have some goddamn respect."

The corner of his mouth twitched.

I held out my phone with the photos of Christmas cakes past.

"Thirty raspberry almond vanilla, thirty red velvet and chocolate alternated with white, forty green Grinch cakes with cranberry-and-cream-cheese filling, fifty vanilla-and-chocolate alternated, and fifty Christmas confetti cakes. All by midnight."

"Do you have an army to help you?"

"I have my grandmother and my mom."

"I like Granny Doyle, but she's been drinking a lot, and if I'm not mistaken, you need those sheet cakes cut lengthwise in half." Anderson's eyes narrowed. "The woman can barely walk."

"Not her."

Grandma Shirley took her spot at the end of the kitchen island, instructing one of her great-nephews to turn on the radio. "I want traditional Christmas music."

"How about a vintage Spotify playlist?" the kid offered.

"No, play the new Snoop Dogg album!" his brother suggested.

I clapped my hands and addressed the gaggle of relatives in the warm kitchen. "Everyone, please stay in the station you're assigned. If you have to leave, then tap out. Don't just wander off and leave a cake half-iced. I'm talking to everyone, but Sawyer, I'm looking at you."

"You're so picky about the cake decorating. It makes my brain hurt. I needed a drink," my cousin complained.

"But did you need three?" Nat asked.

"Anderson, this is going to be a shit show, going by last year." I waved him away. "You might want to take your snack to the dining room."

Anderson cracked his neck then reached for an apron from the set on the wall.

"Ooh!" My cousin Lauren licked her lips. "I might actually decorate more than one cake."

Anderson deftly circled the apron ties around his waist then knotted them.

"You are not on the decorating station," I warned Lauren. "Get your hands off of the icing piper."

Anderson was neatly rolling up his sleeves when I turned back to him.

"This man is a professional." Aunt J whistled. "He cooks. He fixes shit."

"He's got a dick the size of a coke bottle." Granny Doyle raised a glass.

"But does he know how to use a knife?" I looked at him.

"Do you have a knife worth using?"

I whipped open a drawer.

Anderson selected a long serrated knife.

"Do your worst."

"Sharp!" Anderson bellowed as one of my tween cousins tried to reach for the sprinkles.

"Sprinkles need to stay in the sprinkle station," I reminded him.

Normally, I used wooden blocks to keep my knife perfectly level as I sliced the thin sheet cakes into slices.

The first few times Anderson had deftly sliced the cake into two perfectly even, thin sheets, I'd held my breath, waiting for the knife to slip and the cake to be ruined. But the man was a machine.

"Does he fuck like that?" Granny Doyle asked as Anderson quickly sawed through the next sheet cake.

"You are supposed to be assembling boxes," I reminded Gran as I used a four-inch round cake cutter to cut perfect circles out of the sheet cake. My aunts layered them on parchment-paper-covered cardboard and spread the filling on the slices.

A small piece of the scrap cake went to Snowball, who was begging on the floor. The rest went to my younger cousins, who, led by the triplets, were happily making cake pops far away from my cake operation.

"That dog doesn't need any more sugar," Anderson warned me, still laser focused on cake slicing. "There have been two broken windows in the past twenty-four hours."

I was more trusting of randos with my sexy photos than I was with letting people decorate the Christmas cakes. There was a very short list consisting of me, Grandma Shirley, and Mom.

The cakes were piling up at Grandma Shirley's station, though.

Anderson had finished all the slicing ten times faster than I would have.

"Behind!" he barked, scooting past me to the other end of the island.

He grabbed an offset spatula, slid a cake onto one hand, placed it on a cake stand, and set it spinning.

"What are you doing?" I screeched as he scooped up a huge glob of Swiss buttercream frosting.

"Forty Grinch cakes," he said, the white frosting sliding on in a smooth sheet, not a single crumb of the layer cake disturbed.

"Those are actually a complicated cake." I winced. "There is an intricate white-and-red lattice pattern surrounding green hearts over the base frosting layer..."

Cake still spinning, Anderson tossed up a frosting bag, tested the tip on the counter, then like a machine began piping frosting onto the cake.

Grandma Shirley watched in grudging admiration as Anderson deftly piped Swiss buttercream frosting in the intricate lattice pattern on the miniature cake.

"It's not as good as my grandma did it," she finally declared.

"Didn't you say your grandma used to chase your dad around with a meat cleaver?" Sawyer piped up.

Grandma Shirley sniffed. "It was a different time."

Anderson finished the cake and took it to the fridge, which was stuffed with pastry.

"You and you." He tagged two of my younger cousins. "You're on cake patrol."

After watching to make sure my younger cousins were correctly ferrying the chilled cakes to Nat and Lauren, he returned to decorating. They had been banished to assembling boxes at the breakfast table, stamping the finished ones with a custom *MURPHY* calligraphy stamp surrounded by holly.

Anderson picked up several boxes that had already been filled to make more room.

"Corner!" Anderson shouted.

Braeden yelped then cursed as Anderson almost bowled him over.

"The man said corner, Braeden!" Nat yelled. "Felicity, get your useless fiancé out of the kitchen."

My parents and Ian's arrival were marked by arguing in the hallway.

"...care if you don't think it's a career. Dance is my passion. You're letting Evie do whatever the hell she wants."

"Yes, but you are my son."

"I'm also gay, so I can go find some hot piece of ass to fuck me for a free place to stay just as well as Evie can."

"I take it miniature ice-castle golf didn't go well?" Sawyer asked dryly.

My mother began tying on an apron, green eyes flashing in anger.

My dad opened the fridge to grab a beer and cursed when he saw it was full of cakes in varying states of disarray.

"All the drinks are down in the rec room, Dad," I said.

Uncle Ross poked his head out of the basement door. "Girls, are those cake pops ready? Don't worry, Evie. I'm not asking for one of those cakes. I learned my lesson last year," he added cheerfully.

"When's dinner?" My younger cousins had reached their cake limit.

"We'll order pizza." More of my uncles trooped through the kitchen, coolers and grocery bags of snacks in tow.

"You want to come watch the game?" Uncle Hugh slapped Anderson on the shoulder.

Anderson growled low in his throat as his arm was jostled.

"Jesus, fuck." My uncle skirted back, banging into the kitchen counter. "Evie, you can't have a man on that short of a leash. See how wound tight he is? That's not healthy."

"You can go watch the game." My mother dismissed Anderson as he finished the next cake.

"Don't fucking drop it," he warned my tween cousin who reached to transfer it to the fridge to set before it was packed into a box.

The boy nodded. "Yessir."

"You clearly need my help." Anderson didn't look at my mother as he reached for the next cake.

"Actually," my mother said, putting the final touch on the chocolate cake she was decorating, "I am a master at cake decorating, and we've managed just fine without you in years past."

Anderson paused, cake spinning in front of him. He gave my mother's cake a long, critical look. "Is that cake for internal use?"

"I beg your pardon?"

I glanced over. One of the little green holly icing leaves was ever so slightly smaller than all the rest.

"I prefer to do things the right way, but it's your cake." Anderson shrugged dismissively.

"I thought you were just a busboy. What do you know about cake decorating?" My mom's tone was sharp.

Anderson was nonplussed. "Waiter, but the head pastry chef keeps giving people nervous breakdowns, and sometimes, I draw the short straw and have to help him. He cuts off fingers if things aren't perfect." Anderson inspected his own impeccable cake. "The lack of standards in people's work product is sending this country to hell."

"Hear! Hear! Melissa always did cut corners," Grandma Shirley said to him with a sniff.

Mom's sisters cackled.

My mother added more icing to the holly leaf.

"Let Anderson fix it, Melissa. Why don't you go watch TV with the men?" Grandma Shirley said it like an insult, and my mother took it as such.

Mom hadn't even ripped her apron off before Anderson was scraping the top of her cake clean to redo it.

"So much for a wholesome Christmas evening," Melissa said loudly as her sisters snickered.

"Christmas is for the professionals, Anderson." Grandma Shirley sighed. "Her mother can't cook either."

"Your line is amateur hour," Anderson remarked, straightening up and twisting his torso.

The rest of my relatives had wandered off as the boxes of cakes stacked up on the breakfast table and all the cake pops had been dipped in icing.

We were in the Christmas-cake endgame.

Tongue poking out, I carefully piped snowflakes around the rim of the cake in front of me.

Anderson picked up the cake he'd just finished and took it to the fridge. "I'm going to paint that window."

"*Et tu, Brute?*"

"Don't want you to get thrown out ahead of schedule." He kissed the back of my neck.

I was hallucinating swirls of frosting when I finally finished the last cake, using tweezers to carefully set a little edible gold ball at the center of each icing snowflake.

Sure, Anderson might give me shit about putting up with my family's emotional abuse, but this was why. This evening had been perfect—all of us in the kitchen, making memories, spreading Christmas cheer, laughing and joking—multiple generations together.

It was the one time I truly felt like I belonged in the family.

The storage room adjacent to the kitchen had the heat off to keep the cakes cool. In the dark room, Anderson set down the paint can and wordlessly took the cake boxes from me to stack them with the others, which were each tied with a bow.

"Thanks for fixing the window," I said in a rush, "and for baking. We'd honestly—probably just me, actually—be here past midnight trying to finish. But it's still early. The game isn't even in the third period." I looked up at him.

"I guess I should tell you that was... well, that was pretty special, what you did. You're like perfect boyfriend material," I joked.

His mouth turned down. "I'm not that guy."

"What guy?"

"The perfect guy, the one that every girl wants—the sweet, helpful hero hidden under the tough, blackened armor of the villain." He ran a hand through his hair, frustrated. "Believe me. I know bad men—been around them all my life. There's nothing there—no secret passage in the cave leading to the key to save him. It just gets deeper and darker and more claustrophobic until you suffocate inside, trying to find the heart of gold."

"That's dramatic."

"I'm not a good person." His eyes were dark.

"I know."

"I'm a bad man."

"I know."

"And I want to do very bad things to you." He took a step up to me. The heat radiated off him.

"How bad?"

His fingers rested on my neck.

"Is that what you want, Gingersnap?" he asked, his deep voice sending shivers through me that weren't from the winter air. "You want to choke on my cock?"

I swallowed the drool.

"Is that what you've been thinking about all alone when you touch yourself at night, how it would feel for you to be kneeling down in front of me in your soaking-wet panties, tears streaking down your face as I throat-fuck you?"

I mean, I hadn't, but now I would.

I reached for the zipper on his black jeans, feeling the exhalation of his breath on my mouth right before he crushed our lips together.

He kissed me, hungry, fingers insistent at the strings of my apron, tugging it off then my sweater. He pushed my bra down, then his mouth was hot on my nipple.

I bit back a moan.

"No." His teeth grazed the soft skin of my breast. "I want to hear you, hear how good it feels, how much you want me, how much you crave me. You'd come for me easy, wouldn't you?"

"Only," I gasped, "if you leave the helmet on. Give me the full villain treatment."

"Fuck, Gingersnap, you do want me bad." He nipped at my nipple.

I let out a moan.

"Louder," he ordered in his deep baritone. His hand slid under my plaid skirt, up my thighs, spreading them.

I tangled my fingers in his hair.

"I need you to touch my clit."

"You like getting fucked, don't you? You'd spread your legs for me right here. Fucking little slut."

His hand pressed against my soaking-wet panties. A high-pitched whimper escaped my mouth.

Anderson's lips were half-parted as he watched me grind against his hand.

"You'd come just like this, wouldn't you?"

"You don't want me to come on your cock, bad boy?"

He leaned back in, kissing me hot and heavy, my mouth, my neck, my tits.

"Let me feel you," I begged. "You're a bad boy. I want you to use me like a sex doll."

His large hand tangled in my hair, then he was kissing me again, stealing my breath as he rubbed slow circles against the silk fabric of my panties. "Any man ever made you this wet?"

"No," I gasped out.

"You like this, don't you? You like the thought of me claiming you, using you. I want you on your hands and knees, begging me to come all over your ass."

I spread my legs wider, silently coaxing him to do it, to spread me wide-open and fuck me with his huge cock.

"I bet women throw away their whole lives for you," I blurted out when he broke the kiss.

His nostrils flared. "I'm not your goddamn hero. I'm just the guy who fucks you when he feels like it."

"Evie!" My mother's voice was shrill from the hallway outside the door.

"Shit!" I grabbed my sweater.

Before I could pull it over my head, Anderson, hand still in my hair, half dragged me stumbling out into the kitchen. "This who you're looking for?" he boomed over my ineffective screeching.

"Is this the line for the sex carnival ride?" Granny Doyle asked loudly over my cousins' shrieking.

Anderson dumped me onto the floor.

I scrambled into a crouch.

"Damn, he didn't even take off his shirt." Nat fanned herself. "And I think I can barely walk."

"We weren't spying, Evie, honest. Sawyer was looking for you," Aunt J assured me.

Anderson's mouth twitched in a smirk.

"You can spy if you want to. I know your husbands aren't putting out."

That set off my cousins.

I wished Anderson would offer me his jacket, *something*, instead of just standing there while I tried to decide whether I wanted to turn my acne-scarred bare back to my family and run back into the storage room to put on my clothes or if I should just accept my fate and make a break for the stairs.

But what had he said? He wasn't my hero, just the guy who fucks me?

Yeah, fucks me over.

"Felicity's spying because she's not getting any from Limp-Dick McGee over here." Granny Doyle stuck her thumb at Braeden.

"I'm saving myself for marriage," Felicity replied, nose high in the air.

"Or maybe you're just saving yourself for me," Anderson said, grabbing his crotch.

"Do it, Felicity!" my cousins screamed. "Braeden's not worth it."

"You have to have sex with a man who knows what he's doing at least once in your life." Granny Doyle banged the table emphatically.

"Evie's got that covered," Aunt J hooted.

"Don't think you're anything special," my mom said derisively to Anderson, who had a cold, sharp smile on his face. "This isn't the first time I've caught my daughter with a boy in there, and shamefully, it likely won't be the last."

"Boy?" Granny Doyle hiccupped. "That's a full-ass grown man."

"Don't worry, Mrs. Murphy," Anderson drawled. "I was just messing around. I didn't even make her come." Anderson grabbed my jaw and tilted my face up to him. "I like thinking about you walking around, your pussy aching for me." He rubbed his thumb, which had just been on my panties, over my lower lip.

My drunken female cousins and aunts wolf whistled.

"I don't know why," he said to my stunned parents, "you're so concerned. You tried so hard to mold Evie into your perfect daughter, but she's never going to be anything more than a sex-hungry little slut. Your epic, expensive failure spreading her legs for me."

My mother's nostrils flared.

The smirk turned feral. "I could have her eating cum out of my hand."

My chest was tight. I couldn't breathe.

"What the hell is wrong with you?" I choked out.

Anderson grabbed me by the neck, gave me one long, deep kiss, then let me lurch back to the floor, dizzy, mouth dry.

"Don't act like you aren't going to come crawling back to me, begging for my cock, no matter what your parents say."

Chapter 28

ANDERSON

"You fucked up my truck."

"I'm gonna fix it," I snarled, not at all ready to deal with Hudson's bullshit today.

"What the hell even went through it?" he demanded.

"I said I was going to fucking fix it." My skin felt too tight. I could still taste Evie on my mouth.

I should have just fucked her right there. I didn't know why I hadn't—it wasn't like she was some blushing virgin I could traumatize. She was fucking perfect.

And now I might never see her again.

Better to end it this way.

I owed it to my past self to at least leave a bitter impression with her parents.

It was better for Evie if she hated me. I'd seen how she looked at me with stars in her eyes.

Better to break her heart now than on Christmas morning when she realized that I wasn't going to ride in on a white reindeer at the eleventh hour to save her from her family.

I was moving on. I was going on vacation after I returned the last of the recovered money to Aaron. Somewhere warm, with no Christmas.

After grabbing a beer from the fridge, I stood behind Jake's computer. I nodded to the screen.

"So, bad news." Jake grimaced. "Some of the info we got was crap."

"People at the party were probably trying to one-up their family and friends," Talbot interjected.

"This guy?" Jake pulled up a photo of a balding red-headed man with freckles all over his face. "Doesn't even have the clearance at his company to be making insurance decisions."

"Fuck."

"Yeah, fuck."

"So, how bad is it?" Lawrence asked me as I scanned through the checklist of firms that potentially had committed insurance fraud.

"I need another eighty-seven grand."

Talbot winced. "Like before Christmas or on Christmas?"

"Christmas Eve. Two a.m."

"You gotta hit the Bergeson account. That's the only way, man," Lawrence said. "You gotta hit it hard."

I rubbed a hand on the back of my neck. "Fuck." I paced toward the door, which let out into the cold, out to Evie, then back. "Let me just think about this. I need to come up with a plan."

"I have a plan: let's get Braeden super drunk, kidnap him, threaten the info out of him, and go home in time for Christmas," Jake suggested.

"That is not a plan that—"

Eeek!

"Hudson, what the fuck are you doing? You know I hate that sound!" I bellowed.

Lawrence clapped his hands to his ears as Hudson scratched white numbers on the rarely used chalkboard on one wall.

Screee!

He drew a circle around a four-digit number.

"That?" He tapped the chalk. "That is how much money you owe me for my window, Anderson, on top of the money you owe Aaron Richmond."

"Fuck you."

"Also?" He slapped an unmarked white envelope against my chest. "This came for you."

I ripped it open, knowing exactly what I'd find. The only thing on the card was a time and an address.

"Looks like you've been summoned." Lawrence peered over my shoulder.

Talbot patted my shoulder. "Can I have your bike after Aaron kills you?"

Chapter 29

EVIE

"I'm not going to cry."

After months of spilling tears over Braeden, I swore I wasn't going to cry over a boy ever again.

"Anderson's a grown man, definitely not a boy, so maybe I can take the loophole," I decided as I scrubbed the lingering touch of him from my skin in the shower.

He'd used me.

When he was fixing the window and laughing and helping bake cakes, he was just pretending to be nice, pretending to like me.

He was literally only entertaining the blackmail thing because he wanted to fuck with my parents.

I was suddenly exhausted.

I wanted to stay under the warm water until Christmas.

My skin prickled as the water started to get cold.

"Aaahhh!" I screamed in the shower of the tiny bathroom in the half-finished attic.

Instead of spending the money to finish the build, my parents had spent money adopting me. I was reminded of the fact whenever Ian and I had complained about sharing a room when we were younger. Of course the triplets got their own rooms. Three rooms. Once each. So that they could self-actualize, according to the expensive psychologist my parents had hired.

I took a breath.

"I am not bitter. I love my family. And I hate Anderson." I opened the shower door too hard, and it slipped off the track.

Cursing, I slipped and slid on the cracked tile floor as, water dripping into my eyes, I tried to force the door back on the track.

"Stupid." I was stupid, stupid, stupid to think that Anderson actually cared about me.

Clearly, he wasn't a good person. No matter how much I wanted to change him, he was a villain. He probably got off on sticking it to my parents and humiliating me. Anderson had a fucked-up childhood and lived to spread chaos to those of us from good families.

I raced through the freezing-cold attic room to my bed. The saggy mattress buckled under my weight as I climbed under the mound of blankets, curling up into a ball.

My mom was right. It hadn't been the first time I'd been caught kissing a boy in the mudroom, but it was definitely going to be the last.

"New Year's resolution: Evie Murphy is turning over a new leaf. I'm going to get a job, I'm going to try really hard to find a decent boyfriend, and I'm going to find a place to live that isn't me mooching off of family members. And I am never ever thinking or even speaking to Anderson Wynter."

He was not a bad boy. He was a terrible man.

I flopped over onto my back, thinking about the last time I had almost given in to the temptation and fantasized about him.

Not anymore.

He was dead to me.

Too bad my hoo-ha hadn't gotten the memo.

I turned over onto my stomach.

My fresh panties were completely soaked even though I'd been trying my hardest not to think about him.

It was just the unfairness of it—how smug, how sure he had been that of course I wasn't going to be able to resist him.

I sat up in bed, the covers falling off of me.

"Stop thinking. What the hell is your problem?"

My problem was him.

Anderson didn't get to have the final word.

"Lick his cum out of his hand," I grumbled as I stuffed my feet into my boots, zipped up my long, heavy coat over my sleep shirt, and tiptoed down the creaky stairs.

The family members still hanging around late in the evening were watching the game highlights, drinking wine, and playing cards.

So wholesome.

I snuck past them to the back kitchen door.

I just made the bus and sat in my seat, fuming as the bus rumbled through town toward the Gulch and to Anderson.

The entitlement.

The arrogance.

The aggression.

The maleness.

He was the absolute worst.

When I walked up to the converted industrial building where he'd taken me last time, light glowed from one frosted window.

He was there.

"Anderson!" I rammed my fists on the metal. "Anderson, I know you're in there. You don't get to ignore me."

No response, damn him.

"You open this freaking door right the eff—*oof!*"

The door swung open, and I stumbled inside, falling right in front of a shirtless Anderson.

His gray eyes blinked at me as he closed the door.

I scrambled to my feet, brushing off my coat.

"Look who came crawling back, begging for my cock," he sneered.

"That is not what is happening. I'm here to yell at you."

"Yell my name as you come?"

"Screw you. I'm not attracted to you." Despite the cold, my face felt hot. I clenched my hands in their mittens.

He crossed his arms, the motion making his biceps bulge, sending those tattoos dancing.

I launched into my speech. "You pretended to be nice to me to get me to think you were a good person, then you used me."

Anderson snorted. "I didn't use you."

"Yes, you did, for your sick games against my family."

"Gingersnap, if I'd actually used you, you'd have cum dripping out of your ass right now."

My eyes bugged out of my head.

"Now, take off that fucking coat." His deep voice dropped an octave.

"I'm not staying." I hated that my voice trembled.

"Gingersnap." He reached out and tugged at the little knitted snowman on the tassel of the zipper. "I bet you aren't wearing a bra under there." The zipped rasped down. "You were lying alone in your bed, trying to talk yourself out of touching your clit."

"I—"

Suddenly, his hand shot out, grabbing my neck, holding me in place so he could force his other hand between my legs.

Through the flimsy nightgown fabric, he could feel I was soaking wet.

"Knew it." A slash of a smug smirk filled his face.

He leaned in, crushed our mouths together, and pushed my coat down my arms.

His large hands slid up the nightgown. They were everywhere, on my tits, tugging at my panties.

"If you don't take the nightgown off, I'm going to rip it off. Have fun explaining that when you stumble home."

"How do you know I'm sleeping with you?" I croaked, pushing at his waist.

His large hand grabbed a fistful of the nightgown fabric, jerking me forward. My hands splayed over that muscular chest.

"You showed up here, didn't you? You want to act like you're the perfect Murphy princess, but you're not. You want me to fuck you on the floor of this garage."

I fumbled at the buttons at the neckline.

"Time's up." He grabbed the sleep shirt, ripping it straight down the front, buttons popping everywhere.

Then his mouth was kissing me, his tongue sweeping in my mouth. Then his teeth were on my nipples, which were pebble-hard.

I moaned as he stroked me through my soaked panties.

"Greedy little slut." His voice was harsh. "You're going to come for me, aren't you?"

His hand slid under my panties, and a whimper slipped out.

"You know I like to hear you, like to hear you tell me how good that feels, how much you crave it."

My legs trembled as he stroked me. A moan escaped. I didn't want him to know what he was doing to me.

He kissed me roughly as I clung to his tattooed shoulders.

"I could make you come just like this. Is that what you want?"

I bit my lip, trying to keep from crying out.

He kissed me, the hand that had just been stroking my clit gripping my jaw. "You want me to leave you like this?" he growled against my mouth. "You want me to tell you to walk home with your pussy dripping down your legs?"

"Don't leave me like this," I whimpered, hating myself for giving in.

"Then I want to hear you beg."

I squeezed my eyes shut.

He whispered a horrible sensual curse in my ear. "I want to hear how much you want me, where you want me to fuck you, how you want me to fuck you."

I swallowed.

"I want to hear you tell me how you want my cum in your hair and all over your tits and how you'll kneel there, your cunt taking my thick cock as I fuck you raw, fuck you till you can't even scream my name."

Put me on the naughty list, but that was all I wanted for Christmas.

"I want you to hold me down and take me," I choked out. "I'll be a good girl for Christmas and hold my pussy open for you so you can ram your cock into me, every thick, throbbing inch. I won't even touch myself, just hold my pussy open so you can take me."

I reached for his zipper.

He nipped my lip. "You want me to fuck you that bad that you don't even care if you come?"

"I know you'll make me come." I scraped my teeth on his jaw.

"Did Braeden ever make you come?"

Mrs. Claus's tits. "What the hell?"

"Did he," Anderson enunciated, "ever make you come? Did Preston? Did any of those guys you were fucking in the car, in your parents' house, they even make you come?"

"Er… yeah?" I squeaked. "Definitely. Well, not Preston, but er—*eep!*"

He picked me up around the waist, took two large steps, then sat me down facing backward on his motorcycle, which was parked by the closed metal garage door. "You sure they made you come?"

The leather seat had me tilted back. I tried to struggle off the bike, grabbing at the handlebars, my legs splayed open.

Something glinted in his hand. *A switchblade.* He flipped it open.

"Oh my god!" I started screaming. "You're going to murder me, and I'm not wearing a bra. My mother's going to kill me."

He pressed a large hand on my chest, forcing me back as I struggled.

"Police! Help!"

The blade cut through the red panty fabric with a whisper.

He flipped the blade closed with a snap, then he grabbed the cut scrap of fabric, pulling forward, making me feel excruciating pleasure as it slid along my slit.

"I knew this was a fetish for you," I gasped.

"You hoped this would be a fetish for me," he corrected me, tossing the scraps to the floor, then looked at me, those intense silver eyes darkened to a slate gray. His gaze swept down my naked body, from the rapid rise and fall of my tits, down my torso, down to the glistening slit of my cunt.

"You got your pussy all ready for me." His thumb slid briefly along the beginning of my slit.

"Women can do groom for their own personal enjoyment."

"Nah, Gingersnap, you were hoping to have my mouth on your clit."

I gulped and struggled back against the handlebars. I let out a gasp as his fingers traced a line down my slit. His mouth was back on my nipple, sucking it while his fingers played in my pussy.

I couldn't get any purchase to move my legs to close them or lift them up. I just had to lean back and take it, him stroking my hard clit with two fingers. He moved from my tits up to my mouth, kissing me, his tongue tangling with mine, claiming me.

His fingers slid down to push their way into my opening, stroking me like I wished he would fuck me—rough, hard, heavy.

"You are a bad girl," he rumbled. "You're getting my bike all dirty." He added another finger.

I moaned, my nails digging into his hair.

Another long, slow kiss followed as his thumb rubbed my clit, and my hips surged up.

"I don't think I've ever been with a girl with a cunt as juicy as yours, Gingersnap."

I clung to him as his fingers worked between my legs, stroking my clit.

"You like it, don't you? I bet you'd love my cock up your tight little cunt."

I mewled as his fingers twisted around my clit. In me, his fingers moved faster.

"Tell me," he ordered.

"I love getting fucked," I moaned. "I like getting all dirty with cum. I want your cum all over me."

His fingers curled in me, and my back arched up. He leaned down to take my tits again, teeth scraping the nipple as I gasped and my hips ground needy circles against his hand.

He stroked me faster, harder, working my pussy as I begged for his cock, for his cum.

We were going a hundred miles an hour to the cliff edge, then I was gushing all over his hand and the leather seat of the bike as he kept working my clit, milking my orgasm.

"Christmas crackers," I gasped, pushing back my sweaty hair.

Arm and thighs shaking, I tried to haul myself off the bike. Anderson just watched as I struggled.

"I could fuck you just like that." His voice had a dangerous lilt to it.

I stopped moving. "Then do it."

He stepped up to me, grabbed me around the waist with one arm, and lifted me off the bike.

He was kissing me as soon as my feet hit the floor.

I pawed at his zipper.

He slapped my hand then turned me around.

"Bad girls who make a mess on my bike don't get my cock. Now." His large hand on the back of my neck pushed me forward. "Clean it up."

My nose was practically in the wet spot on the leather. He had me bent over the bike, ass in the air. I struggled ineffectively.

"Don't disobey me." He swapped his hand, moving the one on my back of my neck to grab my ass, forcing my legs apart. He stroked my still-raw pussy then slapped me hard on the ass, making me squeal.

"I said clean it. Or you want me to use my belt?"

Damn.

My tongue darted out hesitantly to lick at the juices from my pussy. I got earthy musk and the slight animal scent of the leather. My tongue darted out again, licking long and slow along the leather.

Anderson's fingers were back in my pussy, stroking me hard then moving down to finger fuck me.

I couldn't help it. As much as I didn't want to give him the satisfaction, my hips rocked back against his hand as he added another finger, really working my pussy.

"I bet you want me to fuck you just like this. Your pussy's wet enough. It's dripping down your legs. You want me to make you come again? You want to come on my hand again, Gingersnap?" He twisted his fingers.

My pussy was still raw from moments ago, and all I could do was moan as his fingers stroked my cunt. His fingers tightened in my hair, pressing my face into the leather seat.

"Please fuck me," I begged.

"You made a mess on my bike. Dirty girls don't get cock." His fingers surged up in my cunt, making me cry out. "They get punished." He slapped my pussy hard.

"You can go home after this, your pussy still swollen, wishing you'd had my cock." His knuckles dug into my clit. "But nothing you do to yourself is ever going to feel as good as this, no matter how much you try to touch yourself."

His teeth sank briefly into my bare shoulder.

I was close. I couldn't control my hips as they rocked back against his hands, needing, seeking, wanting.

I let out a sobbing moan.

"I could work your pussy like this all night."

Then I was coming, the leather seat stifling some of my cries as he pumped his fingers into me as I shuddered my orgasm around his hand.

When it was over, I half lay there, draped on the bike, stunned.

He stroked me one more time then twisted my head and wiped his fingers on my mouth and chin.

"Lick it," he ordered.

He let me suck on his fingers for a second then leaned down to kiss me hard, possessively.

His hand dropped, squeezing my ass like he owned it.

I struggled to push myself up, leaning on the bike.

"You don't want to..." I trailed off.

His eyes flicked down my naked body dismissively.

"What? Fuck you? No, I don't want to fuck you. I just wanted to prove that you did secretly want the man who almost killed your brother to destroy your pussy."

He leaned in to spit the words into my ear. "Think about me when you touch yourself tonight. Think about

308 • Alina Jacobs

me the next time you're spreading your legs for one of your brother's shitty friends. Hate me while you try to come. You Murphys need to pay for your sins. You'll never escape me."

He picked up my torn clothes off the floor and threw them at me.

Trying not to shake, I pulled on the nightgown and coat and drew them around me, all under his dismissive gaze.

I hated him. He'd made me come harder than any man had, and while I felt used, I still would bend over on the floor and let him come in me, just like he'd said.

Get it together, Evie.

I had come to get the parting shot. Not get the most mind-bending orgasm of my life.

"You're so full of yourself," I said haughtily. "No one fantasizes about getting fucked on a motorcycle in a shack. It would have been better if it was in a Ferrari in front of a mansion."

Head held high, I strode to the door to do the walk of shame in the snow.

"I hope you don't need a ride home," Anderson called after me. "Be warned—if you mess up my bike, I'll make you clean it up in front of your parents' house."

"You're sick."

"I told you I was a shitty person."

The door slammed in my face.

Stunned, I walked to the bus stop on the corner.

What had I been thinking?

But then, wasn't that how it always went? Find a shitty guy, build him up in my head to be the Nutcracker Prince, then get surprised and shocked when he was just a giant rat?

My phone rang.

"Girls' night!" Granny Doyle whooped when I answered. "I already got Sawyer. The rest of them just want to stay home."

In the background, music blared. Snowball was barking, and Sawyer was screaming, "Watch out for that truck!"

"Boo! Lame. Learn how to drive, asshole!" Granny Doyle laid on the horn.

"Let's go, Evie! You're my fun granddaughter."

"I'm actually at Anderson's."

"Getting railed? I figured. No judgment. You gotta keep him on his toes. I'll pick you up. I'm bringing you a change of clothes. I bet Anderson got cum everywhere."

Chapter 30

ANDERSON

"You'd better be paying."

"Is that frosting in your hair, or are you just happy to see me?"

I sat down across from Aaron at a rickety metal table at the old 1950s horse-racing track on the outskirts of the Gulch, just outside the city limits of Maplewood Falls.

Aaron slid over a shot glass filled with oily, clear alcohol. Bracing myself, I knocked it back.

Coughing, I forced out, "Can't you just call like a normal person?" I pounded my chest as the alcohol went down my throat, burning away the guilt, the anger, the bitterness. But it couldn't burn away the taste of Evie.

She didn't know how close I'd been to throwing her onto the ground and fucking her doggie style until she couldn't hold any more of my cum.

312 • Alina Jacobs

I took two more shots in quick succession, wishing I could just drink the whole bottle.

"We are eight days away from Christmas, and you're still short." Aaron knocked back another of the toxic-waste shots, wincing slightly.

"I'm going to get the money. No problem. I'd have it by now if you hadn't yanked my leash. You're wasting my time."

Aaron fixed his unyielding green eyes on me.

Both of us had grown up in shitty circumstances, but Aaron's childhood made mine look like a multiyear Disneyland trip.

He was used to being hypersensitive to people's micro behaviors. Not doing so could have resulted in being on the receiving end of violence or starvation. The skill was further honed in insurance, where you could save hundreds of millions of dollars by ferreting out when people were lying or withholding part of the truth.

I tried to keep my expression neutral but confident. "I'm very close wrapping up the Bergeson contract. You'll be able to close it out and be home in time for Christmas."

Aaron poured more of the toxic liquid out of the glass bottle and set it back down on the table with a thump.

"And yet I heard you spent the last several days baking cakes, going to parties, and fixing some girl's window."

"She's not *some girl*." I tensed before I could set my expression.

"She the love of your life?" Aaron didn't flinch.

"Of course not." I backtracked. "I'm using her."

"Sounds like she's using you. How much do you normally charge to decorate a house that size? Maybe next Christmas, I'll have you come string lights on my roof."

I resisted the urge to blow it all to hell and throw him to the floor. "Look, I already have my brother up my ass about it," I snarled. "I don't need any more secret summonses. Just let me work. Evie's been a gold mine. I hit like half the list after one party with her."

"Hurry up." Aaron shifted. "I need you to look at that train derailment that was on the news. Close this out so I can fly you out to Idaho. Don't make me have to fire your brother's firm. I already have you all booked out for investigation through Q2." Aaron downed another toxic drink.

"What evidence do you have so far on... what's his name? Braeden?"

"He's a slimy little shit. He made a mistake somewhere. He's cocky. He thinks he's getting one over on me. There's a smoking gun somewhere. He can't stay away from Evie. If he was smart, he would have just left her alone."

Aaron slowly blinked. "What does that have to do with the alleged scammer that intercepted the payment to the Bergeson Real Estate accounts?"

"I just meant—" I tried to force myself not to sound defensive.

"Save it. You're a terrible liar. I don't care if you think you're in love with the daughter of people that would like nothing more than to see you strapped to a yule log and set ablaze, but you work for me. You owe me money, not her."

Technically, she was blackmailing me, but I didn't need to remind Aaron of that. "She's not my redemption arc, if that's what you're after."

"Seems like you can't resist a lost cause." Aaron leaned back and crossed his arms.

"Evie's not a lost cause, despite what her parents think. She's fearless and brassy, and she could do anything except ride a motorcycle. I'm not letting her drive my motorcycle."

I squashed down the image of her coming all over my bike.

Aaron raised an eyebrow. I might as well have just written my feelings on the wall in red paint.

"Can we just get through the part of the meeting where you chew me out, then you can go blab to Grayson?" I snarled. "And he can tell Hudson, and my brother can get in my shit, and then I can tell all of you to fuck off and get back to work?"

A horn blared, tinny over the loudspeaker. The race was starting.

Aaron didn't move. "I don't tell my older brother my business."

"And yet like Santa Claus, he knows when you're sleeping and knows when you're awake. He and Hudson are constantly hanging out, gossiping like two little old ladies."

A snarl settled on the well-dressed man's face. "Is Grayson telling Hudson stuff about me?" Aaron demanded.

"You mean besides that he thinks you spend too much money on takeout brew at your lobby coffee cart?" I poured more of the drink. It was starting to grow on me. Or maybe that was the alcohol, like jet fuel in my veins.

"You tell Hudson that in *America*, we drink coffee, and he can tell Grayson to take his Earl Gray tea and shove it up his ass," Aaron hissed.

"Fucking older brothers, right?" I saluted him with the shot glass.

"The goddamn fucking worst."

The horn blared on the sound system again. The race was over.

It didn't matter who won. Everyone here knew the real reason this racetrack was still operational.

"I think," Aaron said, inspecting the bottle, "that if they actually bothered to age this, it—"

"You sit the fuck down, you fucking old cunt."

"The hell did you say to my grandmother, bootleg Scarface motherfucker!"

I set down my full shot glass, twisting in my seat. "Evie? What the fuck?"

Chapter 31

EVIE

"I thought we were going for a fun girl power night out," I said in confusion as Granny Doyle led us up the concrete stairs with rusty handrails to a 1950s space-age building that had probably been cool seventy years ago but now looked like the site of a horror movie.

The fluorescent lights buzzed and flickered as we stepped inside. Sawyer and I huddled together.

"She died as she lived, covered in crumbs."

Christmas decorations that looked like they had been recycled from a 1970s hoarder house estate sale were tacked up everywhere. A rough-looking Rudolph swung slowly from the ceiling.

"At least if we get kidnapped, I wouldn't have to pay rent," Sawyer whispered.

"Gran, let's go somewhere else," I begged.

"We'll go to the bar after this, girls," Granny Doyle assured us. "Business before pleasure."

"What business? You're retired."

"Dammit, girls, I need y'all to woman the fuck up. Now..." Her voice dropped conspiratorially. "Don't tell your dad, but I've been gambling my social security check. I lost twenty Gs, but I'm getting it all back tonight."

"Getting it back how?"

"Are we here to commit robbery?"

"Reindeer gambling!" Granny Doyle power walked through the dank building.

"Too bad Ian had to go to the theater. We really could have used some protection," Sawyer mumbled as we headed deeper into the dimly lit room packed with metal tables and chairs.

We were the only women in the space. The rest were men—dangerous, rough-looking men—not like Anderson. These guys looked like they'd just crawled out of an eighties mob movie.

At least Gran and Sawyer were appropriately dressed. Yours truly was wearing a skimpy Mrs. Claus costume that I'd fit in way back when I was eighteen, but after a very stressful year, not so much. Gran had claimed she couldn't get up the attic stairs on account of her knees, and this was what she found in the storage closet. It was better than the torn nightgown, and at least she'd brought clean underwear.

I could feel dozens of eyes on me. It would have been less scary if they'd all started catcalling us or making gross sexual comments.

Instead, they watched us, silently, their eyes tracking us.

We were prey.

Snowball growled softly.

Gran didn't seem to care. She led us confidently through the tables of predators.

We made our way to a table next to a dirty glass window overlooking the empty track.

I pulled out my chair, wincing as it screeched against the terrazzo floor.

Sawyer sank into the chair next to me and slouched defensively over the table.

"They have Christmas specials," I whispered. It seemed like a bad idea to talk at a normal volume. "It can't be all bad if they have custom holiday cocktails."

Sawyer frowned at the laminated menu in front of her.

"Where's the staff?" Granny Doyle asked loudly, looking around. "Does anyone work here?"

"Gran, you can't yell at the waitstaff." I glanced up, hoping she hadn't offended some poor minimum-wage worker. As someone who'd been in food service, I knew the last thing you needed at the end of your shift was being yelled at by an entitled elderly patron.

One of the more grizzled men gave a pointed look to another. That man stood up slowly and headed over to our table, chewing a toothpick. He fished in his pocket for a notepad and paper.

"Merry Christmas!" I chirped.

He clicked the ballpoint pen. "What do you want to order?"

"I'll take..." Sawyer's finger trailed down the menu. "What gin do you use in your mistletoe martini?"

The guy shrugged and chewed his toothpick.

"I guess I'll have that."

"What do you recommend?" I asked him, like we were at a fancy vineyard and not a sketchy racetrack.

Gran snatched the menus. "Who cares what you're ordering? I'm here to gamble. How do we place a bet, sonny?"

The man looked over his shoulder at the grizzled hulk sitting at one of the rickety tables then back at us and sighed heavily. "Place a bet at the kiosk up front." He jerked his thumb.

"Can I also have the mistletoe martini?" I called after him as he turned to head to the kitchen.

"I'm going to go place a bet. You girls want to put anything down?" My grandmother stood up.

"Gran!" I raced after her, rounding the corner to where the guy behind the bulletproof glass was scrolling on his phone.

"Are you sure this is a good idea? Usually, I'm like YOLO, but the house always wins."

"I've been researching." Gran tapped her head. "Ten thousand on Dasher." Gran put a wad of cash under the window.

I grimaced as the clerk slowly leaned forward, scooped her cash into a drawer, and handed her a handwritten ticket.

Granny Doyle kissed it as we walked back to the table, where Snowball and Sawyer were waiting.

"I can feel it. Tonight's my lucky night."

"It was your lucky night with Anderson." Sawyer nudged me.

"No, you were right." I lowered my voice. "He is just another man in a long line of terrible men."

"Bet the sex was out of this world, though."

I scrunched down in my seat, hands over my face. "It was so good. But he's such an asshole."

"This is an improvement. Usually, you fall for shitty men who are terrible at sex."

"How big is his ding dong? This big?" Gran mimed with her hands.

A bottle was slammed onto the table along with three shot glasses.

"Um…" I said to the retreating waiter. "I don't think this is our order. We had the mistletoe martini. Okay, well, I guess we'll just drink this."

Gran popped the rubber cork off the bottle and sloshed out a round of shots. "To Dasher!" She lifted her glass.

I could use a drink after the night I'd had. I knocked it back, and flames shot down my throat. "I'm dying," I gasped out.

Sawyer was coughing, grabbing her chest. "I've been poisoned."

Gran smacked her lips and poured herself another shot. "I think it could be a little stronger. They water stuff down at these casinos."

A horn blared, tinny over the speakers.

"The race is starting, girls!" Gran stood up, excited, and moved to the dirty window.

At the end of the track, the gates sprang open.

I heard sleigh bells, then eight reindeer ridden by small men in red Santa jumpsuits tore down the racetrack.

"On Dasher!" Gran screamed as the reindeer galloped down the dirt track. "Go! Go! Go!"

Number Five was in the lead.

"I'm gonna win!" Gran grabbed Sawyer, jumping up and down. "I'm saved! It's a Christmas miracle."

But Number Five was losing gas. The reindeer took the final turn, and Dasher was fading, fading, his hoofed feet losing momentum.

"No!" Gran yelled, banging on the glass as Dasher came in third. "This is some bullshit."

I grabbed her arm. "I told you the house always wins."

"I want my money back."

"I don't think that's how it works."

"This is a scam!" Gran said loudly.

I looked around nervously.

The dangerous men were giving each other glances, all on the edge of their seats.

"I think you need to leave," a guy almost twice my diminutive grandmother's height informed us.

But Gran wasn't backing down. "You all are running an illegal operation here."

"*Gran, please.*"

"There's some money-laundering shit going on here or something. I just know it." She held up a finger. "I'm writing my congressman, and I'm posting on NextDoor about this. You can't be scamming people out of their money. Dasher was winning, and you all had him throw the race at the last dang minute."

"That's a dangerous accusation to make." The man reached over to my grandmother.

"Oh yeah? Well, accuse this!" She grabbed her enormous purse off the chair and swung it at the huge man.

It caught him in the hand with a sickening thud.

"Fuck!" He doubled over, clutching his hand and gritting his teeth against screams of pain. "What the fuck do you have in there, you stupid cunt?" He shoved Gran into the table, sending the bottle of alcohol sloshing. "Give me that."

"Keep your hands off my purse!"

"Help!" the gangster yelled as Gran pummeled him with her bag.

One of his meathead friends raced over, sleeves rolled up.

Snowball sprinted to the closest one, leaped up, and sank her sharp teeth into his crotch.

"Get it off!" He batted at the dog.

Sawyer jumped into the fray, empty liquor bottle swinging.

"Squash the little vermin!" Meathead yelled.

"Snowball! Leave my dog alone!"

Meathead's bigger, meaner brother braved the purse swings to lock Gran in a chokehold.

"Get off!" I jumped on his back, sinking my nails into the soft parts of his face.

He howled a curse, releasing Granny Doyle, but slammed me back against a table, knocking the wind out of me. Then he whirled on me, blood streaming down his face. Bringing my legs up, I kicked at him ineffectively. He grabbed my foot, twisting my ankle in my boot.

"Snowball," I tried to wheeze, my stomach still clenched.

Behind my attacker, Sawyer was whaling away at three huge goons rounding on her.

Meathead's brother yanked, dragging me off the table. I grabbed at it to keep from slamming my head on the floor, sending the table toppling into the chairs as I landed in a jumble on the floor.

"Shit!" I squeaked as his massive boot rose above me. I curled up into a ball, but the kick never came.

I opened my eyes in time to see the goon land with a scream in front of me, his knee bent in a direction it wasn't supposed to.

"You fucking—"

He didn't get to finish because a huge man picked him up by the shirt collar and belt and slammed him into a nearby table.

"Anderson?"

He spared me a brief gray-eyed glance then turned back to the pack of men rounding on us.

Snowball darted through the crush of angry men to snarl at Anderson's feet.

The men in front of us snickered.

"That your dog, Anderson?" they jeered.

They knew each other?

"Fucking puffball."

The odds were not in our favor. Gran was surrounded, and two guys had Sawyer by the arms.

But Evie Murphy goes down with the fucking sleigh, goddammit.

I scrambled to my feet, picking up a metal chair.

"We got this. Right, Anderson?"

"What the fuck? There is no we. Just get the fuck out of here. You and your family."

"I'm not leaving until you all give me my money back!" Gran reached into her purse.

"She's got a gun!" several men yelled.

"I don't have a gun!" Granny Doyle yelled, pulling out the dildo. "But I have a dick, and I will use it."

"What does she mean 'use it'?" the thickheaded goons all muttered.

I took the opening. Yelling a war cry, I hefted my chair and raced straight at the men who held Sawyer. I lived in New York City and constantly had to argue with people trying to scam me in the subway. I had no problem scrapping in the middle of the street.

"Dammit, Evie!" Anderson bellowed behind me.

"Get away from my cousin!" I hollered, smashing the chair into the nearest goon.

Snowball bit a chunk out of one hand that held Sawyer while I slammed the chair into the stomach of the second goon. He stumbled into a table, sending more alcohol spilling and causing more men to jump into the fight.

"I'm fucking done with you little bitches." One goon grabbed me in a bear hug.

I kicked my feet. He threw me into Sawyer, and we both went down, narrowly missing Snowball.

I tried to scramble up. One goon swung a punch at me. Then Anderson was there, taking the hit and giving the goon an uppercut that sent him crumpling to the ground.

It was a mob against one, and the goons all jumped on him. Snowball tried to bite where she could squeeze in. Her fur was speckled with little dots of blood.

"They're going to kill him!" I screamed as the goons whaled on Anderson.

Suddenly, a green-eyed man was flying in like a ninja, kicking one goon in the face, letting Anderson scramble up. Though he was Anderson's size, his hair was brown, not black.

The two men slid in the alcohol pooling on the floor as they fought the ever-growing mob.

Gran was still in the fight, at least, whaling away with the dildo, which was tied to the end of her purse strap.

Something red, white, and green sailed through the air right into the face of the goon twisting my arm. Blood spurted out of his nose.

"Thank you, Aunt Trish!" I picked up the dildo and hurled it. Of course, I was not an anime princess or good at sports.

"What the hell?" the green-eyed man yelled as the dildo sailed past him… and clipped Anderson in the cheek.

"Fuck!"

"Sorry!" I raced over, ducking under the legs of one of the goons.

Anderson's green-eyed friend easily dodged a punch then did some fancy judo move, and the goon was groaning on the ground.

I was shoved to the floor by the green-eyed man before a massive foot could break my ribs.

I grabbed the dildo and brought it down hard on the nearest goon's foot.

He howled, hopping up and down and clutching his leg.

"That's right. I don't need a man to protect me!" I hollered, waving the dildo around. "Come at me, bro!"

Anderson grabbed me, shoving me behind him, as the goons, making the universal sign for *I'm about to kick your ass*, rounded on us.

Anderson readied himself. "I'm going to hold them off. When I say run, you need to run, Gingersnap. You got that? Don't worry about your dog—just run."

"I can't abandon you. Yeah, you're an asshole, but I'm not going to just leave you here. We're in this together."

Anderson cracked his neck.

His friend didn't seem worried at all.

The goons advanced, one of them swinging a crowbar.

Anderson's friend calmly neatened his suit, then he reached into his pocket and pulled out something small, shiny, and pewter. He held it up, whistling sharply.

It took a second for me and the goons to get wise, but then it registered—it was a cigarette lighter.

I was suddenly very aware of just how much the room smelled like alcohol.

"Try me," Anderson's friend said softly.

The man directly in front of him was lying in the pool of spilled liquor. "Oh shit. Mr. Richmond," he whimpered. "Please, don't. Please. *Please*."

Anderson's friend slowly looked around the room at the apprehensive goons.

The ones holding Sawyer slowly let her go. She jerked away from them.

"Are you the owner?" Granny Doyle hustled up to Anderson's friend.

"I..." The brown-haired man seemed slightly confused.

Gran waved her ticket at him. "That race was rigged."

"That sounds serious." Mr. Richmond was solemn.

"Damn right. I lost ten grand."

Anderson blew out an annoyed breath.

"I took this out of your dad's safe, Evie. I was going to try to pay it back after I won my money, but these criminals stole it," Granny Doyle said out of the side of her mouth.

"And you said you were going to file a complaint to the government?" Mr. Richmond added.

"Damn right, I am!"

"Ma'am." The grizzled older man, who had not participated in the fight, stood up, buttoning his suit jacket. "I am very sorry you had a terrible experience at my racetrack." He gave Anderson's friend a pointed look.

Several men were dragging away the injured ones.

"You all need better customer service." Gran put her hands on her hips. "You're not going to get any patrons here if you keep rigging races."

"Of course. Now, since it is Christmas, after all, maybe we could just let bygones be bygones," the grizzled man offered.

"My silence can be bought," Gran declared.

The older man made an imperceptible hand movement. His henchman came over with a suitcase. He opened it, revealing stacks of cash.

"Gran, you can't come home with a suitcase full of money. Dad's going to have a fit."

"Perhaps just the ten thousand?" Anderson's friend murmured.

"I need thirty. Otherwise, there's gonna be lots of uncomfortable questions, like 'Where'd all your savings go?' and 'Do you have dementia?' They're already about to toss Evie onto the street, and I don't have a hot guy who'd be willing to trade casual sex for a place to sleep." She looked out over the still-standing goons. "I don't think any of you would be interested?"

They shifted apprehensively.

The man holding the briefcase counted out thirty grand.

"Pleasure doing business with you." Granny Doyle shoved the cash into her purse.

"My compliments." The grizzled racetrack owner handed her a full bottle of the toxic-smelling alcohol. "I've been dabbling in the art of distillery."

"You're on the right track, son. I can tell you have a nose for it." Granny Doyle patted him on the cheek like he was a little boy. "You gotta let it mature. Oak barrels—that's the ticket."

"Evie, let's get the fuck out of here." Anderson grabbed my arm, hauling me toward the front door, Snowball trotting after us, puffy white tail waving.

Mr. Richmond offered Granny Doyle his arm and Sawyer the other.

Anderson shoved me out the door, into the cold.

"Shots!" Granny Doyle whooped, passing the bottle around.

I took a swig and corked it.

"You should have gotten some cash too," Granny Doyle told me. "Then you wouldn't be homeless."

"Crap!" I turned back to the door. "Do you think they're still handing out free money?"

Anderson blocked me. "You are not going back in there."

"You could have just told me you were going to meet your hot, rich friend and already had plans!" I yelled, kicking snow at him. "I would have just left. It wasn't like I had a U-Haul parked outside your place. I can do a casual hookup like a normal person. You don't have to be such a dick." I poked him hard with the dildo.

His green-eyed friend raised an eyebrow. "Didn't your grandmother say you were homeless? You can't blame the poor man for being concerned."

"Aaron, shut up!" Anderson barked.

"Ooh, Aaron!" I jumped up, wrapping my arms around Mr. Richmond's neck, kissing his cheek noisily. "Thank you for fighting on the dream team!"

It wasn't lost on me that Anderson was looking pissy.

Aaron still had his arms around my waist, holding me up.

"Put her down," Anderson growled.

"He's nervous because he knows you're just my type," I stage-whispered to Aaron.

His perfect mouth parted slightly. "I'm your type?"

"Good-looking and rich? Sonny, you're every woman's type." Granny Doyle cackled.

"Don't try to deny it. I can tell a knockoff from a real Patek Phillip watch." I trailed my fingers along his wrist. "You're like St. Fucking Nick. You could make all my holiday dreams come true. Wave that credit card around, and *bam!* Nice house." I performed arm motions with my sound effects. "*Babam!* Presents under the tree. *Kerpaw!* New bra."

"Aaron doesn't want some broke gold digger." Anderson grabbed my arm to drag me away from his friend.

"I'm not after him for his money. He's got green eyes and red hair." I rubbed my hands together. "I have a fetish," I whispered to Anderson's friend and winked dramatically.

"I don't have red hair." Aaron scowled and touched his head then drew his hand back abruptly when he realized what he was doing.

Anderson pinched his fingers together. "You do a little bit, in the sun."

The door to the racetrack opened a crack, and a wary-looking man stuck his head out. "Mr. Richmond? The boss is on the phone for you."

"Back for round two?" I shouted after him. "Want another ass whoopin' from the dream team? We still have the dildo."

The goon scowled as I waved it around.

Anderson batted my hand down. "Gingersnap, shut the hell up. You run your mouth like you're six-fucking-five. You are going to get me killed."

Chapter 32

ANDERSON

"I see why you're out there hanging Christmas decorations for her," Aaron said, taking a swig from the bottle of homemade liquor that the enforcer had foisted on us after we'd had a call with his boss and assured him that Van de Berg Insurance wasn't going to be ratting out the Vesuvio Syndicate to the Feds and that the women had not been harmed.

"I can't even whack the dog?" one guy nursing a deep bite wound had complained.

His boss had slugged him in the face. "Any more of that, and I'm going to take that finger."

I grabbed the bottle from Aaron. "I told you it wasn't about Evie. It was the job, for you, for your money."

But Aaron didn't drop it. Instead, he seemed intrigued, which was a problem for me.

"Who the hell even dresses like that? She was wearing that skimpy costume, in a mob hangout no less, and then starts a fight she cannot possibly win," he mused as we crunched through the snow back to my place. "She's perfect chaos."

Of course Aaron would be enamored with Evie.

I took a long swig from the bottle.

"Don't tell me you're about to go through a rolling quarter-life crisis. All your uptight workaholic tendencies are coming back to bite you, and you want your own little manic pixie holiday dream-girl doll."

It was too much, too personal. I knew it as soon as the words left my mouth. Aaron and I weren't really friends—even though I was probably one of the few people he spent the most time dealing with on a regular basis that he wasn't related to, aside from Betty.

But I was too drunk to care, and I was prepared to fight just to keep him from going after Evie.

Aaron didn't seem pissed. His smirk widened to a smile. "I was right."

"Fuck you."

"I was right because I'm *always* right. You're fucking in love with her," he scoffed. "You think a nice girl like her wants a guy with a record?"

"Evie lives in an unconverted attic. She has low standards."

"No, she doesn't," Aaron preened. "She said I was just her type."

He laughed as I took a drunken swing at him, grabbing the bottle from me before it could spill.

"Fuck. You."

I leaned against the doorway, taking two tries to unlock it.

Aaron stumbled in behind me as I flicked on the lights.

"Oh, fuck me." Because that was just what this night needed.

Our doppelgangers were waiting for us.

Aaron's older brother Grayson was leaning against one of the heavy wooden worktables, while Hudson flipped through a folder with my files on Braeden and Evie.

"It's like neither of them has a girlfriend they're supposed to be spending time with." Aaron half fell onto the couch.

I snatched the folder away from my brother.

"Were you in a fight?" Hudson demanded.

"Who the fuck are you? You get into fights all the time." I whipped off my shirt, heading to the sink to start washing off the blood.

"Does he have more tattoos?" Grayson asked Hudson. "No wonder he doesn't have any money if he spends it all on body modifications."

Hudson went to the freezer, grabbed several ice packs, and tossed a couple to Grayson.

"Get away from me," Aaron warned his older brother as he approached him.

I pulled the rubber cork off the bottle of homemade liquor.

Hudson sniffed it. "I'm surprised you all can still walk if that's what you're drinking."

"Just let me—"

"Get *off* of me," Aaron complained as Grayson tried to clean up his face.

I took Hudson's offered ice pack and held it to my shoulder.

He pressed another to my face. I tried to tilt my face away, but he reached for my jaw. I raised a hand to him.

334 • Alina Jacobs

"Don't." He shook me. "I will kick the shit out of you, and you'll spend Christmas drinking Pedialyte out of a straw. Again. Jesus, you two are too fuckin' old to be out there getting in bar fights."

"It was the Vesuvio Syndicate's racetrack," Aaron drawled.

"Are these mob guys going to be a problem?" Grayson's tone said that he would make sure they weren't anymore.

"Leave them alone. I don't show up at Richmond Electric and slap the dicks out of your mouths. They're my cash cow." Aaron loosened his tie. "Sometimes I have to remind them I can fuck with more than their money."

Grayson's lips thinned.

"They're a hell of a lot better than the dog-pound people." That was aimed at me. "Because they don't try to fuck me around, and they pay their fucking bills." Aaron scowled.

"Sorry I'm not running around with a psychopath's DNA," I snapped, raising my hands. "You'd have put all those elderly animals on the street. I did that for your soul as much as mine."

"You put white trash in a suit, and it's still white trash." Aaron slapped away the ice pack.

"Aaron doesn't have a dog," Grayson said to me. "He doesn't understand."

"You coddle those Dalmatians." Aaron shoved his brother off as Grayson tried to put antiseptic on his bleeding knuckles, holding his hand away from Grayson.

"Switch," Grayson said to my brother.

Hudson watched him warily as he approached me.

Grayson pulled butterfly bandages out of the first aid kit and sprayed antiseptic on my face while my brother patched up Aaron.

"I'm surprised one of them got you in the eye like this," Grayson said conversationally as he taped the cut under my eye.

"We were up against like twenty violent killers."

Aaron glanced around Hudson, peering at my face. "That wasn't the mob guys. That was a little girl."

"You were fighting a girl?"

"It's the one he likes." Aaron snorted.

That earned me a look from Hudson.

"We were protecting her. It doesn't matter."

"Why are you lying to me?" my older brother demanded. "What are you hiding?"

Hudson and Grayson looked at me expectantly.

"It was an accident," Aaron, that fucker, piped up. "She hit him in the face with a dildo. Of course he's going to lie to you, Hudson. It's fucking embarrassing."

"It did that much damage?" Grayson peered at my face.

"It was reinforced. It's like a hunk of concrete." I mimed. "With rebar."

Hudson swore violently. "That's what went through my truck window, isn't it?"

Chapter 33

EVIE

"Who died?"

"From your mouth to God's typewriter, please, oh please, let Shirley keel over dead as a doornail but not in the punch bowl," Granny Doyle prayed.

"It's not that kind of a viewing party." I shoved Anderson.

He leaned in to kiss the back of my neck. There was still some bruising on his face.

"Is it the kind where your grandmother watches as all these dolls eat our souls?" Anderson remarked as we walked into Grandma Shirley's house.

"That's how you know there's something not right about her. She has all these creepy baby dolls," Granny Doyle whispered to him as she carted the tray of snacks. "The woman peaked when she was pregnant, and it's been downhill ever since. Always trying to relive her glory days and control her children. Not me," Granny Doyle declared loudly. "My best days are ahead of me."

Grandma Shirley was in the living room. "Evie, good, you brought your brute with you. I need the TV set up. I bought a new one. The FedEx delivery boy didn't put it together, said it wasn't allowed."

Granny Doyle used her hand to mock Shirley as she complained.

"Honestly, in my day, men were helpful. You asked them to do something, and they'd do it. You know, my husband never made me pump my own gas."

"Yeah, but he did make you responsible for your own orgasms," Granny Doyle retorted.

"Do not say that word in this house!"

"Orgasm, orgasm, orgasm!" Granny Doyle shouted as Grandma Shirley fled the room.

Snowball pranced next to Anderson as he flipped open a switchblade to unbox the TV.

He frowned down at the dog. "Why is she glowing?"

Snowball's white fur was extra white—like fresh snow on a sunny morning.

"I had to dip her in OxiClean to get the stains out of her fur. You know, from the big fight."

He sighed and shook his head. "I'm not going out with you anymore."

I danced around him. "But we won!"

He grabbed me around the waist, pulled me to him, and growled against my mouth, "You'd have been killed if I wasn't there."

"I could have held my own. Besides, your hot friend Aaron was the one who really saved the day."

"Stay the hell away from Aaron." He released me with the warning.

"Aww, but I was going to ask you for his number, you know, since you're not boyfriend material and all." Laughing, I went into the kitchen to prep the rest of the food for the viewing party.

Grandma Shirley had a huge house, bigger than my parents', and lived all alone. She liked to relive her glory days, as she called it, hence hosting the viewing party for the triplets' Brooke Taylor appearance.

It was also why she insisted on serving individual cream-cheese-and-strawberry-Jell-O salads molded into the shape of a star.

"Did you sneak out and do the nasty with him last night? You know, give him a reward for the fight?" Sawyer joked as she and Ian came into the kitchen.

"Shh! Grandma Shirley will hear you. And no."

"Then why is he in your grandmother's house, putting together her TV?" Sawyer rolled up her sleeves and started stirring the strawberry Jell-O with the softened cream cheese.

"Evie's giving Anderson a blue-balls Christmas."

There was a string of curses from the living room. Snowball barked.

"I don't need sex to get him to like me, because I don't need him to like me. I am responsible for my own emotional happiness." I handed Ian the cream cannoli filling I'd made last night to try to keep myself from running back to Anderson's. Instead, I'd listened to a self-help podcast and made five hundred cannoli shells.

"I need that matchmaking service you were telling me about," I said abruptly as Ian and Sawyer were arguing over whether mini chocolate chips or shaved chocolate was better on the cannoli.

"Wait. You're seriously giving up on Anderson?" Sawyer asked.

"No, I need you to parade him around next Christmas," Ian begged. "I live for St. Henry's annoyance."

"He's not the one. I need to get serious about finding a man," I said firmly.

"I already told you last night, you're never going to find anyone to erase me from you."

I jumped, sending the molds I was setting out scattering. "Don't sneak up on people."

Anderson leaned in and kissed me. "Stop lying to yourself. You'll never get over me. You can't help it. I ruined you for other men." He grabbed my ass, briefly squeezing it while Sawyer and Ian gasped.

"I need the Wi-Fi password to finish setting up the TV, Gingersnap."

"I have it on my phone." I followed him back into the living room, where Grandma Shirley and Granny Doyle were fighting over the remote while Snowball strutted around, barking.

"I am the hostess!" Grandma Shirley was yelling. "And this is my TV!"

"You don't know what you're doing. You think electric typewriters are too newfangled. I've got a secret OnlyFans account, and I'm all over TikTok."

"Gran, just give Anderson the remote."

Still sniping at each other, my grandmothers left the room.

Anderson quickly finished setting up the new smart TV. The biggest I'd ever seen, it took up practically one wall of the living room. He turned it on to the channel that was running reruns of Brooke Taylor's talk show.

I reached down and picked up a chair to start moving the furniture for a better viewing experience.

"I know you're not still trying to convince me that you could have won that fight."

"I had an ace up my sleeve," I told him as he reached over to pluck the chair from me with one hand then grabbed its twin with the other.

"Unless you had a machine gun under your skirt, which I doubt because it was so tight I could practically see your cunt, you weren't making it out of there."

"I would have just flashed them." I pointed at where I wanted the chair to go. "And that would have stopped them cold."

"You cannot be trusted in public."

"Or private," I added, removing the vases and other knickknacks from one of the long tables that would be used to hold food.

His arms circled me from behind. "Oh, I know you can't be trusted in private." His hands came up under my skirt, sliding under my panties.

"Do you want these table cloths on the—oh damn!" Sawyer said. "You really are trying to get on Grandma Shirley's naughty list."

"We're not doing anything." I slapped at Anderson.

He just smirked. "If I wanted it, you'd star in a Christmas porno right here on your grandmother's living room floor."

"Might as well go for it. We all know Grandma Shirley has cut you out of the will," Ian joked, coming in with a box of mothball-smelling table decorations.

Anderson scowled slightly and opened a window as Ian helped me clear the rest of the tables.

"Is this an annual occurrence?" Anderson asked, finishing the furniture rearranging.

"Usually, it's just a movie night, *Miracle on 34th Street.* Mandatory holiday fun."

"Is there drinking?"

"Not officially."

"Sounds festive." He picked up one of the boxes I'd filled with all the travel knickknacks, stacked it with two more, and easily picked them up.

I grabbed another. "We can put these upstairs." I led the way up the wide, dark-stained wood staircase.

Anderson whistled long and low as we walked into my dad's room.

"Did your father have a twin who died or something? Why did your grandmother build a shrine?"

Nothing had changed in my dad's childhood bedroom since he'd moved out for college in the early eighties.

"My grandmother does not like change." I set the box on the desk, which held an Atari. "Also, I think she's secretly hoping he'll divorce my mom and move back home."

"And I thought my family was fucked up." He set the boxes down with a thump on the desk then grabbed the back of his gray T-shirt, pulling it over his head, and cast it onto the back of the desk chair.

"I hope you don't think I came all the way over here with you and put up with your Christmas-decorating bullshit just because I like you." His nose brushed mine.

"I hope you don't think I actually invited you because I wanted you to fuck me."

He nipped my bottom lip. "You do want me to fuck you, don't you, Gingersnap?" He gave me a quick, hard kiss. "You were begging for my cock last night. You would have let me tie you up to the standpipe and leave you there till your hands were numb, your thighs wet. I could fuck your pussy wherever I felt like it. You're a little slut for my cum."

"I hope your cock is as big as your ego, or I'm going to be pretty disappointed."

His hands were on my skirt, pulling at the zipper, tugging the skirt down until it pooled on the floor.

I slipped off my flats to stand barefoot in front of him.

He kissed me hungrily, his fingers hooked into the string of the thong I wore.

I whimpered as he pulled it, the fabric sliding in my wet slit.

"You do want me in your pussy," he whispered against my mouth. "You wouldn't have worn this if you weren't hoping I'd see."

I pulled off my knitted sweater crop top. He reached behind me and pressed hot kisses along my neck and collarbone as he unhooked my bra, letting my tits hang free.

He mouthed them, sucking and teasing as his hands were rough and unyielding over my body, kneading my ass, insistent between my legs.

He pushed me backward. My calves hit the bed, then I sank onto the mattress, legs spread, pussy aching.

Nuzzling the fabric, he slid the panties off, then he grabbed my hips, pulling me forward to the edge of the bed.

"Spread them wide. That's what I want to see." His gray eyes were dark slits. Large hands slid up my thighs, up, up, forcing my legs apart.

My pussy was dripping all over the blue bedspread.

His thumbs dipped into my pussy, spreading my pussy lips to reveal the dark-pink flesh.

My head tipped back, and I leaned on my arms. I was practically gushing thinking about how good he would feel. "Yeah, I want that huge cock in me. Put it in me, bad boy. I want you to fuck me raw."

He didn't unzip his pants. Instead, he leaned in, kissed my navel, and slid his tongue down, down…

I kicked my legs. "Whoa, don't you think that's a little, uh…"

His head rose. "What? Don't tell me you, the girl who was about to flash a room full of dangerous gangsters, who shows up in the middle of the night at the office of the man who almost murdered her brother, and who slept with her cousin's boyfriend, has hang-ups about getting her pussy eaten."

"I-I just—" I stammered.

"Just what?"

"I mean, guys don't really do that."

"'Guys' who? What straight American male doesn't want to eat pussy, especially one as tight as yours?"

"None of the guys I've been with have. You know, it's a mutual thing. I don't really want a man that close."

He made a disgusted noise.

"I just think it's weird!" I protested.

He ignored me. His tongue flicked out, and I practically came right there.

"I think I'd just rather have normal sex." My voice sounded like I'd been huffing helium.

His tongue darted out again, giving me another long lick.

"Kris Kringle on a freakin' shingle."

Then his full mouth was on my pussy. My hips rolled, and I gasped in shock when his tongue curled on my clit.

My hips ached. My pussy wanted nothing more than to come on his face.

"Oh my god, you're gonna to make me come."

His tongue trailed another long lick on my pussy. It was wrong and good and was like nothing I'd ever felt before.

"You're gonna make me come just like this. Freaking—"

"Where, Gingersnap?"

"I want to come on your face—*fuck, Anderson.*"

Then he went down on me for real. His mouth felt ten thousand times better than any cock I'd ever had. My head lolled back, and my elbows trembled as I drowned in him while he licked me, his tongue sweeping down my pussy to lap at my opening then back up to suck my clit.

His head tipped up.

"Why are you stopping?" I moaned.

"Let me hear you. I want to hear how good it is to have your pussy eaten." He nuzzled my breast, sucking on one nipple, tongue swirling around it. "I know you're a greedy little slut. Let me hear it."

I let out a long loud moan as he sank down onto my pussy again. His teeth scraped my clit.

"I want to come on your face!" I cried out. "I want to gush all over your mouth, then I want you to bend me over and bury your cock in me."

His tongue still on my clit, he slid two fingers into my opening, curling them as his tongue made long, slow licks along my slit.

My arms gave out, and I half collapsed onto the pillows.

He added another finger while he lapped at my pussy, drawing snowflake patterns on my throbbing cunt, my juices smearing all over his face.

There was motion outside the partially shut door.

"Make me come like this. I want to come all over you," I whimpered as his fingers pumped in me.

"You sick little—" The door opened to a furious Braeden.

"Shit!" I tried to sit up, tried to pull Anderson off me.

Anderson looked up. He made eye contact with Braeden.

"He just wants to watch," Anderson drawled. "He's never actually seen a woman get her pussy eaten before. Certainly not by him."

"Wait, um—"

I tried to reach for something to cover myself with, but then I couldn't think because Anderson dipped his head back to my cunt, licking me into a frenzy.

"You're fucking disgusting, Evie!" Braeden raged.

"Yeah, you are, Evie," Anderson's deep voice purred. "You're my goddam little porn star."

I couldn't stop the moan that escaped. Couldn't miss the twitch of anger in Braeden's face.

"Your ex misses your tits."

His tongue trailed down to where I longed to have his cock.

"Too bad they're mine now."

My nailed scraped his scalp as his tongue curled on my clit.

"Tell Braeden how much you like me in your pussy."

Braeden's nostrils were flared. I recognized the lust on his face.

"She's putting on a nice little show for you."

I gasped back arching as Anderson slid two fingers in my pussy.

"God Anderson you're such a piece of shit." I whimpered.

Braden made a noise of disgust.

"Don't look at him. Look at me," Anderson ordered, voice slightly muffled between my legs.

"Henry! Come get your fucking sister!" Footsteps raced down the stairs.

His tongue was on my clit now, working it.

My fingers grabbed at his hair, holding him to me as my hips ground against his fingers then surged up, needing to feel him.

I sounded like a porn star as his fingers pumped into me, finger fucking me as he worked my clit, his mouth all over my pussy.

I touched my tits, pinching my nipples, giving in to the sensation of his mouth on my cunt licking me into a frenzy, taking me higher and higher.

My body tightened, then I was coming suddenly, crying out his name as Anderson milked the orgasm with his fingers and tongue.

He leaned in to kiss me, making me taste myself on him.

Footsteps were racing up the stairs.

"You taste so fucking good, and if we weren't about to face the firing squad, I'd go down on you again and see how many times I could get you to come." He squeezed my ass.

I grabbed my skirt and top and threw them on, not bothering with the underwear, tugging my sweater in place just as the door burst open.

"They were having sex right there. You need to get rid of her, Melissa," Braeden complained as my father looked at my rumpled clothes and the wet spot on the bedspread.

I kicked my bra and panties under the bed.

Anderson was unapologetic, wiping at his face like a cat cleaning his whiskers of cream. "You missed the big finale," he drawled to Braeden. "You should have stayed and watched. I bet you've never seen Evie come before."

"Of course I—"

Anderson's eyes lit up with dark glee.

"O-Of course I haven't." Braeden stammered. "Evie's an exhibitionist. She's sex obsessed. She's doing this to ruin Christmas."

"Evie's been here all afternoon!" Granny Doyle hollered, holding a barking, snarling Snowball in front of her like a flamethrower. "Decorating for someone else's party. Braeden's a peeping Tom."

"You see?" Sawyer insisted. "We told you all last Christmas they were together. Braeden is the one obsessed with her."

Anderson's gaze was flicking back and forth between my family members and Braeden.

I held my breath. Was this it? Was it all about to be over?

"Why else would he be so bent out of shape by Evie getting her jolly holiday on if he wasn't jealous that Anderson was fucking his ex?" Ian argued.

"Don't you dare spread lies about my fiancé!" Felicity grabbed Braeden's hand.

"If I'd offered," Anderson said, "if I'd flipped her over and told him to take what he wanted, he'd have dropped his boxers and fucked her." His deathly gray eyes bored into Braeden.

His hand at my waist slid up to cup my still-bare breast under the cropped sweater. Anderson pressed a little kiss to my forehead. "Check his pants. I bet he's hard after watching Evie's little porn display."

"We will do no such thing," Grandma Shirley said.

Granny Doyle rolled up her sleeve and reached out to grab Braeden's crotch.

My ex cursed, and Grandma Shirley almost fainted.

"I think it's a little bit hard, but I can't tell. He's so small."

Ian and Sawyer doubled over laughing.

"You sure you want to go to bat for a man who doesn't eat pussy?" Anderson asked Felicity.

"Think long and hard on that," Granny Doyle said sagely, petting a still-growling Snowball.

"With that weak jaw, not sure he could actually go down on a woman." Sawyer sniffed.

"This is so juvenile," my mother snapped. "Clean yourself up at once, Evie. Stop instigating orgies in your grandmother's house."

"Probably the most excitement this poor old house has ever seen." Granny Doyle cackled.

I hesitated.

"Evie," My mother warned me.

My underwear and bra were still in the room.

I saw Braeden's eyes flick to the bit of fabric sticking out from under the bed.

"What are you waiting for?" My mother turned on Anderson.

"I was actually going to fuck your daughter, ma'am."

Chapter 34

ANDERSON

thudded downstairs under the angry gaze of Evie's parents.

What I'd told her mother wasn't wrong. I did want to fuck Evie. More than anything. More than was healthy.

I parked on the bottom step. Evie ran into me. I grabbed her jaw, kissing her, making her taste the lingering scent of herself on me.

"I'm out of here."

"Same," Granny Doyle declared. "Let's hit a bar." She fist-bumped me.

"Finally, a Christmas miracle," Sawyer said. "I'll pay first round at North Pole Nibbles."

"Let's get out of here." Ian was motioning with his head to the door.

"You're all leaving?" Evie's mother was appalled.

"Well," Evie said, "if Anderson's leaving, then…" She shrugged.

"She's hoping that I'll fuck her after we get drinks."

"You cockblocked your own daughter. What ever happened to the girl code? I thought I raised girls' girls!" Granny Doyle raged.

"Anderson's not staying? He has to." Grandma Shirley pitched a fit, coming into the foyer. "I didn't reserve any of the waiters from the country club. Someone has to manage the food. I can't be in the kitchen all evening."

"Might make the party better for everyone if you were," Granny Doyle muttered.

"But he—"

Dr. Murphy silently shook his head at Evie's mother.

No one wanted to deal with setting off Grandma Shirley.

"Evie, comb your brute's hair and make him presentable. I have the ladies from the junior league coming. They are quite the fans of Brooke Taylor's talk show. Fetch one of your grandfather's ties for Anderson. I must show them that I, of course, know how to entertain. Ian—" She clapped her hands. "You're a minimum-wage disappointment. You'll be working the bar."

"You can hook your old granny Doyle up, right?" Gran elbowed Evie's brother.

"Sawyer, you're not pretty enough to have a public-facing role. You can be with Evie in the kitchen. Anderson, we must find you a white shirt." Grandma Shirley handed out assignments.

The front door opened, bringing in a gust of winter wind and several guests.

"My grandbaby!"

Declan's wife winced as her mother-in-law swooped in. "She's asleep," she warned her.

"Oh, but she wants to wake up to see Grandma."

The baby cried.

Declan's wife gave her husband a pointed look as they followed Melissa into the living room, where the viewing party was kicking off.

Evie looked longingly upstairs.

"Evie, do not ruin this night for your grandmother or the triplets," her father warned her under his breath as he passed her.

I nuzzled her neck as she squeezed past me.

"Just sneak out the side door," she whispered to me.

I grabbed the back of her neck and kissed her.

"Pass. I like thinking about you walking around in the kitchen, tits out, pussy dripping, just waiting for my cock."

"He doesn't look like a murderer."

Shirley's elderly friends crowded around me as the Brooke Taylor slash Murphy triplet holiday extravaganza played on a loop on the new TV.

"He's hot!" One old woman grabbed one of my biceps, squeezing appreciatively.

I grunted as another pinched below the belt.

Extricating myself, I said smoothly, "Your friend Shirley will fire me if I let the hors d'oeuvres run out."

I pushed through the crush of Murphys. I'd hoped that I'd glean something useful, something to cover the last eighty-seven grand to clear off the ledger.

The clock was ticking. All my chips were on the Bergeson Real Estate account. My brothers were running analysis on the data from Preston. If Braeden had messaged him about Evie, there might be something on the Bergeson account too.

I just needed a hit, one hit, then I was free. Off to Idaho, sure, but free-ish.

Evie was in the kitchen, the snowman apron she wore giving her tits some support.

If I were her real boyfriend, I'd sneak back upstairs to rescue her bra and panties. But her mother was guarding the stairs in between chatting with her relatives.

And I didn't care about Evie that much, right? It was just animalistic sexual attraction.

Evie scooted freshly cooked hors d'oeuvres onto a platter.

"I got it." Sawyer picked up the tray. "I need to see if Ian can sneak us some drinks."

"We're out of napkins," I told Evie, grabbing a handful from the stack by the sink. "I think some of the old ladies are stuffing them into their purses."

"We need the special Christmas ones," she said as I followed her into the pantry.

She reached up for the napkins, her cropped sweater riding up.

She's not wearing any panties under that skirt.

Evie squeaked when I grabbed her wrists.

"You don't know what you're doing to me," I whispered, kissing her neck, my hand against her throat, tilting her head back. "Watching you walk around, knowing I can just slip my hand under your skirt and run my fingers in your pussy." My hands slid up her warm thighs. I hissed as they made contact with the hot slit. "Fuck, Evie."

She whimpered as I stroked her pussy, which was aching and dripping and craving my cock.

I knew I shouldn't, but I unzipped my pants.

"Let me see," she whimpered softly. "I need to see your cock."

"Feel it," I breathed, rubbing the head of my cock in her hot cunt. "You feel that?"

Another whimper.

I squeezed her breast, which was braless and huge under the thick cropped sweater.

It would feel so perfect, so right, to spread her legs a little further, thrust into her, and let everyone in the party hear her scream as I took her cunt.

She ground her pussy back against my cock, making me curse. I let her squeeze her pussy lips around my dick, swallowing a curse and the desire for her.

My phone rang, stopping me from doing something I'd regret later.

"Yeah?" I answered it, zipping up while Evie hastily fixed her clothes.

Jake sounded excited. "Looks like we're getting hits on Preston's data. You gotta get in here."

"You're leaving?" Evie asked.

"I am still trying to nail Brandon to a yule log." I leaned in and kissed her to cover the easy lie.

"The audio. You were able to fix it?" Her face lit up. "We almost got him!"

I felt like shit.

She was counting on me, and I was just going to what? Fuck her over?

I knew how that felt.

"Getting there." I went to the fridge and swiped one of the Christmas cakes on the shelf.

I almost dropped the cake when Evie wrapped her arms around me, kissing me as if I was just home from war on Christmas morning.

"I—" She hesitated, her eyes shining. "Thank you. You really are my hero."

I felt like shit when I opened the door to the field office, stamping off the snow, then headed into the warm garage.

"Ooh, and he brought cake."

"There's an audio file on the server. You only get this if you can clean it up for me," I warned Jake.

I opened the box to show him the cake.

Jake rubbed his hands together.

"Done. Now, look at this shit." My brother swung a chair around for me and faced the large monitors.

"We managed to recover some deleted files on Preston's hard drive. Braeden is bragging to Preston in this text chain." Jake pointed at a message highlighted in green. "A lot of the context is corrupted, but Braeden mentions someone named Bee. She comes up a lot, and he sent Preston an attachment that we weren't able to recover. But I bet it's incriminating." Jake was excited. "We've been trying to find someone named Bee. We checked all the Bergeson company databases and the Venetian Shades company databases where Braeden works. There's four hundred twenty women with a name that starts with the letter *B*."

"*B, B...*" I paced around the office, racking my brain and parsing past conversations with Evie and her relatives.

What about Aunt Bianca, who didn't like Aunt Trish and had made snide comments about her lack of children and a husband?

"Check Bianca Murphy."

Jake pulled up her Facebook page. "Boom. Works at Bergeson Real Estate. And she's having a Christmas party tomorrow. One last Christmas party."

And one more chance to have Evie before I never saw her again.

Chapter 35

EVIE

"It's beginning to look a lot like Christmas revenge!" I sang.

In less than a week, I was going to stand up in front of my family and set all of Braeden's lies on fire. I'd be welcomed back into the family, be in the middle of the Christmas photos, the first to open presents.

And it was all because of him.

Anderson kicked the snow off his boots and unzipped his jacket as he stepped into the warm kitchen.

Sawyer wouldn't approve, but I couldn't help but throw my arms around him and kiss him passionately. "You came back!"

His face softened briefly, and he nuzzled the side of my hair.

"You have your aunt Bianca's party tonight." He set his helmet on the table. "Figured I owed you for bailing."

I squeezed my arms around his waist. "You were doing important work." I lowered my voice, saying, "How does it sound? Can I hear it? I almost don't believe it."

"There's one more piece of evidence we need. You heard your family yesterday," he warned me. "Braeden's not going to go down easy. We need to drown them in evidence. Once people have preconceived notions in their head about who they think someone is, they'd rather believe the lie than the truth. We have to build the case."

I ran to the fridge to get him a beer.

"We got a lead off that data we copied from Preston," he said then took a sip. "Your aunt Bianca might have what we need."

"Why would she—"

He held a finger to his lips.

"I don't know, but we can't afford to ignore any clues. We don't have the time, and the stakes are too high."

"Thank god you're here." Uncle Jaime urged us inside. "Your cousins all scattered, freaking little traitors. She's been up my ass all day about the decorations. Like, woman, it's just a poker game—beer, chips, Velveeta cheese dip, those meatball things in the Crock-Pot."

Anderson held up my oversize Crock-Pot.

"God bless you, Evie. Are they ready?" My uncle hugged me.

"You can have one," I promised.

He followed us into the kitchen, where Aunt Bianca had trays of party snacks ready. Anderson set the Crock-Pot on the counter and plugged it in.

Uncle Jaime grabbed a small ramekin out of the cabinet and practically bounced like a little kid as I dished him up a few meatballs.

"So good," he mumbled as he spooned one into his mouth. "And you made the cheese dip."

"It's not a traditional Christmas dish, but it does have Rotel tomatoes, sausage, and green peppers in it, so they're holiday colors."

Uncle Jaime scooped a tortilla chip into the dip.

"Don't care. Haven't eaten all day." He closed his eyes happily. "Sausage and cheese. Don't make my mistake," he warned Anderson, "and go for the girl you think everyone's going to be impressed by. It wears off fast. Find someone who cooks you a big greasy breakfast and doesn't scream at you the morning of your own holiday party. Stick with Evie. She knows how to make the meatballs." He grabbed a newspaper. "If anyone asks, I'm on the toilet."

"Evie, you're here!" Aunt Bianca floated into the kitchen from the dining room entry. "Have you seen my husband or my children?"

She had been one of the last daughters-in-law to marry into the Murphy clan but was determined to be the best.

Even Grandma Shirley would admit when she'd had a bit too much to drink that even she found Aunt Bianca's desire for tradition to be a bit much.

My aunt looked up at Anderson looming behind me. "You brought your 'brute,' as Shirley would say." She giggled, covering her mouth. "Sorry. Shouldn't have said that."

"Don't be. She just likes to call me that in bed," Anderson purred.

"My word." Aunt Bianca fanned her cleavage, prominent in her 1950s dress. "I'm going to go freshen up, then we can set up for the party."

"Where is her home office?" Anderson asked quietly as we set out the card tables in the living room.

I pointed up above us. "It's right off the master."

His mouth was a thin line. "We'll have to wait until the party is starting."

The holiday poker evening was a big deal in the Murphy clan. Uncle Jaime had hosted it ever since he'd sold his startup and bought a huge house down the street from his older brother.

"This is the bougiest fucking poker evening I've ever been to," another uncle complained.

"They just keep getting more elaborate every year." His cousin shook his head.

"Shh!" Uncle Jaime said. "I can barely take a shit in peace as it is."

"Are those tablecloths on a poker table?" His brother scowled.

"Merry Christmas!" Aunt Bianca trilled, greeting the arriving guests.

Sawyer and Ian slumped in behind their respective parental units.

Henry was immediately surrounded by a swarm of my uncles.

"I don't want him starting off at my table. I'm going to lose."

"You can't eat all of the meatballs," my dad said as his brothers jostled for food.

Anderson stood quietly in the corner of the room, waiting and watching.

"I cannot believe you willingly came over here." Ian unwound the scarf from his neck and hugged me.

"I could say the same about you."

"Ian's licking his wounds," Sawyer remarked.

"Still no lead role?"

"As if I'm going to sit there like a wallflower, waiting for my chance to be an understudy. I told him he could shove his promises into the crawl space with the rest of the waterlogged decorations."

"We'll be out of here soon, and you can go wallow," Sawyer said soothingly.

"I'm not wallowing. I'm plotting Winston's demise."

"I want to max out my credit card at Nutcracker Nibbles," Sawyer said. "They have scallop crudité."

"Can't. I'm here on a spy mission," I whispered to her. I grimaced and looked back at Anderson.

He still had that laser-focused look on his face.

"How much money is in the pot?" Granny Doyle took a wad of cash out of her purse.

"Mom!" Melissa raced after her. "Bianca, are you really allowing gambling?"

My dad's brothers erupted in protest.

"We always play for money."

"What the hell is this?"

"I'm hosting next year if you all keep trying to ruin Christmas poker night."

"Let's do strip poker!" Granny Doyle hooted, which set off the family.

364 • Alina Jacobs

Anderson gave me a pointed look, then those gray eyes flicked to the kitchen.

Looking around furtively, I followed him up the back servants' staircase to the second floor.

Somehow, even though Anderson was, like, three times my size, he was still moving more quietly than I was.

Unfortunately, Bianca's home office was right above the living room and in full view from the foyer for anyone who looked up to admire the ornate chandelier. Anderson pressed his back against the wall, keeping to the shadows of the hallway that led to the bedrooms.

The front door opened, and Felicity and Braeden arrived with Aunt Lisa.

"Merry Christmas!" People exchanged hearty greetings. "You buying into the pot?"

The voices faded away.

Anderson held a hand by his waist, palm down. Without looking at me, he motioned and slid against the wall while I followed less gracefully.

The doorbell rang.

Anderson clapped a hand to my mouth, stifling my shriek, and dragged me into Aunt Bianca's home office then shut the door softly right as more guests entered the foyer.

"I don't see how you can do this as a full-time job," I whispered, bending over and feeling lightheaded as Anderson took careful steps to the laptop on the desk.

He opened it. "Pin," he muttered, looking around on the desk, then started opening drawers.

"There." I pointed at a pink Post-it with passwords written on it.

He typed in the date of Aunt Bianca's wedding year.

"In." He plugged in a hard drive and set the entire contents of the laptop to copy over to it. "Twenty-seven minutes."

Antsy, I crossed my arms, rocking on the balls of my feet.

"Stop that," Anderson hissed.

"The poker game is starting soon. People will be looking for us. Maybe I should go down there so they don't get suspicious."

"Gingersnap." He grabbed the back of my neck, kissing me. "Shut the hell up." He pulled his T-shirt over his head then kissed me again. "You're not going anywhere. You're my cover story."

"I'm your what?"

He took my hand, pushing it against the bulge in his pants. "If anyone asks, you're here to swallow my cum."

His head bent down to claim my mouth again. "You like the thought of that, don't you?" The kiss deepened. His tongue tangled with mine. "Do you want to swallow it, or do you just want it all over you face and tits? I know where I want it." He kissed my neck, nipping my earlobe. "I want it leaking out of your ass."

I swallowed a moan. I wasn't doing *that* with Anderson while my family was downstairs.

He reached over, tugging at my blouse slightly as he undid the top button. His tattooed fingers were warm as they brushed against my skin.

"You have the nicest fucking tits I've ever seen." He cupped my breasts under my bra, squeezing gently, then he turned back to the laptop.

I reached for the buttons.

"Leave it undone," Anderson ordered in a low tone, eyes not leaving the screen. "We need to be prepared in case someone comes."

Standing there in my aunt's home office, I tried to be as cool as possible and not drool over Anderson's expanse of tattooed, muscled chest.

He turned around, crossed his arms, and leaned back against the edge of the desk. "Twenty-three minutes." He jerked his chin. "Take off your skirt."

It puddled at my feet.

"Are you going to fuck me now?" I slid my palms up his ripped black jeans.

"Only if I have to." He hooked a finger under the waistband of my panties and let it snap back against my skin.

I slipped my bra off but kept the sheer blouse on, draped over my breasts, alluringly, I hoped.

"This is just for show, Evie. I'm not doing this with you in your aunt's house. I'm working." Those gray eyes remained cold.

I wanted to see him lose control. Feel the same addictive pleasure mixed with shame of not being able to control your desires.

I leaned in, just a thin layer of air between us.

My tongue flicked out.

He grabbed my jaw before I could run my tongue down the ridges of muscle. "Don't touch me." He shoved me off.

"So you get to fuck with me however you want, but you can't take it when someone does it to you? How disappointing."

"I know what you're doing." He hands dropped to clench the edge of the desk, the lines of his body dangerously taut. "You live in your dad's house, and you don't even have a driver's license," he sneered. "You're not impressive enough to pull that independent sex goddess shtick."

I was done with men like him. As soon as I blew up Braeden's life like he'd blown up mine, I was joining a feminist commune.

I ran my fingers over my tits, kneading them, playing with them, and rolling the nipples between my fingers. Pushing one up and bending my head down, I ran my tongue over the nipple.

His mouth parted as I sucked my nipple, then his jaw clenched.

"Nice trick, Gingersnap." His tone was dismissive, but his eyes were those of a starving man.

My fingers trailed down, down to my panties. My head tipped back. "So good," I breathed as my hand slipped below the thin band of lace.

A scowl settled on his chiseled features, but his eyes didn't leave me, tracking the hand that moved under the sheer lace.

"You have me so wet," I groaned as I stroked my pussy, fingers sliding into the hot wet slit. "Is the bad boy hard enough to fuck me the way I want to be fucked?" I pulled my hand out of my panties. "Taste it." My fingers slid over the slash of his mouth.

He grabbed my wrist as I tried to force my fingers between his lips, clenching it so tight I thought he'd break it. "Don't fuck with me, Evie." His deep voice lowered an octave.

"Or what?" I trailed my nails down his chest. Taunting a polar bear would be safer.

His head cocked, and he stilled. Then I heard a sound outside in the hall too.

Someone was coming.

"On your knees," Anderson ordered. He grabbed my head, forcing me down in front of him.

The edge of the carpet dug into my knees.

He undid his belt with one hand, the other hand half closing the laptop lid. He wasn't even fully erect, and it was already the biggest cock I'd ever seen in my life.

"You ever sucked dick, or are you scared of that too?" he crooned as my head pushed back against his hand.

"I don't know if I—"

"Do it now, or I'll choke you with it." There was a threat laced in the words.

The footsteps grew louder.

Circumcised was all I registered before I had that throbbing cock in my mouth.

"That's right, Evie Murphy." His voice sounded strained as his hips thrust that thick, huge cock into my mouth.

Before I could gag, he tugged my hair, pulling me off of him. Then his hips snapped again, forcing that huge length down my throat so hard I saw snowflakes.

"Take it. Choke on my cock. I want my cum dripping out of your mouth, all over your tits."

The door opened. I screamed against the cock in my mouth.

The hand in my hair held me in place as I gagged. Anderson turned his head slowly, his cock in my mouth somehow growing even bigger.

"My word!" Aunt Bianca said breathlessly as I panted through my nose.

"Sorry," Anderson said, though he did not sound sorry. He slowly pulled me off of him. His cock came out of my mouth with a pop as I gasped for breath.

"Oh!" My aunt's hands fluttered, and she took a good, long look at Anderson's erect cock. "Oh my, you are having a merry Christmas indeed." She hiccupped and took a long drink of her wine, eyes still on his cock. "I don't want you to miss the poker game, Anderson, so I'll just delay us a little bit since you look like a man who can last." She licked her lips.

The door slammed.

"That was close." I stood up—or tried to.

His large hands fisted in my hair. "I'm not done, Gingersnap. Open your pretty little mouth and finish sucking my cock."

I licked my lips and leaned forward.

"Shit." He cursed as my tongue flicked out against the head of his cock. "I really want to fuck your tight little cunt." His deep voice sent thrills of desire through me.

I put my lips around the head of his cock, just sucking the tip.

"I thought I told you to stop fucking with me."

Then he buried the full length in my mouth, making me groan. My jaw ached as he fucked my mouth. My pussy dripped as I thought about him fucking my cunt like that.

"I don't know why your family hates you so much," he crooned. "You're a good little girl, taking my cock like this."

I wanted to beg him, wanted to plead with him to fuck me, give me relief.

I pulled my head back, wondering for a split second if he'd let me. His grip on my hair loosened, and I slipped off his cock.

"Can't take it?"

I was satisfied that his breathing was as ragged as mine. "I need you in my pussy."

Hand tangled in my hair, he pulled me upright. But instead of giving me his cock, he tipped me forward.

His fingers dug into my pussy, stroking my slit.

"I want you in my pussy," I begged.

Fingers tangled in my hair, he guided me back to his cock.

"Keep going."

I moaned around his cock as those thick fingers plunged into my pussy. He was rough, rougher than he'd been on the motorcycle. Between the cock in my mouth and him stroking my clit, it wasn't long before I was gushing all over his hand. He yanked me off of him before I could bite down, covering my mouth to stifle the screams.

"How did you not come yet?" I gasped, and he pushed me down to my knees again.

"Guess you have more work to do." I half collapsed on the floor in front of him, pushing up my tits, squeezing them around his cock.

"You don't want to swallow my cum?"

I gasped as he fucked my tits. "I want your cum all over me, then I want it in me."

"Fuck, Evie." His hand gripped the back of my neck as his hips jerked against my tits while I squeezed.

"You're making me so wet again," I whimpered as his control crumbled. "I bet you could—" My breath hitched. "Could make me come just like this."

"Goddamn," he swore as he came all over my face and tits.

His tattooed chest rose and fell. He nodded. "Do your trick again."

I was aching for his cock as I lapped and licked his cum off my tits while he watched, eyes as dark as coal. Nipple in my mouth, I widened my knees, stroking myself as I sucked his cum clean. Too soon, I was shuddering on my own hand.

He kissed me hard, silencing my cries.

"When I finally fuck you, Gingersnap, you're not going to be able to walk." He squeezed my breast then swiped my cheek, smearing his cum on my mouth.

"Look who's eating cum out of my hand," he said with a smirk as he disengaged the hard drive.

"Asshole."

"That where you want me to fuck you?"

Aunt Bianca gave Anderson a hungry look when we snuck back downstairs after cleaning up in the bathroom.

"Don't worry." He winked at me. "If she starts giving you any trouble, I'll fuck her in the powder room."

It was so casual the way he said it, like what we'd just done hadn't meant anything to him.

It probably didn't. It was just a distraction, just part of the plan.

You're blackmailing him, remember? Not dating him.

With guys like Anderson, sex was just another currency to be bartered and traded.

Anderson grabbed his leather jacket off the coat peg by the door and patted the hard drive in his pocket. "Let's go."

In the living room, poker chips clacked. Seventies guitar music played until my mother complained, and it was switched to Christmas carols.

"It's family poker night."

"You're staying?" Anderson gave me a questioning look. A look of disappointment, really.

Who cares what he thinks?

"I can't leave Sawyer and Ian to face it alone. The table needs one more sacrificial lamb."

He frowned.

"Okay, so here's the deal: Game nights suck generally. Games with my family, especially, aren't the greatest."

A dark eyebrow rose. "What happened to 'The Murphys are the best family in the world, and you don't know what real Christmas is unless you're a Murphy'?"

"That does not apply to poker night."

He followed me into the living room.

"We just try to survive it, and that means throwing the game early." I poured myself a drink. "There is an art to losing. Especially if you're at a table with Whiney Wendell, who is a terrible poker player."

I pointed at the watercolor seating chart Aunt Bianca had made.

"Anderson!" Bianca fluttered around him. He offered her a smoldering smile that promised deep, dirty pleasure. Her eyes flicked down to his crotch, then she hastily held her wineglass to her mouth.

"I didn't know you were coming. I don't have you on the chart."

"He can have my spot!" me and the other two Murphy Misfits shouted in unison.

"I'm up first!" Sawyer yelled, kicking Ian so he fell down hard in his chair.

Anderson took her seat.

Uncle Jaime clinked his spoon against his beer bottle. "First round of the poker tournament begins now."

"You're not even trying," Anderson complained as, on the first hand, I pushed all my chips to the center of the table. "I know you don't have anything higher than double kings."

"You don't know. I might have a royal flush." I smiled at him.

"Yeah," Ian added, "me too. All in."

Whiney Wendell pushed up his glasses. "It's statistically unlikely that both of you have a royal flush."

Anderson made a disgusted noise and said, "Fold."

"No, just put the rest of your fucking chips in." I tried to move his chips, but he slapped my hand.

"Just bet," Sawyer urged us, offering me snacks on her plate. "Then we can all do something else."

Ian and I laid our cards on the table.

"Why are you betting on those cards?" Anderson was appalled.

"Because I want to hang out by the bathtub of meatballs," I replied.

"Well, Ian wins." Anderson threw up his hands.

"Dammit!" Ian said.

"Evie, he gets all your chips."

"Ugh." Ian's head flopped onto the table.

"If you'd just bet your fucking chips," I hissed at Anderson as he laid down three kings, "Ian could be eating meatballs too."

"I didn't know what you had," he argued.

"You should have just asked."

"That's cheating!"

"Who cares? It's holiday poker death roulette."

Anderson shuffled the cards like he was a blackjack shark and dealt them out.

Ian didn't even look at his cards. "All in."

I poked Anderson. He held his hand close to his chest.

"Stop looking at my cards. You're going to tell him."

"Oh my god!" Sawyer pushed me. "He's a card guy. You like a card guy."

"No, I don't like him."

"That's not what she said when she was coming on my—"

"Mom! They're having grown-up conversations," Wendell complained.

"Why did you put my poor baby at that table, Bianca?" Aunt Abby chastised her. "He's going to get corrupted."

"Can we hurry this along?" Ian begged.

"Wendell, Evie will show you her tits if you go all in," Sawyer said around her cheese dip.

"Really?"

"Evie." Anderson was horrified.

"You were about to fuck Bianca in the powder room."

"I'm sorry. He what?" Aunt J asked, turning around in her chair.

"We should switch to strip poker," Granny Doyle declared.

"Anderson isn't wearing any underwear," Aunt Bianca blurted out, "so that's hardly fair."

Anderson smirked.

My mom looked pained at the table with her sisters, who were falling over themselves, giggling like teen girls at a boy band concert.

Cards were laid down. Anderson had two pairs, Ian had nothing, and Wendell had a pair of jacks.

"Game over. Anderson wins."

"I want to see her tits."

Anderson slammed his hand down hard on the table, right in front of Wendell, making the chips jump. "You sure about that?"

My cousin shook his head.

My mom's sisters viciously flirted with Anderson as we waited for the rest of the tables to declare a winner. Grandma Shirley was managing the clocks so that we weren't there until three a.m. like that one Christmas.

"See? If you'd just let Wendell win," I hissed, digging my finger into his hip, "we could have been out of here."

Anderson had this look in his eye, though, the same one that Snowball would get when she saw the FedEx guy.

He was out for blood.

My family didn't stand a chance.

Chapter 36

ANDERSON

"**S**omeone sounds like he just got laid." Hudson was acerbic when I answered the phone.

"No."

"Liar."

"I mean, yes, but I just won a poker tournament." I let the door to Bianca's house slam behind me.

After playing poker with Aaron, the Murphys were laughably easy. I'd won table after table, beating Evie's mother, wiping the floor with her father, then finally, in what my sister Elsa would call karmic justice, I'd faced Henry— and won the pot.

"You used to be better at this," I'd told him before pocketing the stack of cash while Evie's aunts fawned over me.

"Really? Was the pot eighty-seven thousand dollars?"

"No, but it did enable me to clean out the data of a woman who is the source of fraud on the Bergeson account."

"So you've crossed off the last item on the ledger? Aaron wants to send you to Idaho. It's a big contract."

"Not yet," I backtracked, lowering my voice. "I'm going to review the data over the next couple of days and cross-reference it, but I think we're close to closing it out."

"I'm concerned by the timetable."

"Worry about your own shit, and stop calling me just to chew me out."

"I need you in New Jersey. All hands on deck for the Svensson PharmaTech account."

Evie was standing on the porch, waiting for me to come back inside, jumping up and down, arms crossed over herself to keep warm.

I leaned in to kiss her, savoring the taste. If I got what I needed off these files, this was it. She and I and her shitty family were done. "Have to head out for a job."

Her face fell. "Do you think you'll be back for Braeden and Felicity's engagement party? Please?" she added at the expression on my face. "I know I'm supposed to be getting more evidence, but I can't be there by myself. Not with him."

"Just skip it."

But her big brown eyes dissolved my defenses.

"Fine. I'll be there. I promise."

"You'd better not fuck this up," Hudson warned me.

I'd been on my hands and knees on a giant tarp, sifting through mountains of trash for the last five hours.

"It's picking through trash." I tossed a slimy banana peel aside.

"No, the thing for Aaron."

"I'd be able to finish it up tonight, except you have me here, cleaning garbage."

Hudson kicked the banana peel at me. "Just hurry the fuck up."

I would have gone through the Bianca files tonight, should have, but Evie needed me at the engagement party.

I'd stay a few hours then start the mind-numbing task of analyzing the data. Then that was it. It was over. I was going to Idaho, and this holiday with the Murphys would be the memory of a nightmare.

That was what it was, right? Evie was a nightmare, right?

The snow fell softly around me as I walked up to the Murphys' house.

"You're here!" The front door slammed, then Evie flung herself into my arms.

I spun her around as she kissed my face, giddy. Snowball jumped around us, barking.

"Of course I'm here. Why wouldn't I be?"

"I don't know." She beamed then hugged me again.

I kissed the top of her head, drawing her under my arm as we headed into the warm house.

"Did Felicity seriously allow your parents to host her couples' shower?"

"My mom offered to make it up to her for my ruining her surprise engagement announcement."

"Felicity's not worried you'll poison the guests after being locked in the kitchen all day?"

"It wasn't all day. I also submitted a job application to Target."

The living room and dining room were packed with Murphy family and with Felicity and Braeden's friends.

"Evie," her mother called.

"Keep an eye out for Aunt J. She just dumped her boyfriend," Evie whispered.

I kissed her one more time before she ran off to the kitchen.

Her uncles and cousins were huddled together, talking hockey.

"If you haven't been playing together regularly, keep it simple." I interjected the suggestion as, with sleight of hand, I returned the phone I'd swapped at a previous family party, putting the broken one in my pocket. "Hard offense, keep the puck down low, and crash the net for rebounds. Keep it up, and wear them down."

Evie's uncle clapped me on the back. "This man hockeys! We're putting you on our team."

"Something tells me your sister's probably not going to like that, Todd," his brother-in-law quipped.

"It's my hockey game at my lake house." Todd sniffed.

"I'll pass. I don't want my balls eaten on Christmas morning, thanks." And I sure as fuck wasn't spending my free time playing hockey with the Murphys. They probably couldn't even play.

I headed over to the table to grab a scotch.

Several frat boys who'd aged out of their fraternity but still wanted any excuse to relive their glory days were already smashed. They loudly brayed to each other about how much they hated their bosses and who had attractive coworkers.

I half listened to them, running my plan for analyzing the Bianca Murphy data. And trying not to think about how I was going to have to leave Evie forever after tonight.

Would she hate me?

Of course she would. I'd seen the way she looked at me. I was going to break her heart.

It's her own fault for falling for me.

One of them gave me a bleary-eyed look.

"You Felicity's friend? Never seen you before."

"This guy looks like he fucks." Another of the frat boys slapped me on the shoulder.

"Bet you were one of Felicity's old hookups, weren't you?" One of them swayed.

"She's not putting out for Braeden. Probably because you're banging her, I bet."

"Like Braeden isn't cheating on her," I sneered before I could stop the words.

But Braeden's friends weren't offended.

"Oh, he knows everything!" More braying laughter came with slaps on the back.

"Braeden's a beast! He always has more than one girl at a time." His frat brother guffawed.

"Gotta respect the hustle, bro."

"How does he have the time?" I sipped my scotch casually, slipped my hand into my pocket, pulled out my phone, pretended like I was just checking my text messages, and hit record on the phone. "Especially when he's about to get married."

"He makes time. He's got one in the works right now," the frat brother confided.

"Seriously?"

He nodded. "It's this girl he was with last year."

"Is it some lot lizard he dredged up?" I mimicked their mocking laughter.

The frat brother with a beer belly whipped out his phone. "I took a video of her. She's not bad-looking. Nice tits. Young. Impressionable."

He flipped through video on his phone then hit Play.

There, as I suspected, was a video of Evie centered in the frame.

The frat boy and Braeden were talking as the video, slightly shaky, zoomed out from Evie. They were in some off-Broadway theater.

She glanced toward the camera. She looked so happy and in love.

"See?" The phone video picked up Braeden's voice. "Look at her. She wants me. She'll do anything. I'll keep her as a sidepiece. Felicity won't find out."

The phone camera panned. Braeden's face appeared in the frame briefly. "She's some barely legal college dropout. I just have to buy her some cheap shit, and she's so impressed."

"She have any friends?" another guy not in the frame asked.

It took everything in me not to yank the phone out of the guy's pudgy hand, stalk through the room to where Braeden was giving some embellished story to his relatives, and kick the phone through the back of his throat.

"Hm." I took a sip of my drink to keep the disgust off my face. "Respect."

"She looks even better without her shirt." The frat idiot snickered, swiping to another app to open up a photo, *the* photo, of Evie topless.

I was pretty sure I could get Jake to help me bury their bodies if I bought him a cheeseburger.

I smoothly took his phone. "Let me get a copy?"

"Knock yourself out."

Three taps, and I had the video sent to my email.

Case closed. That was it. Braeden was done. And I was going to skin him alive in front of his family.

"Thanks." I toasted the frat guy.

Evie was in the kitchen, scooping whipped cream into a bowl. I didn't want her here, didn't want them anywhere near her.

I grabbed her hand. "We're leaving." I ignored her protests.

"Why?"

"Because I'm about to burn this place down."

Chapter 37

EVIE

Anderson dragged me out the back door.

"I didn't get anything to eat."

"I have something better than food."

"Your cock?" I joked.

"Your salvation."

"What?"

"Not here."

I wrapped my arms around his torso as the motorcycle sped to the converted old garage.

Resting my hands on his broad shoulders, I managed to get off the bike without falling over this time.

Anderson sprang off the bike, long legs cutting a path through the snowy night. One hand flicked on the lights in the garage. The other pulled off his helmet.

"What's the big break? Did you get one of his friends to say something?"

"Better." Using a voice command, he turned on the TV that was hanging on one wall, then he hit a button on a keyboard.

On the TV was a video taken at Ian's dance theater.

"That's from last year. Sawyer and I organized a family outing to go see Ian in the *Nutcracker*. The owner promised him he would get to be on that night. Of course, he wasn't."

I stood there watching the video.

Anderson's arms were crossed. He looked away from me as the clip played.

"Holy shit!"

"Evie…"

"That rat-faced bastard. I knew it. I knew I wasn't crazy! Braeden's been fucking with me this whole time. We need to go back to the party and play this for everyone."

"No. I'm waiting on someone who's processing that recording. Then we'll have all the evidence we need to bury him." Anderson paced in front of the TV. "The frat idiot had your photo. Braeden sent it to all his friends."

He seemed dangerous, predatory, as he paced, agitated, in the dim lighting. The motorcycle gear moved on him like blackened armor. "I don't want them to have your picture. I don't even want them to look at you or think about you."

"Who cares? This is awesome. We have evidence."

"I care. *Because you're mine!*" The roar echoed off the concrete floor in the gray space.

I froze.

"You're mine, and I will fucking kill anyone who tries to take you or hurt you."

"We're not—" I swallowed.

He was breathing hard. He looked crazy, irrational.

"We're not like that, right? Like, it's my own delusions."

He grabbed my hair, half dragging me up to him so he could whisper against my mouth. "I want to carve your name in my skin."

"That sounds drastic."

"You drive men crazy." His teeth were at my neck.

"I think you were already insane."

"You didn't have a problem last night when you were licking my cum from your tits."

"That was…" I winced. "It was part of the mission. I don't actually fantasize about being with you or anything."

At least I wouldn't any longer.

Now that this nightmare was almost over, now that I was so close to… what had Anderson called it? My salvation? It would be snatching defeat from the jaws of victory if I slept with him now. This was my chance to wipe the slate clean.

"I think I should just go back to the party."

One gloved hand shot out to my throat. "Don't lie to me. You want me." The leather scraped my skin as he drew his hand down.

"But my family…" Even with all the excuses, I couldn't bring myself to say, *No, stop, don't*. Because. Put me on the naughty list, but I wanted this. Wanted him.

"You've wanted me to fuck you since you caught me in your parents' house." His deep voice was so smug, so self-assured.

"That's not true," I croaked.

Off came my sweater, the gloves rough under my bra against my tits. Then his hands were on my hips, seeking, pulling the skirt.

"Take it fucking off before I destroy it."

I needed to make better choices, which would include not dropping my clothes on Anderson Wynter's floor.

But the way he kissed me, like he wanted me, like I was everything, like I was the most intoxicating thing he'd ever had? I didn't want to walk out of there.

Maybe he could just, you know, eat me out, then I'd have some clarity and could resist the walking, snarling bad choice personified.

I kicked off my flats and stood on his boots so I could kiss him, arms wrapped around his neck, my bare skin pressed against the sharp ridges of his motorcycle jacket.

He kissed me long, slow, hungrily, his heavy gloved hands at my waist, my ass, between my thighs.

"Don't tell me," he whispered, an edge of a threat in his deep voice, "that you don't want me to fuck your tight little cunt."

I did.

"I don't."

He grabbed my hair. "Liar."

Then I was being forced down on my knees.

"Suck my cock. I want you to get me nice and hard for when I fuck you."

Hands shaking, I undid his belt buckle, breathing on his cock as I slowly pulled down the zipper. He was already half-hard.

My tongue flicked out to the tip. He hissed, then I took the thick length in my mouth.

His gloves rubbed slow circles in my scalp as I took the cock in my mouth, trying to convince myself that I totally wasn't turned on by this, that I wasn't thinking about his cock in my pussy.

I moaned, not able to stop the fantasy of him spreading me, filling me.

He cursed and ripped me off of him.

"Had enough?"

In answer, he threw me forward. My knees banged the hard concrete. My hands stung.

His gloves were rough as they scraped my pussy, pushing inside me, on my clit.

I rocked against his hand.

"Spread your legs."

The concrete scraped my knees.

"More." His thick gloves gripped my thighs.

I arched back against him as he buried his face in my pussy, lapping my clit as his thick gloves pushed inside me.

This was what I needed—him to make me come, then I'd walk out of there, away from him.

My hips ground back against his face as he licked and sucked on my clit. Then I was coming, my high-pitched cries echoing around the dark space.

Panting, I crawled forward.

He stood up. His shadow darkened the floor in front of me. Then his heavy boots were kicking my legs wider.

"Let me see your dripping cunt."

Just because my family already thought I was sleeping with him didn't mean that I actually had to do it, right? *I would know* that I'd committed the ultimate betrayal.

Maybe he'll just jack off on me.

But even the thought of his hot cum all over my ass and pussy was enough to have me wet and aching for him.

The tip of his cock was hard and thick at my opening. I let out a moan, arching up for him.

He took me raw.

I groaned as his thick, hard length claimed my pussy, filling me all the way to the hilt.

"You're so big." I whimpered as that thick length pulled out. I didn't have a second to catch my breath before he rammed into me once, twice, then pulled out.

"Forgot a condom?" My pussy ached.

"I was just getting my dick wet."

The glove was back in my pussy, in the wetness, smearing it all over my ass.

"You're mine, no one else's."

I panted as his thick cock pushed against me *there*, *higher*.

"Tell me you want my cum up your ass, Gingersnap. Tell me how much of a slut you are that you'd let the man you hate fuck your ass." He ground against me.

"Shit," I mewled, my sweat-soaked hair plastered to my face.

"Tell me." He stroked my clit again.

Velcro rasped, then the gloves thumped onto the floor next to me.

He was right, though, wasn't he?

I was the worst Murphy. I always made terrible decisions.

They already think I'm sleeping with him, my brain tried to rationalize when he rocked his cock against me.

I heard the telltale sound of a cap opening. Then oil-slick fingers were *there*. He held me in place as he slid one finger into my ass while I shuddered.

"What are you going to do if I say no?" I whimpered as he inserted another finger.

"I'll jack off on your tits and call your grandmother to come get you."

"Shit." My hips rocked back against his hand. His fingers curled.

"I'm not giving you my cock unless you beg me for it." He added another finger, stretching me.

The moan came out low and needy. "Take me with that big cock. Make me feel every inch. Fill me with your hot cum. You know I'm a little slut for it. It tasted *so good*. Now I want it in me."

"Fuck, Gingersnap." His fingers slid out as I groaned.

"I'm a bad girl, and I'll kneel here for you, cum dripping out of me until you're done fucking me, then I'll lick it up."

The thick head of his cock pushed at my opening.

"Use me," I begged. The hating myself would come later.

I'd done this before—hello, poor decision-maker with abandonment issues. But never with a man with a cock as thick and huge as Anderson's.

I saw Christmas lights as he pushed into me inch by thick, unrelenting inch.

"You're gonna take all of me, aren't you?" His hand came down hard to slap my ass. Then in one move, he thrust the rest of the way into me.

The breath left my body. I couldn't even cry out.

He gave me a second to get used to him, then he was pulling out as I groaned.

"Too big for you?" He stroked my clit then thrust into my ass again as I took him to the hilt, the moan coming from deep in me.

"I like that little noise you make when you take my cock up your ass," the deep voice growled as I let out a little whimper. "Your ass is so fucking tight." He thrust into me again. "It feels even better than your pussy."

Then he was fucking me, rutting in me, his balls slapping against my ass, the zipper of his pants scraping my thighs as he filled me.

I cried his name as he took me, my elbows shaking, hips aching, the insane pleasure building deep inside me.

Anderson shifted. One hand grabbed my neck, pressing my face down into the concrete floor, my ass in the air just for him.

He fucked me wildly, like he'd been waiting years for this.

"Take it. Take my huge cock," he snarled.

I'd never been fucked like that, not in my pussy and certainly not up my ass.

His huge cock filled me, dominated me, made me his.

"You like that, don't you?" he hissed in my ear, jerking my head. "You like a cock in your ass."

His hand moved to my clit, stroking me as the thrusts got more erratic.

"Please," I said as he rammed into me. "I want your hot cum in my—"

Suddenly, I was gushing on his hand, coming around his cock.

He pounded into me, drawing it out. I moaned as he bucked into me, hard, then he was spilling thick, hot cum up my ass. I clenched around him, milking his cock in me, filling me up.

He half collapsed on me for a moment, pressing hot kisses on my rapidly cooling skin.

I whimpered as he pulled out.

"You." He slapped my ass. "Are the best fuck I have ever had."

"Hate fucks are the best fucks," I slurred. "I can almost forgive you for ruining my Christmas after that."

"You did like my cock up your ass, didn't you? I could have fucked you on the floor that night in the study, and you would have taken my cum just like this." He sounded almost mesmerized.

Then he scooped me up, and my arms looped around his neck.

My foot banged on a lamp as he brought my legs up around his waist. My nails scraped in his hair, and my nose bumped his as I kissed him.

He thumped me against a nearby wall, the rough plaster digging into my bare back.

I heard a condom packet rip as he sucked on my breast, teeth nipping the soft skin.

"You want my cock in your pussy, don't you?"

I arched against him, then he thrust into me, fucking me against the wall.

"I hate you so fucking much, Evie Murphy," he snarled into my ear as he jackhammered into me. "You and your whole fucking family." He thrust into me, his cock hitting my clit. "You ruined my fucking life. And here you are, my cum dripping out of your ass, all over my fucking floor." He kissed me hard. "You gonna come for me, Evie? You gonna let me come in your tight little cunt?"

I bit down on his ear. "Your cock feels so good in my pussy. I want to come. I need to come," I begged as he pounded into me.

Then I was shuddering my orgasm, pussy clenching on his cock.

Not him.

"You always make me so wet. Fuck, Evie." He adjusted the angle so he could really fuck me, hitting that perfect spot deep inside me.

"Come on. I know you can come again. I know how much of a little slut you are."

I hissed, twisting against him, the pleasure excruciating.

When he put his mouth on my tits again, I was done. I cried out, a gushing mess coming all over him. He grunted, spilling into the condom as he pounded into me.

He kissed me as he drew out of me.

My legs trembled as I sank onto the floor, still trying to catch my breath. In my blurry vision, his heavy black boots walked away from me as he went to toss the condom.

I had never ever in my life been fucked like that. I'd done some dumb shit, but I'd never had anal with a guy when the only scraps of information I had about him were all bad news.

Anderson came back, tossing a wet towel at me. "Clean up. You're dripping cum and your pussy juices all over my floor."

"Ah yes," I said, wiping myself off quickly. "Your beautiful dirty concrete floor. Wouldn't want to mess that up."

He reached down to squeeze my breast, pinching the nipple.

"I see now why my birth mom threw away her entire future just to fuck the wrong man," I quipped.

"That's real dark for the holidays, Gingersnap." A fridge door slammed.

Anderson sat down in a worn leather chair a few feet away from me, beer in hand. He did that boot trick with the bottle cap and sipped the drink while he watched me slowly drag myself upright.

"Such a gentleman."

"I like watching my handiwork." He smirked, taking another long pull of the beer.

Before I could stop them, the words tumbled out. "We could—"

"What?"

Stay, get married, fall in love...

"Get the big reveal ready," I finished lamely.

"I have actual work to do, you know," he said, reaching for his laptop. Instead of opening it, he tracked me with his eyes as I pulled on my skirt, struggled to stuff my boobs into my bra, which had technically been too small when I bought it, found my sweater, and padded around the room, looking for my panties.

"Want this?" He held up the scrap of lacy thong, twirling it around on his finger.

I straddled his knee. "Give it back."

He pressed the fabric to his face then handed it back to me.

I felt awkward putting them on in front of him, so I just stuffed them into my skirt pocket.

"What the fuck are you doing?"

"Leaving," I snapped at him.

"I don't want you walking out of here with no panties on." His face was dark.

Making a big show of it, I pulled the panties out of my pocket, took aim, and let them sail across the room to hit him in the chest.

"Have fun jacking off by yourself, loser."

"*Evie.*" He had shifted forward in his seat like he was going to stand up.

I turned, my back against the door.

Don't run to him, I ordered myself. *Have some sense of self-respect.*

I was about to move out of the shithole that was my life. This was a new dawn for Evie Murphy. Shoot, I might get a bedroom.

"Girls who do anal on the first date don't stick around, asshole. I'm not cooking you breakfast in the morning."

He grinned slyly. "You will if I show up."

The party was winding down.

No one seemed to have noticed I was gone. I slipped back inside and pulled on my apron. I felt fucked—like fucked and satisfied but also fucked like *Oh fuck!* because that had been the hottest thing I'd ever done, and also *fucked* because, well, Sawyer had been right.

All the hormones and pheromones and the feel of that huge, muscular body all around me had my attachment issues planning a holiday wedding.

"This always happens," I reminded myself.

I dumped dish soap into the sink and started scrubbing.

"He doesn't love you. He hates you. Said so himself." I flipped over the pan. "Get it together, Evie Murphy."

"You were getting fucked by him, weren't you?"

I yelped. The dish soap dropped into the sink.

Braeden was *right there*.

"You're a horny little girl who can't even stay at my engagement party for an hour before you run off to be a pussy pocket for that murderer."

"Shut up, Braeden. I'm busy. Go away."

He grabbed my hips.

"If this is you being jealous, you trying to send me a message, trying to win me back, it's working, Evie."

I pushed off his hands, but he just laughed.

"You can be my little puck bunny after the game tomorrow."

Chapter 38

ANDERSON

'd crossed a line.

Actually, it wasn't just a line—I'd strapped a rocket to the back of a convertible and gone straight over the Mississippi River.

I kicked the rag she'd used across the floor.

What the fuck had I done?

Whatever.

I was searching these Bianca files, giving Aaron his last deliverable, then I was fucking off to Idaho.

I wished, though, as I opened up the Bianca files to start scanning them for the evidence, that I'd asked Evie to stay. I'd have given anything to be curled up next to her, warm under the blankets instead of standing here in the chilly room, eyes fatiguing as I flicked through file after file, trying to find something that would clear my ledger.

When day started to break, the pale-pink light glowing in the clerestory window of the converted garage, Aaron called.

I ignored it, grabbing my jacket and my helmet.

Was it too early to go over there?

Probably.

But I could rationalize it.

Bianca had four terabytes of data on her computer, none of it organized. A lot of it was videos of her cat and her kids. She wrote everything down, so I knew there was evidence there, buried under a thousand low-quality cat memes.

However, if she didn't have evidence, or if I needed more data, I'd need Evie to access it. So I couldn't ghost her yet.

I had to go see her. The job required it.

Evie stood in the kitchen, balancing on one leg in over-size Rudolph slippers, the nose giving off a faint glow while Snowball jumped around, pretending to attack them.

She was mixing up some sort of custard with egg beaters. She didn't hear me when I opened the door or when I crossed the small Christmas-themed carpet over the tile floor, didn't notice till I stood behind her, inhaling her scent, which was sweet like cookies and cake and Christmas.

She did scream when my hands circled her waist. The beaters dropped into the bowl, spattering her with the filling mixture.

I grabbed them and switched it off.

"Oh my god." She let out a shaky breath.

I leaned in and kissed her, tasting the slightly tart filling mixture, not hugging her so I didn't get the filling all over my motorcycle gear.

Snowball bounced around me, yapping, tail wagging.

I bent down to greet the little dog. She jumped up, licking the few spatters of custard that speckled my face.

"You're not going to let me say hi to your mama first?"

Evie was still clutching her mixing bowl.

I stood up, an apology already ready to jump off my tongue.

You are not like that.

"I'm—didn't mean to frighten you."

"You didn't," she said in a rush. "I just didn't expect you to be over here."

She didn't look at me.

"I can go."

"No, no, I'm making breakfast."

The corner of my mouth twitched. "I thought you said girls who do anal on the first date don't cook breakfast."

"This is a communal-breakfast thing, not specially for you." She batted my hands away, but I tilted her face up to kiss her.

She didn't seem that into it.

Fuck, I didn't want her like that with me. Mad? Hating me? Furious? Sure.

But not sad.

"Look, I'm—" I ran a hand over the back of my neck. "I'm sorry. I didn't mean—I just had to see you."

"Oh, for startling me? Don't worry about it. For some reason, I thought you were someone else." She forced out a laugh.

"No, I mean last night."

"It's not as sexy if you apologize for giving a girl the lay of a lifetime," she teased. "Besides, I'm not spending the night at your place. That would be crazy. I mean, can you imagine? My mother would have a heart attack."

"Yeah."

Then…

"Who did you think I was?"

"No one."

I rewound to the concern, no, *the fear*, in her eyes—how off-balance she was. Uncertain.

"Gingersnap."

"It's nothing. Can you take Snowball out? She's trying to chew up my slippers."

I grabbed Evie and shook her roughly. "*Tell me!*"

"Stop yelling at me!"

"*Then fucking tell me!*" I bellowed.

"It's nothing. It's just—"

I grabbed her jaw.

"I know you said I was supposed to act like prey, but Braeden just won't leave me alone."

I stilled. "That means we're winning."

"Yeah." Her eyes flicked to the stairs. "Yeah, right, we're winning. I'm being dumb."

I released her.

"Can I get a microphone with a camera on it in case he shows up in my bedroom again in the middle of the night?" She was trying to sound jokey but couldn't disguise the desperate edge.

"*He what?*"

"Well, you know…"

"That motherfucker."

I couldn't do it—too many sleepless nights, too much pressure building, and now *Braeden*, that fucking worm, that fucking cockroach, was in her room, scaring her, and I *wasn't there.*

"I'm going to fucking kill him."

"No, just calm down," she pleaded. "You said this was part of the plan."

"Him in your bedroom isn't part of the fucking plan. He doesn't get to be in your bed."

She must have been scared… was still scared.

I should have been there. I should never have let her leave yesterday, and I never would again.

Voices sounded in the hallway.

"Sawyer, help!" Evie begged as her cousin burst into the kitchen, followed by more Murphys.

"Get the fuck out of my way, Evie," I ordered.

"Just drop that knife."

I looked down at my hand to the honed chef's knife there.

"Get the hell away from her," Sawyer demanded, fumbling in her purse for mace.

The Murphys freaked out.

"Don't shoot that in here!"

"Call the police!"

"I'm not going to hurt her." I threw the knife away.

Her uncles gasped. One of them grabbed his kid as the knife seemed to sprout out of the wall.

"That was my good knife," Evie complained.

"I'll buy you a new one."

"Whoa," her uncle Todd said, approaching me, hands up. "Whoa, big guy."

"What did you do to set him off?" Braeden's nasally whine sounded from the doorway.

My head snapped up.

Evie whispered something to Sawyer.

"Jesus, you're a scary dude." Her other uncle took a can of beer out of the fridge and rolled it along the floor to me. "I'd hate to be whoever you were about to go after."

"I hope it wasn't Henry," someone else said.

Her family was nervous, apprehensive.

"That would really set my sister-in-law off."

"He doesn't need that. He needs some herbal tea," Sawyer said sourly, kicking the can away.

"No, he needs to save that aggression for the hockey game," Todd insisted.

"You're not seriously putting him in the hockey game. You want him to play with us?" Braeden yelped.

"I want him on my team, not on your team," one of Evie's cousins joked.

"Breakfast will be out soon." Evie tried to dissipate the tension.

"No sugar," her uncle insisted. "We need protein."

"The French toast isn't for you, and when you try to steal mine," his wife added, "I'm going to remind you."

I glared at Braeden until he followed the rest of the Murphys out of the kitchen.

Evie and her cousin were whispering while I tried to relax my shoulders.

Sawyer finally turned to me. "You need to leave."

"I'm not fucking leaving her."

"You pulled a knife on her," Sawyer argued.

"I didn't pull it. She had it on the counter."

"This is a huge overreaction," Evie said.

"You need to stop making excuses for the toxic men in your life," Sawyer warned her.

Aaron called me again while I helped Evie with breakfast. I sent it to voicemail. I should go back and keep reviewing the Bianca files, but I wasn't leaving Evie alone.

She's not the job.

I stacked the platters of steaming food, resting the over-size trays on my shoulder as I ferried the dishes to the dining room.

Her uncles were using pieces of bacon to lay out hockey plays.

"You're on team Grinch. Get your number from my mom," one of Evie's uncles told me around a bite of the ham-and-pepper stir-fry.

"I'm not playing."

"The fuck?"

Several of her male cousins glared at me.

"Evie!" her uncle yelled back to the kitchen. "What the hell are you doing bringing a man who cannot play hockey into this house?"

"I didn't say I couldn't play." I was offended. "Just that I'm not."

"Scaredy cat." Her brother Declan ribbed me, grinning, his baby bouncing on his knee.

"Might want to calm that down. You didn't see him with that knife earlier," his cousin warned him.

Granny Doyle made chicken noises at me.

Evie hurried in and set a platter of fresh French toast on the buffet. "Anderson has to work. Leave him alone."

"Did you not put out last night, Evie?" Her aunt Jennifer asked then turned to me with a predatory smile. "I bet I can give you some motivation to play."

"Is there money on this game or something?" I frowned.

"There damn well can be." Granny Doyle threw down a stack of cash.

"Gambling at a family hockey game." Shirley harrumphed.

"There's going to be fighting and fucking at this game too." One of Melissa's sisters winked at me as she plaited her hair.

"This is supposed to be a wholesome holiday event," Melissa told her.

"Booo!" Melissa's other sisters yelled at her from the other end of the table, where they were wrapping their knuckles with tape.

"This isn't a family-friendly event. Children are not playing," one of them said.

Jennifer swiped black grease under her eyes. "Anderson's scared. Leave him alone."

"I'm not scared," I sputtered.

"Yeah, he is." Sawyer was calmly sipping her coffee from the doorway. "Anderson's never played against girls before. His balls are shriveling up as we speak."

"He's supposed to be on my team. Don't psych him out too hard," Victoria said cheerfully.

"No offense, but I'm pretty sure I can beat a bunch of girls at hockey."

Chapter 39

EVIE

"**T**ake his testicle!" Granny Doyle screamed, throwing her clipboard to the ground as Aunt J crashed into Uncle Hugh.

My dad looked on nervously, waiting with a first aid kit.

"Don't fucking let him this close to goal!" Sawyer screamed at one of my cousins when Team Grinch sent the puck flying toward the goal.

"What the hell are you all doing? I should have just sent Evie out there, the way you're playing," the Team Scrooge coach yelled at his players.

Bundled up against the cold, I poured out spiked hot chocolate for the spectators.

Katie sprinted by on her skates then pivoted, stealing the puck from Anderson.

"Anderson, get it the fuck together!" Granny Doyle hollered at him. "She's a twelve-year-old girl. Kill her!"

Katie sent the puck flying just as Aunt Virginia tackled her.

"Bitch! Don't knock down my daughter." Aunt Heather went after her sister.

"Fight! Fight! Fight!" the crowd chanted.

Declan's wife patted her first aid kit.

"Just as exciting as the emergency room?" I joked.

"The men are better looking." She smirked at me.

"Cunt punt that bitch into next week, J!" Granny Doyle whooped.

The family members who, like me, were not hockey inclined, sat on the makeshift bleachers lining the lake behind Uncle Todd's huge lodge.

The kids who were too young to play cutthroat holiday hockey bounced between a little patch of ice where they could hit the puck around and the refreshment table I'd set up with hot food and beverages.

"Oof!" Uncle Ross slammed into Anderson.

"I thought you were supposed to be a killer." Aunt J laid into Anderson. "This is a shit show. Man the fuck up."

"Your boyfriend is embarrassing the family." Ian adjusted his sunglasses.

"He's not my boyfriend," I replied automatically.

But if he wasn't, then why was he here?

Anderson finally got over his mental hurdle and was barreling down the rink, ice spraying from his skates as he bulldozed thorough my family members, taking a shot on goal.

Team Grinch roared when the puck bounced off the back of the net.

"That's what I'm fucking talking about!" Aunt J slapped him on the helmet.

Then Team Grinch was flying.

Anderson passed Sawyer's little sister the puck. She took a swing on goal and was promptly tackled by several of my cousins.

"Walk it off!" Sawyer yelled at her as the younger girl smashed one of our cousins with her hockey stick.

Skating backward, Anderson grabbed the girl by the back of the jersey, setting her on her feet, and patted her helmet. She took off after the puck.

"If he was someone I didn't actively hate, I'd say that was adorable."

"I thought you weren't doing this," Ian said under his breath.

"I can objectively think that a man could be good father material."

"Anderson's not father or husband material."

As the game went on, Anderson seemed relaxed and in his element, like he was having fun. When he could, he tossed the puck to one of my younger cousins, setting them up so they had a chance to score.

"Be careful with him. He just finished his residency," my dad pleaded as Anderson and Declan crashed into each other, racing for a puck.

"Fuck you," Declan said good-naturedly as Anderson helped him up.

My dad the surgeon, who basically saw mobility-ending injuries all over the ice, had his hands over his face.

"Grow some balls, Brian!" his brother, sporting a newly earned black eye, ribbed.

"I have medevac on speed dial," my dad replied.

"Evie, come get your brother," Anderson shouted to me with a wink and a smile. There was something boyish about him as he flew on the ice, like I was seeing a glimpse of the real him.

"I was right," I said firmly. "There is a good person under the grumpy, Christmas-hating exterior. Anderson just needed the right woman to help him see the joy in Christmas."

"As a man, I'm just going to remind you," Ian said in warning, "that this is how the bad boys get you. They make you believe that you're the only one in the world who can change them, then they blame you when you fail."

When I turned back to the ice, Anderson and Braeden were racing for the puck.

I froze as the two men hurtled toward me.

Anderson reached it first, taking a swing and sending the puck zooming across the ice. The motion sent him banging into Braeden, who crashed into me headfirst like a missile, bowling me head over heels.

"Shit, Evie." Grabbing me around the waist, Anderson picked me up out of the snow while I sputtered. He dusted me off and set me back on my feet.

"You tried to kill me, you fucking piece of shit." The edge of Braeden's skate clipped me as he tackled Anderson, sending both men crashing to the hard ice.

Anderson was up immediately.

Both teams skated over, hesitating a moment as Anderson rammed his knee into Braeden's ribs then tackled him, slamming his head back against the ice. If Braeden hadn't been wearing a helmet, he'd be dead.

This wasn't the normal good-natured hockey rough-housing. Anderson was out for a pound of flesh.

"You do not ever touch her." His fist slammed into Braeden's nose with a sickening crunch. Blood spurted. "She's mine."

"That's the monster you brought here, Evie!" My mom was shrill.

I screamed as Henry grabbed Anderson around the neck before he could punch Braeden again.

Braeden's teammates pulled him out of the way as the two men went at each other, fighting like they must have been trained to in the Marines.

"I told you, don't go after my sister or my friends. Your problem is with me." Henry kicked Anderson's knee.

"Your friend deserved to have his face sliced off." Anderson spit blood with the words.

Henry lunged, but Anderson slammed his gloved fist into Henry's chin. My brother wasn't fazed, just wrapped Anderson in a headlock.

"Do something!" my mom yelled at my uncles as the two men struggled on the ice.

Uncle Todd ineffectively tried to hit Anderson with his hockey stick.

"Oh, for fuck's sake, grab him." Aunt J pushed into the fray with the rest of my aunts, many of them hardened nurses, pulling apart the swinging men.

Anderson bared his teeth as Aunt J inspected him and Henry for injuries.

"Calm the fuck down!" she barked before Henry could go after Anderson again.

She shooed away my anxious father. "They're fine. Skate it off, boys."

"You're a cardiac surgeon. You don't know," my dad sputtered.

Aunt J gave him the finger then slapped at his hand when he reached for Henry.

My brother was still glaring murderously at Anderson.

"Relax, Henry," Anderson said, his gray eyes dangerously calm. "It's just a game, right?" He skated backward, those ghostly eyes lingering on me.

Team Scrooge dumped Braeden next to me so Reagan could patch him up.

Hands trembling, I poured myself a cup of bourbon hot chocolate.

Ian gave me a concerned look. "You sure you want to tame that beast?"

"She shoots! She scores!" Uncle Ken yelled into the microphone as Ashley made the final goal before the buzzer sounded.

"Hell yeah!" Aunt J and Uncle Hugh whooped as team Grinch raced over to Ashley.

Anderson picked up the tween girl, lifting her above his head. She hoisted her hockey stick high while her team cheered.

I couldn't stop grinning, and I didn't even like hockey.

"You're a damn good goalie." Anderson shook Sawyer's hand. "Respect. I've never had to work that hard for a goal."

"I'm trying to convince her to move back home and play hockey on our rec league team," Aunt J said as Team Grinch skated over for refreshments. "Why she'd rather wax labia than play hockey is beyond me."

My dad fussed around the players, applying ice and bandages and checking for sprains and fractures.

"You should be dead after taking a puck like that to the face," Declan's wife said cheerfully as she mopped dried blood off the gash on Anderson's cheek.

"Just another scar for his collection," my uncle joked.

From up the hill, there were screams and a flash of light. Anderson tensed.

"Finally got that bonfire started, I see," my uncle chortled.

"Told ya—a little kerosene, and that's all she wrote." Granny Doyle slapped her clipboard.

"Got a hamburger with your name on it," Uncle Todd said to Anderson.

The larger man's eyes flicked to the black truck parked under the trees. "I should work."

"You found a man just like your father, Evie—work and more boring work. For shame." Granny Doyle shook her head.

"There's nothing wrong with Brian," my mom argued.

Aunt J made a face. "Evie, take that stick out of your boyfriend's ass and tell him to come have a drink."

"It's not one of those cocktails you made, is it, Evie?" Anderson draped a sweaty arm over my shoulder.

"Everyone likes my Holly Jolly Hot Toddies," I argued as my family trooped up the hill to the bonfire, which was dangerously close to the hay bale seats.

"Bet you haven't had a workout like that since the last time you hooked up with Evie," Granny Doyly whooped, slapping Anderson's butt as he leaned over to grab the hay bales before they turned into an inferno.

He sat down heavily on one of them, looking relaxed and happy. I handed him a drink.

"It's a scotch, asshole," I said when he looked at it mistrustfully.

He pulled me down onto his lap, sloshing the drink slightly, so he could kiss me.

My mom's cousin Justin slapped Anderson on the shoulder then grabbed one of his kids before he could lean too close to the fire to roast his marshmallow. "Great game, man."

"You ever thought about going pro?" his brother interjected.

"I'm too old for that shit."

Uncle Todd handed him a plate with three hamburgers piled high with toppings.

Anderson took a huge bite of one.

"Someone would hire you just to fight people," my mom's cousin joked.

"Evie, you think you can keep him around till next Christmas?" Uncle Todd nudged me.

Anderson wiped his mouth.

"Not sure if he likes me that much." I laughed like it was a joke and not my insecurities talking.

Anderson gave me a look I couldn't read. It definitely wasn't hatred.

"Then propose to him," my aunt demanded, scooping a mound of butternut squash salad onto Anderson's plate.

"Evie's not that old. She doesn't need to be proposing to a man yet," Granny Doyle insisted from where she was glugging a bottle of gin into the punch.

"Gran, that is a delicate recipe to ensure all the flavors are harmonious—" I began.

"You can't taste the booze."

Anderson stood up.

"You're leaving?"

He looked at me, the firelight flickering on his face, then he leaned in and kissed the top of my head then my cheek then my mouth. "I'm just getting your grandmother to spike my drink. I'm not ready to leave you yet."

Chapter 40

EVIE

"**Y**ou have to break up with him."

I wiped melted cheese and relish from the corner of my mouth. Anderson had left half an hour ago, saying he really had to work and that he'd see me soon. Then he'd kissed me furiously in the shadows under the snow-covered evergreens.

Henry sat down on the hale bale across from mine. His face was still bruised around his jaw from where he and his helmet had been slammed into the ice by Anderson.

"Anderson isn't good for you." Henry leaned forward. "I'm not asking you anymore, Evie. I'm telling you as your older brother. Break up with Anderson Wynter. *Now*. He's going to hurt you. He's going to hurt this family."

Over his shoulder, I saw Sawyer and Ian making their way over.

"I'm not doing this to be controlling," Henry added, patronizing bastard.

"Really?" Ian asked, standing beside me. "Because it kind of feels misogynistic and controlling."

Henry looked up at him, scowling, then back down at me. "Anderson doesn't love you, Evie. He doesn't care about you, and he certainly doesn't respect you."

"And you're what? The protective older brother? That's a first," Ian shot at him. "I bet you're just jealous because Anderson kicked your ass in front of everyone."

Henry rested his hand on my shoulder. "Don't be naive, Evie. A man like Anderson doesn't fall in love, especially not with a girl like you. He's just using you to get to me."

"A girl like her?" Sawyer demanded.

"Evie's awesome. Of course Anderson wants her." Ian shoved our brother's arm off me.

"You're not going to fight me, Ian," Henry scoffed.

"I will." Sawyer rolled up her sleeves.

Henry looked down his long, thin nose at her then stood up, adjusting his jacket. "Break up with him, Evie. I'm warning you."

Braeden dragged Henry to the rec room after we'd arrived home. "You need a drink."

Ian helped me ferry the empty coolers to the kitchen. Sawyer had already left for an early-morning wedding in Connecticut. The triplets had gone to Cousin Nat's for a sleepover, and Granny Doyle was going "out on the town," as she put it.

Ian took a call in the living room to talk one of his cast members off a ledge, who was complaining loudly and angrily into the phone receiver that the theater owner hadn't paid the power bill.

"Four more days until Christmas," Ian reminded her.

Four more days.

The anxiety churned.

I turned on the water in the sink full blast and started scrubbing pans.

I had no job. I was still on my parents' shit list, and now my brother hated me. I'd put all my chips on Anderson.

And it worked, I reminded myself.

We had proof against Braeden.

A rush of joy filled me as I imagined the big reveal.

Anderson would make a big, dramatic speech, and Braeden would be thrown out.

My family would tell Anderson how clever and brave he was for helping me and how he must really truly love me.

Or must be blackmailed.

We were more than blackmail buddies, right? We'd had sex multiple times. He'd played hockey with my family, decorated cakes, and fixed my window. Even Snowball liked him. That meant something. Anderson wasn't just using me, right?

At least not any more than I was using him.

Braeden's braying laugh filtered up from the rec room, making me jump.

After tiptoeing over to the door to the basement stairs, I shut it softly. I wished I'd asked Anderson to install a lock on the attic door the last time he'd been here.

I wished Anderson was here.

Opening the cabinet, I stashed away the last of the now-clean platters.

I would have gone to Nat's if I'd realized Braeden was going to be here all night. She and my aunts were all helping the triplets get ready for their big-girl jobs at Svensson PharmaTech, giving girl-boss advice.

I didn't have anything to contribute. I'd just be the awkward third wheel in the corner like I was at most sleepovers.

I tried to channel Anderson and quietly creep up the stairs to my attic bedroom, worried that Braeden would hear me go upstairs.

I lay there in the dark.

I should sleep. We had the mandatory holiday hike tomorrow. Good, wholesome Christmas fun in the blinding snow in the mountains.

But I was afraid. Braeden's car was still parked in front of the house. That meant he was still here, in the house. What if Henry let him stay the night? Braeden could come up to the attic whenever he wanted to.

I pulled the covers over my head. The clock ticked.

My alarm would sound in a few hours so I could pack hiking snacks.

The house creaked.

"It's just your imagination." I curled up under the comforter.

Just as my heart started to slow, I heard another creak.

Someone was coming up the stairs.

I pulled the covers down to my nose.

The latch on the attic door didn't catch properly, and a thin strip of yellow light from the bulb in the stairwell splayed out over the plywood nailed to the bare joists.

Suddenly, a shadow blackened out the light. The door creaked open.

"Go away!" I yelled.

There was a heavy sigh.

The silhouette in the door was too broad shouldered to be Braeden.

The man turned away.

"Wait!" I scrambled out of the saggy bed and hopped across the cold room.

Anderson paused a few steps below me on the narrow stairs.

"Wait, please. I thought—"

A scowl marred his handsome face. "You thought I was him."

"He's in the rec room. I'm surprised he and Henry didn't go after you when you snuck in."

"I came in through the window."

"The window?" I hissed. "My parents could have seen you." Grabbing his jacket sleeve, I looked around furtively. "They're going to flip their shit if they find you here."

"Guess you'll have to be quiet, then, when I'm making you come." He dragged me to him.

I tumbled off the narrow step into his arms, and he carried me up the last couple of steps. He set me down on the rough plywood floor, kissing my face, my hands, my hair.

His head almost bumped the low attic ceiling as he maneuvered me back toward the bed.

"I thought you had to work." I panted as his hands were everywhere, pulling off my nightgown, on my tits, and cupping my ass.

"I can't concentrate." He nipped my lip. "All I can think about is you coming on my face." He pushed me back onto the bed. The mattress bowed under me.

He struggled out of his heavy leather jacket and tossed it onto the floor with his motorcycle gloves. He pulled his T-shirt over his head then leaned forward, gripped the back of my head, and kissed me, his tongue slipping into my mouth while his other hand worked his belt buckle loose.

"I want your pussy so fucking bad, Gingersnap." His belt buckle hit the floor with a dull thump.

Anderson mouthed me through my panties then stood up, kicking off his pants.

"You are really playing with fire, riding that motorcycle with no underwear."

"I thought you liked riding my bike with no panties." He straddled me on the bed, leaning down to kiss me, his cock thick and hard against my thigh.

His fingers pushed my panties to the side so he could stroke my pussy.

"Don't make me come yet." I kissed his chin, whimpering as he rolled two fingers around my clit.

"You giving the orders now?"

I dragged him down by his hair so I could nip his lower lip. "Yeah, I am."

"You sure you want to boss me around?"

"Haven't you heard? I make terrible and impulsive decisions."

"Fine." He rolled off me and put his hands behind his head. "Let me see what you come up with."

"You think I can't come up with something better than getting my ass fucked in your shitty garage?" I asked casually, straddling him.

Sitting back on my thighs, I drew my hands down the array of tattoos.

"Boring."

I grabbed his cock, twisting it.

He swore. His hands came down to grab my hips, and his head tipped back.

"Take off your panties, Gingersnap. I want to see your cunt."

I had to do some gymnastics to remove them. I was definitely going to start yoga again as soon as I got some disposable income.

His fingers digging into my ass, he hauled me up to him. As he held me hovering above him, his tongue flicked out to lap at my dripping slit.

"Definitely the sweetest cunt I've ever tasted." He gave me another long, slow lick.

I held on to the squeaky metal bedframe for dear life.

His strong arms kept me from sinking onto his face. His tongue dipped into my opening then traced up my pussy to my clit, circling it, teasing it. He mouthed me harder, his tongue licking my whole pussy then sucking and licking my clit until I was coming all over his face with deep, throaty moans.

"Turn around so I can eat your ass out too."

He started again after I turned, his tongue on my clit, in my pussy, at my opening, then higher.

So worth the painful waxing to listen to him tell me how nice and smooth I was and how he could eat my ass out all night.

"All night?" I moaned as he tongue fucked me.

I had to lean forward to rest my hands on that massive chest. My thighs ached, my hips burned, but still, he ate me out. I rocked back against his face, my hips making needy circles as his tongue took me higher, higher, then I was coming all over his chin.

I army crawled off him and turned around. He grabbed me under the arms to pull me up to him.

Panting, I slid two fingers into his mouth. He sucked on them.

"Now I want you to fuck my pussy raw."

"Yeah, you do."

"Wait," I yelped as he had us flipped, condom in hand. I took it from him. "You only get to fuck me if you're wearing that helmet." I kissed him. "And the boots." I bit his lip. "And the gloves."

I lay back on the rumpled blankets, humming happily as I watched him work his feet into his heavy boots, buckle them, then pull on the gloves, one hand then the other.

In the soft glow of the light that came through the doorway, his muscles rippled as he reached for the black motorcycle helmet.

"Wait." I gestured him forward then kissed him long and slow. "Now do it."

The helmet came down, hiding his face, now a mask of black on the ripped body. With the tattoos and the helmet, he was every stalker-boy romance fantasy come to life.

"Gimme, gimme!" Gleeful, I rubbed my hands together.

He took a step toward me. The floor creaked.

I raked my nails down his washboard abs, running my tongue down his thick shaft, nuzzling his balls, which I wanted shooting his hot cum into me.

His hand was heavy on my head as I gave him another long, slow lick down his cock.

"No." The deep voice, muffled by the helmet, was doing all the things for me. "I want to fuck your pussy. Put the condom on," he ordered. "If you don't, I'm going to throw you onto the floor and fuck your ass instead."

Not that I didn't crave it, but I wanted to watch my fantasy come to life.

Looking up at the faceless helmet, I slid the condom onto his thick cock, rolling the heavy balls in my hand one more time.

His gloved hands gripped my shoulders. He shoved me back onto the bed and ran those heavy gloves down my chest, over my tits, and down to my hips. Gripping my thighs, he spread my legs for him, angling me up.

His thick cock jutted out in front of him. Then he slammed it into me.

Clutching at the quilt, I couldn't stop the cry that escaped as that pussy-splitting cock filled my aching cunt.

"Oh, it's so big. I forgot how big it was," I whimpered as he thrust into me again and again, forcing me to take all of him.

The deep voice hidden behind the helmet was making me crazy, talking dirty to me. "You like my cock in your tight little cunt, don't you?"

"Yeah," I gasped out as he hit that perfect spot deep in me.

He rutted into me, holding me on the edge of mind-numbing pleasure.

"I'm gonna fuck your tight little pussy raw, Gingersnap."

"Make me come," I begged the faceless helmet, clawing at his thighs and running my hands over my breasts.

He grabbed my hands, forcing them above my head so he could fuck me into the mattress, the bed screeching as the screws loosened.

I wrapped my legs around his waist, urging him deeper.

The helmet bumped against my chin. My teeth clacked together. The hard plastic was cold against my cheek and neck as he held me down, the rhythm more erratic. Then he was shuddering in me.

I cried his name, fogging up the tinted visor of the helmet as I came around his cock while he pounded into me, milking the orgasm.

I pulled off the helmet, needing to see his face. I smooched his brow, laced my fingers in his dark, damp hair, and kissed that mouth to keep myself from telling him how perfect he was.

He pushed himself off the bed—one side was definitely lower than the other—stood up, and tossed the condom.

"Is the bad boy running scared?"

He shook out his hair then put the helmet back on.

Just seeing him standing there in my bedroom, cock half hard already, was enough to make me want him again.

I stood up as gracefully as I could manage, which wasn't all that much.

"I want to make myself come all over that helmet," I said breathily, and the helmet did a little shake of surprise.

I blew him a kiss then jumped on him, making him stagger backward as I pressed his helmet down against my tits. "Then I want you to fuck my ass so hard that I—*aaahh!*"

I screamed as the floor gave way with a loud crack.

"Shit!" Anderson swore, then we were falling, my arms scraping the plywood as Anderson fell through the insulation and the ceiling of the bedroom below—my parents' bedroom.

My mother screamed, her fancy lotion in her hand, as Anderson's naked body crashed through her ceiling, plaster raining down around him as we crash-landed on the antique white settee. The short legs splintered, and the cushions thumped to the floor.

Anderson lay there stunned, the black helmet not moving, his arms still protectively around me.

I scrambled off of him to stagger in the wreckage of the bedroom, dust and bits of fluffy pink insulation in my hair, while my mother yelled over and over, "Oh my god! Oh my god!"

My father shouted from the bathroom, which was partially blocked by the collapsed ceiling, "What happened? Was it a raccoon?"

"Really? A raccoon, Brian?" my mother shouted. "It's Evie." She glared at me. "Put some clothes on, for God's sake."

I reached for a nearby blanket.

"Not my good blanket."

"What am I supposed to wear?"

Footsteps echoed up the stairs.

Anderson finally managed to rally enough to pull himself upright, out of the wreckage of the settee.

"Damn." Granny Doyle whistled low as she regarded the scene. "I wish a naked man would crash through my ceiling. You didn't tell me that was a perk at *chez Murphy*, Brian."

My father was stunned. A piece of plaster landed on the floor in front of him as his mouth moved silently up and down.

"Brian, do something!" my mother raged.

"Holy shit."

There were curses and the sounds of phones taking photos as more of my family members crowded in my parents' bedroom doorway.

"I told you, Evie!" Henry yelled at me as I cowered behind Anderson, who seemed nonplussed to be standing stark naked with his fake girlfriend's family staring at him. "I told you to dump him."

"You can't dump that." Nat slapped Henry on the back of the head.

"You can dump that in my bed," Aunt J crowed.

"My bedroom was right next door," Granny Doyle wailed. "Ten feet over, Anderson. You have terrible aim."

"Don't care if he comes all over the walls," Aunt J was saying.

"Wait. That's a thing that happens?" Alana whispered.

"Have you girls been drinking?" my mother demanded.

The triplets tried really hard to look sober.

"Jennifer…"

"They're grown-ass women, Mel."

Anderson pulled off his helmet, rolling his neck and shoulders. He didn't even cover himself with it, just let it hang from one hand.

"You're not even using a condom!" my mother sputtered.

"See, Melissa?" Granny Doyle hooted. "For all your big talk about hating Anderson, you couldn't help but steal a peek."

"Girls, don't look," my mother ordered my sisters.

But my sisters and my cousins were all staring.

"Take it from experience," Aunt J said sagely. "That's not even fully erect."

Alexis crossed her legs. "How does that even fit in you, Evie?"

"We are not having this conversation." I covered my eyes.

"Thank you." Henry threw up his hands.

"You are free to leave, Henry," my cousin stated.

"Or stay," Granny Doyle said, "No judgment. Being bisexual is perfectly okay. Live your truth."

Anderson winked at him. Henry sputtered a "Fuck you" and stomped out, Braeden behind him.

My dad threw a towel at Anderson.

He handed it to me.

"We came to steal you for a girls' night, Evie." Alissa giggled as her sister took a swig from a bottle Granny Doyle was passing around. "But you already have it covered."

"You're taking them out, Mom?" Melissa complained.

"Duh, Aunt Mel." Nat rolled her eyes while Lauren took slow-motion video of Anderson as he flexed his muscles for her.

I held my towel tighter. It was unfortunately a hand towel, and I was a full-coverage type of girl.

"They can't go to a big-girl job without ever having seen a penis," Aunt J argued. "There are rich guys in Harrogate. They can't be the office virgins if they're going to find a hubby."

"You're going to lose your virginity?" my mother screeched.

"I bet Evie can tell you a thing or two about that," Granny Doyly hooted.

Anderson gave me a self-satisfied smirk.

"I need a drink," my mother moaned.

"I told you when you redid the house you should have installed a wet bar in your bedroom." Granny Doyle sniffed.

"Wait. They didn't finish that attic, but they also didn't put in a wet bar?" Anderson frowned.

"It's because Brian can't do shit," Granny Doyle said to Anderson. "They paid out the ass for a terrible contractor."

He shook his head.

My mother's hand fluttered to her chest.

"Where's that penis flask?" Granny Doyle asked. "Mel, you need to lighten up. This is a good thing."

"My ceiling…"

"You needed to redecorate anyway. Maybe Brooke Taylor could do a segment on your home renovation."

"I'll come fix it for you," Anderson offered, picking a piece of insulation off his abs.

"Then Brooke really will come." Lauren grinned.

The triplets giggled. "Yeah, she will."

My sisters collapsed with laughter.

"Anderson only works if you flash your titties at him," Granny Doyle said and lifted up her shirt. "There's your deposit."

Anderson recoiled.

"Evie, put your bra on and comb your hair," Aunt J ordered. "The strip club cover charge goes up at midnight."

"Strip clubs? You need to clean up this mess right now!" my mom yelled.

"Just hang in my room, Mom." Alana dragged my arm. "We need Evie to come to girls' night. She's the one who can point out the nice dicks."

Chapter 41

ANDERSON

"You're really going to owe us when this is all over," Talbot said cheerfully.

I'd carted the worst of the debris out of the bedroom last night before I left to review the Bianca files.

Not that I'd found anything incriminating. I'd finally bitten the bullet and begged for more favors from my brothers.

"Whatever. Text me if you find anything," I told him, grabbing my jacket.

"You're not going to stay?"

"He's going to go hang out with his girlfriend," Lawrence singsonged.

"His ass is the one going to Idaho, where he's going to have to use a hairdryer to keep his balls from freezing to his dick. He needs to get laid while he can."

"There but for the grace of god." Talbot shook his head as he began reviewing the files. "Lucky for you, Hudson has us doing remote surveillance right now, and I can help keep Aaron from killing you."

The Murphy women were tired and hungover when I arrived at the Murphy house. All except for Melissa, who looked like she was going to call the cops on me if I so much as coughed in her direction.

"Look who took pity on you," Ian said to Evie as I grabbed her hand and placed a freshly made foil-wrapped breakfast sandwich in it.

"I am not eating that." She made a face.

"Coffee." I set the cup down.

"Can I get a ham-and-cheese omelet?" one of her younger cousins asked me as I set a platter of grilled onions and potatoes on the table.

"You can eat that, or you can starve," I growled.

My phone rang as I was heading back to the kitchen. Aaron.

I sent it to voicemail. I had two fucking days. He could leave me the hell alone. With my brothers helping me, I was getting that data by tonight.

"Who's ready for the hike?" Melissa asked when I came back with the rest of the food.

There was groaning from everyone at the table except for Jennifer, who flashed a thumbs-up while she scooped the uneaten potatoes from Evie's plate.

"Why are you so chipper, Aunt J?" Evie blinked blearily. "Can we shut the blinds?"

I ran my hand through her tousled hair.

"I'm a doctor, so I can give myself an IV." Jennifer unwrapped Evie's breakfast sandwich.

"If I ever have a heart attack, just let me die in the street if you're the only doctor," I told her.

"A-fucking-men, Anderson," Dr. Murphy said then scuttled out of the room when his wife glared at him.

"Are you coming, Anderson?" Evie called.

I loped over to her.

"I'll help you unload your picnic, but then I have to run." I kissed her to keep her from asking me what I was working on then kissed her again just because I could. "I wish I could stay," I murmured.

She wrinkled her nose. "Do you?"

"Hiking is fun."

"It's a holiday death march in the snow. I might manage a third of a mile, then I'm sneaking off."

"You walked more than that with me."

"Yeah, because there was food and a warm house at the end, not a snowy outcropping, and you carried me part of the way." She wrinkled her nose when I picked her up, hugging her soft body to me. "I am an indoor kid."

Snowball raced crazy eights in the snow.

I draped my arm over Evie's shoulders as we walked back to my truck.

"You have got to bring more booze than that," Granny Doyle complained as I ferried the rest of the baskets and coolers up the short hill to the picnic area with its view over the river that led to the falls.

"You hear that? We're light on liquid refreshments!" Evie said loudly, grabbing her purse. "Just to be safe, we need to run to the store. You guys can start the hike without us."

"I'm coming too," Ian called.

"You're a dancer. You're supposed to be in shape." Evie struggled with her brother as they raced down the path to the car.

"Ian," his mother chastised him. "You are not skipping out on this hike. It's a family affair."

"Evie's skipping," one of the triplets complained.

"No, she isn't!" Evie called. "Be right there!"

"*Not!*" she muttered and shot me a conspiratorial grin.

"Take Snowball," Evie begged Ian as the dog tore across the clearing, startling the several Irish setters prancing gracefully through the snow. "She needs a walk. *Please?*"

"I'll put it on your tab," her brother said, herding the dog away from the car.

"If you wait a minute, I can drop you off," I offered.

"You drive too slowly." Granny Doyle honked the horn. "Get in. We're going to the liquor store!"

Evie looked around furtively and jumped into the car. "Go, go, go!"

She blew me a kiss out the open window.

I picked up the last of the boxes of food.

"Is that my Mercedes?" Dr. Murphy asked as the tires squealed on the snow. "You need to keep your mom from taking my car."

"I told you to hide your keys." Melissa stretched out her legs. "Now, for today's hike." Melissa began addressing the rest of the family. "This is not a sightseeing tour. We need to reach the top of the falls in three hours."

I set the last of the boxes down on the picnic table bench and grabbed my phone to text my brothers.

Snowball barked as I headed down the trail.

Behind me, snow crunched.

"Fuck off, Henry," I said, not even looking back.

"What is your fucking endgame?" He reached for me.

I didn't stop.

My phone was ringing, probably my brothers calling to complain.

I shoved off Henry's arm.

He slid in front of me, blocking me.

"Henry!" his mother called, insistent.

"Seriously?" he exploded. "I know you're just trying to fuck with me, Anderson. What the hell do you want?"

"This isn't about you." I kept my voice level.

In the distance, Granny Doyle was speeding the Mercedes down the hill.

Henry laughed derisively. "What? Is it about Evie? Please. I know you. You don't love her. You don't care about her. You're going to break her heart to hurt me. Admit it." He shoved me. "Answer me."

"Fight! Fight!" his cousins chanted.

"Do not fight him, Henry," his dad warned him.

"I'm calling the police!" Shirley thundered.

The Mercedes was fishtailing down the icy road.

"Get out of my way." I shouldered him aside. "Steer into the skid!" I yelled, though it wasn't like either of the women in the car could hear me. "Dammit." I raced off, cutting crossways through the woods.

The car was out of control. It spun and veered sharply off the road, sliding down the snowy embankment nose-first.

It has to stop. There's brush. It has to stop.

Yells of shock echoed in the woods behind me as I ran, pulling off my heavy jacket and pushing myself into a dead sprint.

Ice cracked.

Henry and several of his family members raced behind me through the snowy woods, the snow muffling the fury of our footfalls.

"Call 911!" I shouted as the car slid into the icy river.

"Mom!" Melissa cried.

"Evie's in there." Ian was desperate as we pulled up to the gouge that cut down the snowy hill.

"Henry, you have to save them," one of the triplets begged.

But the eldest Murphy son stood frozen at the edge of the embankment, where the car had plunged through the ice.

I had already kicked my boots off, utility knife in hand.

Snowball appeared next to me.

"If you go in, you're on your own," I warned the dog.

Then I took two steps down the hill, aimed, and jumped into the jagged hole in the ice.

This is gonna hurt.

Chapter 42

EVIE

clawed at the airbag in front of me. The glowing dials on the car dashboard didn't do much against the murky blue light.

"Dad's going to be so pissed about his car." I knew I was panicking. "I think we need to call 911. Where's my phone? Oh my gosh, did I forget my phone?"

I yelped as something cold lapped at my feet.

Water.

"There's water in the car."

"We have to break the window." Granny Doyle hammered on the glass. "Dammit, doesn't your dad have a crowbar in here? This is why I told your mother to marry a man who can do things around the house."

"If we die, then I don't have to worry about finding a job." A desperate laugh escaped my throat.

"We need to control our breathing. We're going to run out of oxygen. I figure we've got at least an hour—"

"This isn't a submarine!" I screamed.

"It's German engineering."

"We are the least prepared people for this type of a disaster. Oh my god, I need to call Ian."

Gran grabbed my purse and flung it at the glass.

"Where is that dildo Trish gave you? That's what we need."

"I don't know!" I shrieked. The water was at my calves now.

"I watched a YouTube video about this. We're going to be fine. This is fine. We just have to wait for the water to fill the car, then we hold our breath, then we open the doors."

My breath game out in nervous gasps. I wasn't the most coordinated. "You have what? A minute before you pass out underwater? I'm not going to be able to get the door open. Help!" I screamed as I ineffectively banged on the glass. "I am doing weight training if we get out of here."

"Fuck that. I'm buying a shotgun. And a Jeep."

Crack!

I screamed, "We're going to die!"

Out of the darkness, a knife appeared.

Crack!

A spider web formed where the knife had hit the glass. A face appeared in the dark water. Gray eyes peered at the crack.

"Anderson!" I screamed, banging on the other side of the glass.

Crack!

The glass fractured across the length of the windshield. His fist, wrapped in a leather belt, pummeled the glass, shattering it enough to make an Evie-sized hole.

"Take her first. I'm going down with the ship," Granny Doyle declared as the cold, dark water poured in through the cracked glass.

I took deep gulps of air, then the icy water was over my head. Disoriented, I tried to swim to the light as a firm hand on my jacket collar tugged me upward.

"Gran!" I cried as soon as I could take a breath. I gasped as icy air burned my lungs.

Anderson, eyes the same color as the gray ice around us, blinked at me, then he disappeared.

"Anderson!" I screamed.

Something that looked like a half-drowned white rat paddled around me then disappeared under the water.

On the shore, my family was panicking.

"Help!" I screamed.

"Evie, swim to shore." Ian gestured wildly. "Swim!"

"I can't!"

"Evie Murphy, I paid good money for you to have swim lessons. Why are you still in the water? Henry, go get her," my mom shouted.

Anderson was down there. So was my grandmother. I pushed the ice around, ducking my head underwater, trying to find him.

Bubbles brushed my face, then he was surfacing in front of me, Granny Doyle in his arms.

"Come on. She needs to go to the hospital." He flipped onto his back.

Hands numb, I hung on to his shirt as he kicked us to the shallows, where the ice had collected.

Breaking through the ice sheet, he carried Granny Doyle's lifeless body on his shoulders.

The doctors in the family immediately jumped into action as Anderson set her down on a cleared patch of snow.

I collapsed in the icy shallows. Anderson picked me up.

"It's my *Titanic* moment." My teeth chattered as he had to half drag me out of the water.

"I have your jacket." Ian tried to hand it to Anderson as he stripped me out of my water-logged clothes.

"Put it on her."

"Gran!" I cried as I shivered. "She's dead, oh god!"

My aunt was on the phone with medevac.

"Someone save her!" I begged no one in particular as Anderson rubbed me through his warm jacket.

My dad tipped Gran's head back to give a rescue breath.

Granny Doyle's hand came up to slap his face. My dad cursed.

"I thought Anderson was saving my life. If it's just going to be you giving mouth-to-mouth, Brian, don't bother."

"Of course the lord couldn't have given us a Christmas miracle for once in this family." Grandma Shirley stared up at the sky.

"Fuck yeah, I'm back, baby!" Granny Doyle whooped as Aunt Jennifer draped a silver thermal blanket around her. She peered over the icy river where somewhere in the depths, a black Mercedes lurked. "You needed a new car anyway, Brian. Maybe you can buy a truck like Anderson's."

"I hate to ask, but you didn't happen to rescue the dog, did you?" Sawyer asked delicately.

"Snowball!" I cried. "I knew I saw her! Snowball!" I raced into the lake.

"Do not go back in there." Anderson threw me back into the snow, which was actually weirdly warm compared to the water.

"My dog!" I sobbed. "She tried to save me."

"Missy's about to have puppies," my uncle offered sympathetically. "You can have one."

"Evie doesn't need another dog." My dad had snapped into his detached-surgeon mode as the disaster unfolded.

"You can have one of my cats," Aunt Trish offered.

"You are moving out today if you bring home one of those cats, Evie," my mother warned me.

"I shouldn't. I'm a horrible dog mom," I blubbered as Anderson petted my frozen hair. "This is the worst Christmas ever."

"Looks like you're actually getting a Christmas miracle." He tipped my chin up.

Snowball paddled furiously against the current toward to the edge of the shore, teeth clamped on the strap of my purse.

"Leave it!" Anderson yelled at the dog.

Snowball ignored him and continued to paddle toward us.

"You going to go jump in there this time?" Aunt Victoria asked Henry, who seemed like he was in shock.

"Goddammit," Anderson swore then waded into the icy water, scooped out Snowball and my bag, and dumped both next to me on the ground.

"Who's a brave girl?" I hugged the sopping-wet dog.

"You need to be thanking your brave boy," Aunt J joked.

My other aunts whistled as Anderson peeled of his already-freezing wet shirt, and my uncles congratulated him.

"He's goddamn Superman."

"He just jumped right in there."

Nat stuck her phone in my face. The video of Anderson jumping into the icy water to rescue me played.

"Hell yeah!" Lauren whooped. "It's going viral. I just posted it."

"I told you I was posting my video." Nat shoved her. "I need to be an influencer."

"I'm the one who needs some extra income," I said around my chattering teeth.

Anderson, moving stiffly, dragged me up, his arm still around me.

Frost formed on his eyelashes as he wrapped me in his dry jacket, trying to keep me close to him.

It didn't seem real, what had just happened.

"You need to get warm."

"You don't have any shoes."

"I'll be fine. I just need you to be okay, Evie." His freezing hand stroked my face as his eyes searched mine.

"At least the hike is canceled!"

Chapter 43

ANDERSON

"Evie, your hair!" her mother yelled, rushing over with a towel.

"Crap." Evie blew on the singed ends of her hair, which she was drying in front of the fire.

"Can you please…" I blew out a breath. "Try not to get yourself killed for the rest of the day?"

"I'm going to have to tell Brooke you can't be on her talk show," Melissa tutted. "Where is Sawyer? You burnt off half your hair. Sawyer!"

Evie sat down on the loveseat closest to the fire, and I handed her the mug of tea I was carrying.

"Drink," I ordered. "You're still cold."

She took a long drink then leaned against me. "It's not that bad, is it?" Evie asked, worry in her eyes as she ran her fingers through her tangled hair.

I tugged at the singed curls. "I think you'd look cute with a short haircut, Gingersnap."

I sat in front of the fire, wearing in a loaner pair of pants, the chill of the icy water finally starting to fade.

I'd never forget the pure terror, the need to save that had been a gun at my neck forcing me into action.

I pulled her closer to me. "Don't do that again."

"Ride shotgun while Granny Doyle is driving? I think my dad's going to shred her license."

"No." I squeezed my eyes shut, seeing only the murky icy water. I breathed in the holiday scent of her. "Don't leave me. Don't almost die. I can't—"

She grabbed my hand. "If you want to stay with me, then buckle up, asshole." She smiled up at me. "I have a pretty bad track record."

I rested my forehead against hers, stared into her eyes.

"I can't lose you. And I could have." What if I hadn't been there? What if she'd just drowned while her useless family watched on the shore? I'd have shown up to her house wondering, waiting, only to have my heart ripped out, leaving an Evie-sized hole.

One of Granny Doyle's sons shoved a plate with a huge square of lasagna in front of me.

"Uncle Hugh, he doesn't eat carbs." Evie sighed beside me on the couch, the warm mug of tea cradled in her hands.

"My bad, Anderson," he said jovially. "You want a burger? You want Chinese? We can get you anything you want."

"We owe you," his brother said, muscling in. He draped a blanket around my shoulders like I was a prizefighter.

"I'm grilling steak because I actually care that we're not burying Mom and Evie, unlike you," Todd shot at him as two of his sons traipsed through the house with a bag of charcoal.

Evie had a freaked-out look in her eyes at the mention of Christmas burials.

I'd been expecting it. I drew her close to me.

This was why I had to stay.

"What are you doing?" Jennifer chased her brothers away from me. "Someone get this man a drink."

"Get him a medal. He saved Christmas!" Her sister ruffled my hair.

"Evie, you are disaster prone. Get that hot water away from that man's balls," Jennifer scolded her.

"Eat," I urged Evie, taking the mug from her.

"I'm actually not that hungry. Funny. A near-death experience was all I needed to kick-start that New Year's weight loss resolution." She fidgeted with the plate, running her thumb over the holly pattern on the edge.

I cut off a piece of the lasagna and held it up to her mouth.

She leaned in and took the bite. She still had that freaked out, wide-eyed look as she chewed.

The front door burst open to the sound of Granny Doyle giving an impassioned interview to several reporters then slammed shut.

I fed Evie another bite of lasagna as more aunts piled into the living room.

"My husband said you wanted Chinese food." A piping-hot bag was sat next to me.

"I—"

"He doesn't want that," her sister-in-law argued. "I made you potato-and-bacon soup. You need something warm."

"He needs a drink."

"Just give him the bottle."

"Not that swill Brian has." One of her aunts pulled a bottle out of her purse and handed it to me.

"If Evie shits the bed," her aunt assured me, "I have several daughters. You can give them a try. You are a part of this family now."

"I think I'll stick with the one I have." I squeezed Evie.

"As you can see, the hero of Maplewood Falls is shirtless and recovering," Nat announced, phone out. "Yes, we are taking donations, Sparkledolphin32."

"Are you live streaming this?" Evie cried as she licked the lasagna plate.

"Ooh, is that CNN I see in the comments?" Nat asked. "The rescue video is copywritten, by the way. Call me for licensing fees!"

Evie's small, soft body was warm against me. I fished in the takeout sack and handed her an egg roll.

Snowball jumped up on my lap, licking her small black nose.

"You made a difficult situation even worse," I reminded the dog.

She set one small paw on my hand.

I opened the top container and selected a piece of beef.

"She saved my phone." Evie scratched the little dog behind the ears as she scarfed down the snack.

"My phone. Shit." I patted my pockets.

My wallet and keys had been in my jacket, but my phone? At the bottom of the river.

"I have to run." I kissed Evie's warm mouth.

"You're leaving? But you didn't get steak."

"Save it for me."

My brothers were grim faced when I raced into the garage, leaving the truck parked askew out front in the gravel lot.

"No jokes about the daring rescue? I didn't think you'd be that worried about me. You know I can handle a river." I set my keys on the table.

Jake crossed his arms. He didn't smile. "We found something on the Bianca files."

"Fuck yeah." I pumped a fist. "So that's it. It's done. Give me your phone. I need to call Aaron."

"I wouldn't do that." Talbot held out a hand.

Lawrence pointed at the screen behind him. "She's keeping secrets."

"Yeah, a secret affair. That's the reason she and Braeden were hiding messages," Jake explained.

"Fuck." I slumped down onto the threadbare couch.

"They've been hooking up on the down-low for months. She's got tons of evidence—homemade pornos, sexy text messages, chat logs between them, talking about how she's going to meet him at the tropical resort where he and Felicity are having their honeymoon so they can hook up."

"Damn."

"Nothing, however, on the insurance fraud," Jake added.

"I'm fucked."

My mouth was dry. Suddenly, I was glad I hadn't eaten much of the offered food. I was going to puke.

"This can't be happening. The files were supposed to be there." I pushed Lawrence away from the computer. "There has to be something there. Aaron's going to kill me."

"Unless Santa wants to bring you an early Christmas miracle, you're totally fucked, dude."

I sat there in the chilly garage, drinking, after my brothers had packed up and left, finishing up Braeden's destruction. Jake had cleaned up the audio file.

I shouldn't be wasting my time on this.

I needed to run. Should already have packed my shit and set off to get as far away from Aaron as possible.

I closed my eyes.

Then I'd have to leave Evie, the only good thing I had left in my life.

I hauled myself up.

"Leave," I urged myself.

The little train that I'd finally fixed so that it would run again sat on a piece of track. I picked it up. It needed one more coat of paint.

"Leave her. Leave this."

I took out the paint, not sure if I could leave a piece of my heart behind or if I'd even survive.

EVIE

The box of unused Christmas decorations thumped on the floor of the small guest bedroom.

"Are you moving out early?" Ian asked as I crawled next to him in the bed with the rest of the leftover Chinese food and some cake pops.

"It's my thank-you present to Anderson." I scooped up some of the sesame chicken. "I'm decorating his house."

Sawyer pulled a cake pop out of her mouth. "I don't think Anderson is that wholesome."

"You think he's not going to like the scarf I knitted him for Christmas?" I cried.

"I think he'll like it if it comes with a blow job." Ian grabbed a fork.

"I thought my mom threw out this Christmas tree years ago." Sawyer pulled out a slightly dilapidated miniature Christmas tree predecorated with lights.

"Waste not, want not."

"That man jumped into a freezing river and saved you from drowning, and in thanks, you ate all his food, let Granny Doyle ambush him in the front yard for an interview, and now you're going to dump holiday garbage in his living room?" Ian raised an eyebrow.

"No, she's not. I need him on my hockey team next year." Sawyer picked up a hand-knitted Rudolph ornament made by yours truly.

"You need to make Christmas ornament of your boobs, not this. Where's your Cricut?"

"Don't you think that's a little cheap? He did risk his life for me," I argued.

"It's a nudie pic," Ian declared, pointing a cake pop at me. "It's at the top of every American male's Christmas list."

"Anderson probably just saved you because his military training took over or whatever." Sawyer stole a piece of chicken. "Didn't you say he hates you? Anderson is not a good guy."

"He's a hero. The bad-boy stuff is just an act." I was fervent. "All he needed was a woman to save him, and that woman was me. We saved each other."

"It's the shock and the cold." Ian held a hand to my forehead.

"Evie, you're blackmailing him, remember?" Sawyer shook me. "Anderson does not like you. You cannot give him your heart for Christmas."

"He risked his life for me. What if…" I licked my lips then dared to say the words. "What if he's in love with me?"

"Yikes." Ian made a face. "Evie, you can't show up at a man's house in the middle of the night to tell him you're in love with him."

"Just surprise him with crotchless panties and the left-over steak," Sawyer urged me. "At the very least, wait until he torches Braeden. Then you can scare him off with your declarations of love."

"Too late," Ian said. "She's already planning their wedding."

"Evie." Sawyer clapped her hands. "You're so close to finishing the year on a high note. Just keep it together for a few more days."

"He rescued me!"

"You always fall too hard for the wrong men."

"I know you think Anderson's the wrong man, but I believe there's something more there," I argued.

"There is only sexual attraction. Now, let's redirect." Sawyer reached into her backpack and pulled out a pink bag decorated with white Christmas trees.

"Aww, did the bride give you thank-you gifts?" Ian cooed.

Sawyer snorted. "The bride fired the maid of honor in front of the whole wedding party and told me I could take her goodie bag."

"Is this a butt plug?" Ian dumped the bag out onto the bed.

"Ooh, a cookie!" I grabbed it.

Sawyer slapped at my hand.

She clicked a pair of tweezers at me and plucked a stray hair off my chin.

"Ow!"

"You need to be on your A game." My cousin ripped out another hair. "This is thank-you-for-saving-my-life sex."

"Not I-want-to-spend-the-rest-of-my-life-with-you sex," Ian warned me.

Anderson was shirtless and barefoot, black jeans slung low on his hips, when he opened the door. He stared at me blankly for a moment, then his eyes narrowed.

In the cold and after upping my blood sugar, I could see my cousin's point of view. It wasn't my best idea to show up at Anderson's house with a used Christmas tree. Thank god Sawyer had my back.

I dropped the box and shoved it aside.

Anderson's eyes slid off me.

"Ignore that." I fumbled with the zipper of my coat.

The door slammed behind me as Anderson knelt down in front of the box. "What are you doing, Evie?"

"I was going to put a little down-home festive cheer in your life then let you fuck me in these crotchless panties."

He inspected the Christmas tree.

"But if you want to decorate first, we can do that too." I grabbed it out of his hand, fished for the cable, plugged it in, then fluffed out the branches. The lights warmed up the gloom, and Christmas carols filtered out of the base of the tree as it slowly spun. "Voila! Instant Christmas." I set his present under the tree.

"No, what are you doing, Evie?"

"I also brought you your steak. Not your Chinese. Sorry. Ian and I ate that already."

He regarded me, silent. He looked exhausted.

I reached up to run my fingers on his rough jaw.

"You might be the best thing that ever happened to me." He nuzzled my hand.

"The tree's not that nice." My voice was soft.

Anderson kissed the tips of my fingers. "Evie, I'm falling for you."

He stared at me a moment while I trembled, off-balance.

He sighed. "I am so fucked."

"That's my line."

Chapter 45

ANDERSON

S he tugged off her jacket, shy almost, and laid it on the armrest of the sofa.

My life was collapsing around me, leaving only her.

I blinked, not believing it.

"I can't lose you, Evie." I cupped her face, brushing my forehead against hers. "You're all I have."

"You didn't lose me," she whispered. "You saved me. That means you get to keep me."

I hoisted her up, kissing her. She wrapped her arms around my neck as I lost myself in the sensation of her. Her legs kicked as I carried her up the narrow metal staircase.

Frank Sinatra crooned from downstairs as I laid Evie on the bed, her clothes bright red against the gray military blanket.

I hovered over her, drinking her in.

This might be my last Christmas on earth, but fuck it if I wasn't going to spend the rest of my miserable life with her.

I hesitated slightly as I unbuttoned her shirtdress, giving her skin the barest brush of my lips. "You're everything I've always wanted."

Kissing her long and slowly, I swept my tongue into her mouth as I unhooked her lacy red bra. Her breast was soft and full in my mouth, the nipple hardening quickly under my tongue.

"Shit, Gingersnap, you weren't lying about the panties."

She gasped as I stroked her slit. "That's how bad I want your cock."

Hooking one leg over my shoulder, I buried my face in the hot, slick warmth of her, licking her, memorizing her.

Her fingertips rubbed little circles in my scalp, and her hips rocked against me as I mouthed her, swirling my tongue against her clit.

Reaching up, I cupped her breast, pinching her nipple as I ran my tongue roughly over her clit, bringing her closer and closer until she was shuddering while I milked her orgasm.

"You're stupidly good at that," she groaned.

My pocket vibrated. I sent Aaron's call to my new burner to voicemail then shrugged off my jeans.

Nuzzling her navel, I pulled the panties down and grabbed a condom from the nightstand.

She was ready for me. Her hips surged up to meet me as I thrust into her, burying myself in the familiar tightness.

I let her pussy flex around my hard length, pulled out, and slid in again, kissing her as I sank into her.

She wrapped her arms around my neck as I made love to her slowly. She was perfect under me—her mouth, her tits, her hips, her thighs gripping my waist as she took my cock. Perfect.

She arched against me as I angled her hips up, hitting deep inside of her.

"Fuck me," she begged as I gave her another long, slow thrust. "No, I want you to wreck my pussy."

I pulled out of her, and she whimpered, reaching for me.

"You want me to ruin your cunt?"

"Yes, fuck me. *Please.*" She squealed when I flipped her around, her hips at the edge of the bed.

"Spread your legs." I kicked at her ankles, and she widened her knees.

"Wider. More. I want to see your pussy."

Moaning, she reached behind her, toes gripping the wood floor as she spread her ass and pussy for me.

I rubbed her swollen dark-pink cunt while she moaned, throwing her head back. My cock ached for her pussy.

"I'm gonna enjoy this."

She jumped against the bed as I surged into her, jack-hammering into her with my hard cock, her pussy placed perfectly for me.

"You feel so good in my pussy," she moaned.

I hunched over her, resting my fists on the bed, keeping up the unrelenting pace.

"Harder! Fuck me harder!"

I pounded into her as she moaned and squealed under me, her tight little cunt clenching as she took my cock, then she was coming around me.

"Make me come again," she begged.

I flipped her over, and she grabbed at my arms.

"I want to see your face when you come, screaming my name, Gingersnap."

She nodded, eyes glazed in pleasure.

Then I was in her again.

Little gasps came out of her swollen mouth as I brought her closer and closer, her pussy so tight around me, her tits soft against my chest as I claimed her, reminded her that she belonged to me, that her pussy, her tits, her whole body was mine.

"Fuck Evie," I chanted as I buried my cock in her, over and over again, "fuck, I love you. Fuck, I never want to lose you."

She twisted under me, fingers digging into my neck, then she was coming, chanting my name, tight little pussy clenching and rippling around my cock as I fucked the orgasm into her until I couldn't take it anymore and my balls clenched as I surged into her.

I kissed her as I spilled in her, needing to feel every piece of her.

She smiled at me as I kissed her eyelids, her chin, her neck.

I pulled her up on the bed with me and wrapped the blanket around us.

"You're unfairly good at this," she murmured.

I tucked her hair behind her ear.

I needed to toss the condom and really needed to figure out some sort of plan for dealing with Aaron's violent displeasure.

But what could I do?

Nothing.

So why not spend my last hours here with her?

"I love you," I whispered, trailing my fingertips along the soft underside of her arm, up and around to summit the swell of her breast.

She smiled against my chest. "Say it again."

"I love you," I promised, pressing soft kisses to her temple. "Run away with me."

"Run away where?"

I cradled her head against my chest, letting her hear my heartbeat only for her. "Anywhere."

Before I could doze off, I forced myself up.

Evie pulled me back to her. "I hope you're leaving because you're bringing leftovers."

"Something better."

I tossed the condom on my way downstairs then grabbed a bottle of wine on my way back with the tablet.

She was still warm under the blanket. I propped the tablet up on a pillow.

"Merry Christmas." I kissed her softly. "Braeden's going to burn tomorrow."

"We're doing it!" Her eyes lit up.

"I've got everything on a flash drive." I set it carefully between her breasts.

"Have it plugged into the TV, then tell your family you made a video of fun family memories you want to share. They'll be gathered around to watch as Braeden's life implodes."

She squeezed me briefly, gleeful.

"It starts with him at Ian's theater." I hit Play on the tablet. "Then it segues into the text he sent Preston, tastefully censored, by the way." I kissed her nipple.

"The disembodied Rudolph heads are a nice touch."

"And the grand finale is his and Bianca's affair."

"Damn, you really are an evil villain."

I kissed her fingertips. "Yes, but I'm your villain."

I laced our fingers together. "And after, as everyone falls apart, I'll take your hand, and we'll walk out the door. You'll climb onto the back of my bike, and hopefully, you won't fall—"

"Snowball will come too."

"Snowball will be there, too, and you can take one of those raggedy Christmas trees, if you want." I smiled, eyes half-closed, as she swatted me.

"We'll ride and ride, maybe south or out west, and we won't stop until we see a little town. There will be a hardware store that an old man is trying to sell. We'll remind him of him and his late wife. He'll hand us the keys and wish us good luck. You'll open a café next door. We'll buy a big rambling farmhouse. You can have all those dogs and kids from foster care. They'll be a little prickly at first, but you'll win them over."

"No, you'll win them over."

"We'll have a garden. Some chickens. I'll tell you I love you every day and make love to you every night. You'll be so happy."

"I love it." Her eyes shone. "Play it again."

Evie was there in the frame, smiling that gorgeous smile, mouthing *I love you* in the video as she whispered the words to me.

"Again," Evie said happily, kissing me, tucking herself under my chin so I could smell the Christmas scent of her hair.

"You saved me." She kissed my collarbone, smiling up at me as the video version smiled at the camera.

The video looped.

Evie ran her toes up and down my calf, making happy noises as Braeden's impending destruction played.

But I wasn't watching her or Braeden's fucking face in the frame.

No, I was watching the top right-hand corner, where a familiar man with red hair and a dancer's costume was talking furtively with a heavyset man in a suit.

And I knew—knew from instinct honed from almost a decade of working on insurance fraud cases, working up close and personal with Aaron, knew because the evidence was clicking into place—snippets of conversation, complaints from Ian, an overheard phone conversation...

There was something there.

Chapter 46

EVIE

"Someone got laid."

"It's better than that." I sighed happily. "I'm in love. Last night, Anderson helped me put up the decorations I'd brought, then we'd made love all night. Yes, made love, not just hooked up. We even went out for breakfast in the morning and looked at farmhouse floor plans on his phone."

My cousin's face fell. "No. You didn't, Evie."

"I did, and I'm so glad." I beamed. "Because he said he loved me. Technically, he said it first."

"And we're not concerned about that at all?" Ian winced.

"No, we're going to run away together after the big reveal." I twirled happily.

"It's cloudy outside," Ian said flatly.

"You don't even know this man." Sawyer grabbed me.

"We're meant to be together. No one understands me like he does. He's my everything," I gushed.

Across the room at my parents' dinner party, Anderson was listening intently as my younger cousins were excitedly talking hockey with him.

"He saved me. He's got this whole insane presentation that's going to blow the lid off Braeden. I'll be free!"

"Yes, but you won't have to move out, remember?" Sawyer was desperate.

I had my future with Anderson all planned out. "I'm moving out anyway. We're going to ride off into the sunset and buy a farmhouse."

Sawyer pressed her hands together. "I feel like this might get you on a true crime podcast, Evie. Don't you think you want to slow down?"

"I don't need to. He's used, like, all the love languages on me."

"It's not a bingo card." Ian pursed his lips.

"Why don't you wait until Braeden gets his ass kicked out the door then reevaluate how you feel about Anderson?" Sawyer wasn't giving up.

"I don't need to reevaluate. Anderson's my perfect Christmas. He's my Hallmark romance. He's my happily ever after."

He noticed me watching him from across the room and winked at me.

I swooned.

Ian grimaced.

"I just don't think you should be making life-changing decisions two days before Christmas. This is an emotional time..."

"It's not a decision. It's fate," I explained as I fumbled the USB drive into the port on the back of the dark TV. "Do you guys see the remote for this TV?" I asked, searching around.

"If you don't find it, I have a remote control app on my phone," Ian said, patting his pants pockets. "Wait. Shit, where's my phone? Did you see my phone?"

"Did you leave it upstairs?" I asked.

We traipsed up the steps to search in the small guest room.

Nothing.

"Didn't you have it in the car when we went to get ice?" I asked.

"Right, yeah, it's probably in Sawyer's car."

"You waiting on your boyfriend to call?" my cousin teased.

Ian shoved Sawyer as we raced down the stairs.

"The director promised I would dance the Nutcracker Prince this season."

"He can't keep stringing you along," Sawyer said as we pushed out the front door. "You're a much better dancer than that clubfooted loser they keep casting."

"Right? My lines are so much better than his."

Sawyer and Ian searched her car as my second cousin pulled up behind them.

"You're here!" Excited, she wrapped her scarf around her. "I can't believe I missed the hike. Nat texted me, and I was all, like, I don't want to hike in the cold. And then I missed it. Oh my god, he's even bigger in person," she gasped.

Anderson was walking down the porch steps, motorcycle helmet in hand.

"You're leaving?"

464 • Alina Jacobs

"There you are." He leaned in to kiss me dizzy while my second cousin wolf whistled.

"I have to check on something at one of the venues. I'll be back." He trailed his fingers in my hair.

"You promise?"

"He's not a soft trust-fund kid Evie." My second cousin rolled her eyes. "Your man works for a living. Make sure you come back," she said to Anderson. "I had a three-hour drive, and I was promised eye candy for my troubles."

His gray eyes didn't even flicker.

He kissed me again. "I'll be back as soon as I can."

I winced as his motorcycle roared.

Henry was waiting in the foyer when we all trooped inside, glowering at the front door.

"You didn't say something to him, did you?" Ian snapped at him.

Henry ignored him and turned on his heel.

"We're not holding dinner for Anderson," my mom called from the dining room.

"The man's a hero. Let him have hot food," her sister said.

"The roast will get dry."

I sent him a text.

Evie: *You want us to wait on dinner for you?*

Of course he isn't going to answer, dummy. He's riding.

"Evie? The kids are hungry," Mom said.

"I guess we can eat."

I called him again and again through dinner, where I sat banished at the kids table, trying to keep my younger cousins from stabbing each other with their forks.

Evie: *Please come back soon. We have to do the reveal.*
Evie: *I can't do this by myself.*

This was the last time the entire family was going to be together until Christmas day. And that would be too late. I was going to be thrown out into the street in thirty-six hours.

It was now or never.

Anderson needed to be here.

The Yorkshire pudding sat like rocks in my stomach.

"Everyone is about to go downstairs to watch hockey," Ian hissed at me. "Where is he? You need to do the big reveal. Now."

"I need him here." I called him again. It went straight to voicemail.

I gulped down the rest of my wine. "Maybe he had a motorcycle accident."

"Or maybe he is a lying piece of shit like all the other men you are attracted to, Evie." Sawyer grabbed my shoulder.

"But he did it. He found the evidence to bury Braeden. I don't believe he'd screw me over. He loves me." I looked at the TV. "I should go look for him." I blinked back tears. "That's what a good girlfriend would do."

Sawyer shook me. "Snap out of it. Anderson's hated the Murphys for years. He's not fucking Santa Claus. He's a bad man. He's not crashing through the roof to save you."

I needed him to come. I needed the happily ever after to my holiday romance.

I refused to believe he wasn't coming, because if he didn't come back, that meant there was something wrong with me. That I was really, truly unlovable.

Chapter 47

ANDERSON

The ghost of Christmas future played a funeral dirge as I clicked through the files I'd copied over from the phone I'd stolen from Ian.

There was no question.

The Starlight Theater had committed insurance fraud, to the tune of a 1.2-million-dollar payout. It was all there on Ian's phone—the text messages and the emails.

Ian had caught the director purposefully damaging theater equipment for the insurance money. The director had promised him a lead dance role if he kept his mouth shut.

However, the director reneged on his promise, leading Ian to complain about the lack of a role materializing. Evie's brother had photos and video evidence, receipts, invoices, and proof of work orders being inflated.

There was enough not just to bury the company but also to send people to jail.

I tried to control my breathing. I sounded like a victim. I was not a victim.

The old analogue clock ticked as the minute hand crept closer to twelve. I had four more hours to get Aaron the last of his money.

And ruin Evie's life.

Again.

Ian was her favorite brother. She would hate me forever if I was the reason he was sent to jail.

Evie was everything to me. The only good thing that I had. Was I ready to just throw that away?

I reached for the external hard drive I'd copied the data to.

I had to destroy it, had to protect her and Ian. I'd suffer whatever consequences Aaron threw at me if it meant I could shield her. I pulled out the blender to destroy the phone and the hard drive.

"*Don't kill him!*" There was yelling outside my front door and the sound of someone trying to kick it down.

"*I have a key, Hudson, Jesus.*"

"What the fuck, Anderson?" My eldest brother stormed into the garage. "The fuck is wrong with you?"

He shoved me back against the counter.

"You've been in a downhill spiral all year—lying about the status of a case to a client, getting caught on a job, and now you just give up? You should have told me the Bianca files were a bust. We could have done something. You're fucked. You know that? Your deadline is in four hours."

"Three hours and fifty-five minutes," I corrected him.

Hudson raised an arm to punch me.

"Oh shit." Jake huffed out a laugh. "Bro. It's a Christmas miracle."

"This wasn't on the list," Talbot said, picking up my notepad with the Starlight Theater name circled and the evidence listed out underneath in neat bullets.

I tilted my head.

It was like I was watching the whole scene from outside my body, like Ebenezer Scrooge being forced to confront the consequences of all his bad decisions.

"I can't give that to Aaron," I said quietly.

"You fucking what?" Hudson snarled in my face.

"Evie will be heartbroken."

"Evie? Evie *Murphy*?" Lawrence asked. "You're throwing away everything for her?"

"We're in love. We're going to buy a farmhouse," I said simply.

"You're not buying a farmhouse, Anderson." Hudson paced in front of me.

"He probably took one too many hits to the head." Jake shined a flashlight in my eyes.

"You're not in love with her. She doesn't love you. You tried to kill her brother," Lawrence argued with me. "She was never really going to love you. She's manipulating you. She tried to blackmail you, remember?"

Hudson made a disgusted noise. "You've completely lost your edge."

"Maybe I just finally found happiness."

"What about us?" Talbot asked softly. "Is she worth more to you than us—your brothers, your family?"

And just like that, I snapped back into myself.

Aaron would make Hudson pay—make my brothers pay—if I ran off. I grabbed the blender and shoved it back into the cabinet.

My brothers watched me warily.

I'd already sacrificed enough for the Murphys. They all looked out for each other, closing ranks around each other.

I couldn't afford to stick my neck out for another Murphy, and I damn well sure wasn't sacrificing my brothers for one of them.

"Get out of my way." I grabbed my helmet.

"Are you seriously running?" Hudson demanded as I shoved past him.

"No, asshole. I'm going to New York City."

Chapter 48

EVIE

"Oh, Evie, you were supposed to be watching them."
My mother cut through the white noise in my
head to scold me about letting one of my little
cousins smear whipped cream all over himself.

"He's six. He should know how to eat with a fork," I
said, duly wiping off his hands.

I was frozen in my chair.

"Where'd Hot Stuff run off to?" Granny Doyle asked,
coming by with a bottle of eggnog-flavored vodka.

"You need to cut her off." My dad was arguing with my
mom near the Christmas tree. "She already wrecked one
car."

"He has to work," I said, my voice sounding far away,
"but he'll by later."

Maybe.

Hopefully.

Except it was turning into a horrible repeat of last Christmas, when the man of my dreams had left me flopping around on the back of a sleigh.

Sawyer was right. I had never ever in my life picked a nice, normal man. They were all complete life-ruining assholes. Why couldn't Anderson just show up?

"You ready for your big moment?" Ian's face was concerned.

Snowball stamped her tiny feet next to me.

I grabbed the bottle of vodka, twisted the top off, and took a huge swallow. Then another.

"I don't need a man to save Christmas." I wiped the back of my arm over my mouth. "God, that stuff is nasty."

Sawyer sniffed it. "I think it smells even worse than last year."

I took another big swallow for fortification. The alcohol was working.

I didn't need Anderson.

I had this.

The toasts were starting.

I downed glass after glass of champagne as the Murphys all told each other how awesome they were, my dad professed his love to my mother, one cousin even announced they were adopting a puppy, and Aunt Amy made a mildly passive-aggressive toast about her daughter-in-law. Then...

"I have a toast!" I stood up, swaying drunkenly.

"Maybe we should move this to tomorrow." Sawyer tried to tug the hem of my shirt. "Or just send it in the group chat and be done with it."

"No. I'm making my announcement." I stumbled toward the TV and pressed the remote.

I pressed it again.

"Damn remote." I banged it on my hand while my family looked on in confusion. "How do I turn this on?"

"Evie, sit down."

I ducked around my mom. Snowball yapped at her when she tried to approach me.

"This is your mother's fault, Mel. She gave Evie a whole bottle of vodka," Dad hissed.

The TV flared to life.

Finally.

I hoisted my glass and turned the volume up as high as it could go.

"In this holiday season of giving, I want to acknowledge one man here who has made this last year one to remember."

"Is it Anderson?"

"No, he left."

"What?" My cousins asked.

"If I'd known he wasn't going to be here, I wouldn't have come. I'd have stayed at the retirement home." My great-aunt thumped her walker on the ground.

"I thought I was going to see a shirtless man."

"I have something better than a shirtless man." I made a grand gesture to the TV.

"A naked one?" my aunt asked hopefully.

"No. I'm making a presentation here."

"Hurry up, Evie! The game is about to start!" my uncle bellowed.

Several of my cousins pulled out their phones, and a couple called outside to family members who'd wandered off and were going to miss the drama.

"Braeden." I pointed at him. "This time last year, you stood here in front of everyone and lied."

474 • Alina Jacobs

"Evie, that is enough!" There were two splotches of red on my mom's cheeks.

"You told me you loved me. You told me we were going to be together forever." My voice cracked. But instead of Braeden, I was thinking of Anderson. "You made me imagine a future with you, but the entire time, you were just using me. Exhibit A."

"Those better not be your—"

"Damn, those are nice tits!" Granny Doyle toasted me.

My family erupted in a fit of giggles.

"Wait. No—" I didn't have Anderson's flair for the dramatic or his timing. "I need to start it over at the beginning. You have to see it from the start."

My family did hear the audio recording loud and clear of Braeden telling me all about how he wanted to start an affair with me if I'd just get with Preston.

"You." Felicity turned on him.

"She's lying. This is a deep fake. That's not me," my ex insisted. "Evie, are you trying to ruin Christmas?"

"She's trying to break up my daughter's marriage!" Aunt Lisa screeched.

"Exactly." Braeden was emphatic.

"He's been lying!" I yelled. "He was lying last year."

"Evie, get out of the way. I can't see the screen," my cousins complained.

"Lies! It's all lies!" Braeden thundered.

"Oh my god, you were sleeping with my fiancé?" Felicity screeched. "Those text messages are from three days ago." Felicity pointed at the screenshots. "It was Evie's underwear I found in the back of the closet, wasn't it? You're having an affair, Braeden."

"Can't you fucking read?" Sawyer yelled at her. "Those text messages aren't Evie's. They're Aunt Bianca's."

My aunt burst into tears. "I was being neglected. I knew it was wrong. I was going to break up with him."

"That's not what you said the other night." Sawyer underlined the text message with her palm.

"Really?" Granny Doyle put on her reading glasses, peering at the screen. "Can't you pause it, Evie?"

"Yeah, I can't see that," my family complained.

"Are there subtitles?" someone asked.

"I'm trying." I mashed the buttons on the remote.

"You ruined my marriage, Evie!" Aunt Bianca screeched.

My cousins, her children, were in shock.

Uncle Jaime sat down heavily in a chair. "My family... I thought we were in love."

"Family? Your mother is a monster!" Aunt Bianca raged at him as her daughter hugged her dad protectively and her son burst into tears. "And you just let her railroad me. I had to do what I needed to do for my mental health."

The video finally looped over.

"You see?" I shouted, pointing. "This is from last year. Braeden admits he was lying. I didn't try to steal him."

"You admit you were sleeping with my fiancé? All of you are cheaters. You, Braeden, and Bianca—need to get the hell out." Felicity pointed at the door.

"I am the victim." I beat my chest.

"You are a home-wrecker."

"Let's watch it again." I made an exaggerated gesture to the screen. "Then you will see," I enunciated, "that I did not know he was with you."

"Turn that off. I do not want to see your sex tape."

"It's a *sext*, mom, not a sex tape. Why are you mad at me, Felicity? I saved you from marrying a cheater."

Felicity scoffed. "You should have told me sooner instead of trying for some big dramatic moment. How long did you know about this?"

"Since *last year* when none of you believed me."

Uncle Jaime was completely hysterical while Aunt Bianca continued to list out Grandma Shirley grievances.

"She said my gravy didn't have enough cream, and you just hid in the pantry."

"You had an affair with our cousin's boyfriend, Mom," her daughter argued. "And I could forgive it if it was Anderson. I mean, no offense..." She turned to her boyfriend. "But I'd sleep with him if I had a chance."

He shrugged. "Yeah, I mean, I wouldn't blame you." He handed Uncle Jaime a wet towel for his face.

"It was a cry for help!" Aunt Bianca wailed.

"Throw her out," several cousins chanted.

"You are so selfish, Evie," Felicity berated me.

"So selfish." Aunt Bianca crossed her arms. "What about the girl code?"

"What about my apology? I am not a home-wrecker!"

"You wrecked my home." My cousin scowled at me.

"This isn't how this is supposed to go!" I wailed.

"Of course not, Evie." My mother pulled the plug on the TV as it looped to my tit shot again. "It never does. You could have just informed us like a mature adult instead of manufacturing this big, dramatic moment."

"I appreciate the drama." Granny Doyle raised a hand while Nat and Lauren nodded.

"Baby," Braeden whined to Felicity. "You can't believe these falsehoods."

"I'm not stupid, Braeden." Felicity took the ring off her finger. "I'm keeping the diamond and all the wedding gifts. You can come by the day after Christmas to pick up your shit from the side of the road."

"You better give me that ring back!"

Felicity's dad and my uncles were rolling up their sleeves. One of my cousins passed out hockey sticks.

"Shit!" I said as Snowball charged at Braeden, who yelled, racing first to the door then to a window, struggling to escape.

"I knew I never liked Bianca," Grandma Shirley was saying shrilly to her crying son. "I told you not to marry her. Just like I told you not to adopt, Brian."

"But Evie has a nice rack!" My twelve-year-old boy cousins devolved into a fit of giggles while my aunt whacked at them with a newspaper.

"Evie, clean up this mess you made," my mother snapped at me. "Honestly, every single year, there's something with you. Will I never have a nice Christmas?"

"The game is starting!" Sean bellowed.

I stood there, stunned, in the middle of the living room as my family slowly cleared out.

"Do I still have to move out?" I asked my dad hysterically.

"Yes, Evie. We set a boundary. You clearly"—he gestured to the arguing Murphys—"need to grow up. This was excessively immature. I'd blame Anderson, but honestly, I have a feeling that even he got tired of your nonsense just like the rest of us have."

"I don't have a job, though," I said in a small voice. "I don't have anywhere to go."

"Then I suggest you grow up and figure it out."

This was my big moment—I'd been waiting forever, and it was a bust. A disaster. Just like the rest of my life.

Anderson would have done it better. Where was he? How could he betray me? If he'd been here, my family would have been cheering me on. Then we'd ride off to a perfect happily ever after.

Tears prickled at my eyes.

Why had he abandoned me?

Chapter 49

ANDERSON

O ne of the few single-family homes on the island of Manhattan loomed against the dark sky like a mausoleum.

My family used to have a house like this down the street...a hundred fifty years ago.

I'd raced down to Manhattan from Rhode Island, and now there was twenty minutes until the deadline was up.

Hesitating, I stood in front of the ornately carved double doors of the house. Mansion, really.

This was it.

The text messages I'd been ignoring had grown more and more heart wrenching, with the final *Welp, I did it* letting me know the reveal hadn't gone well.

I could just sit out here for the next twenty minutes, run out the clock, go back to Evie, apologize for missing the reveal, sweep her off her feet, tell her I still wanted to run away with her... and leave my brothers to clean up the fallout.

I was suddenly sick of this—sick of the cold, sick of the lying, sick of seeing people at their worst, sick of the sleepless nights and the deception and the pretending to be normal when I was anything but.

I raised a fist and pounded on the door.

Because I was exactly what Evie's parents had always said I was—a bad man.

I slammed my fist against the door again, and it slid open a crack.

The inside was dimly lit, flickering gas lamps casting shadows on the checkered marble floor, the paintings of disapproving Victorians that cost more than my bike, and the empty suits of armor.

Following the sound of arguing, I made my way down the wide hallway to a room more ornate than the foyer. A Christmas tree glimmered in one corner. Aaron and his half brothers were crowded around a table. Two black-and-white dogs were sprawled in front of the hearth.

Betty sat on an armchair near the tree, sorting through the piles of corporate Christmas gifts sent to Aaron and writing thank-you notes.

What a beautiful evening to set fire to my own life.

"And twenty minutes to spare." Aaron, glass of scotch in hand, glided over the rug.

I didn't say a word. There wasn't anything to say.

It was my own fucking fault, wasn't it? At the end of the day, I didn't have anyone to blame but myself.

We lived with our choices, or we didn't.

"Christmas cookie?" Betty offered, sliding a plate of Hershey's Kisses cookies toward me.

Silently, I shook my head.

"I don't know why Hudson was so concerned," Aaron said, cold green eyes flicking to Grayson, who was texting someone. "He was always going to come through. You can't buy this type of loyalty."

I carefully set the folder with the printouts, evidence highlights, and flash drive with the full report on the table.

"Starlight Theater, one-point-two million in fraud."

Aaron's eyes widened—it was startling. Normally, he would never let that much unfiltered emotion show.

Picking up the paperwork, he quickly controlled himself.

"That wasn't on the list." Aaron flipped through the evidence. "We need to find out who's account that was," he said to Betty, scowling.

"Could be an inside job, kiddo."

None of that was my problem. Just another person's life I'd thrown a live grenade at.

"I want a receipt."

Aaron's black leather-bound book sat on a nearby sofa. He picked it up and opened it to the page tallying up the payment for my sins. His fountain pen scratched on the cream paper as he wrote in the seven-figure number then tallied up the rows.

"Anderson always overdelivers." He signed his name with a flourish then carefully ripped the page out of the book, handing it to me.

I knew the drill.

The Dalmatians wagged their tails at me as I approached—terrible guard dogs. Snowball would never— and tossed the paper into the fire, watching as the flames licked it and turned it to ash.

"The plane is waiting to take you to Idaho." Aaron's green eyes glittered in the firelight.

"That so?" I walked past him to the door.

"I'll have the files sent to you."

I spun around in the doorway, walking backward. "Yeah... I'm..." I spread my hands. "I'm done. I'm not working for you anymore."

"Aaron's sparking personality drove a stake through another relationship? Shocking," one of his brothers drawled.

Stalking after me, Aaron slammed the door on his laughing siblings. He crossed his arms and regarded me. "You're not going to quit."

I stared back at him. I was so fucking done.

"Take Christmas." Aaron nodded. "You can go to Idaho the day after."

I turned on my heel. "Find someone else, Aaron."

"Look who's off the naughty list!" Jake crowed when I walked into the Brooklyn field office.

I set my helmet down and slumped into a chair.

Aaron wasn't going to sit on that information, and Betty had insomnia. As soon as nine a.m. hit in, oh, six hours, Aaron was dropping a nuke on that theater. Then it was over. Evie was out of my life forever, left with only the bitter knowledge of my betrayal.

Lawrence tousled my hair. "I thought you were going to Idaho."

"Aaron said to take Christmas." My voice sounded dull.

"Aw, Hudson, we can all open presents under the tree at your house."

"I didn't get you anything." Hudson shrugged Jake off.

"Aaron's going soft," Talbot remarked.

"No, he's not," Hudson scoffed. "He needs to give me a credit since you got him more money back than was originally discussed. You should have brought a check back for all the shit you caused me, Anderson. You almost tanked this company. This isn't a charity. Van de Berg needs to pay the difference."

Tuning him out, I stared out the window at the snowy city street.

She didn't have to know it was me. I still had Ian's phone. I could give it back. No one had to know. This thing we had could still work, right? Evie was forgiving—to a fault, really. I wasn't that good of a person. I could take advantage of her good nature, right?

"You need a break, man." Talbot set a bottle of spiced rum in front of me. "We can get cheap tickets to the Bahamas, Jamaica, somewhere warm."

"Somewhere with pretty girls in bikinis," Jake added, slicing off the wax seal on the liquor.

I didn't want a girl in a bikini. I wanted a girl in a homemade knitted sweater with snowflakes on her eyelashes. "I am never going to be able to live without her."

"B Squad just finished the big Svensson PharmaTech job," Jake said. "They're all meeting at Demarcus's place. Christmas party? We can celebrate your freedom."

I hauled myself off the couch.

"I hope you're going to get my money from Aaron," Hudson called. "Anderson. Anderson?"

My helmet fit me like a second skin.

I turned to my older brother. "Get the money yourself. I'm done, Hudson."

Chapter 50

EVIE

maneuvered around the hole in the attic where Anderson had laid out new plywood. I didn't trust it.

My three sisters stirred. They were sleeping in the bed while Ian and I slept curled up like hamsters on the broken settee Anderson had carried up to the attic before he'd disappeared out of my life.

"Are you making French toast?" Alana asked sleepily.

"Uncle Jaime really likes fried chicken, biscuits, and gravy. Since I kind of wrecked his life, I figure we should cater to him in his time of need."

Ian unfolded his long legs off the couch and lifted one ankle up to his neck, stretching. "I should have just slept on the floor."

Yep, Uncle Jaime had refused to return home with Aunt Bianca. His children had stayed for moral support, and two of his type A, mildly sociopathic attorney older sisters had stayed to "plan the execution," as they put it. As such, we'd all lost the downstairs bedrooms. Not to mention, my parents' room was uninhabitable. We were tight on space at chez Murphy.

Snowball zoomed down the steps in front of me, looking around, ears perked by the time we reached the kitchen.

"Sorry, I don't know where he is," I said, letting Snowball out into the yard.

Was my father right? Had I driven him off?

Anderson hadn't responded to my increasingly unhinged text messages. I refused to believe he was gone for good. He'd come back. He had to. He'd said he loved me.

But so had Braeden.

At least I didn't have to see my ex again.

The sausage for the gravy browned in the pan, filling the kitchen with meaty, spicy smells.

"This asshole," Ian complained as he checked his email on my old laptop since we still hadn't found his phone. "This is my last shot to dance the Nutcracker Prince. At this point, do I even want to still work at the Starlight Theater?"

"Aren't you guys doing *Swan Lake* next? Maybe the director will let you be Prince Siegfried."

"Watch him cast his latest boyfriend with the terrible turnout." The keys clacked rapidly as Ian wrote an angry email.

I dropped the battered chicken into the hot oil, jumping when it spattered.

The house smelled like fresh biscuits when my family started piling into the dining room. Fresh sprigs of evergreen boughs and sprays of red holly berries made the dining room festive. Not that the atmosphere was all that cheery.

"Jaime doesn't need herbal tea," Granny Doyle insisted as I ferried out the platters of piping-hot chicken. "He needs alcohol, a hooker, and some of that experimental heart medication that drug salesman Jennifer was sleeping with used to run around trying to pimp out." She dumped half of Uncle Jaime's orange juice into the pitcher and poured a generous glug of vodka into his cup.

"Is your big-dick boyfriend coming?" Aunt J asked me as one of Uncle Jaime's sisters assembled a biscuit for him and the other tried to force-feed him hashbrowns.

"I think he might be busy," I said weakly.

"Does he know you made fried chicken?" Uncle Todd asked.

The buffet was piled with food. I even had some homemade jam left from my ill-fated job at an artisanal jam store that had turned out to be a money-losing vanity project headed by some tech billionaire's wife.

"You need to get her out of the house," Aunt Steph, the lawyer, was telling Jaime, slamming her knife down on the table for emphasis.

"I bet Anderson could get her out." Uncle Hugh chuckled.

"They wouldn't get me to leave anywhere if he was living there," Aunt J declared.

"Move Aunt Trish and all those cats in," Declan joked.

"I have to get the rest of the fruit salad." I scuttled back to the kitchen.

Your girl was already on thin ice. I did not need to be associated with the breakup of Uncle Jaime's marriage. Better to stay in my safe space and pray that Anderson showed up to whisk me away to our future.

The doorbell rang.

It was him! He'd come back.

I raced through the house, yelling, "I'll get it!" Hands trembling, I opened the front door. "Is someone expecting a delivery?"

The pudgy, red-faced man sputtered, "A delivery? Out of my way. Where is he? Where is Ian? Ian!" he bellowed, going first into the living room, surprising my cousins, then to the dining room.

"Winston?" My brother stood up.

Grandma Shirley screamed as the heavyset man bullied up to Ian, grabbing the taller man by the front of his shirt.

"Get the hell off my grandson!" Granny Doyle put up her fists.

Winston shoved Ian. "You imbecile."

"You never gave me the Nutcracker Prince role. You said you were, and you fucking lied." Ian was indignant.

"You didn't have to tell Van de Berg Insurance about…" He lowered his voice and furtively licked his lips. "*What we did.*"

"I didn't tell them shit."

"They raided the Starlight Theater!" Winston wailed. "We're being shut down. They're investigating. They're crawling all over my poor late father's dream."

"Sounds like karma."

"Don't you *understand*?" Winston shouted. "We're going to prison."

"I'm not going to prison. You are." Ian crossed his arms.

"You were colluding. You knew all about what I was doing, and you didn't report it. It's a criminal offense."

Ian's eyes widened with shock. "But they can't prove anything."

"They have copies of your text messages, your emails. There's a warrant. It's a felony, boy." Winston shook him. "We're ruined."

"I'm going to prison." Ian pressed a hand to his throat. "I can't go to prison."

"No, you're not." My aunts jumped into action.

Ian leaned heavily against the table. "I didn't tell them. I don't understand how this happened."

"Don't say anything," my aunt instructed him.

Ian started babbling. "I didn't do anything. They couldn't know. I just wanted a lead role. I just wanted to be the Nutcracker Prince. How did they know?"

"They probably hacked your phone, and now we're ruined." Winston sobbed.

"You might be," my aunt said coolly. "But Ian, we are going down to New York City. Keep your mouth shut, boy."

"The phone," I whimpered before I could stop myself.

"*The phone.*" Ian was breathing heavily. "He took my phone. That's why it's missing. Oh my god, Evie, your fucking fake-ass boyfriend is sending me to prison."

"Wait, your *fake* boyfriend?" Aunt Steph pounced. "Fake how?"

"Er... semantics?"

"She was blackmailing him," Ian said bitterly. "Anderson was here in Dad's study the night of Aunt J's party. Evie caught him and blackmailed him to get back at Braeden. He's been hacking all of your phones."

My family was in an uproar.

"It wasn't really hacking. He just memorized the pin numbers. It's more social engineering," I said faintly.

"I knew it!" Henry snarled, slamming his hands on the table. "I knew he wasn't here because he loved you. He planned this whole thing to get back at us, to get back at me, and you invited him here, Evie, invited him into our family."

"Henry's right, Evie," Ian spat, "and you know how much I hate to admit that. This is your fault."

Ian, my favorite brother, the Murphy sibling who was always in my corner, shook with anger.

He was mad at me. *Me*—Evie. His little sister. He'd always been there for me. When my mom had been more concerned with taking care of the newborn triplets, Ian had taken care of me. He'd cheered me up when the girls in middle school teased me, made me feel better after my mom and dad yelled at me after another detention, had come out as gay to take the heat off me when I flunked eighth grade and had to do summer school, and had let me crash at his place when I didn't have rent money.

Ian couldn't hate me.

"I'm sorry, Ian." My voice sounded small. "I didn't mean to. Sawyer?"

My cousin just shook her head.

"Dad's right," Ian spat. "You never mean to. You just make terrible decision after terrible, ill-thought-out decision, and the rest of us have to live with the consequences. You ruined my life, Evie."

Tears, hot and fat, rolled down my cheeks.

Outside, a motorcycle roared.

I slipped out of the dining room while my family shouted over each other, comparing notes about missing phones, about my weird behavior, about Anderson. All while Aunt Steph and Aunt Virginia made calls to their attorney friends, trying to glean more information about the case.

"Pass the collection plate for Ian's bail money," Sean joked, carrying his hat around, which earned him a swat from an aunt.

"Anderson saved my life." Granny Doyle was still in my corner. "That has to mean something."

"That's the most egregious offense, in my book." Grandma Shirley was shrill.

My mother sobbed. "My son is going to prison. What will the neighbors think?"

I intercepted Anderson on the porch.

He took one look at my tear-stained face and knew.

"Evie." He cupped my face. "I am so sorry. I—"

"I don't care!" I raged at him through the tears. "My brother's going to prison because of you."

"No." He shook his head. "I'll fix it. I'll talk to Aaron."

"Aaron?" I screeched. "You set this whole thing up. Henry was right. You were trying to ruin us."

"I didn't want to. It wasn't my intention."

"Of course it was. My family was right about you. You're a liar. You used me. You said you loved me."

"It wasn't a lie, Evie. I do love you." He took my hands in his gloved ones. "I never thought I was going to be anything other than a fucked-up man wandering from one horrible, soul-destroying job to the next. You made me feel like I was normal, like I was home." His grip tightened. "I love you, Evie. We're meant to be. Don't you see?" He pressed my hands to his lips. "I think I can make you happy. I can at least love you more than you've ever been. We're made for each other, Evie, just two fuckups in a fucked-up world. Let me take you away. Let me rescue you. I want the farmhouse with you, the kids, and the dogs."

I wrenched my hands away. Behind me, Snowball growled.

"You went after my brother. You hurt Ian."

Anderson looked crushed. "I'll fix it. I promise. I believe in our future. You and me, together. And Ian can come too."

Angry, I wiped away my tears. "Ian isn't coming. Ian hates me. You sold him out. You used me so you could get back at us."

Anderson's gray eyes flicked up to the angry faces of my family watching from the windows and open doorway then back to me. "Your family doesn't appreciate you, but I do. I see the real you, Evie, and I love her more than anything in the world."

"My parents were right about you," I forced out. "You are evil. You're a bad person. I should have called the police when I saw you in Dad's study and let you rot in jail. You're a liar and a thief, and you almost killed my brother. I hate you, Anderson Wynter. I will never be with you. I will always, *always* choose my family over you. You mean nothing to me."

The planes of his face froze, and his eyes chilled.

"And my parents were right about me too," I added. "I'm immature, I make bad decisions, I'm a loser and a screwup, and I'm not worthy of being in this family. But I'm going to make better choices, starting now. And that means I'm removing you from my life."

He made a disgusted noise. "Seriously? You're going to choose them over me? *Them.*" Anderson pointed at the spectators. "They don't care about you, Gingersnap. You want to talk about people using you? Look around. These people aren't your family. They don't like you. They don't respect you. They wouldn't toss a grenade into a lake to free you from the ice. Not you, Granny Doyle—I know you're cool."

My grandmother gave a little bow.

"The rest of them?" His gray eyes pierced into me. "They despise you, Evie. They laugh about you behind your back. They think you're useless, worthless, and they'd be more than happy if you disappeared for Christmas. The Murphys are shitty, horrible people. They drag you down. They keep you from being who you were meant to be." He gave me a longing look. "I would do *anything* for you. I love you. *I know you.* I can make you happy, *really happy*—no strings attached. Evie, choose me. Choose us. We are meant to be."

I squared my shoulders. "You're wrong, Anderson. They are my family. I am a Murphy, and you will never be good enough for me. Now, get off my porch."

Chapter 51

ANDERSON

"I need the Idaho case files."

Aaron looked up. Behind him, beyond the expanse of glass on the upper floors of the Van de Berg Insurance tower, stretched the snowy skyline of Manhattan.

He set down his pen. "Betty said you'd be back after you slept."

"I didn't sleep. I'll sleep on the plane."

Aaron called up the train derailment files.

This was a legitimate, aboveboard, on-the-books project—no secrecy or late-night bar meetings needed.

Aaron plugged in a blank SD card.

"I need a favor," I said, helmet clenched against my chest—not too tight. My heart was gone, and if I pushed too hard, my chest was going to cave in the empty space.

"Hudson already voiced his displeasure about the free work you gave Van de Berg. Betty's processing the payment."

"No, I need—" Here I went again, sticking my neck out for a Murphy. What the hell was wrong with me? Evie hated me. I shouldn't care about Ian. She would always turn her back on me. She'd said so. She was a Murphy.

I didn't have to say it. Aaron read it on my face.

"You think giving her brother a stay of execution is going to make her love you?"

The printer whirred.

"Ian doesn't deserve to go to prison for something he didn't do." I stood in front of Aaron at parade rest. "He didn't report it because the director promised him a lead role."

"Those Murphys and their blackmail." Aaron picked up the papers and slipped them into a folder. "Don't worry. Ian Murphy's lawyers have already been in contact with us. He'll testify against the director, and there won't be a mark on his record. Van de Berg insures a number of tours for larger musical artists. I'll have Betty put in a word for Ian."

"Thanks. I owe you," I said duly.

Aaron set his pen down. "He's so sad. And on Christmas too. Here I thought you would have enjoyed my gift."

"You want me to get on my knees and thank you for not sending my... for sending Evie's brother to prison?"

"Contrary to popular belief, I am trying to not be such an asshole. Apparently, there have been complaints launched—"

"You're doing a real fantastic job of that, Aaron." I was exhausted.

"You know, trying to branch out. Betty thinks I need friends who aren't my brothers. We're a bit enmeshed. Don't know if you picked up on that."

I snorted. "Yeah, join the club."

"I thought you'd be happy to finally have a chance for revenge."

"What?" I sat down heavily in the guest chair.

"Revenge." A self-satisfied smirk settled in the corners of his mouth. "It wasn't an accident which names were on that list. I knew you'd appreciate ruining the Murphys for Christmas."

"I don't understand."

"I like to know who I'm working with. I read your military file." He leaned back in his chair. "Trust me. I know when people are lying about the cause of a disaster. It's not surprising that the US government has a terrible investigation team," he sneered. "The private sector runs rings around them. Speaking of—the Idaho case." Aaron handed me the folder.

"I'll get on this." I was reeling.

"The plane will collect you at seven a.m. on December twenty-sixth. Rumor has it Hudson has some terrible Christmas celebration planned tomorrow. Ever since they got girlfriends, he and Grayson are really working on healing their inner child. I hate it."

"I'd rather go to Idaho."

"Wouldn't we all."

"Don't worry about your friend," Betty called as I shut Aaron's door behind me. "Me and Taylor Swift are cool. I texted her about a kickass dancer."

"Thanks, Betty. Have a merry Christmas."

"I'd offer you a cookie," Betty said, opening up her desk drawer. "But I think you need this more." She handed me a small bottle of vodka. "Merry Christmas, sugar."

I pocketed it as I rode the elevator down.

The lobby was an empty stage set, decorated impeccably for the holidays with no one there to enjoy it.

My heavy boots echoed in the empty space.

"I hate Christmas."

I hated it even more back in Maplewood Falls in the field office.

The decorations Evie had made were still up, a reminder of the night I'd told her I loved her, when I'd painted a false picture of our happy ending.

A laugh escaped my throat.

I was so delusional. I was just as bad as Evie.

The man Evie had said she loved wasn't real. Could never be real.

I picked up the little train I'd fixed up for Evie. The paint was dry. Not that it mattered.

I set up the tracks around the Christmas tree she'd brought and watched it go round and round in circles.

I had wanted to tell her when she opened it that it would be the first piece of the miniature Christmas village I'd make her to decorate our home.

I should burn it.

The Christmas tree spun slowly in its base, lights drifting along the walls, twinkling among the Christmas decorations.

"You have to take this down."

I grabbed a trash bag, tossed old food containers from the fridge, then hesitated when I reached for the wreath in the window.

I sat down on the couch, bag at my feet.

My life, my future—cold and empty—stretched before me. I didn't even need a silent ghost to show me that I'd fucked up to know.

When I picked the miniature locomotive off the track, the wheels spun a bit then stopped.

Smashing it with a hammer and walking away would be the smart move.

What the hell was I thinking? That she was going to choose me over her precious family? That the two weeks we'd spent together meant something?

I walked around the garage, train in hand, finally settling on simple brown butcher paper.

I wasn't as good as my sister, Elsa, who could wrap a Christmas present with her eyes closed in five seconds, but it didn't look half-bad.

I broke off a piece of the garland Evie had draped over the cabinets above the small kitchenette, stuck the dark-green sprig under the butcher's string, and set the little package back under her tree.

"I never got to spend Christmas with her."

There was alcohol in the fridge.

I wondered if that was how my father had started. Had life just been too much, and he'd looked for comfort at the bottom of a bottle of scotch?

I closed the fridge.

I couldn't stay here.

The Idaho files were still in my bag. If I started driving now, I could be there by Christmas.

The phone rang in my ear headset as I was thirty miles out of town.

"I'm on a job."

The line was static for a moment, then Hudson sighed, weary. "Grayson told me what Aaron did. Where are you? Come home."

Chapter 52

EVIE

Ah, Christmas Eve.

This time last year, I was being sent to my room, everyone believing that I'd been a crazy stalker after my cousin's boyfriend.

It had been hands down the worst day of my entire life, including that time in seventh grade when I'd firmly believed that Nathaniel Whitman III was secretly in love with me but too afraid to show it, and I kissed him in front of everyone at the awards ceremony.

Are you seeing a pattern here? Because I was, in retrospect.

I'd thought Anderson was different, believed him when he'd said he loved me, and let myself dream of a future when I didn't have to go through life dragging along the weighted refuse of all my poor decisions. I'd thought I could have a clean slate, that I could be someone else, that I could finally live up to the promise of the first Murphy daughter.

Anderson had made me feel whole—two fucked-up people in a fucked-up world. We were made for each other. Or so I'd thought. But he wasn't special. He was just like all the other shitty men and boys I'd flung myself at.

No more. I was firmly on Team Murphy.

Blinking back angry, heartbroken tears, I turned back to the Scotch eggs I was making for Christmas Eve appetizers.

Sawyer opened the door to the kitchen, hesitant, letting in the hubbub from the front rooms along with Snowball.

The fluffy white dog went to my feet to beg for scraps.

"Man, Evie, you're not having any kind of Christmas." Sawyer wrapped me in a big hug.

I sniffled in her arms.

"You don't have to pretend to be nice to me. You should probably go comfort Ian."

"Ian is such a drama queen." She released me. "The insurance company's not pressing charges as long as he testifies against his boss. Your mom, of course, is beside herself."

"I really screwed up." I picked up the next soft-boiled egg to wrap sausage around it. "I should never have trusted Anderson. You were right. He's a bad person."

"He did some good stuff. Honestly, aside from trying to kill Henry and almost getting Ian sent to prison, he's my favorite of all the terrible guys you hooked up with. At least the man could play hockey."

"Ian's never going to forgive me."

"Ian's living for the drama. He did an interpretive Nutcracker Prince dance in the middle of Times Square." She smirked. "He called it his fired-for-Christmas dance and posted it online. He already got two hundred likes. Uncle

Brian is mad because he was hoping this would be a wakeup call for Ian to go get a real career. Instead, he's doubling down."

"I can't trust myself," I said sadly. "It felt so real. It felt like he really wanted to build a life with me, like we were really going to be a team, like we were in love."

Snowball wound around my ankles to sit on my foot.

"I'm done with men," I promised. "I'm never letting this happen again. I'm a changed woman."

"Yeah, until the next guy."

"There won't be a next guy." I flicked the switch to turn on the deep fryer.

"Never change, Evie Murphy."

It was my best dinner yet.

Like a Norman Rockwell painting, my family gathered around the table laden with food—a beef Wellington, a giant roasted turkey, and a glistening ham the stars of the Christmas Eve dinner.

"You really know how to bring out a crowd," Granny Doyle said, patting me on the shoulder as I wiped a speck of sauce off the edge of a platter with the corner of my apron. "Folks I haven't seen in a decade showed up pretending like they were invited."

My mom was soaking up the attention, while several of her sisters scoffed in the corner.

The Murphys were a perfect family. I was so lucky to have been adopted by my parents, and I vowed then and there I was going to do everything I could do be worthy of them.

"Can we eat?" Declan called out over the hubbub. "I'm starving."

"We need to have a toast first." My father raised his glass.

"Wait!" I shouted, jumping onto an ottoman and almost falling off.

"Aw yeah!" An out-of-town cousin whooped.

The others pumped their fists.

The phone cameras focused on me as I pinwheeled my arms, trying to right my balance.

"Um." I swallowed. "Before we get started on dinner, I just wanted to say a few words."

"Haven't you done enough, Evie?" my mother demanded.

"Let her speak!" Granny Doyle yelled, incurring chants from my more inebriated cousins.

My mother took an angry sip of her wine.

"By now, everyone knows that I invited the Grinch into Whoville, and he almost ruined Christmas," I began. "I just want to formally apologize to the entire family. My actions were not reflective of how I was raised. I'm going to do better in the future."

My mother seemed skeptical.

"Henry." I addressed my eldest brother. "I have to apologize to you. I shouldn't have brought the man who tried to kill you home for Christmas. It was cruel of me, and I'm sorry."

Henry's cheeks were hollowed in annoyance or anger or maybe flat-out hatred at this point.

"Ian, I know you'll never forgive me for ruining your dance career, but I am so sorry, and I will make it up to you."

My brother crossed his arms. "Apology not accepted."

Sawyer kicked him.

My voice cracked. I tried to keep it together.

"I'm committed this next year to doing everything I can to make it up to you all. You need a party planned, dinner cooked, house decorated, children babysat? I'm there."

My family made appreciative noises.

Henry had his arms crossed. I guess I'd hurt him way more than I'd realized.

I doubled down. "In the spirit of being a Murphy, I'd like to offer my service to help Gabe and Madeline grow their family. Maybe something good can come out of this."

"I'm going to be a grandma!" Aunt Kerry screamed.

Suddenly, it was happening: People were proud of me! They loved me! My aunt hugged me, and my cousins were excited. I was back in my family's good graces. I'd done it. Deliriously happy, I accepted the adulation.

My mom was telling everyone how I had birthing hips and she would personally make sure I didn't ruin the baby.

"You need to be careful," one of the family doctors was saying. "You've never had a baby before, Evie. This isn't a joke."

"They're not paying her," several cousins whispered.

"I'd need to be paid to get pregnant again after birthing his big ass," Aunt Virginia said, grabbing the back of her son's head.

"Does this mean you're going on a date with Whiney Wendell?" Nat asked then tipped back the last of the wine in her glass.

"Mom, they're not supposed to call me that," my cousin complained to Aunt Abby.

I gulped. "I mean, in the spirit of being a good Murphy… why not?"

"No!" Henry shouted.

"Nothing's wrong with my Wendie." His mom was offended.

"No," Henry said, pushing through the crowd. "Evie's not going on a date with Wendell. She's not having your fucking baby, Gabe. You have more than enough money to hire someone. She's not washing your cars or cooking your food."

"Henry, I fucked up," I told him gently. "I need to make amends."

"You didn't fuck up, Evie. You're not a bad person. You're not a bad Murphy. You *didn't do* anything wrong." He closed his eyes and took a breath, like he was in excruciating pain.

"The truth is…" His mouth moved, but no sound came out.

"I—Anderson didn't try to kill me." He doubled over like the lie had been the only thing holding him together, and now that the truth was out, he was falling apart.

"I don't understand." My hands shook.

Henry half straightened.

"I fucked up, back there in the desert. I fucked up. I was messing with something I shouldn't have. Anderson saved my life. *He saved me.* I'd be dead without him. Mom, I'm sorry. I begged him not to say anything, not to snitch on me, because I didn't want to get an NJP. Anderson just shook my hand and swore he wouldn't say a word." Henry gave our parents a pleading look. "I didn't want you all to be disappointed in me, Dad. And then you were there, at the hospital, both of you."

He took a gulping breath while our family watched in shock.

"You don't understand," he said to our horrified family. "They were *both there*. I had them all to myself, and they kept treating me like a hero, like I was their favorite person in the world—taking care of me. The military kept saying Anderson was at fault, and I knew I should fess up, knew it was wrong, but I just wanted…"

"You wanted to bask in the unconditional love," I said weakly.

He nodded. "You know what it was like with seven of us. I was the eldest. I wasn't supposed to need our parents. Yet suddenly, for once in my life, I had Mom and Dad's love and attention. All of it. All for me. It was addicting. I didn't think anyone was going to get hurt until it was too late. I thought Anderson was going to tell them what really happened. I kept thinking he'd save himself up until they hauled him away to jail."

I was shaking. I felt sick.

This isn't happening.

"I can't let you throw your life away for a lie, Evie." Tears shone in his eyes.

"I, um…" I rolled my apron under my hands, twisting the hem. "See, the problem is…" I said, not able to look at the grief, the heartbreak, the guilt in my brother's eyes. Because even though we weren't related, even though we didn't look anything alike, I knew I'd see my own expression mirrored in his.

"The problem is that I already did throw my life away for the lie. I threw him away, and I told him I hated him, and I told him he was bad and that I could never love a man like him, and I already lost him, Henry, so it's too late. It's over."

I stepped off the ottoman.

"I am so, so sorry," Henry said.

My mother let out a sob.

I untied my apron.

"I knew it!" Aunt Amy shouted. "I knew it. You always acted like the perfect wife and mother, and the rest of us just shouldn't even bother. Turns out your son sent an innocent man to prison. Mom." She turned to Granny Doyle. "Are you just going to let her get away with this?"

"It's not a good look, Mel," Granny Doyle said, shaking her head. "That poor bastard."

"We can't tell anyone!" my mother cried. "You can't tell anyone, Henry. You'll lose your job. You'll lose everything. Your father and I worked so hard. We'll pay Anderson off. Send him a gift basket."

"He's not going to say anything," Henry said dully.

"Well, that's fine. That's good, then." My mother wiped her eyes. "It's like this never happened. Let's all have dinner."

"I have to tell people, Mom," Henry said gently. "I can't keep lying."

"But your job!"

"Control your children, Melissa!" Grandma Shirley thundered. "I knew you weren't good enough for my son. And now you've dragged the Murphy name through the mud. We'll be the laughingstock of the town. We'll all have to move. We'll be ostracized, sued. I should never have let you marry my Brian. You have managed to raise both a liar *and* a slut. You don't deserve the Murphy name."

"Oh, shut the hell up!" Granny Doyle interrupted. "My daughter didn't ruin the Murphy name. You want to know why? Because Brian's not a Murphy."

Gasps of surprise came from my father's siblings.

"That red hair wasn't a recessive gene. It was just the gardener in a pair of skintight jeans."

"Lies! Slander!" Grandma Shirley screeched.

My dad's brother poured him a stiff drink.

"It is true! I know because I slept with him too!" Granny Doyle declared.

"Oh my god!" Aunt J exclaimed. "Mel, did you marry your brother?"

My mom grabbed the bottle of vodka and downed several swallows.

"Nah," Granny Doyle said. "I know how to use a condom. Also, I did a DNA test just to be sure because I'm hip with the times. Now who's the slut—but not in a slut-shaming way!"

"You see what you did?" My mother shouted at Henry. "You ruined Christmas."

Henry clapped a hand over his mouth.

Granny Doyle dumped out a wine bucket and handed it to him just in time for Henry to puke.

"Christmas is ruined." My mom sobbed as my dad stroked her back.

"Henry didn't ruin Christmas, Mom!" I yelled at her. "And neither did I. You ruined Christmas. You and Dad, because you ruin everything."

"How dare you, Evie?"

"You push and play favorites, and all your love comes with conditions no one can meet without cheating. You have impossible standards. You criticize constantly. You tear people down and make them doubt themselves. You're horrible parents. You failed us. You failed Henry, you failed Ian, and you failed me."

Henry clutched his sterling-silver puke bucket.

"Anderson was right. You all never accepted me. None of you," I said to the Murphys. "I'm just an interloper. I tried so hard to be a good Murphy. So hard. I gave everything, and it means nothing. You don't want me in this family. You never did. I didn't see it until it was too late, and now I've lost the best thing that ever happened to me. My one shot at true love. And yeah, he'd never be the perfect son-in-law, but I'm not the perfect daughter. So he and I can run away and be fuckups together, or we would if I hadn't believed you and screwed it up!"

"Evie, you can't leave," my father ordered as I headed to the door.

I grabbed my coat. Snowball came running.

"Evie, I'm warning you. We need to all talk this out like adults."

"Guess what, *Dad*?" I zipped up my coat. "It's Christmas Fucking Eve, and I didn't get a job. That means per your 'boundaries,' I have to get my shit and get out." I wrenched the front door open. "Which I am more than happy to do. I hope you have a merry fucking Murphy Christmas."

Chapter 53

ANDERSON

"Why didn't you tell me?" My older brother sat in front of me, wearing the same blank expression he used when giving bad news to clients.

"Because I gave my word," I said simply. "I promised."

Hudson shook his head. "Henry Murphy."

"He was my friend. I don't leave my friends out to hang."

"I can't fucking believe this. You spent that Christmas in jail. I was so..." My brother shook his head like he was trying to get rid of the memory.

"I know they sent you to prison after that fire." I rested a hand on his shoulder. "But it wasn't like that. I just read books. I had my own cell."

"My little brother. Little Andy."

"Hudson, I'm—" My voice cracked. "I'm sorry."

Hudson crushed me to his chest.

His girlfriend, Gracie, came in with a tray of steaming herbal tea. She rubbed Hudson's back, making sympathetic noises.

"I've been working on a new drone design. You can strap a flamethrower to it, and we can burn down his house," Lawrence joked.

"Didn't Anderson spend all day decorating it?" Jake asked.

"Okay, so we just jump him in the parking lot." Talbot cracked his knuckles.

"Just leave it alone," I ordered them.

"I'm not going to leave it alone." Hudson bared his teeth. "I'm going to bury him. I'm writing a letter."

Lawrence and Jake collapsed in fits of giggles.

"He's writing a strongly worded letter."

"Gracie, you neutered him."

Gracie sniffed. "Never underestimate the power of a strongly worded email."

"When Elsa comes into town, she'll help us beat the shit out of him," Talbot said confidently.

I checked my watch. "I'd better go pick her up."

Tinny carols filtered over the sound system at the ancient bus station in the heart of the Gulch.

The doors creaked at the bus terminal as I pushed out to the bus parking. In the fifties, someone had envisioned this bus station as the way of the future. Now the tapered columns and streamlined overhangs just looked shabby, the neon lights flickering, the chrome accents dulled from years of salt and grime.

A bus cranked its diesel engine and puttered away, revealing a red-haired man sitting on a bench. He looked up at me.

"Finally come for your revenge?" he called.

I loped over to him, dodging piles of soggy garbage.

"Nah, I'm here to pick up my sister."

"You guys have a big Christmas planned?" Henry asked, face drawn.

"My brother is trying and failing to fix up his house. So we're going be eating frozen beans for Christmas and performing manual labor."

"Oh." Henry glanced down at the bag on his lap.

"I told my family." His eyes met mine, hurt on his face. "I told them what I did to you. How I fucked you over. I am so sorry, Anderson. You didn't deserve that. I know this doesn't help you, but I'm sorry I fucked up your life."

"Hey, you don't get to take credit for shit I did all by my lonesome," I joked.

"Do you think you can forgive Evie?," Henry asked quietly. "It's not her fault—she was defending me. Not that I deserved it."

I gave him a crooked smile. "Like I said, don't take credit for shit I fucked up all by myself."

"I'm going to make it right," Henry said firmly.

"Don't do anything stupid." I frowned. "You hear me?" I shook his shoulder. "I didn't save your life just for you to ruin Christmas."

"I wasn't. Just trying to psych myself up to do the right thing," he assured me. "Be the better person and live up to my own hype."

"Sometimes that's overrated. Ask me how I know."

"You're the best person I know. You're honorable. Brave. You know how to do shit. You're who I always wanted to be." Henry made a helpless gesture.

"Like I said, it's overrated."

"Why'd you do it? Why'd you accept the blame?"

I shrugged my shoulders helplessly. "Because I thought we were friends. I thought we were brothers."

Henry was crushed. "I'm sorry I let them believe the lie. I didn't think anyone would be hurt by it. I thought you were going to tell them." Henry looked so devastated.

I sighed. I was suddenly bone-achingly exhausted. "They separated us. I thought that you and I were going to keep ten toes on the ground. I wasn't going to rat you out. I'm not a snitch."

"I already sent in my resignation letter and notified the government since I work on high-security projects." Henry patted his laptop bag. "I'm going to lose my job and my security clearance when they all get back from vacation."

"They work holidays at the Pentagon," I told him. "So they'll tell you bright and early Christmas morning. Ask me how I know."

Henry let out a long breath. "So it's over. I still feel like shit but at least not a lying piece of shit."

"That's progress."

"You know, what I really regret the most is throwing away our friendship."

"Maybe in the New Year, if you survive your bus ride, we can shoot some pucks?" I offered.

"Why are you forgiving me?" Henry asked.

I shrugged. "It's Christmas. I'm moved by the holiday spirit."

A bus with an inflatable Santa in the window pulled up with a screech.

"All yous, get off the bus!" the driver yelled. "Final stop, Maplewood Falls. I am a man of a certain age. I am not carrying anyone off this bus. It is going straight to the depot."

My sister bounded off the bus. She saw Henry and immediately slugged him in the jaw. "Fuck you, asshole."

"Shit," he yelped.

"Elsa!"

My little sister hugged me. "I need to get my bags before someone steals them."

"What the hell did you bring?" I grumbled, dragging her overstuffed suitcases out of the under-bus storage.

On the bench, Henry watched sadly, rubbing his jaw.

"Do not invite him for Christmas dinner," Elsa hissed at me. "Hudson is right. You are going soft. The holidays are not an excuse to wimp out. Now, hurry up—I have a moose roast that's probably defrosting."

Chapter 54

EVIE

"There she is!" Ian crowed when he and Sawyer rushed over to the table I'd been occupying for the last couple of hours at the Winter Wonderland Café.

Sawyer dumped a duffel bag and my purse onto the bench beside me. Snowbell barked her displeasure as the bag strap hit her snout.

"We packed up your stuff. I didn't take some of those Christmas decorations you've been carting around because I think you need a fresh slate."

Ian scooped me up, hugging me, and spun me around. "You get all the drinks, Evie. That was fucking epic!"

"I'm sorry, Ian," I began.

He brushed it off. "Don't be. All is forgiven! My video is going viral, and Taylor Swift wants me to be in her next video. Aaah!" Several people turned to look as Ian screamed. "She commented on my post! I have ten thousand likes, by the way. Best. Christmas. Ever. Drinks! We need drinks! Let's celebrate."

"We have eggnog cider on tap," the waitress said as she came by. "The bartender doesn't feel like making cocktails. We're trying to talk him off a ledge, so that's what we have."

"Sounds revolting. We'll take a round," Ian said cheerfully.

"Oh my god, you should have been there after you left." Sawyer scooted in next to me on the bench.

"She didn't just leave. She made an exit." Ian snapped his fingers. "Ugh, I just want to throw a shoe at you, girl."

The waitress came by with our noxious-smelling drinks.

Ian made a face. "We should have stolen a bottle of gin on the way out."

"Granny Doyle was telling everyone about Grandma Shirley's affair," Sawyer relayed. "Also, Uncle Jaime and Aunt J got caught in one of the triplets' rooms, making snow angels. Grandma Shirley is pissed because she's losing another of her precious sons to Granny Doyle's spawn."

"Dad's been drinking," Ian butted in.

"Your *mom* has been drinking too. Shit, *my god*," Sawyer added.

"Great-Aunt Eleanor took the entire beef Wellington and tried to walk out the door, and Grandma Shirley's second cousin whacked her with a cane, and she fell."

"She's fine, though. The fire department came," Sawyer assured me.

"They were so hot." Ian fanned himself.

"So hot!" Sawyer clapped her hands.

"Felicity's trying to make it all about her, of course," Ian added.

"Of course."

"And Henry. Saint Henry. He tucked his tail between his legs and left in disgrace! He is now the most hated Murphy. Ding-dong, the witch is dead! Rome has fallen." Ian lifted his glass. "A toast, to Evie, who dethroned Saint Henry and made this the best Christmas ever!"

"Whoo," I said, not really feeling it, as we clinked glasses. I sipped the drink.

Ian sighed.

Sawyer spun her glass around on its coaster.

Ian crossed his arms. The smile left his face. "Best Christmas ever," my brother said again.

"Yeah." My voice was dull. I wanted to go home. But not back to my parents'. Home was with Anderson, but I'd ruined it. For all my impassioned speech, the reality was that I was a fuckup. Who screwed up true love?

Evie Murphy, that's who.

"You know, the dream of this day has kept me going through some dark moments. Now I'm living it." Ian spun his glass in his hand, letting the Christmas lights reflect off the amber liquid. "I'm not the least favorite Murphy son anymore." Ian took a sip of his drink. "But now that my dream came true, I don't feel good. I just feel shitty."

"Yeah." I looked down at the table.

More silence followed.

"Saint Henry." Ian poked at the foam in his glass.

"I think..." Sawyer began.

"Ugh, yeah, I know." Ian made a disgusted noise. "I know."

Henry, bag on his lap, sat on a cold metal bench at the bus station in the bad part of town.

"Who's that wonderful boy!" Ian sang, his inner theater kid on full display.

Henry shrank.

The three of us joined hands and danced around him, chanting, "Murphy Misfit! Murphy Misfit!" while Snowball barked.

Sawyer threw a fistful of M&Ms at Henry.

"Hey." Henry winced as the red, white, and green candies bounced off of his coat.

"I declare you," Ian said solemnly, "King of the Misfits. You have done what no man has ever done—dethroned our mightiest queen—Evie Murphy."

"Murphy Misfits!" We all begin chanting again.

"My liege." Ian swept into a graceful dancer's bow. "We await your proclamation."

"You all are crazy," Henry said with a small smile.

"And fucked up."

"And disappointments." Sawyer added.

"And so are you." I blew Henry a kiss.

"But we day drink." Ian shrugged.

"And night drink."

"And occasionally dumpster dive."

"Snowball is surprisingly good about scaring away the rats," I said.

"I thought you all hated me. Especially you, Evie," Henry said softly.

"Of course not."

"A little." Ian shrugged. "Just a smidge."

"I was a shitty brother," Henry said, rubbing his arm. "You don't have to invite me into your club."

"It's a way of life." Sawyer ruffled his hair.

"I need to go and manage the implosion of my life." Henry's shoulders sagged.

"Nah." Ian dragged Henry to his feet. "You need a drink."

Chapter 55

ANDERSON

"**C**an you freaking believe it?" Elsa was chugging her third coffee since she'd been ushered into Hudson's half-finished house. "I swear to god, if I hadn't shown up, Henry'd be here right now, eating our food."

"Why aren't you more upset about this, Anderson?" Talbot demanded.

"What does it matter?" I pulled the bottle of scotch closer to me. I finally let myself have the drink I was craving, pouring the glass full of scotch.

"Do you want a straw with that?" Jake asked.

Hudson sat next to me at the table, his leg bumping mine, concern on his face.

Lawrence slid a baked brie that Gracie had left us out of the oven. "You can't sit here and drink by yourself."

"I'm with the five people who will never, ever leave me alone," I reminded him.

Jake put me in a headlock.

Talbot tried to stuff a cracker dripping with cheese into my mouth. "You need to eat something."

"Open his mouth." Lawrence reached for my jaw.

"Get off me," I snarled at my brothers as they tried to force me to eat.

I coughed as Elsa almost choked me with a cracker.

"Idaho's looking more and more attractive by the hour, huh, bro?" Jake asked cheerfully.

"The cold, lonely, flat expanse." Talbot stretched his arm out in front of me.

"Maybe you'll find someone new there. Forget about Evie," Lawrence said.

"I can't forget about her," I said helplessly.

"I never thought you'd get shacked up." Lawrence cut off a steaming piece of the cheese.

"I didn't think any woman would tolerate you." Jake stole Lawrence's cracker.

"She was perfectly imperfect, and I traded her for…" I shrugged. "Nothing, really."

"That Idaho contract's not nothing," Hudson reminded me.

I took another long drink of the burning scotch.

"Grayson said you were quitting." Hudson narrowed his eyes.

"You two are like two gossiping old women," Talbot said.

Hudson threw a cracker at Talbot with surprising accuracy and hit him dead on the nose.

"Ow!"

"I don't have anything to quit to. I fucked up. I should have…" I sighed and finished the last of the scotch. "I should have done things differently. Should have done everything differently. I can't be too mad at Henry at the end of the day. I did the exact same thing—sold out someone who was good to me. It's like upside-down karma or something."

Elsa looked worried.

I nudged her. "It's the holidays. No daylight, the oncoming existential crisis of another year over, wondering if anything will change as you stare into a bleak future."

"He's been listening to all those philosophy podcasts," Lawrence quipped.

"Gotta watch reality TV, my man." Elsa tapped the side of her head. "You feel so much better about yourself when you're watching two anorexics scream at each other about overpriced bridesmaid dresses."

Jake clapped his hands over my ears. "We're supposed to be cheering him up, not encouraging him to slit his wrists."

"We should go out," Talbot suggested.

"In Maplewood Falls?" Lawrence poured me another scotch.

"There's the Christmas market," Elsa suggested.

"If we go to Breaker Street, we could get him in a bar fight," Hudson deadpanned.

"I'm not spending Christmas in the hospital with you two again," Talbot said flatly. "Heartbreak or not, you're on your own."

"Look on the bright side. At least you only lost two and a half-ish weeks of your life with her," Elsa said brightly. "You can't fall in love with someone in two and a half weeks."

"But I did," I said helplessly.

"You need to put Evie behind you," Lawrence said. "And you need to put heat in your house, Hudson."

Chapter 56

EVIE

"Hurry up, hurry up, hurry up." I rubbed my arms as Snowball sniffed around a frozen bush in the park off the town square.

She suddenly put her hackles up and growled.

"No, Snowball!"

She took off down the path, and I raced after her.

For a second, my heart leaped. Maybe it was Anderson. Maybe he'd come back.

"Evie."

Snowball parked herself between me and Braeden. He swung a foot at her. I screamed, but Snowball was ready and tore a hole in his leather shoe.

"Damn dog," Braeden said.

"Are you stalking me?" I demanded.

"Of course you're going to make this all about you." Braeden shifted his weight to take a step toward me then

528 • Alina Jacobs

thought better of it when Snowball growled. "You ruin my life, and then you sic your dog on me?"

"*I ruined your life?*" I shrieked. "You lied. You said you loved me. You told my family I was crazy. You blacklisted me around town."

"I never lied. I did love you. I do love you. Felicity didn't mean anything to me. You and I were always meant to be together." Braeden grabbed me. "You don't have any options, Evie. You alienated your whole family. I heard what happened. I'm your only chance. Now, I'm willing to be generous. You can live with me rent-free, but you need to be a good girlfriend—clean, cook, do my laundry, and make sure you keep yourself pretty so I have something to look forward to, if you know what I mean."

"Translation from fuckboy to English is that you'll let me stay with you if I'll be your bang maid." I wrenched my arm away from him. "I'd rather live under a bridge than live with you."

"You won't last a day before you're begging me to take you back."

"Get the fuck away from my sister!" Henry yelled, running up, Ian and Declan close behind him. He bodychecked Braeden.

"Fuck off, Henry," Braeden snarled. "This is between me and Evie. I heard you got disowned. I knew you were huffing your own shit. You're not going to do anything to me."

"Really?" Henry drawled. "'Cause from where I'm standing, I got nothing to lose. I'll gladly spend Christmas in jail if it means I get to break your fucking jaw."

My brothers crowded in front of me, Declan and Ian on either side of Henry.

Braeden took an apprehensive step back then another. "Fuck you, Murphys."

Declan pelted Braeden's retreating back with a snowball. "And stay out!"

"What are you doing here, Declan?" I asked when he gave me a happy smile. "What about your wife? What about Christmas dinner?"

"Funny," Declan said as we trooped back to the town square. "About that. Raegan hates Murphy family functions. The only reason we went as much as we did was because she felt sorry for you."

"Why would she care about me?" I protested. "She's got the first grandbaby, a high-paying career, and a nice house. She's like a celebrity. I'm not even on her radar."

"Seriously, Evie?" Declan stopped abruptly, and Henry almost crashed into him. "You literally lived at our house for like four months."

"Err, yeah, sorry about that. I didn't realize it had been that long."

"Raegan said you were the only reason she felt like she made it through." Declan cocked his head. "You cooked and did laundry and took care of the baby at night."

"I was up anyway, doom scrolling social media."

"You actually helped," Declan said. "Everyone else showed up to hold the baby. You cleaned our bathroom, like, daily. You're her favorite Murphy, probably even above me."

"Oh, I—well."

"Raegan says she not going to any more Murphy family functions since you quit the family."

"Yikes. I bet Mom's not happy." Ian made a face.

"I have not dropped that bomb yet," Declan admitted.

"Evie!"

I wheezed as my three sisters threw themselves at me.

"Ian says we're going drinking."

"But not at the place where the bartender quit," Sawyer clarified, coming up behind them. "I want to go to that raw bar."

"No, I want french fries," Declan said.

"Evie can pick," Alana said. "I'm paying. Got some Christmas money."

"Everyone was so trashed at the Christmas Eve party," Alexis added. "Great-Aunt Evelyn got confused and thought we were quintuplets and not triplets."

"So here's your cut." Alissa stuffed a wad of cash into my jacket pocket. "But we're still paying."

"Don't you want to stay with the family?" I asked them, confused at why my sisters wanted to crash a Murphy Misfits evening of wallowing in your alcohol.

The triplets all talked at once.

"Aunt J was going to come," Alana said.

"We were going to try the strip club again because the last time we went, Alexis wouldn't uncover her eyes," Alissa complained.

"I told her she can't be in pharmaceutical testing if she can't handle the naked body." Alexis pointed a finger at Alana.

"You said you vomited in your mouth when that guy took off his jock strap," her sister reminded her.

"Aren't you, like, twelve?" Henry frowned. "Why were you at a strip club?"

"Granny Doyle," they chorused.

"But she couldn't come out tonight. She's trying to convince Uncle Jaime that he should totally move on with Aunt J."

"Grandma Shirley is not having it."

"She been calling Aunt Bianca, trying to get her to come back," Alexis said as we walked down Main Street.

"Aunt Virginia said if that woman steps in the house, she's going to take out her kneecap."

"Aunt V can play hockey. You know she's not lying," Sawyer stated as we stood outside of the upscale pub, Mistletoe & Mug.

I turned to the triplets. "I appreciate the dinner offer, but you should probably go back to Mom and Dad's. You don't want to be contaminated by us." I pointed at the Murphy Misfits.

"Oh." Alana sagged. "You don't want us here. That's okay. We can go."

Her sisters looked sad.

"No, I mean, I just didn't think you'd want to hang out with us lame Murphys," I said in a rush.

"What?" the triplets cried. "Lame?"

"You're so cool."

"You have a dog."

"And you always have a boyfriend."

"'Boyfriend' is a strong word," Sawyer said.

"You know how to cook and waitress and tend bar and craft," the triplets chattered.

"You live in Manhattan."

"Your life is so exciting."

"My life is a mess!" I cried. "I can't do anything right."

"No way. You dance to the beat of your own drum." Alana did a dance move.

"Ugh, stop, you're embarrassing us." Her sister pushed her.

"You can actually dance," Alexis added.

"She cannot." Ian sniffed.

"We saw you with Anderson."

"Swoon!"

"So epic."

"You don't give a fuck what Mom and Dad think."

"You live your own life."

"Yeah, you three"—Alana pointed at me, Ian, and Sawyer—"are always doing cool stuff together."

"I'm so jelly of your lives."

"Seriously?" I couldn't believe what I was hearing.

"It's so exciting!"

"Ooh, you should come to Harrogate with us! We can all be roommates." Alexis threw her arm around me.

"What? No! Mom and Dad coddle them," Declan whined to me. "They need to learn to be independent. I have a baby. I need the help."

"So long as you don't become a surrogate for fuckin' Gabe." Henry scowled as we piled into the restaurant. "I'll be supportive of all your choices."

"Can we please order some french fries?" Declan begged.

"You should have the lobster roll, Evie," Alana said.

"Many people at this table are unemployed or underemployed, so let's be mindful with our choices!" Sawyer said.

"I told you, we're paying."

"Aunt J helped us sign up for credit cards."

"You gotta be careful with those things," I warned them. "Pro tip: they do expect you to pay them back eventually."

Snowball, who I'd snuck into the restaurant, popped her head out of my coat.

"Just stay, Snowball. Snowball!"

The Pomeranian took off and sprinted through the pub.

"Dammit." I raced after her, dodging a waitress.

"Just going to the bathroom," I called, like she didn't see the contraband dog trying to get to...

"*Anderson.*"

The little white dog showered the huge man with doggie kisses, her wagging tail a blur as Anderson gave her happy pets and greetings.

Those silvery eyes fixed on me. The smile fell from his face.

Anderson sure seemed a lot happier to see Snowball than me.

I really had lost him forever.

Chapter 57

ANDERSON

"This is nice. We should hang out more," Jake said happily as we walked in a group down Main Street. The Christmas market was in full swing even though it was almost midnight, and people were out.

"I don't like you all that much," I growled.

"He got his poor heart broken, and now he's bitter and damaged," Talbot joked.

It was, of course, a beautiful night. Some clouds were moving in, and it wasn't too cold for snow. The decorations in the quaint shop windows made Maplewood Falls look like one of those miniature Victorian Christmas villages. We just needed a little train with a smiling girl in a red coat.

"Most people are home with their families. I don't think it's a flex to be out drinking on Christmas Eve," I told my siblings.

"We're out with family." Elsa grabbed my arm.

Family—what I thought I was going to have with Evie.

"A dog would be good for you," Lawrence suggested.

"He doesn't have time for a dog. He should get a cat," Hudson said.

"No, get a cool pet like a snake," Talbot suggested.

"This is where we're getting drinks?" I frowned when we stopped in front of one of the ubiquitous Christmas-themed establishments in Maplewood Falls.

"I want french fries," Jake explained.

"We can make french fries at home." Hudson opened the door to the Christmas-bedecked pub.

"Okay, Mom." Lawrence rolled his eyes.

"Please. Mom would never."

We followed Hudson into the pub.

Something small and white rocketed through the restaurant.

"Is that a Furby?" Jake asked then the little white dog jumped into my arms, licking my face and yelping happily.

"Oh my god, it's so cuuute! How do you know my brother?" Elsa cooed at the dog. "Anderson, you have a cute little friend."

Snowball immediately growled at my sister when she tried to pet her.

"You don't let up at all, do you, Snowball?"

She went back to being a happy cute dog as I hugged her to my face.

"Snowball, no! Shit."

"You aren't supposed to have dogs in the restaurant," a patron chastised.

"Restaurant? Really?"

Then I was face-to-face with Evie.

She had melting snow in her hair and a bright-red scarf around her neck.

I should cup her face, tell her I was sorry, and beg her to forgive me, but instead, I stood there drinking her in, wondering if it was the last time I'd ever see her.

"Oh."

Evie stared down at her shoes. "Anderson, you're here! I didn't think… Must be the magic of Christmas." She forced a laugh.

I didn't even smile.

My heart was breaking all over again. "Evie…"

"Oh hell no." Elsa unzipped her jacket and quickly tied up her hair. "I'm about to cut this bitch right here."

"For fuck—" I held out an arm, but Elsa threw down her bag and her jacket and took off through the narrow path between the tables.

"Stop her!" I bellowed.

"Why?" Hudson asked with a shrug. "Fuck him."

"They're going to kill Henry!" Evie screamed as Jake, Lawrence, and Talbot followed Elsa, sprinting over tables and sending plates flying. Diners screamed.

Sawyer picked up a chair and swung it at my brothers as Lawrence threw a punch at Henry.

"You sold out my big brother!" Elsa raged, ducking the chair and going after Henry.

I charged through the crowd of drunk patrons, Snowball bouncing like a mountain goat off of surprised drinkers.

Sawyer had one of my brothers in a headlock. The triplets were ineffectively throwing coasters at Lawrence. Snowball took a chunk out of my middle brother's hand, making him pull the punch he'd been aiming at Henry.

Talbot continued to pummel Henry and got a kick in the face from Ian. Evie jumped on his back before he could grab Ian. Declan hit Jake in the face with the napkin dispenser as he tried to pry Sawyer off Lawrence.

"Get the fuck off!" I waded through my brothers, blocking one of Jake's punches. I kicked my foot out and swept him off his feet. He landed in a heap on the floor. "Elsa, I'm warning you…"

She gave me the finger. When she tried to go for Henry again, Snowball blocked her.

"Oh no, adorable little doggie, I wanted us to be friends!"

Snowball showed more teeth.

"Hudson, are you going to fucking help?" I threw myself in front of Henry before Talbot could stomp on him.

My eldest brother helped Henry up, dusted him off, rolled his shoulders, then hauled back and slammed an uppercut into Henry's jaw.

Henry grunted and staggered back, knocking over a table full of drinks.

I grabbed Hudson's arm. "Gracie is going to kill you if she has to bail you out of jail," I warned my brother.

"I think she'll understand."

"Out!" The bar owner, heavyset and dressed like Santa, came after us, swinging an axe.

My siblings and the Murphys all dove out of the way.

"I didn't get my french fries!"

"You're banned for life!" the bar owner hollered, hefting the axe. "I don't ever want to see you here again. And no," he said to Evie, "you can forget about ever getting a job here."

"Dammit, that was my one lead," Evie said as we were thrown out of the bar.

My siblings milled around on the cold sidewalk.

Jake, ignoring the blood running down his nose, immediately started flirting with the giggling redheaded triplets.

"Open your mouth," Sawyer instructed Henry and pulled out her phone flashlight. "You better still have all your teeth. People who just gave up their dental insurance shouldn't be bar fighting."

"*You* were fighting," Henry protested.

"I didn't get hit, because I don't fight like a little bitch."

Evie pulled out an oversize embroidered handkerchief and dabbed at Henry's face, making concerned noises.

I guessed she really did mean what she'd said. She was choosing the Murphys over me. What we had—well, what I'd thought we had—wasn't real. It was just my own delusions.

"Let's go," I said to my siblings.

"Wait," one of the triplets called to Jake. "We were going to go party tonight."

"Oh yeah?" he grinned.

"No." I dragged him back by his collar. "They are too young and inexperienced for you. You don't want to waste your time on someone like him," I shot at over my shoulder at Evie's sisters. "Find men with real jobs and retirement savings who don't get in bar fights."

"Anderson," Henry called as I followed my siblings down Main Street.

He was whispering something to Evie and pointing at me.

"What?" It came out harsh.

Evie cringed.

Henry gave her a gentle shove in my direction.

Chapter 58

EVIE

Standing in the middle of Main Street, the first few flakes of white Christmas snow falling around him, Anderson was everything I'd always wanted—my Christmas dream.

And he hated me.

His entire family hated me. They were never going to forgive me.

Shoot, I wouldn't. But I at least needed to apologize.

I stopped a few feet away from him, the snow and all the things unsaid a barrier between us.

"No wonder you hate the Murphys," I joked weakly. "We really are out to screw you over."

He crossed his arms.

My face fell.

"I am really sorry, Anderson," I said lamely. "I don't think that really cuts it, though. It doesn't change anything or fix the past. I'd like to say I can do better in the future, but you're probably tired of me by now." Tears pricked at the corners of my eyes. "I made a lot of terrible decisions, but the one I'll always regret the most is hurting you and throwing away the best thing that ever happened to me."

"Evie." He took a step toward me. "Evie, no, I'm sorry I betrayed you. I had to pay off a debt." He shook his head sadly. "It doesn't matter. It's just excuses."

"You could have told me. I understand about owing people money." I pulled at my mittens. "I still haven't paid Sawyer back for groceries. I would have understood."

"I owed Aaron a lot more than grocery money." He gave me a wan smile.

"He helped a senior-dog rescue get one over on an insurance company!" Anderson's sister cupped her hands around her mouth and shouted. "This man is a legend."

"*Elsa.*" Anderson turned back to me. "I shouldn't have sacrificed your brother like that. I know what he means to you. I'd go scorched-earth on anyone who did that to my sibling. I can't blame you."

"For senior dogs?" I scoffed. "Ian can handle it."

"You were right, though," he said, resigned. "I'm not a good person."

"But I wasn't," I choked out. "You're perfect. You're the most perfect man in the world. You saw me for me. You saved my life. You fixed my window. You believed I was better than the family fuckup. Maybe... I don't know. Maybe after Christmas, we could get coffee or something? Not at that place you hate and no candy canes—I think I'm getting a little tired of Christmas too." The tears were rolling down my cheeks now. "I don't want to lose you."

I couldn't read his expression.

"I can't, Evie. I have another job booked. I'm leaving."

"Oh." My shoulders sagged. All the energy left my body, and I just felt so empty and cold. "Right. I guess real adults have work, don't they?"

He didn't say anything. Just turned and walked away.

"Have a good holiday," I called after him.

"Have a nice life, Evie Murphy." The words were almost lost on the wind.

I shuffled back to my siblings.

"What are you doing?" one of the triplets asked. They were all freaking out.

"He hates me," I said, sobbing.

"Since when does Evie Murphy give up?" Henry smiled at me.

"I—" I looked back at Anderson, the dark figure retreating.

No, I wasn't giving up.

"Evie Murphy goes down with the ship." I wiped my eyes.

"Did you like it?" I yelled, racing back down the street.

He turned, a questioning look on his face.

"Did you like your present?" I added.

He shook his head

"Oh." I stopped short.

"I didn't open it," he explained. "It's not Christmas."

"It is now." I pointed at the clock on the city hall tower. It was snowing harder now.

"You know, the funny thing is," I called after him. "I think my father might have been right all these years about me not applying myself, about being a loser."

"Don't believe what he says about you, Evie."

"I don't want to give up on you. I know it's stupid and delusional, but I want you. I want the farmhouse and the dogs and the holidays by the fire and the kids and the store. I know you hate me, and you'll never really forgive me, but I'll never give up on us. I love you. It's so unfair how much I love you. I love you more than I've ever loved anyone, and it's crazy because I know you loved me more than that, and I fucked it up." I wiped at my wet face with my mitten. "You were right, Anderson. No one ever loved me like you did. And I wish…" The tears were freezing on my cheeks. "I really wish I hadn't thrown it away."

"*Evie.*" Anderson was there, gathering me in his arms. "I don't hate you. I told you I love you. You and me? We were made for each other." He shook me gently.

"Then why are you leaving?"

"Only because I can't stand being near you but not being able to have you." He cupped my face and wiped at my eyes. "I used to wish that I'd made better choices, been luckier, richer, but I wouldn't change a thing, because if I had, then I wouldn't have met you. You're the best thing that's ever happened to me. I will never love anyone like I love you."

"Are you sure you don't hate me?" I warbled, not daring to believe it. Like my dream would get yanked away from me if I loved it too hard.

He leaned in, hesitated, then gave me a crooked smile. "What would it matter? Didn't I tell you I never hated anyone like I did you?"

He closed the distance and kissed me then, not like he hated me but like he loved me, like he'd always love me, like he'd come home for Christmas.

The triplets cheered, and Henry whistled as Anderson spun me around in the snow, like he'd never let me go.

The Wynter siblings scoffed.

"You sure this is a good idea?" one of them muttered.

"Of course it's not," Sawyer deadpanned. "Evie makes terrible decisions. This is going to blow up in our faces, but on the bright side, we now have a ringer for family hockey matches!"

"You play hockey?" Elsa screeched, racing toward Sawyer.

"Goalie."

"Me too! Oh my god, finally, a sane woman in this town." They fist-bumped.

"Look, I know that my family really screwed over your brother," I said to Anderson's less enthusiastic siblings, "but I promise I won't ever hurt him. In fact, I'm going to come to Idaho with him to be a supportive girlfriend."

"No, you're not," he said quickly.

"Fine. I will knit you socks while I wait. He doesn't know it," I whispered to his brothers, "but I'm going to show up anyway because I'm unemployed and homeless."

"Real catch there, Anderson." Hudson smirked.

Anderson kissed me.

"Well, I'm not unemployed," Declan declared. "I have to go to my holiday shift at the emergency room. Sawyer, you're my ride."

"And I thought my job sucked," Jake muttered.

I grabbed Anderson's hand. "I want to see you open your Christmas present."

He kissed me. "No, I want to see you open your Christmas present."

"You got me a Christmas present!"

"Do not scream like that," he said, wincing.

"You mean unless I'm riding your dick?" I poked him in the chest while my sisters shrieked.

"I'm going to make you walk."

Chapter 59

EVIE

"I want to ride you like I rode your bike." Evie wrapped her arms around my waist, beaming up at me as we strolled down Main Street.

I let her kiss me before taking back control.

"That's what I walked out of my mom's holiday party for."

"I wish I could have seen that."

"It was pretty epic!" Evie said cheerfully.

I set the helmet on her head then got on the bike, Snowball tucked into my jacket.

Evie's arms came around my waist, squeezing me tight, then lower.

"I told you, not while I'm driving." I slapped at her hands.

"I'll do it when I'm driving!"

"You will never drive this motorcycle."

I grabbed her thigh, caressing her, then pulled the throttle, sending the bike roaring down Main Street.

When we arrived at the field office, the snow had let up.

I slow-clapped as Evie managed to make it off the bike without falling over.

She took a bow. "I'm ready to open my present." She was giddy as I unlocked the door.

She dragged me down by the front of my jacket.

"Hurry down my chimney, Santa baby."

I ripped off my helmet and threw it onto the floor, then I was on her.

"That's why I want the bad boy," she murmured, "not some boring corporate finance guy."

She stripped off her sweater while I pulled off my heavy motorcycle jacket. Then I was on her tits, burying my face in her ample chest, making her whimper as I took a nipple into my mouth.

"What would you have done without me?" I nipped her ear.

"You think I can't get off without you, bad boy?" She dug her nails into my neck, making me hiss.

I ran my hands down her soft skin as she slid her skirt down.

"Nuh-uh." She wagged her finger at me as she slid her panties down.

"How many Christmas-themed pairs of underwear to you even own?" I unzipped my pants, my cock already rock hard for her.

"These..." She kicked off the panties. "Are swimsuit bottoms." Then she sank down and straddled the helmet.

"What the fuck?"

She ground her pussy against it, moaning like she was riding my face. Which I guessed she sort of was.

"See?" Her voice had this high-pitched, breathy tone. "I didn't really need you to get off." Her legs spread wider as she rubbed her clit and pussy all over my helmet.

I stepped behind her. Her ass was in the air as she leaned forward and grabbed the edge of the couch so she could really rock her clit against the smooth plastic.

"You're fucking with me," I growled, grabbing her hips.

"Just your helmet."

Spreading her pussy lips, I slammed my raw cock into her cunt, fucking her as she ground her clit against the motorcycle helmet.

It felt so good to be in her without a condom. I needed to either get one or recalibrate. Otherwise, we might be making another major life-altering decision.

She groaned as I pulled out. "I need to feel your cum in me."

I grabbed the bottle of lube I'd used the other night and popped the cap.

"You know just what I like, Santa." Her eyelashes fluttered as my oil-slick cock poked at her ass.

I slapped her ass hard, making her jump. "Don't call me that."

"But you're about to send good things down my chimney."

I cut off whatever crazy thing she was going to say next when I slid my huge cock into her ass. She arched up against me while bearing down on the helmet, legs spread as wide as they could go, coaxing me in.

"Shit," she gasped as I slid out again, the motion making her clit rub against the smooth plastic helmet. "I forgot how huge you were."

As my thick cock filled her again, I ground her against the helmet, then she was coming all over it as my cock slid into her ass to the hilt.

Still in her, I pulled her up by the hips. She grabbed the helmet for leverage as I took her ass, jackhammering into her, my balls slapping against her as I made her feel every thick inch of me.

"Still think you're about to have a wholesome Christmas?" I grunted as I took her ass while she jerked as I fucked her.

"I'm gonna have a—" She let out a loud cry. "A very—"

I slammed into her again.

"Merry—"

I grabbed one of her tits, squeezing it as I buried my cock in her.

"Christmas!"

I felt her orgasm around me, then I was coming in her, spilling every drop—the pent-up anger, the stress, and above all, how much I loved her.

I pulled out of her, spun her around, wrapped her in my arms, and carried her the two steps to the couch, kissing her and telling her, "I love you. I can't live without you. I need you. Don't ever leave me."

She straddled me on the couch and kissed my mouth, nipping it. "I love you, Anderson, and if you keep giving that kind of performance, you're going to have me showing up in your bed whether you expected me or not."

With two fingers, I stroked her still-swollen clit. "I want to make you come again," I murmured against her mouth.

A condom packet ripped.

She straddled me and didn't even have to prepare, just sank her tight little pussy down onto my thick length.

My hands came up to cup her tits, squeezing her nipples.

As she balanced on my arms, I held her upright so I could thrust my huge cock up into her pussy.

"I love you." I thrust up into her. "I love you, Evie." I felt it as we connected.

She leaned forward, our chins bumping, and kissed me as I made love to her slowly, powerfully.

I didn't want it to ever end.

Her hand came up to cup my head. "I love you so much," she whispered.

"And I really—" She rocked her clit against my cock as I slid out of her. "Really love you in my pussy."

My hands dug into her ass, then I was shuddering in her as she came around my cock.

Evie collapsed onto my chest, red-and-white-striped fingernails tracing the tattoos there.

"I need to get one of your name." I kissed her hair.

"Now who's making impulsive, crazy decisions?" She nuzzled me under my chin. "The fastest way to doom a relationship is to get a tattoo."

She rolled over onto her side and pointed at a rose tattoo on her hip. "I've replaced several names there already."

I slapped her lightly on the side. "I should have gotten you a tattoo removal for Christmas."

"As soon as I get my first ungarnished paycheck from my yet-materialized job, I'm getting 'Anderson wuz hur' tattooed on my ass."

"Please don't."

"Mr. I Covered Myself With Shitty Tattoos has opinions!" She opened one eye and grinned at me.

I kissed her roughly then softer.

"We can't both make the same fuckups, Gingersnap. We need to balance each other out."

"You really don't hate me?" she whispered.

I trailed my fingers up and down her arms. "You're terrible at blackmailing, Evie Murphy."

"You were going to run away to Idaho."

"After I licked my wounds, I would have come back. I didn't really want to believe I'd lost you."

"You weren't giving up?"

I kissed her nose. "I had some light stalking planned. You know, leaving notes and flowers in the box you were going to live in under the bridge."

She grinned. "I knew it!"

"You didn't know anything."

"You are a good person," she crowed. "Even Snowball likes you. Shit, Snowball!" she yelped, sitting up.

I grunted when her knee dug into my side.

"Spoke too soon." Evie made a face as she saw the dog gnawing on the fridge.

"She wants her present."

"You got Snowball a present?" Evie squealed, then she was all over me, kissing me.

Cradling her in my arms, I stood up from the couch, not wanting to let her go. But I had to set her down to open the fridge.

Evie wrapped a gray military blanket around herself.

"Can you handle this, Snowball?" I asked when I pulled a huge bone out of the fridge.

The dog spun in crazy circles as I set it on the floor for her.

"It's almost as big as she is!" Evie exclaimed.

Snowball did her damnedest to pick the bone up, tipping to one side as she made a wavering path to the little Christmas tree.

"Prezzies!" Evie clapped her hands as I handed her a little brown wrapped package. She carefully untied the string.

For a second, I wished I'd gotten her something else, anything else, but then her face lit up.

"A train." Her eyes melted as she looked up at me. She made a heart with her hands. "You made this."

"Refurbished it."

"There's me and Snowball!" She pointed at the little figures in the cab of the locomotive. "It's so perfect." She kissed my chest.

I set the train on the little track that ran around the miniature Christmas tree. It let out a shrill whistle.

Evie clapped her hands in delight.

Snowball looked up from chewing on her bone.

"I'll make you a whole village when we have our farmhouse," I promised.

"I love it!" She was mesmerized as the train went round and round on its little track. "We're really going to do it, aren't we?" She grabbed my hand. "We're really together forever."

I leaned in and kissed her, needing her to know how much I wanted forever. "You already tried to get rid of me a few times," I reminded her, "and it didn't stick."

She made a face.

"What?"

"I wish I'd gotten you something nicer. Actually, disregard my present. Sawyer was right. I miscalculated."

"Now I want it." I grabbed the soft package and tore into the wrapping paper, ignoring Evie's protests.

"It matches your eyes." Evie grimaced when I pulled out the soft scarf.

I draped it around my neck. "Gray's my favorite color."

"I think that's my line."

I was about to convince her to come on my face when her phone went off, blaring with the "Jingle Bells" ringtone.

"Ignore it."

She grabbed the phone while I peppered kisses down her back.

"Ooh! We're going to go throw a Christmas lunch."

"For the Murphys." My voice was flat.

Evie winced. "Not all of them—the cool people. A small lunch, like ten folks."

"With your family? I doubt it."

Chapter 60

EVIE

"You seriously should have just said no." Declan's wife hurried up to us when my boyfriend—*Yep, boyfriend!*—parked his motorcycle in front of her house. "It was an early-morning text message. I seriously shouldn't have sent it."

"There are only so many Christmases we have on this earth," I declared. "You have to make the most of them."

My baby niece reached for me, babbling.

Anderson let Snowball out to sniff the snow.

Raegan handed me the baby.

"You can't already be giving your mom trouble," I teased my niece.

"She's just like you." Raegan grinned, linking her arm with mine. "Not sure if she'll bring home one of those." She lowered her voice as Anderson tried to corral Snowball from racing across the street toward someone's Christmas yard art.

"So what are we working with?" I asked as we trooped into the house.

There was a half-decorated Christmas tree in the corner that desperately needed water, and a box of decorations my mom had sent home with Declan a few weeks ago on the coffee table.

"I'm not that great at entertaining, but my parents are at my sister's for Christmas since this was Declan's year for the family holiday, but thank god that's not happening." Regan wrinkled her nose. "No offense."

"Absolutely none taken," Anderson said dryly.

"We can make do. It's not that many of us, right?" she added.

"I can make magic," I promised.

"And coffee?" Raegan was hopeful.

"You need some protein too." I tried to hand the baby back. She was teething on a crocheted teething ring I'd made.

"Hard pass. I will take that coffee, though."

"You can help me decorate." Anderson held out his arms for the baby, who screeched happily when he hoisted her over his head.

"I hit the grocery store after we got the hell out of the imploding house of Murphy," Reagan said as I followed her to the messy kitchen. "Freaking epic, by the way."

Their house had a beautiful open living-kitchen-dining area. On the other side of the space, Anderson had the baby under one arm, narrating what he was doing as he deftly hung up lights around the window.

I dumped out the stale coffee in the pot and washed it out. The pot gurgled as I started cleaning the messy kitchen. "Declan needs to step up."

"It was a mutual failing."

"Do we have enough food?" Anderson called.

I opened the fridge. "Is that the Christmas Eve ham?"

"Everyone was stealing food." Raegan was unapologetic. "I wanted the mac 'n' cheese, but your uncle Todd snatched it."

Anderson nodded to the window. "No, *that*."

Reagan and I raced out as Aunt J parked behind Anderson's motorcycle.

"Woo!" My aunt held up a bottle of wine in each hand. "I heard there was a secret Christmas party."

Nat and Lauren shuffled up, yawning. "Can we get an invite?"

"Up to Evie." Declan's wife nodded.

"Don't bust your tits cooking, Evie!" Aunt J trilled. "I stole this out of my sister's house." She waved for me to follow her to the car.

Uncle Jaime gave me a sheepish "Hello" and opened the trunk, which was packed full of food, much of which I'd made yesterday.

My family members carried the dishes inside as another car screeched up in front of the house. The triplets spilled out, groaning, while Granny Doyle looked spry and chipper.

"Hell yeah, now this is a Christmas party—booze and shirtless men."

"Shirtless?"

Anderson was carefully peeling off his spit-up-covered T-shirt.

"Better him than me," Reagan said cheerfully, taking the baby back.

While I washed off his shirt, my female family members used the excuse to give Anderson very long Merry Christmas hugs.

"I think your grandmother touched my junk," he muttered to me, reaching for an apron.

"Damn, that makes him look even sexier," Aunt J said as she and Lauren grabbed a big stockpot and started dumping wine into it for holiday sangria.

"Oh thank god, only the cool people are here." Ian and Sawyer breezed in, Henry slinking behind them.

"I'm shocked you're up this early, Ian," I joked.

"Never went to bed!"

Anderson gave Ian a guilty look. "I'm really sorry, man."

"Don't even worry about him. Taylor Swift liked his video and might hire him," Sawyer cut in.

"Aaron's assistant offered to put in a good word for him," Anderson explained.

"I'm sorry. Your friend knows Taylor Swift?" Sawyer was shocked. "Can he get me a job?"

"He needs to give Henry a job." Granny Doyle bustled in for more ice for the wet bar.

"He's not giving Henry a job, Gran," I said loudly, sliding the casseroles into the oven to start heating up.

"We can't have multiple unemployed people in this family. My social security check doesn't stretch that far."

"Especially if you're spending it on strip clubs and gambling." Sawyer looked up at the ceiling.

"At my age, you gotta get action where you can." She peered into the pot Lauren was stirring while simultaneously scrolling on her phone and poured in a splash of bourbon. "It always needs more alcohol."

"You can be my new social media manager," Ian offered Henry.

"There's that Christmas spirit." Sawyer punched his arm.

"What's the pay?" Henry gave him a crooked smile.

"You can sleep on the floor on my half of the split bed-room I rent."

"Fine. Why not?"

"I thought I was sleeping there!" I cried to Ian.

"You have got to get your life together, Gingersnap." Anderson shook his head.

"Don't worry, Evie." Alana slid onto a barstool. "You're moving in with your boyfriend!"

Anderson hissed. "I hate to be the bearer of bad news, but the garage is technically a field office."

"You don't own the bat cave?" My mouth fell open.

"My brothers and employees will be taking over after Christmas," Anderson explained. "We're going to be dealing with top-secret information."

"I'm getting evicted again. Merry fucking Christmas."

"That's okay. She can move in here." Declan, looking tired in his scrubs, announced, sliding on a stool at the kitchen island.

Alexis hit him with a towel. "You need to step up, Declan. Your house is filthy."

My cousins moved to hang out in Declan's living room as I prepped the Christmas lunch.

More people knocked on the door as the morning wore on.

Granny Doyle and Snowball deputized themselves as bouncers.

"Only cool people get to come to this Christmas." Gran opened the door a crack. "Don't show up empty-handed."

"I have half a bottle of gin," Uncle Russ said.

"I'll allow it."

"I have a casserole!" A friendly-looking woman and two pugs, all wearing matching sweaters, followed my uncles into the house, along with Anderson's siblings. "Thought you might need some food, but you've got it covered."

"You all can't be here if you're going to start a fight," Anderson warned his unapologetic siblings. "Gracie, you should take them back with you."

"I'm bouncing from holiday party to holiday party, accepting food and accolades from my adoring fans." His brother Jake spread his arms. "Ladies, I have arrived."

Aunt J looked him up and down coolly. "Do you play hockey like your brother?"

"Better!" Jake waggled his eyebrows.

"Hm." My aunt sniffed. "Not saying much."

"Damn."

"You said I was good," Anderson protested.

"We'll have another game after lunch—boys against girls."

"Hell yeah! New favorite family." Elsa flopped down next to Sawyer on the crowded couch.

"Merry Christmas, Murphys!"

I dropped the block of cheese I was grating.

"Brooke Taylor!" I screamed as she swanned through the front door in a cloud of perfume.

"I feel a migraine coming." Aunt Trish sank onto a sofa, almost squashing one of the cats she'd insisted on bringing.

"I saw you on TV." Elsa was astounded.

"I love your show," Gracie gushed. "I can't believe you're here!"

"I'm single, my parents are in Tahiti for Christmas, and you can't go to a bar on Christmas morning. I mean, what is that, even?" She headed to the wet bar but stopped short when she saw all of Anderson's younger brothers. "Is there an after-Christmas sale, by any chance? Because I want three for one."

Granny Doyle snorted. "Don't look too excited, boys. You couldn't handle her."

"Full disclosure." Brooke took a sip of her mistletoe martini. "We thought this might go a little bit better if I was here."

"Hell no! You all are not invited, especially you, Shirley!" Granny Doyle yelled as my parents and grandmother hovered in the doorway.

Anderson moved to stand protectively next to me.

Stubbornly, I moved to stand in front of him.

"Gingersnap..."

I held my arm out when he tried to bypass me.

"I don't have anything to say to you," I told my parents. "All your efforts to make me independent and not a freeloader have paid off. Congratulations. I won't ever sleep in your house or eat your food or take so much as a bag of garbage from you ever again."

My dad looked guilty. My mother sighed.

"I know you don't have anything to say to us, Evie. But we have something to say to you, if you want to hear it."

"No, I don't," I said then immediately regretted it because I was insanely curious.

"Fine." My mom turned to Anderson. "We owe you an apology," she said formally. "And a thank you. You saved our son's life all those years ago, and we've treated you horribly since then. You are obviously an honorable man, and now you've saved the lives of two of our children and my mother. I owe you a debt of gratitude."

"I know that I said over the last few weeks," my father added, "that you weren't good enough for my daughter, but—"

"She's not good enough for him?" Sawyer interjected.

"That is not what I was going to say." My dad took a breath. "Anderson, I couldn't think of anyone better for my wonderful daughter to fall in love with."

He turned to me. "Evie, I know you didn't want to hear this, but I have to say it. You're right. We have been unfair to you and hard on you. Your mom and I never treated you like an individual, and that's a failing on our part." He smiled sadly. "I remember when the adoption agency worker first placed you in my arms. Your mom and I were so excited to finally have a daughter. I held you against my chest and promised to be the best dad ever. Clearly, I failed at that, and I am sorry."

"I never really understood you." My mother made a helpless gesture. "And I never tried to either. I regret that. I wanted a strong, confident daughter who wouldn't take crap from anyone, but I couldn't actually handle her once I got her. I'm sorry, Evie."

My parents stood there for an awkward moment while the rest of my inebriated family members watched, stunned.

"If you're waiting for a dinner invitation, you're not getting one," I said finally.

My parents, especially my dad, seemed sad.

"I also own you an apology. I obviously misjudged you, young man." Grandma Shirley squeezed her handbag. "Though not on the cake decorating. You are better than my mother was, certainly better than any of my children or grandchildren, though Evie is a close second." Grandma Shirley cleared her throat. "While I understand I'm not welcome for Christmas, I'd like to invite you for dinner when your schedule allows, Anderson. You and Evie. I'd like to get to know the newest member of the Murphy family."

She pushed her handbag onto her shoulder. "Well. Merry Christmas."

"One last thing before we go." My father had a pained expression on his face. "We understand, Anderson, that our daughter threw a piece of ceramic usable artwork at your vehicle, damaging it."

"She what?" Anderson squinted.

"You mean the dildo?" Aunt Trish asked dreamily from the couch.

Granny Doyle sat it on the table. "Just in case someone's car goes in the river, this thing could come in handy."

"To that end, we have replaced your truck," my father concluded.

"Damn!" Anderson's brothers crowded around the doors and windows with my male cousins.

"Sweet ride."

"That's a nicer truck than Hudson's."

"Where's Evie's gift?" Alana piped up.

My mom blinked.

I crossed my arms.

"We got Evie a job," my mom said primly.

"No, thanks. I'm going to be a stay-at-home girlfriend in Idaho."

"No." Anderson shook his head. "You're not."

"You don't want to come work in Manhattan with me?" Brooke asked sweetly. "Mel said you would love to be my new creative assistant."

Someone was screaming.

Anderson winced.

"Oh my god! Are you serious? But I don't have a degree."

"You have a good eye for decorating and cooking. I'm starting my own cable network, and we need content, like, now. Dog-sweater knitting, a book club, subscription boxes, jams, the works! And December will be all Christmas, all the time. We're redoing your mother's house." Brooke turned and looked my boyfriend up and down. "I don't suppose you'd be up for recreating the cause of the ceiling collapse, Anderson?"

"I'd be glad to be his body double, ma'am," one of his brothers offered.

"How's the pay?" my father asked.

"Mediocre." Brooke took a long pull of her drink.

"I'll take it!" I pumped a fist.

"It's a quick train ride to Harrogate. You can come visit us!" one of the triplets said, excited.

"I thought you were going to be taking care of your new man, Evie," Grandma Shirley said pointedly. "If you don't, someone else will."

"Now, that, we can agree on." Granny Doyle toasted her.

"Can we eat so we can play hockey?" one of my cousins complained.

"I guess you can stay," I said begrudgingly to my parents—partially because it was Christmas and I needed some good karma and also because I wanted Brooke Taylor to have Christmas dinner with me.

Henry passed our parents to lay out the food on the dining table, pointedly not acknowledging them.

Ian scooted a barstool aside. "Did you tell them the good news?" he asked Henry.

"You're still employed?" My mom was hopeful.

"No, just got the 'Merry Christmas, you lost your security clearance' email," Henry said.

"Told you they work holidays." Anderson carved the turkey, the dogs begging at his feet.

"I asked them to amend your discharge information," Henry said to Anderson, still sounding guilty.

Anderson just grunted.

"Henry's going to be my new social media manager," Ian announced brightly.

My mother clamped her mouth shut.

"That sounds like fun," my father forced out. "And I'm sure Ian will be glad to have someone capable heading his team."

"I do actually know about algorithms," Henry warned Ian. "You're not just going to fart around. There'll be a schedule, and I'm tracking your numbers. This isn't going to be like whatever bullshit you and Evie pull."

"If you need money for rent..." My mom opened her purse.

"You never offered Evie and Ian rent money," Henry reminded her pointedly.

"Don't worry about Evie," Brooke said. "This is going to be a very intensive job, so she can and should sleep at the office."

"Why don't we pay to get your license back so you can finally drive again?" my mom offered.

"I don't want her driving my truck," Anderson said flatly.

"No problem. I'll get a motorcycle license."

"No!" Anderson and my parents said at once.

"Ye of little faith."

My family filled their plates. Nat and Lauren tried to convince Brooke Taylor to give them a show on her new cable network while Granny Doyle and Grandma Shirley squabbled over where I was going to live. My cousins and Anderson's siblings talked hockey strategy while the cats tried to jump onto the counter, and Aunt Trish sketched out potential set designs for Brooke. My family members who, like Declan, had just ended their hospital shifts all talked loudly and in excruciating detail about the patients they'd seen.

Finally, I dragged Anderson out the back door.

"That's the problem with open floor plans," I said, loosening my apron. "You can't hide in the kitchen."

"Already planning for our farmhouse?"

"Or maybe a lodge near the falls. But more likely a shack in the woods. We'll wear lots of sweaters. It will be like Laura Ingalls Wilder."

Anderson looked down at me. "Gingersnap, we're not living in a shack. I haven't been working for free all this time."

"I feel like that's a dig at me. But I can contribute, you know."

Anderson raised an eyebrow and tugged one of the curls that had escaped my bun. "Don't you have a laundry list of people you owe money to?"

"Yeah, but I'm going to win it all back gambling on reindeer racing."

He kissed me, smiling. "I love you. Trust me when I say I can get you your dream house wherever you want."

"I love you, and my dream home is wherever you are." I sank into his arms. "But just to clarify… wherever?"

He thought for a moment. "Not Manhattan. That's between you and Santa."

Merry Christmas!

A SHORT HOLIDAY ROMANTIC COMEDY

ELF

BUILDS A

SHELF

Chapter 1

EVIE

"I thought you were turning over a new leaf—you know, making better decisions." Ian crossed his arms.

"I'm not an architect, but I really wish you had consulted us before you bought the place." Sawyer sighed.

A slate shingle slid down the roof of the rambling gothic farmhouse to explode on the ground in front of us.

"I didn't want him to spend all his money on a house, and it was a good deal," I explained desperately.

"Yeah, because it's haunted by Old Widow Weatherby." Sawyer spit on the ground.

"What can you expect from someone who gets her dog out of a trash can?"

My friends and I gazed up at the dilapidated house.

"If some enterprising person wanted to clear out the thicket of blackberry brambles, you'd have a stunning view of the lake." I rocked on my heels.

"Isn't there a cemetery back there?" Ian looked alarmed.

"You could have bought a house in town."

"The dream was a farmhouse," I said determinedly.

"There is a lot of land." Sawyer poked at a nearby blackberry bush. In the summer, it would be overloaded with berries. Now, in December, it was Sleeping Beauty's protective barrier.

A few days ago, when we'd seen the house—it was the first house we'd officially looked at now that Anderson had his dishonorable discharge reversed and could qualify for a VA loan—I'd fallen in love immediately.

I'd insisted, begged, and pleaded that this be our forever home.

Had Anderson asked me if I wanted to look at other options?

Yes, but I was in love. Now I was a homeowner.

"Oh god, I'm a homeowner." I whimpered. "Do you think it's too late to get a refund?"

"You already signed the paperwork," Ian reminded me.

The gravel crunched behind us as a truck pulled up, and the Wynter siblings jumped out.

Anderson gave me what felt like a perfunctory kiss.

"There it is."

The house creaked, and the wind moaned, seeming to say, *Disaster… this is a disasteeer, Evie Murphyyy…*

"Hudson, you need to give Anderson a raise." Jake slapped his brother on the back.

"You're going to live in a dump?" Talbot made a face.

"It feels like home!" Elsa said cheerily.

"Our childhood home was in worse shape than this," Anderson reminded them.

"Is that the one that burned down?" I asked in horror.

Oh no. I'd brought up his childhood trauma.

"It's going to look great when it's fixed up." I was sweating, even though it was icy outside. "We're going to paint it and put in a kitchen."

"'We' who?" Ian asked.

"'We, Anderson,' it sounds like." His brothers ribbed him.

"It's in better shape inside."

"Evie, your delusions know no bounds," Ian said as we shined flashlights around the empty house. The Widow Weatherby had lived here as a recluse for the last twenty years. Her estate had cleared out the furniture, knickknacks, and other possessions.

I pulled at a piece of peeling wallpaper, which squeaked, sending Snowball barking.

"The foundation's pretty solid," I whispered as we creaked up the wide staircase. "New paint. Some fairy lights. It will look great. We can put the Christmas tree there. Clear the bats out of the fireplace."

"Why don't you just tear it down and build something like Uncle Todd's house?" Sawyer asked as we peeked into an old bedroom. There was a painting of a clown dressed up as Santa Claus still on the wall. Presumably, the movers had refused to touch it.

"I convinced the estate to sell the house to us with an impassioned plea of how I wanted to use it for future foster kids. The widow wanted it to become a real home, not a vacation property. She loved this house."

Anderson tapped a plaster wall with his boot. The whole thing shuddered then collapsed in a puff of dust. "She really should have taken better care of it, then."

"He hates the house, and he hates me!" I wailed over Jingle Bell Juleps at the Twinkle Taproom.

"You really do know how to pick 'em." Ian licked his spoon.

"It didn't look so bad the first time we saw it!" I cried. "And I know he's going to think I want him to renovate it all by himself."

"That's going to take years, Evie," Sawyer said. "Can't you guys hire a crew?"

"Brook Taylor wasn't lying about the pay being mediocre." I guzzled my drink, the alcohol not helping the panic, only making me feel even worse. "Anderson is going to resent me, then he's going to wish he'd never met me, then I'm going to wake up one morning, and he'll be gone. I'll be all alone."

"No, you won't. Widow Weatherby's ghost will keep you company." Ian snickered.

"Just figure out how to renovate without putting too much on him, and you'll be fine," Sawyer assured me. "You could get a better-paying job—you have experience now. Then you'd qualify for a home renovation loan."

"I'm buying a lottery ticket," I decided.

Sawyer pinched her nose. "Not exactly what I meant."

With the smells of dinner filling a swanky, newly renovated historic apartment a few nights later, I finished typing up a summary of a meeting with an interior design personality for Brooke. Then I took a sip of very good wine and set the stemware on a marble counter. No, I was not living out my Carrie Bradshaw dreams. I was pet sitting. Brooke Taylor was a brand-new dog mom, one who also didn't want to cancel her girls' ski trip.

When the doorbell rang, Snowball started barking, which set off the Pomeranian puppy, who looked like and had the brain cell count of a large cotton ball. I hid my losing scratch-off ticket in the trash can—should have just bought a cruffin—then rushed to open the door.

"You're back!" I flung my arms around Anderson.

He smelled like the winter woods.

I melted in his arms. I didn't want to lose him. I was going to figure out a plan for that house—one that didn't rely on him.

"Dinner's almost ready—chicken fried steak, mac 'n' cheese, and greens."

My boyfriend sat down on one of the dining room chairs, watching me as I made the gravy. He scooped the dogs up on his lap so they could cover his black clothes with dog hair. He seemed world-weary.

"Tough day on the job?"

"Just long." He rubbed a hand on the back of his neck.

I handed him a beer. He wrapped his arms around my waist briefly, nuzzling my chest, and slid his hand under my apron.

"So, about the house..." he began.

After a lifetime of disappointing my loved ones, I was not a person who liked to have difficult conversations. In fact, I went out of my way to avoid them.

"Don't even worry about the house." Suddenly, I had a flash of genius. "I have a plan for it. We could be house flippers. We'll fix it up then sell it for a profit."

Anderson drew back from me. "So now you don't want the house?" He scowled. "You just had me buy it." He hissed when Peanut the puppy nipped him playfully.

"I just think it's a lot of house." I petted the wiggly puppy. "What are we even going to do with all that space? I might have gotten ahead of myself a bit, is all."

"Uh-huh." He stood up, taking another swig of the beer. "I'm going to take the dogs out."

The puppy chewed on his jacket zipper. Snowball was unimpressed.

I felt like crap. Anderson was furious with me. I'd really screwed up.

Chapter 2

ANDERSON

"That's the look of a man who doesn't want to admit I was right."

"Fuck off, Aaron." I sighed, setting a folder of information on his desk along with a hard drive.

"You should have steered her to something more manageable." Aaron could be such a prick sometimes.

"It's not about being manageable. Now she's rethinking our whole future." I tried to sound calm. Inside, I was a tempest.

Aaron sat back in his chair. "I thought you were about to propose to her."

"Now I don't know if I should. She had this dream for us, and now she just wants to renovate the house and flip it and move on. From the house? From me? Who knows."

"You're overreacting. Isn't that place haunted?" Aaron deadpanned. "Flipping that disaster is the most sensible idea your girlfriend's had yet."

"Why are up my ass all the time?"

Aaron turned his cold green eyes on me.

"I'm just going to hold off on proposing to her."

"No, propose to her now, fix up the house, and sell it. If you both survive that, then you'll be good the rest of your lives. Statistically, renovating a house is one of the leading causes of relationships ending."

"What the hell do you know about relationships?"

"It's not love. Its statistics."

"I don't know…"

"Or you could not propose to her and continue to be an emo piece of shit, and when she eventually dumps you for greener pastures, I'll be there to mop up the tears."

"Fuck you." I was on the edge of my seat.

Aaron cocked an eyebrow.

I exploded. "Stay the fuck away from my girlfriend!" I slammed my hands down on the desk.

Aaron just grinned up at me. "There he is. Betty's picked out some rings for you. Trust her taste."

I gave him the finger.

"Also, you might want to wear a suit when you ask her father for his blessing."

I stopped short in the doorway and whirled around. "I'm not asking her fucking father."

"You can't just propose to her without asking *someone*."

"She's a grown woman," I argued.

"From a nice family," Aaron added. "With a very traditional grandmother. You need to get the blessing from some member of the family so you don't ostracize her."

I rubbed my jaw.

I could tolerate the Murphys and even enjoyed spending time with some of her relatives in small doses and when hockey was involved. But it just rankled that, after everything, I needed to ask one of them for her hand in marriage.

"Surely there's someone over there who can check the box," Aaron prodded.

Did I want to take Evie with the rest of her family, though?

Chapter 3

EVIE

Anderson seemed like he was in an even worse mood a few days later when I had gathered a ragtag group of volunteers to help clear out some of the brambles.

My boyfriend, wearing a thick canvas long-sleeved shirt, a skullcap over his dark hair, and a tool belt looped around his waist, strode through the house and around the property. He was followed by Ian, notepad in hand, writing down a list of the repairs needed and doing everything to avoid clearing brush.

"Don't worry. I'm typing this up with pictures," Ian said as Anderson tapped the rotting wood on the porch posts with thinly veiled irritation. He made a big show of turning to yet another empty page in his notebook.

"You been feeding that man, Evie?" Granny Doyle asked pointedly as Anderson's heavy boots stomped down the steps.

A stiff breeze picked up.

That's not ominous.

"Evie, the puppy!"

Anderson raced after a white ball of fluff as it tumbled across the bare yard. He finally grabbed it when she got caught on the cut brambles. Anderson made soothing noises as he untangled Peanut.

"Now he thinks I'm a terrible dog mom," I groaned, "and probably a terrible human mom too."

"I thought you wanted to adopt teenagers, not a helpless baby," Sawyer said, dumping thorny brambles onto the pile.

"Probably for the best." Granny Doyle patted my arm.

I was sore that evening when I was alone back in Brooke's swanky condo, blow-drying Peanut after giving her a bath.

Anderson hadn't wanted to come back to New York with me, grunting some excuse.

I blinked back tears.

"How's my baby?" The door flew open, and Brooke Traylor swept in, dumping shopping bags all over the floor. "Did you get dirty?" My boss greeted the still-damp puppy.

"I took her with me and Anderson to work on our house," I explained.

"You bought a house!" Brooke gave me a spine-breaking hug.

"It's not an exciting house."

"As long as you have a hunky husband willing to work shirtless on it, you have it made, girl. Wine." She clapped her hands. "Metrics. How did all my ski selfies do? What about the one with the bachelorette? Book her for Tuesday's show. Peanut, were you good for Evie?"

I tried to manage Brooke as she jumped from topic to topic.

"There's smoked salmon dip in the bag." She pointed with her wineglass. "Did I tell you I was thinking about getting a cat?"

"Really?" I picked up a dripping bag while Snowball licked her chops.

"The house, Evie, where is it?"

I handed her my phone. Brooke swiped through while I started unpacking all of her bags.

"Anderson doesn't seriously want to fix all this up by himself? Oh, smoked salmon. Eat this!"

"I don't think he does," I said carefully.

"Of course he doesn't." Brooke was flippant. "It's such a big house."

I was crushed.

"I fucked up. I pressured him into buying," I admitted. I was not crying in front of my idol.

"Mm-hmm." Brooke didn't seem like she was listening. She was using my phone to text someone.

"Never mind. I'm going to clean it up as best as possible and sell it."

"Uh-huh."

Jeez, these A-listers really were walking personality disorders. I didn't know how my mom had dealt with Brooke all these years.

"Do you have a picture of Anderson on here?" she asked, swiping through my photos. "A shirtless one. Never mind! Found it! Yummy."

"I actually was going to go…"

"No, you have to stay. We need to have girl talk. I have to tell you all about my trip." She slid a wineglass over to me. "And we're going to discuss your new show."

"I'm sorry. My what?" I spilled wine all over the marble counter, cursed, and grabbed for a rag.

"Your notes said that designer, Leslie, would be a great host. Your new house is perfect. Anderson can make appearances. Snowball too. Tell your people not to clear any more brush out."

"Not that much was actually done," I admitted. The cleanup had been a bust.

"You'll be the producer, especially since you have a free place to stay in Maplewood Falls. That will keep costs down. Start booking sponsors for the products in the home." Brooke beamed. "Look at us being boss babes!"

"I don't think people use that term anymore."

"Your mom's going to be so excited to have you move back. You'll be one of the first people to stay up in the new attic suite."

Brooke grabbed me and took a few quick selfies.

At least I had a solution to the house problem, but I wasn't sure how Anderson was going to take it.

And I definitely wasn't sure if I was going to survive living at my parents' house for the year it would take to do the construction.

But it would be worth it if it meant I wouldn't drive off Anderson, right?

Chapter 4

ANDERSON

"**Y**ou're naming your firstborn son after me, aren't you?" Jake asked as we watched the drone surveillance footage.

"Sure," I lied. Evie wanted to adopt, and I wasn't changing a thirteen-year-old's name. Or at least that had been the plan. Now? Who knew.

My plan was still to propose. For now.

The least bad option to ask for a blessing was Granny Doyle. That meant I needed Evie's parents out of the house when it happened.

"Clear. Move out," Jake said as her parents finally left in evening finery to go to some Christmas concert you wouldn't catch me dead at.

I could hear the TV blaring through the front door when I walked up the steps.

No one answered when I knocked, so I used a key Evie's parents had insisted on giving me and let myself in.

Granny Doyle was sprawled out on the couch, three cocktails deep, watching a holiday baking show.

"No one wants to eat goat brain smothered in eggnog custard, you moron. Oh shit," she slurred when she noticed me in the doorway.

The old woman was piss drunk.

"It's two in the afternoon."

"You didn't see nothing." She swayed on the couch. "Evie's not here, but you can leave a message."

"I actually came to talk to you."

"Don't worry," she said, pouring out the rest of the cocktail from the shaker into her glass. "You can just dump the cat Trish gave you back in her house. She won't notice."

"She didn't give me a cat."

"Didn't give you a cat yet."

I sat down on the ottoman in front of Granny Doyle.

"Look," I said seriously, "I've been thinking about this thing between Evie and me. I love her, and I want to spend the rest of my life with her. I wanted to ask your blessing before I propose."

"You want permission to tap that ass on the regular." She fist-bumped me and hiccupped. "Permission to be awesome granted. I tell you what, when I got married, I—" She slumped over on the couch.

"Fuck."

She wasn't dead, was she? I looked around wildly. I needed to call 911. I needed to do CPR.

Granny Doyle sat straight back up with a loud snort while I jumped backward.

"...Telling me it wasn't justified, you see?"

"I think you need to sober up."

"I take a shot whenever they do something stupid like season a goddamn steak with cupcake sprinkles like a fucking communist."

"How about some coffee," I said, racing to the kitchen.

Evie wasn't going to marry me if I let her grandmother get blackout drunk and hurt herself.

The coffeepot hissed as I searched around for something to soak up the alcohol.

There were ingredients in Evie's parents' house to make poutine, and after a short while, I carried a plate out to Granny Doyle... who had a half-empty bottle of bourbon next to her.

I swore under my breath.

"That will go perfect with this." She slapped my thigh.

"Evie's going to be glad to lead you around by a cock ring. When's the wedding? I want to be a flower girl. Flower power." She stuffed a forkful of the poutine into her mouth. "It's funny—when you say poutine, it sounds like pussy."

Granny Doyle took another swig from the bourbon bottle. "I'm just pregaming for the bridge holiday party."

"Look," I said as she craned her head to see the TV screen. "Please don't say anything about this to anyone. The proposal is tomorrow, and I don't want to ruin the surprise for Evie."

"You make a mean fried cheese curd, my friend."

This was a fucking disaster. Had she even heard a word I'd said?

"Squeak, squeak!" Granny Doyle took a bite out of a cheese curd. "Goddammit, now my dentures are loose."

I couldn't trust it. This barely counted as getting a blessing.

But it would have to be good enough.

Then I worried—if I told Evie and she asked her grandmother, and Granny Doyle gave her the blank look she was giving me right now, Evie would think I was lying. That wasn't how I wanted to start off our marriage.

"Parents incoming!" Jake yelled in my ear. "Go out the window!"

Too late.

"Anderson! My favorite future son-in-law!" Evie's mom said as she and her husband breezed in.

"Spending quality time with Mel's mother?" Dr. Murphy asked.

"She was like this when I got here. I tried to sober her up," I explained.

"That's right! You lost!" Granny Doyle yelled at the TV, where Sprinkle Boy was being shown the door.

The Murphys gave me big friendly smiles.

I almost preferred her parents when they were mean to me. This was off-putting.

Maybe I should just ask them.

No.

"Do you want to stay for dinner?" Melissa offered.

"We had pussy for dinner." Granny Doyle took another noisy bite of the snack I'd made her.

"We did not. And I actually have to go." I stood up.

"Shirley will be so sad to have missed you," Melissa said.

Shirley.

"Say hello to Evie for us!" her dad called.

"Tell her we're proud of her!" Melissa added.

Shirley's house was postcard-perfect. I crept around to peer in the window just to make sure she was alone. I didn't need any Murphys ruining the surprise.

"I have a gun!" the old woman yelled from inside the house.

I swore and made my way back to the front door.

"Anderson," she said when she opened it. "I just made tea."

We sat in the formal living room. There were doilies everywhere—the plate sat on a doily, the spoon had its own doily, the damn doily napkins had doilies.

Shirley stirred her tea.

I picked up the dainty bone china with its Christmas motif as gingerly as if I were disarming a bomb.

"I assume this is about that travesty of a house." Shirley sipped her tea.

"It's going to be beautiful once I've fixed it up." I bristled, defensive.

"Of that, I have no doubt. You're certainly the handiest in the family. No, Mrs. Weatherby was a kook. She lied to everyone and said her husband had died, but he ran out on her with a waitress. I can't blame the poor man." The old woman's mouth turned as if she'd eaten something distasteful. "And now you're living in that disaster."

"Not living there yet."

"Please note I am leaving you and Evie my home when I die. I highly suggest you vacate Mrs. Weatherby's home once that occurs."

I tried not to choke on the hot tea, which was already a big ask, considering it tasted like I was drinking liquid pinecones.

"You're the only one skilled enough in this family to handle it." She handed me a doily.

I set down the teacup. "I actually came here," I said, "with a request."

"How much do you need? My checkbook is in my purse in the study. Go get it."

"No, I don't need money."

"So you found the money Mrs. Weatherby hid? Rumors, of course, though I always did wonder."

I hated this town.

"I wanted to ask your blessing to propose to Evie."

"You didn't ask her father?"

"No." I waited.

"Well." Shirley preened. "I am flattered to be the one asked. Do make sure that proposal is top-notch. I don't want any of that nonsense you see people putting all over Facebook for my granddaughter."

I wondered, though, as I worked to put up lights on the house for the big proposal—what if everyone was wrong? What if I was wrong and Evie didn't want to spend the rest of her life with me?

What then?

Chapter 5

EVIE

"**I**t even has a breakfast bar."

"Yep, Mom, I was a producer on the show."

You didn't keep Melissa Murphy down for long. She was not having one of her children estranged, let alone three, and had thrown herself into a full-on support-ive-mom role.

"Brooke also told me about your idea for a Mother's Day program about the difficult relationship daughters have with their mothers as they head out into the adult world. I think that would be a wonderful opportunity for us. Very clever idea, Evie. Well-done."

"I was not thinking about us for that."

"I hear you're moving home for a little bit. I must admit that your father and I were concerned when you bullied poor Anderson into buying that house—"

"There was no bullying. Nobody bullied anyone."

My mom sniffed. "He loves you, you know, Evie. He'd do anything for you. You need to be more careful with his heart."

"Anderson is fine." *Right?*

"I should have known my creative go-getter daughter had a plan! I told Brooke to do a magazine special. Don't you think that's a great idea?" she asked as we entered the newly redone attic suite.

"All ready for you. There's a sitting area. Everything is insulated. The floor is reinforced. Brand-new bed. Anderson can stretch out. It's a custom-size mattress, Evie. You need that in your new house, don't forget. And Anderson can come stay here too."

"Anderson is going to leave me if I tell him he has to move in here with you and Dad."

"Nonsense, Evie. We bought him a truck. Not to mention I got a very good deal on a high-end grill for his Christmas present. Though, maybe I should wait. Yes, I think I should. He'll probably want an outdoor kitchen. Write that down on your list for your home renovation."

Ian: *You're not moving back home, are you?*
Evie: *It's the only solution to the house problem.*
Sawyer: *Does Anderson know?*
Evie: *I'm making this sacrifice for all of us.*

"Mom," I interrupted. "I actually have to go to the house to, you know, take some pictures for preproduction. Brooke wants to move fast."

"I'm glad to see you taking this job seriously, Evie," my dad said as I rushed down the stairs. "Brooke is very pleased with your work. Now your own show? That's a big step up. Your mom and I are very proud of you."

"Yep. Gotta go!"

"Why don't you take the Range Rover?"

"I can just take my beater car."

"We don't even know if your airbags work, dear," my mom clucked.

My dad went to his safe, punched in a passcode, and then handed me the keys. "Just take it."

I drove fifteen miles an hour, cars lined up behind me.

"I am not scratching the paint!" I yelled out the window as a minivan sped past me, honking the horn. "It's a brand-new car."

I regretted running away from my parents as soon as I drove down the overgrown dark driveway.

It was still light out but barely. Everything had an eerie moody light.

"I do not own a haunted house. I do not own a haunted house."

The meager piles of bramble were in the future fire pit that Sean had made instead of helping cut brush.

"We have a solution. It's fine."

Since I was there anyway, I snapped photos of the house interior. I'd need to get a copy of Ian's list. Should I call a priest, too, just to be extra careful?

Something thudded in the house.

Yeah, definitely calling a priest.

There were pounding noises like from the inside of a coffin.

I yelped, and Snowball barked.

"We're leaving now." I raced through the house to the front door.

It slammed before I could cross the threshold. I pulled on the handle, but it popped off.

There was more thudding and creepy wailing.

A cold breeze chilled the back of my neck as I tried frantically to open the door.

"It's the Widow Weatherby!" I cowered on the floor, hands over my eyes. "Don't drag me to the underworld!"

"Evie?"

I opened my eyes to see a confused Anderson, half in shadow. He picked me up, cradling me in his strong arms.

"I didn't know you were here," I gasped.

"I parked in the back," he said, carrying me through the chilly house.

The black pickup truck waited in the overgrown back garden. We sat in the cab. I resisted the urge to turn on the music. Anderson seemed a little tense.

"I just want to—"

"I need to—"

"You first."

I took a deep breath. "I know that you're really mad about the house, and I'm sorry I pushed you into it. And—"

"*Evie.*" He cupped my face, staring into my eyes. "You think I'm mad about the house?"

"You've been stomping and snarling."

"Gingersnap, I already told you I love you. I want the kids and the Christmas magic. I don't know about horses with this elevation change, but we could do goats and chickens. I want that with you. We're supposed to be together. I believe, anyway."

"But it's a lot of house."

"Shirley told me she's giving her house to us after she dies, so we could set up Evie's Unlicensed Orphanage there."

"Why were you talking with her?"

"Never mind." He stared into my eyes. "I don't want to trap you with me if that's not what you want."

"I'm not trapped here with you. You're trapped here with me, buddy."

Be serious, Evie.

"I love you, Anderson," I said honestly. "I keep thinking maybe I'm not good enough for you."

"You're everything to me, Evie." He leaned in and kissed me softly on my forehead, nose, and mouth. "I love you," he whispered.

"Okay," I whispered. "I love you, too, and good girl-friends don't make their boyfriends do free manual labor, so I—"

"That's not what you said the other night." He gave a smoldering grin.

"Wait, I was going to tell you—" I gasped as he kissed me harder.

His hands moved to the zipper of my jacket.

"I have a solution to the house—"

"I don't want to talk about the house when I'm about to fuck you," he said, hoisting me.

Then I was tumbling into the back seat of the truck.

"So much better than sex on the back of a motorcycle." I panted on my hands and knees as he pulled my tights and panties down.

"You came just fine all over my motorcycle," he reminded me right before he buried his mouth in my cunt.

My cries fogged up the window as he worked my pussy, poking his tongue into my opening and sweeping down to my clit.

"I will never, ever get tired," he said as a condom packet tore, "of being in your cunt."

Then he thrust into me, filling me. My tights kept my knees together even though I wanted to spread my legs for him.

He thrust into my tight pussy as I held on to the door handle to keep from banging my nose on the glass as he fucked me. He reached under my sweater to pinch and play with my tits as he buried his cock in me over and over until I could barely speak enough to beg him to go deeper.

Stroking my slit, he increased the pace, unrelenting, until I was coming with a cry as he jackhammered into me. Moaning, I just had to take it as that thick length drew out the pleasure until he was shuddering in me, his teeth clamped on my shoulder.

"What did I say, Gingersnap?" He slapped my ass then let his fingers linger briefly on my pussy. "You're such a good fuck."

I struggled over the center console to land in the passenger seat. He climbed next to me, facing me, kissing my neck as I talked.

"Keep that in mind," I said, breathing hard. "Brooke Taylor wants to fund the whole renovation as part of a new show. So you don't have to do anything."

"Huh." He sat back. His gray eyes flicked to the clock on the radio. "Do you want me to drive you to your car?"

Shit, he hated the show idea.

"No, I can walk." I blew out a breath.

"I just need some time…" He rubbed his jaw.

I slid out of the cab of the truck to make the long walk to my car.

"Evie…"

"Don't worry. That's not the first time a guy's kicked me out of the car after bumping uglies," I joked.

He swore, but I trotted into the house, pulling at my clothes.

When I got out to the front of the house, though, it had been transformed into a winter wonderland.

"Congratulations!" my family yelled, jumping out from behind trees, bushes, and tables of food.

"I'm so confused. Why are you here?"

"Not to do any more yard work. I'll tell you that," Aunt J said.

I blinked against the dazzling lights strung all over the front of the house.

"Sorry, Evie." Anderson stood in the doorway of the house. "I was going to change my shirt."

"Oh no. We're early," someone yelled.

"How did you screw this up?" My family started squabbling.

I turned back to Anderson to ask him, *What the hell?*, but he was down on one knee in front of me.

"Evie," he said as I clapped my hands over my mouth. "I'd like to say I loved you from the minute I saw you, but we both know that's not true." A smile twitched at his mouth. "You're unlike anyone I've ever met. You're brazen and crazy and beautiful and perfect, and you're loyal to a fault. I've never loved anyone like you, and I don't think I ever will again. So I need you to be my wife. Please say yes."

"I can't believe you did all this for me," I choked out as he held a sparkling ring out to me. "You're so perfect, Anderson. I don't deserve you." I was sobbing now.

"Evie, I don't deserve you."

"Great. Neither of you deserves each other, so just say yes already, Evie!" Ian yelled.

"Yes, I want to marry you, Anderson!"

He slid the ring onto my finger as I jumped up and down, then I jumped into his arms while he laughed and swung me around.

"This is amazing. How did you get everyone here?"

He cleared his throat.

"My bad, Anderson," Granny Doyle piped up. "I had to tell J. She's my ride or die. And then Shirley was telling everyone that you asked her for her blessing and not me, and I had to set that record right the fuck straight."

"You asked my grandmothers?" I was teary-eyed.

"I didn't think you remembered," Anderson said to Granny Doyle as he carried me down the steps.

"I didn't have that much to drink." Granny Doyle snorted. "Still had my bra on."

"Will you do the honors?" one of my cousins asked as Sawyer and Ian draped tinsel all over me.

I was handed a container of kerosene.

"Bonfire! Bonfire!" my cousins chanted

"Anderson, this is how much I love you." I declared, holding the lighter to the kerosene-soaked bramble branches.

And then the fireball erupted.

I watched those dry brambles burn like an inferno from the ground, where Anderson had thrown us clear of the flames.

Sawyer hissed, and Ian covered his eyes.

"Let's make sure the wedding is set far enough in the future for those eyebrows to grow back," my mother said finally.

Anderson kissed me. "I have a Sharpie in my toolbox. No one will notice."

The End

Acknowledgements

A big thank you to Red Adept Editing for editing and proofreading.

And finally a big thank you to all the readers! I had a great time writing this hilarious book! Please try not to choke on your wine while reading!!!

About the Author

If you like steamy romantic comedy novels with a creative streak, then I'm your girl!

Architect by day, writer by night, I love matcha green tea, chocolate, and books! So many books...

Sign up for my mailing list to get special bonus content, free books, giveaways, and more!

http://alinajacobs.com/mailinglist.html

Made in United States
Troutdale, OR
11/17/2024

24952921R00339